SECRETS OF

GREENOAK

WOODS

Brenda Jane Davies

For my Mum and Dad x

Contents

Chapter 1

1816 St Merryn, Cornwall

Benjamin jolted awake with a shock of fear so intense he gasped and broke into a sweat. As his eyes adjusted to the deep darkness of his bedroom, he drew a slow breath and let the terror running through his veins calm and settle. He did this almost every night; he should be used to it by now.

Somewhere in the distance, amongst the far-off trees in Greenoak Woods, he heard a chilling scream. But waking to screams was nothing new either. If they weren't in the woods, they were in his head.

The distant shrieks became louder. He clamped his hands over his ears and concentrated on the sound his surging blood made, like the sea rushing in. Too late; the shrill cries had pierced his mind and would not leave. They made him think of his mother. He gripped the bedsheets, unable to breathe. She had screamed like that just before she died.

Benjamin couldn't sleep now. He jumped out of bed, dressing quickly and stuffing his feet into his worn black boots. He couldn't stay here with only his thoughts for company. It hurt. It hurt too much.

He whistled for Jess. She sprang to her feet like she'd been waiting for him and nuzzled his hand. Her coat was sleek and smooth when he gave her head a rub, but her face and body were marked by white scars, much like his own.

'Come on, Jess, let's get out of here.' Throwing on his jacket and ramming his hat down on his head, he opened the cottage door and peered outside. The whisper of surf across the sand on an ebb tide met him, and a cold moon floated low in the dark sky. The screams from the woods continued.

Jess pricked up her ears and whined.

'Go, Jess, go!'

She sprinted for Greenoak Woods, and he slammed the cottage door behind him and ran after her.

Jess waited for him at the edge of the brooding forest, darting off again as soon as he caught up with her. He followed into the shadowed blackness, where a light wind prowled around the trees, making their leaves tremble. He liked this darkness where he was just one more ghostly shape, a living phantom haunting these woods.

Again, Jess waited for him to catch up before plunging down the mossy path's throat. He followed at full pelt, jumping fallen logs and skidding on wet leaves. He felt free like this. It was the thrill of knowing he was going to do something he shouldn't, and it drove him like an overwhelming madness.

But as he ran towards the screams, images flickered into his vision. A curtain of copper-coloured hair; slender wrists so easy to restrain, so easy to bruise. He wrapped his knuckles against his forehead and tried to knock the

2

memory out of his brain, but it refused to budge and filled him with shame and sorrow.

Jess barked from somewhere deep in the woods. He focused on the sound and followed it. He found her waiting patiently beside a thick patch of brambles with a trembling, twitching rabbit, one of its hind legs caught in a rusty gin trap. With bulging eyes and lips curled back in agony and fright, the rabbit screamed again. The sound was so human, so full of despair, it dropped him to his knees. The metallic smell of blood and musty brown earth rose from the ground.

Removing his jacket, he slung it over the rabbit. The silence was instant, but the creature continued to quiver, his jacket shaking from the tremors. The serrated jaws of the trap were crusty with dried blood and fur when he gripped them and prised them apart, freeing the snared leg. He let the trap snap shut. Holding Jess by the scruff of her neck, he whipped his jacket off the rabbit and watched it spring into the air and lope off, dragging a broken leg behind it and disappearing beneath the tangle of brambles.

A noise behind him made him spin in a half-crouch and peer into the dark shadows. Nothing. Then he heard it again, the sound of twigs snapping under feet. Like the rabbit, he sprang into action, shrugging on his jacket and moving deeper into the woods to stand stock still in the trees. Just one more dark shadow amongst other shadows. He glanced at Jess, but she lay flat on the ground; she knew when to be quiet.

He spied a figure moving through the woods. So, Samuel was in the woods tonight too, up to no good. Again. Why else would someone be out alone at night? He glanced up at the face of the man in the moon, who scowled down

3

at him. Yes, yes, so he was here as well, but unlike Samuel, it wasn't the woods that drew him; it was the night, the darkness, the screams. Particularly the screams.

If Samuel was here, Mary might come too. Oh God, she might be on her way right now. At the thought of Mary, he pushed the sleeve of his jacket up to his left arm and picked at the crusty scabs there, plucked and scraped until he levered off each itchy one with his fingernail. The wounds were now raw and pinpricks of blood bubbled to the surface, but he couldn't stop; he craved the sparks of pain that flew along his fragile skin.

Samuel was casually propped against an oak tree before him. He hated Samuel so much that it made him shiver with rage. The secrets they shared were foul and dirty and coated him like a layer of grime he could never wash off. He bowed his head and hunched his shoulders to wait and listen.

Like he was expecting something bad to happen.

Chapter 2

In the kitchen at Goodtoknow Farm, Mary slumped on a dark oak settle. She leant her head against its high back, stretched her toes towards the fireplace, and let her eyes rove over the faces of those sat with her. Her sister's fair hair, twisted into a thick braid, draped over one shoulder like a skein of silk. Her father and grandfather supped homemade beer, and gentle ribbons of pipe tobacco spiralled lazily towards the ceiling. She breathed in the sweet woody smell and thought of Samuel, of how tobacco smoke often clung to his hair and clothes, and she allowed her mouth to curve into a soft smile.

Her grandfather knocked his pipe against the fire grate and cleared his throat. 'You looks pale, Lizzie, like a little ghost sat beside our Mary. Are you well?'

Mary clutched a handful of her skirt and twisted it in her hand as she glanced across at her sister. Elizabeth's pale, waxen skin was stained with dark hollows under her eyes, like a corpse. Her eyes met Mary's briefly before she replied, 'I'm fine, just a headache.'

'Go to bed, then. I can help Mary finish down here.'

'No, Gramfer, you go. I'm fine, really.'

Mary wiped her clammy hands down the sides of her skirt and smoothed out the creases. What was it her grandfather always said? Worrying was pointless; it changed nothing. It didn't help. Easy for him to say. She watched Elizabeth pick at the frayed skin around her fingernails; she'd have nothing left of them soon.

A memory of the two of them surfaced, and she smiled. Two silly young girls hiding in the hay barn, watching the farm boys wash after a dirty day's work. Stifling giggles whilst the boys stripped to their waists, or further if they were lucky. Two conspirators together, always and forever. Who'd have guessed it would come to this? Poor Elizabeth—it wasn't her fault that they were both snared in a tangled mess and escape was going to be painful, if it was even possible.

Mary's grandfather groaned and pushed himself out of his chair. 'I'm off to bed, then.'

'Aye, me too,' answered her father.

Mary jumped up and bent to kiss her grandfather on the cheek, then rose on tiptoes to reach her father, who stroked the side of her face with his thumb. Her height she got from her father, but her dark hair and eyes were her mother's. She looked just like her mother; her father thought so too, and she saw the pain in his eyes whenever he looked at her.

As they left the kitchen, Mary picked up a candlestick from the lintel above the fireplace and frowned at the family Bible that lay in judgement on its shelf beside the fire. She reached out to run her fingertips across the worn dark cover and shivered. She turned away, her eyes concentrating on the smoky trail of light in her hands. 'Take this, Lizzie, and go to bed. Get some sleep.'

Lizzie furrowed her brow. 'Sleep. What's that?'

'You look worn out.'

'Are you coming?'

Mary shook her head. 'I've got chores to do.'

'What chores?'

Mary couldn't think of a convincing reply, so she shook her head. She didn't care if Elizabeth guessed where she was going.

'Don't be long. Please.'

Mary heard the tremor in that *please*, saw the candlelight quiver. Her chest sank with the weight of them. 'I won't. Promise.'

With a sigh, Elizabeth turned and drifted out of the kitchen.

Mary tapped her foot, waiting for the tread of footsteps on the old wooden stairs, then the creak, creak, creak of floorboards above her head. Now she could go. She longed to leave. That's what love did to her—drove her frantic. Seeing him would help her get through the next few months; she couldn't do it without him. Leaving the low fire burning in the grate, she skipped to the kitchen door, opened it a crack, and slipped out.

The late September night chilled her skin. The moon loitered in the dark sky and splashed a soft mellow glow of light onto the ground. Mary picked up her skirts and ran, ran because she loved to make her footsteps pound in time with her heartbeat, because it made her blood thunder through her veins, and because she would reach him that much quicker. She sprinted up the farm track and past the field of stubbled wheat towards Greenoak Woods. At the woods, she didn't stop running. Filling her lungs with its damp breath, its earthy incense, she leapt over fallen tree trunks, familiar with this path and weightless with anticipation.

She slowed as she turned off the track, then stopped, panting, breathless. He was already here, up

7

ahead, his back against a broad leafy tree. *Samuel.* Holding her breath, she waited. He shifted to face her. Yes, he sensed her. Of course he did.

He pushed himself off the tree and opened his arms wide.

Mary exhaled and dashed towards him, laughing. She jumped into his arms, knowing he would catch her. With a gasp, she wrapped her arms around his neck and buried her face in his chest. She closed her eyes and revelled in his smell of sea spray, of sweat. He gave a low chuckle with his lips pressed up against her ear, and shivers rippled down her spine. He clutched a strand of her hair and ran it through his fingers. His touch surged through every fibre of her body; he might as well be caressing her bare skin.

Samuel tugged her hair and pulled her face up to meet his. He grazed his stubbled chin across her cheek, exposed her neck, and trailed kisses over her throat. Her pulse quickened, and her grip tightened. He licked around her lips before he pressed his mouth to hers, plunged his shameless tongue deep inside, and slid his hand behind her neck to hold her firm. She opened up to him and let him taste her, whimpering when he flicked his tongue against the roof of her mouth. Her own tongue twined around his, stroking with a driving need. His kiss tasted of rum, honey sweet and hot as a sultry summer evening. Her worries dissipated in a shimmering haze.

His hand travelled down her body, squeezed her buttocks, and pinned her against him. Needing to touch, she pulled at his shirt and freed it from his trousers. She slid her hand inside to stroke the smooth, hard contours of his chest, knowing he would want more.

A muffled crack of a snapping branch made her break away from his kiss. Wide-eyed, she whispered up at him, 'Is someone out there, watching?'

He raised his head and frowned at something—or was it someone—over her shoulder, then bent his lips close to hers. 'No, it's only a deer.'

Helpless to control her own desire, she ran her hand down his chest to his stomach.

He moaned softly. 'Oh, maid, you know I can't stand it. I have to have more.'

Mary giggled. 'I know it, and I don't mind.' She glided her free hand down his side, his waist, and over his crotch to grip his thick, stiff erection. He gasped and jumped, and she smiled into the hollow of his throat.

'Oh God. I love you, maid.'

He placed his powerful hands on her shoulders and nudged her to her knees whilst she unbuckled his trousers, which slid to the floor with her.

Chapter 3

B enjamin held his breath and slunk behind a twisted oak tree, rooted to the spot in the cold, still silence of the night. Had he been seen? He didn't think so, better not have been; he didn't want them knowing he watched in the shadows. He didn't want her knowing, anyway. He couldn't care less about Samuel.

He pursed his lips to let out a controlled breath and glanced down at Jess. She was flat on the ground, her ears alert. He could rely on her to be quiet. He inched his head away from the tree and risked a look.

The waxing moon hung heavy in the night sky, blurred beneath a dark pall of cloud. He glimpsed only indistinct, shadowy figures, shapeless shapes. Even so, they pressed up against each other, caressing, kissing. Benjamin returned to cower behind the oak. He shouldn't be watching, tormenting himself. Why did he stay? Because he had promised himself he would always make sure she was safe. But really, she didn't look like she was in trouble. And safe from whom? Would she really be safe with him?

Again, an image swam behind his eyelids. Large hazel eyes wide with fright, hiding behind thick copper hair. Benjamin gripped the rough bark and slammed his head against the tree. What the fuck was he doing? He craned his neck and took another look.

The clouds parted like a curtain, and a swathe of moonlight fell across them to reveal an intimate scene between two lovers. She sank to her knees, his trousers bunched into a knot around his ankles.

Benjamin watched, digging his nails into the gnarled bark. If she struggled, if she pushed him off or tried to get away, he would help her. He would. But she wouldn't. She never did. Like a starving man, he devoured the sight, sweat slithering down his chest and back, his breath coming in shallow pants. Swallowing down the bitterness that rose in his stomach, he dragged his fingers down the rough bark until they bled. This was what he wanted her to do to him, dammit; her touch was all he could think about.

Benjamin pushed himself up against the tree, his own rock-hard erection painful as he thrust it against the coarse bark, his flimsy trousers no protection. Breathless, he reached inside his trousers and pumped up and down in a steady rhythm whilst ravenously watching them. He came quickly and stifled a cry.

Horrified, he gazed down at the sticky mess in his hand and flinched. He was disgusting. He wanted to be sick. Pushing himself off the tree, he backed away from them, waiting until he was certain they couldn't hear him before he turned, stumbled, and ran.

At the edge of the woods, he fell onto his knees and retched, bringing up nothing but bile. He wiped his hands clean on the damp grass before fleeing back to his cottage and flinging open the door. It slammed hard behind him, and he slumped against it to steady his breath. He rubbed his eyes, and his vision swam back into focus.

A soft orange glow from the fire in the hearth beckoned him. What he needed was the warmth of a roaring blaze. He threw some wood on the fire before collapsing onto a chair. Bright flames cavorted against the soot-blackened fireplace, and beside him was a table with a bottle of brandy and a glass goblet. The bottle clink, clink, clinked against the glass as he poured a drink with trembling hands. Lifting the glass to his lips, he threw it down his throat and waited. Heat tracked down his chest, his body blazing as the liquid fire journeyed through him. Then it was gone. He reached for the bottle, poured another, and took measured mouthfuls until he drained the glass.

Oh, his existence was worthless, and he only had himself to blame because he spent it like a thief in the night, a coward. Why did he go? Because he had to stop them screaming. The rabbits caught in the poacher's gin traps sounded human. Their cries ripped through his cottage, through his head. Screaming out at him in pain and suffering. Because when he woke, he thought the screams were made by his mother; they sounded just like her cries for help. He should have left when he saw Mary. She never needed him.

His eyes rested on an unlit tallow candle standing in its holder on the smoke-stained lintel above the fireplace. As if possessed, he rose, reached for it, and leant towards the fire. The wick caught; it gave a subdued, dim light that left a trail of vapour as he set it on the table beside him and sat down.

Focusing on the flame, he rolled up the shirt sleeve on his left arm and lost control of his breathing. With eyes half-closed, he held his wrist over the flickering light and sighed, soothed by the familiar acrid smell of burnt flesh and singed hairs. He clenched his teeth and dug his nails into the palm of his shaking hand. Balling his other hand into a fist, he slammed it hard against his thigh and screwed up his face. *Wait, keep it there. Wait.* Sweat soaked his shirt, pain seared his body, and he focused on it until the despair in his head dissolved, until he had control. Only then did he remove his hand and let his head slump on the back of the chair.

He wished he could disappear. This had to stop; he was destroying himself.

It was time to stop.

Chapter 4

Grace, the bonesetter walked towards her cottage, away from St Merryn. It had been a good day, hard but good. She'd treated a family with worms, dressed a cut finger, and lanced a boil. A big boil on a big behind. She laughed and shook her head to free it of the image. And then she saw him, Benjamin, running from the direction of Greenoak Woods. His arms hugged his body as he stumbled and lurched like he was trying to hold in pressure. A man shunned or scorned by most of the village, and for no good reason. But still, this wasn't the first time she'd seen him out alone late at night. She'd heard the rumours, but she was always hearing rumours.

As she neared her cottage, she glimpsed a figure slumped against her door, so slender it could be a child. But no, she recognised her, and this wasn't a child. The figure moved aside as Grace approached but said nothing, so Grace opened the door and let herself in, leaving it ajar.

Once inside, the bonesetter went to her chair by the window overlooking the beach she loved so much. She kicked at the legs so it turned and faced into the room instead, then plopped down, making the chair legs wobble, and watched the door.

The slight young girl inched into the cottage and edged towards her. She wore a thick grey woollen shawl crossed in front and tied behind. Grace glanced down at her

14

own legs and imagined wrapping that shawl around one of her own hefty thighs. It might fit. Just.

As the girl crumpled into a seat, Grace tilted her head and studied her. Everything about this girl was grey apart from her hair. She looked as if all the air had leaked out of her body, her copper hair falling across her pale face like a shield. The girl remained perfectly still except for her hands, which performed an intricate dance as they clasped and twisted together.

With a shaky voice, the girl uttered words that caught the bonesetter's attention and sent chills down her spine.

'I'm pregnant, but it wasn't my fault. He forced himself on me, and now I have a bairn I don't want and can't have. No one must find out.'

Grace shook her head as if denying what she'd heard could make the words go away, but it was no use; they called out for attention because she alone knew this had happened before to other young women. It happened too often. She turned her gaze away from the girl to stare blankly at nothing, to gather her thoughts. When she looked back, the girl raised her bowed head to ask the question they all asked.

'Can you help me? Please, you're the only one who can.'

She expected the request but didn't reply. This couldn't go on; something had to be done.

'Please, I need help. Please.'

The bonesetter could no longer bear to look at her beseeching hollow-eyed stare. She'd seen that look of despair before; the pain they held was the type that destroyed a woman, so she dropped her head to look at her

15

empty hands. This girl was, what? Sixteen or seventeen years old, but she looked so much younger. She would, of course, do what she always did—offer to take the baby, to care for it after it was born. But fear and shame always made them say no to that suggestion; they were as desperate to get rid of them as she was to keep them. Being pregnant and unmarried was the worst possible condition they could find themselves in. They would be forever tarnished, and the child too, no matter that it wasn't their fault. Grace took a deep, slow breath. 'Tell me how it happened.'

Perhaps the girl would refuse to tell. Sometimes they did, the scar of humiliation sealing their lips. But no, between stutters and hiccups, she unwrapped her secret and laid it bare, her sobs and tremors making her delicate hands flutter like a fragile bird.

'And you've no idea who it was?'

They never knew or claimed not to know, saying it was dark, they couldn't see, so Grace caught her breath when the girl replied.

'Oh, I know who it was.'

'Who?'

The girl bent her slender young body towards her and, as her voice sank to barely a sigh, she whispered his name.

***

THE BONESETTER TRIED to disguise a yawn with the back of her hand. It was early, but that wasn't the problem. She hadn't slept well the previous night because now she knew a secret but didn't know what to do about it. The worry of it kept gnawing at her.

The village was quiet today. It was too early for the morning risers, but the door to the cottage she needed was wide open, waiting for her to enter. She ducked under the lintel and took in the scene. A man slumped in a chair in the centre of the room, groaning and holding his hand to his face with two other men stood beside him. She gave a sympathetic smile, but secretly she couldn't wait to get started. She enjoyed this bit the most, giving relief from pain.

She rummaged around in her bulky, worn-out leather bag. *Where was it?* That was the trouble with sausage-sized fingers—they sometimes got in the way. She pushed aside unwanted objects until her nails tapped against a long, cold, thin metal item. A tooth key. She extracted it from the bag and held it up. *Yes, this one should do.*

Stepping up to the chair in front of her, she held the key at arm's length. 'This one will fit you.'

The occupant of the chair groaned and moaned, gripping the side of his face with one grubby hand.

She cracked her knuckles. 'Let's do it.' She advanced towards him, prised his legs apart with a knee to get in between them, then wriggled her hips so she could get as close to him as possible. He slithered down in the chair, his legs splayed out wide. Grace brought one of her knees up and rested it on his chest, then nodded to the two men, who pinned his arms down on either side of the chair. It was time to start.

When he opened his mouth, she turned her face and tried not to gag as his putrid breath wafted over her. She

17

pushed hard to force the key over the decayed tooth. Good, very good, now it was trapped. Taking her time, she turned the key. The tooth was broken, rotten, so it should come out, but she didn't want to shatter it and spend all night picking out the pieces from his bleeding gum. She turned it again, and the man let out a scream. 'Do you want me to come back later, after breakfast? I don't mind. It's very early in the morning.'

He moaned but shook his head, screwing his eyes shut.

Grace swivelled the key once more, listening for the unmistakable crunch of breaking bone, but she couldn't hear anything above his deafening bellows of pain. Ah, that was it. It rippled through her fingers, the jerk then the crack of bone. Now it was time to pull.

Despite his cries, she pushed her knee into his chest and wrenched and wrestled with the tooth. With a sucking, popping sound, it burst free. She flew backwards, hit the back wall of the cottage with a thud, and took a minute to steady herself. At least she hadn't landed on the floor; getting up again was always a challenge. She examined the tooth and nodded. A clean break, no gum or jawbone attached. A skilful job. She stomped back to the chair, brandishing the blackened tooth before her, and gazed down at its owner.

His beetroot-red face gasped for breath, and he held his chest with his now free hands, bright blood spilling down his chin. 'You nearly killed me. Broke some ribs, I reckon.'

Cocking her head, she considered his words. She did sometimes forget how much pressure she was capable of creating, and compared to her, he was scrawny. She prodded his chest, and he swatted her hand away. Broken ribs? She didn't think so. He couldn't really complain, anyway. She never charged much for her services, just bartered for food usually. Most of the villagers could not afford anything else. They needed her; who else would do this for so little?

She passed him a compress made of marigold, yarrow, and comfrey. He could clean himself up. She'd done enough. She turned to leave but hesitated when one of the men said, 'That bloody Carnarton boy. I'll wring his bloody neck if I catch him.'

They meant Benjamin. Someone or other was always moaning about Benjamin. 'What's he supposed to have done this time?' she asked.

'Same as always. Let all me rabbits out of the traps last night. Was food for our table. I'll kill him.'

'Might not be him,' Grace said.

'It is, gibbet boy. He's strange, that one.'

'Don't call him that. It isn't his fault what his da did. His scars run deep.'

'It's no excuse. What's he doing out every night, anyway? He shouldn't be there, and because of him, we've no rabbits to pay you with now.'

'I can wait.' She scratched at her scalp, then her arms, the itch spreading. She needed to get out.

Escaping outside, she breathed in the clean morning air until it filled her lungs.

Oh, Benjamin. They were right; it had to stop. She had to make it stop.

Chapter 5

As dawn light stealthily crept under his curtains and into his bedroom, Benjamin stirred and prised open one eye. A chorus of birdsong erupted outside and woke him further. He cranked open both eyes, raised his arms languorously, and stretched out his body like a lazy cat. He opened his mouth in a wide noisy yawn, then shook his head to clear it of sleep.

Memories of the previous night came back to him, the details crowding his mind. Oh God, he was a damned fool. He brought his arms down and examined his new blisters. They bubbled red and raw on his skin. He skimmed them with his fingertips, then pushed down so pain lanced through him. Closing his eyes, he sank back against the pillow. Better, that was better. It was only agony that held him together.

Benjamin sat up in bed and shivered. Rubbing the sleep from his eyes, he snatched his clothes and threw them on before the cold morning air bit into his body. Perched on the edge of his bed, he stretched out a hand for his old black boots and forced his feet into them, his toes crushed up inside, and tied the strings he used for laces. His jacket strained as he pulled it taut across his shoulders and snapped as another stitch broke. *Damn, was he getting bigger?* Well, too bad. There wasn't money for another jacket. This one would have to do.

Now, where was Jess? He found her in the kitchen lapping up water from her bowl and leant against the doorframe to watch, his arms folded. No better way to waste time, but he didn't have time to waste. Striding to the cottage door, he opened it and stooped under the low lintel. A blast of cold air greeted him, tainted with the briny scent of the ocean. He gulped it down and listened to the thundering voice of the sea.

Waves exploded against the rocks below the cliff, then roared up the beach. The sound filled his head, the melancholy, constant surge of the sea. If he could rip his heart out and let the sea take it, he would. Just to stop himself feeling.

Following the direction of the wind, Benjamin walked around the outside of the cottage to the water pump and stuck his head under. Icy cold water splashed over his head and took his breath away, making him gasp. He stayed under. He turned his face into the water, opened his mouth, and shocked the last remnants of sleep away.

Jess rounded the corner and jumped up at him, placing big paws on his shoulders and making him stagger backwards under her weight. 'Steady, girl, you're too big for that. You'll knock me over.'

He picked up a stick and wound his arm back. He flung it hard, lifting his feet off the ground with the effort. He left her to run after it and sauntered back inside, staying just long enough to grab his hat and run his fingers through his wet hair to release the curls and knots. The front door banged shut behind him. With long swinging steps, he strode inland, away from the cliffs and the sea, towards work.

When he reached the edge of the muddy, furrowed field called Upper Meadow, Jess gave a low rumble. Benjamin stopped, squinted, then frowned. Samuel Treleggan crossed the field in front of him.

Damn. He knelt on one knee and pretended to retie his bootlaces. The last thing he wanted to do was catch up with Samuel. He kept his head down but raised his eyes, watching as Samuel sauntered towards a group of women and children. They stooped low, busily picking stones off the field. The women stopped their work as Samuel approached. They hitched themselves upright, keeping their hands on their backs. They gathered around, looking up at him as he tilted his head back and laughed. He leant towards the young girls, and their faces flushed as they giggled.

It was just because he was tall and broad and probably handsome—if you liked piercing, unflinching blue eyes. Benjamin scowled.

Samuel left the women, ran a hand through his fair hair to push his fringe off his face, and strolled over to talk to some labourers hard at work lifting potatoes. They also stopped their work, slapped him on the back, and even shook his hand. He was most likely telling them about his latest daring smuggling run, of how much they would all get from it. Or bragging about his father again. He thought that having the local bailiff for a father made him better than most. Well, it didn't. Oh God, how they all loved Samuel. Or pretended to, anyway.

Samuel crossed the field and disappeared out of sight. Only then did Benjamin rise and follow the same path, pulling his hat down low. He kept his head bowed, and crept past the women and children. But they spotted him, yelling, 'Gibbet boy, where's our rabbits?'

He stuffed his hands in his pockets and walked on. A stone thumped into his shoulder, then another hit his back, so he picked up his pace until he was out of range.

When the labourers caught sight of him, they shook their fists, then turned their backs. Shrugging, he kept his eyes on the ground and glanced at Jess, who padded beside him. Who needed friends when they had a dog like her? They could all go to hell. Anyway, he preferred to be ignored. He was practised at being unobserved and used to being alone.

At the end of the field, he paused and leant on a five-bar gate with one foot on the bottom rung, his arms folded across the top. Spread out in the valley below lay Goodtoknow Farm. Looked at from here, it reminded him of one of Mary's intricate tapestries—the one hanging in the farmhouse kitchen, the one he ran his fingers across when no one looked. As daylight fought and won for dominance of the morning, he just made out the stream uncoiling like blue thread through the lush meadows and rich brown fields. There was something about this farm that called out to him and drew him in. It wasn't just Mary; an invisible strand had unravelled and wound around him. Perhaps it had something to do with the family who ran the farm. But the tenant farmer, Mary's father, didn't know he even existed. Since the death of his wife, Jane, Mary's father rarely noticed anyone anymore, too wrapped up in his grief.

Ah, Jane. Now, Jane he had liked, and God knew he didn't like many people. After the death of his mother and the hanging of his father, he'd come to this farm.

23

Apprenticed at six years of age to work all day and sleep in the barn at night. The first time he had met Jane, she had stroked his head and brushed one finger under his chin to tilt his face so she could look at him. To his surprise, he'd let her, not flinching away like he usually did. She'd looked, really looked, past the skin and bones and into his soul, and she'd liked what she saw. For that reason, he liked her too.

He thumped the top of the gate and vaulted over, waiting for Jess to follow. They took Sandy Lane down to the farmhouse. Passing a copse of copper beech trees, he kicked the crisp fallen leaves and watched the wind scoop up the brittle brown heap and bring them back to life to dance and whirl around him. His eyes on the leaves, he was far too late to notice Samuel, who emerged from behind a tree brandishing a large branch. Samuel gripped it in both hands, swung it like a bat, and slammed it hard into Benjamin's stomach.

Doubled over from the impact, Benjamin landed on his knees and grasped at short, wheezing gulps of air, then lunged and grabbed hold of Jess before she sprang for Samuel. She bared her teeth and growled.

'Keep that dog off me, gibbet boy, or I'll hurt her. I know what she used to be, a bait dog, so keep her off,' Samuel shouted as he swung the branch above Benjamin's head. 'And in case you're wondering, that was for spying on people when you should be minding your own business. Always out at night creeping around, snooping, prying. I know you've been watching me and Mary, little sneak. I know you were there last night. If I catch you again, I'll break your arm. Or I'll tell my da. Tell him you don't deserve that tied cottage.'

Staying down, Benjamin held onto Jess and caught his breath.

Seconds crawled by.

The branch hovered inches above his head. He stared at it, waiting. Samuel threw the branch down with a clatter. 'A coward and a freak, that's what you are.' He turned and left.

With a groan, Benjamin staggered to his feet and muttered, 'The lubber-headed fool. Call Jess off, or you'll hurt her. I called her off to stop her from killing you!' He shouted out the last line since Samuel was out of earshot, then spat on the ground, which still bore the imprint of Samuel's boots.

To calm Jess, he bent and wrapped his arms around her, stroking her head. 'Yes, you were a bait dog until I rescued you. Left for dead, but I nursed you back to life. Like me, you have the scars to prove it. I know you'd give your life for me. He's got no idea how powerful you are, but he's a fool.'

He rose and stumbled after Samuel, clenching his jaw and cracking his knuckles. Everyone loved that bloody man, everyone but him. He hated him with a passion. Not just because he shared a foul secret with him and not just because Samuel secretly met Mary, but because Samuel was not the man everyone thought he was.

Why didn't Mary's heart reveal what her eyes couldn't see?

Why was it he alone saw the real person?

**

BENJAMIN TRUDGED TO work, holding his stomach and cursing Samuel with every stride he took. When he reached the farm and passed the cattle barn, a voice called out to him. A voice he loved. His pulse quickened. He raised his head and held his stomach tight because a yearning ran through him that made his muscles spasm.

'Benjamin, I need you.'

Oh, how he wished that were true.

Entering the old wooden barn, he passed rusting scythes and tin buckets. As he inhaled the earthy scent of the dirt floor, animals, and manure, he paused to look for her.

The soft peaceful sound of oxen breathing, chewing, and shifting their weight came from his right side, but Benjamin turned to look down the other side of the barn. In the dim light swirling with dust, he found her. She stood with her back to an open window. Her straw bonnet, secured with sky-blue ribbons, framed her lovely face. His heart lurched. She was almost as tall as him, her dark hair tied into a braid. He imagined it coiling down her back to her waist. But she wasn't alone.

'Come here. You're helping me today. We've got to winnow the corn. Elizabeth is feeling ill, so you'll have to take her place.'

She stood with another labourer and, of course, Samuel. His heart sank, but he went to her without hesitation. Even though Samuel's arctic-blue eyes narrowed, he answered her call. Not taking his eyes off Mary, he drew near. Now he could watch and listen to her all day, and he lowered his face to hide a smile.

A white winnowing sheet lay stretched out on the barn floor, piled high with dusty golden corn. The barn

26

doors opposite the window were wide open. A stiff breeze blew through the barn and made the pale blue ribbons on Mary's hat flutter like streamers behind her.

Benjamin reached his place as a streak of weak morning sunlight ran across the floor to land at his feet. He bent and picked up the corner of the sheet opposite Mary and waited for her command. Waited while Samuel dropped his corner to stroll over and brush aside her strands of escaping hair, leaning down with his lips beside her ear. Whilst Samuel talked, she covered her mouth and laughed, glancing up at Benjamin to laugh again.

What lies was he telling her now? Benjamin spied on them from beneath his lowered hat. He kicked at the shaft of light, and it shrank away.

Eventually, Samuel walked back to his corner, and Mary counted down. 'Three, two, one.'

The sheet rose in the air, and as the corn flew up high, the wind caught the chaff and toyed with it, carried it away, and left shiny, plump golden nuggets of grain to sink back down. The barn filled with dusty, hazy air as the task was repeated in a rhythmic pace. Benjamin coughed, sneezed, and screwed up his eyes, ignoring the grime-covered skin that he desperately wanted to scratch and claw clean.

Still coughing, he glimpsed Mary through the blur of chaff as she watched Samuel. He scowled and shifted his gaze. God, he wished he'd go away and never come back. He wished she would look at him like that. He wished . . .

He yanked hard on the sheet and sent his turmoil of thoughts to spin with the chaff, to circle the barn and be blown away by the wind. He raised his face and closed his eyes to let the breeze blow the ache from his head until the

27

only thought that remained was the only one that mattered. He loved her, and he had to do something about it.

'Benjamin, pay attention. You don't get paid to sleep at work.'

His eyes snapped opened. Her words stung more than any sticks or stones.

Chapter 6

Elizabeth gazed out of her bedroom window at the full moon. A harvest moon. She licked her finger and pressed it to the glass, listening to the squeak it made as she traced the moon's outline in the square pane. Her mother always said it was female, that the waxing moon stood for fertility, completeness. It certainly could be; it looked swollen and fat. And such a bright orange, more like a cold sun in the dark night sky.

Her left hand curled into a fist around a strip of fabric the same colour as the moon. Ignoring it, she looked out of the window.

Across from the farm track that stretched into the darkness like a slash of grit grey, the wheat field unfolded, just a dark patch of stubble now. Her eyes, drawn to the track, slid up, up, up to the woods. *Those damned woods.* The very thought of them made her insides ball into a tight knot and caused droplets of moisture to bead across her forehead. With her free hand, she wiped the sheen of sweat off her face and wrenched at the top of her nightdress to free the ties around her neck.

She threw open the window, and hung her head out to breathe in the cool night air. A mild evening breeze caressed her hot face and ruffled the lace on her cotton nightdress. Dark clouds drifted across the moon, sailing past in ragged formation, and the moonlight dimmed.

She stared at the cattle huddled below. Their breath rose like a mist in the night as they snorted and jostled for the best position against the farmhouse wall, wanting to suck the heat out of it. The farm was calm and peaceful as if wrapped up in a warm blanket, but she remained trapped beneath, smothered.

Sticking out her left hand she uncurled her fist, finger by slow finger, to reveal the orange ribbon. One of Mary's favourites. The wind plucked it up and let it fall, tumbling onto the cattle below. It caught on the head of one shaggy beast, dangled and swayed until shaken free, when it fluttered to the ground and was trampled in the mud. Ruined. Mary would be upset, and she didn't care because she partly blamed Mary for this nightmare. Mostly she blamed herself.

She should have run. But she didn't.

She should have screamed. But she didn't.

She should have fought. But she didn't.

And who would believe her, anyway? Just a girl, hardly a woman, she didn't count for much.

Elizabeth took another look at the woods, and the dread of what was to come made her cry. She dug her nails into her palms and squeezed her eyes shut, brushing away damp tears with the back of her hand. Feeling sorry for herself was pointless.

She closed the window and shutter and plunged the room into darkness, except for two bobbing yellow candle lights. One beside her bed, one beside Mary's. The outline of Mary's face flickered in and out of the light until Mary blew out the candle and vanished into the darkness.

Elizabeth rubbed her arms and paced back and forth beside the window. And where was her mother when she needed her? Needed her more than at any other time in her life? Gone. Perhaps it was just as well; she couldn't have helped and would have guessed the truth. She always had. So that left Mary. What if Mary let her down? It would make no difference to her plan; she would do it herself because anger propelled her, that and the need for this to be over, finished and forgotten.

She slicked clammy hands down her nightdress, and focused on her candle. When she reached her bed she crawled under the covers and blew out the flame.

In the darkness, floorboards creaked, a door slammed, and someone coughed—her grandfather? Then silence. She nibbled her nails. If only sleep would claim and drug her too instead of fears and doubts gnawing away all night.

Her body arched as an ache rippled through her stomach.

She smiled in the night and pushed her fists into her belly until the dull pain became a searing hot spasm that made her grip the bedclothes and curl up into a tight ball. She didn't care about the pain; she welcomed it. It brought an end to her torment.

Chapter 7

Mary woke from a brief fitful sleep and cried out at the memory of her dream, of someone creeping about in the night. A hand clamped over her mouth to keep her quiet, and panic crawled up her spine. She opened her eyes wide but saw only darkness. A familiar flowery scent tickled her nose, and soft tendrils of hair stroked her cheek. Her sister's breath, warm and ragged, whispered in her ear, 'I think it's time.'

Time? Impossible. Shaking her head, Mary sat bolt upright. 'No, it can't be. It's too soon, far too soon. We have months to wait yet.'

Elizabeth gasped and stifled a moan. 'It's time.'

Mary rubbed her eyes and swallowed. This wasn't right; she had months before she had to face this ordeal. She couldn't do this now. She wasn't ready. Fear crawled out of the pit of her stomach and tethered her to the bed.

Elizabeth tugged at the bedclothes. 'Come on, I can't wait.'

Mary fought the urge to refuse and bury herself beneath the bedclothes. She swallowed down the cry because her sister needed her and because she'd made a promise to her mother to always take care of her sister. How could anyone break a promise made to a dying mother? No, she had no choice.

Allowing herself a sigh, she pushed the blankets back and eased out of bed. Mary groped for the clothes neatly folded on her chair and pulled on her dress. She slid her feet into her flat black shoes and stopped dead. If she put them on now, the wooden soles would make too much noise. Mary kicked them off and picked them up in one hand. Rising, she took a few faltering steps towards the door, paused and returned to the bed; kneeling down and reaching underneath for a hidden canvas bag. Her hands found and wrapped around the handle. Thank God this, at least, was ready. She got to her feet and took a deep breath but had to grip her stomach hard to stop herself falling apart. She squeezed her eyes shut to close off tears. With outstretched arms, Mary inched her way through the dark towards the bedroom door, where her sister's trembling body waited for her. Reaching for Elizabeth's hand, she squeezed, a reassurance she didn't feel.

Mary crept onto the landing and waited, listening to long, drawn-out snores and snuffles coming from her father and grandfather's rooms, then slunk along the hallway and blinked in the dark. It was no use; no light stole through the shutters. Stretching out a hand, Mary fumbled for the familiar wooden newel post at the top of the stairs. Elizabeth's hand clenched hers so hard her knuckles popped, dragging her backwards and downwards to the cold hard floor. Mary gently dropped her shoes and bag and placed a hand over Elizabeth's mouth, smoothing her hair. Elizabeth shuddered beneath her. *What pain and fear must she be in? She was only fifteen, for God's sake.* Mary shook her head and pushed her own dread aside.

After minutes that felt like hours, Elizabeth rose, and so Mary did the same. Tiptoeing to the top of the stairs, she put a bare foot on the top step. It creaked. Mary paused, but Elizabeth gave her back a push. She descended, sliding her hand down the smooth wooden bannister, keeping her feet close to the wall and pausing at every groan the old stairs made, prodded by Elizabeth every time she did. The worn dents in each tread were familiar, but when had they become so noisy?

On reaching the kitchen, she held Elizabeth's damp hand as she crossed to the front door, her toes curling up on the cold flagstone floor. A noise from above caught her breath. Mary froze.

Elizabeth whispered, 'Go.'

But Mary couldn't move. Above her head came a thump. Was someone else getting out of bed? Feet stomped, and a door handle rattled.

Mary's body jumped into action. She prised open the front door just wide enough to let them through. Pulling Elizabeth out, she closed the door with a click behind her. The mild evening welcomed her. She sucked in the night air to fill her lungs and calm her beating heart.

'Wait,' Elizabeth whispered and fell to her knees again.

Taking the opportunity to slip on her shoes, she waited until Elizabeth could move, then pulled her sister's arm over her shoulders and carried her away from the farmhouse, shoving aside the cattle to head towards Greenoak Woods.

The full moon hung like a lantern, its bleached light spilling down to guide the way, but the woods struck her as dark and menacing this night, and she had to enter them using an old but unfamiliar track. She'd practised this route though, once—no, twice.

Mary supported her sister, stumbling through the stubble, all that was left of the wheat field, and gazed across at the dark woods again. *Could the moonlight penetrate the trees? Should she go back for a light?* No, too late. Someone might see her, and she knew the way. She just had to stay calm and not panic.

Mary entered the shadowy woods and hauled her sister along with her, gasping with the effort and not daring to stop. She kept moving, but now she wasn't sure. They had to leave the old path and join a simple track, but where? She turned her head to-and-fro but didn't recognise anything. *Oh God, which way?*

Elizabeth tugged her dress and pointed to a small opening on their right. Was that it? Mary had no idea but took it anyway. They moved deeper into the woods, and the moonlight dimmed. Mary glanced up at the sky, and a pall of darkness sneaked across the moon, enveloping her in inky black. She stopped dead and waited for the clouds to move, but Elizabeth murmured, 'Keep moving. Straight ahead.'

Mary took a tentative blind step forwards, then another. The pale moonlight unhurriedly returned, but the woods remained eerily hushed. Something was wrong. The track petered out with no evidence anything ever trod this way. They were surely lost. A muscle spasm crossed her eyes, and she winced. The dense trees loomed up above her head, and the shadows deepened.

What was that lurking amongst the trees? It looked like the dark outline of a hunched figure waiting to pounce. The forest floor smelt of damp, rotten compost. Mary glanced at Elizabeth. It was Elizabeth who was terrified of these woods, even refusing to enter them during the day when there was nothing to fear, so what courage did it take for her to enter them now? She took another look through the trees and puffed out her cheeks. It was just a stunted, decayed tree stump marooned in the forest. Her shoulders relaxed. No, there was nothing to fear from these woods, not ever.

Mary continued, fighting her way through dense branches. Ignoring the stabbing pain from her aching muscles, she pulled her sister onwards until a spiked thicket barred her way. She recognised this place.

Mary staggered and pushed herself and her quivering sister through the tight clump of prickly bushes, the thorns drawing rivulets of blood as they scraped across her skin. But they were here, their secret place, a place where no one came. An old abandoned mine shaft with the scattered derelict ruins of a stone house.

Sitting her sister down on the dry grass beside a low stone wall, she brushed Elizabeth's damp hair off her brow, cupped her small face, and focused on Elizabeth's frightened grey eyes. 'I'll be as quick as I can. Hold on, dearest. Hold on.'

Elizabeth's eyes held her own briefly before they glazed over, and she moaned. Mary reached into the canvas bag and withdrew a thick folded cotton rag and pressed it into her sister's moist hand.

Oh Lord, she wasn't ready for this. Mary trampled over the grass and weeds to the old mine shaft and knelt down. A foul stench made her gag and hold a hand to her nose. She brushed unruly leaves away and recoiled at the putrid pile of hair and bones underneath, where maggots still crawled over the remaining tissue. The corpse of some dead animal. Disgusting. She kicked it away, but the rancid smell remained. She pinched her nose tight and got to her feet, glancing across at Elizabeth, who squatted on the ground, watching her.

Mary got back down on her knees and winced. Rocks dug into her flesh, but she reached out for the massive stone slab cover lodged on top of the disused shaft and pushed, grunting with the effort. She could do this; she'd done it before. Her muscles screamed in pain. Stopping to wipe the sweat from her eyes with her sleeve, she took a rest.

The crack of twigs breaking under someone's creeping feet strangled the breath in her throat. She strained to hear, listening to the sounds around her. The trees whispered their secrets above her head, the plaintive vibrato call of a tawny owl floated eerily through the night, and the rustle of small animals stirred in the undergrowth. She heard Elizabeth's shallow panting. Nothing else.

Releasing her breath, she returned to the stone, forcing her arms straight. She strained, the tendons in her neck like wire. The slab scraped and rasped along the floor. Just a small gap, a little more would be enough. Her hands scratched and bleeding, she groaned long and low and pushed. It was done. That part, anyway.

Brushing at the damp, loose stones and blood that stuck to and stained her hands and dress, she sat back on her heels and gaped at the hole. *Did she really intend to go through with this?* She wanted more time to decide, to make another plan. A cold hard knot settled in her stomach. She glanced at her sister again. It would be better not to let her know. Mary dragged herself to her feet.

Elizabeth clamped the cotton rag between her teeth, smothering any screams. Beads of sweat clung to her forehead and top lip. She shuddered. Removing the rag, she pursed her lips and forced air out, screwing her face up in pain. She squatted on the ground, holding onto the tumbledown wall with one hand, her flimsy cotton dress pulled up around her waist.

Mary grabbed the canvas bag. She withdrew a tattered muslin cloth and laid it on the ground between her sister's legs.

Elizabeth doubled over and sank to the floor, panting, her legs bent, and let out a long, low moan.

Dear Lizzie, if I could share this pain, I would. If I could take this burden, I would.

A gush of water swept over Mary's feet as Elizabeth's waters broke. She sat and rubbed Elizabeth's legs, waiting for the contractions to intensify. Mary tussled with her prayers but lost.

Slivers of sweat trickled down Mary's back, and her hands shook. Nearly time, but she wasn't ready for this. At seventeen, she'd never delivered a child before; what made her think she could do this now? She'd rehearsed this in her head every night but would have to draw on all her experience on the farm to help her. Would it be like helping ewes deliver their lambs?

When the time came, would it be like killing a chicken by wringing its neck?

Oh God, it was the baby's head. 'I can see the baby's head. The baby's coming. Push, Elizabeth; keep pushing.' Mary watched in silence, her shaking hands now steady, her tense muscles now still, her breath even as she helped Elizabeth's baby slither into the world.

A boy! She picked him up. His tiny, defenceless body took her breath away. She could fit the whole of him on one hand. She scanned him. Perfect. Covered in blood and mucus and impossibly small, smaller than any baby she'd ever seen. And lifeless. If he'd been a newborn lamb, she would calmly tickle his nose with straw, but he was no lamb. She cleared his mouth, and he jolted and made a soft mewling noise like a kitten as if pleading with her that he too could be quiet.

This was life, a brand new life in her hands, at her mercy. She grabbed the cloth and wiped him clean.

'Do it. Do it now before it cries. You must do it; you promised,' Elizabeth hissed at her.

'No.' Mary drew in her breath and held it. She had promised. They had planned every last detail together, even this. But holding him changed everything. What ifs flooded her brain. What if they changed the plan? What if they left the baby at the church? What if they left the baby with the bonesetter? What if . . . She swallowed hard as hysteria rose up in her throat. There had to be another way. There was another way.

'Don't you make me do it, Mary. You said. You promised. I'm begging you, please.' Elizabeth sobbed hard. 'This has to be over now; it has to be. Just do it, finish it.'

Mary wiped her palms together, slick with sweat, and a shiver slid down her spine.

He was at her mercy.

'I can't do it. I can't,' she wept. And hadn't she always known she never would?

'I'll never forgive you,' Elizabeth cried out, her voice as cold, as bleak as death itself.

Mary jerked her head. There it was again, the snap of breaking twigs. Someone was out there. The baby let out a feeble wail, and she held him against her body, pressed him to her breast to stifle his cries. 'I heard a noise. I think someone's watching.'

'I heard no noise. It's nobody. You're wasting time. Hand it to me. I'll do it. I knew I'd have to.' Elizabeth's voice sounded flat, unemotional.

'No.' Mary shook her head and held him even tighter.

'Give it to me; it has to go. I don't want any part of that man remaining, reminding me.'

As Elizabeth grabbed at Mary's arm, Mary fell backwards, gripping the baby. Determined not to let him go, she pushed herself out of Elizabeth's reach.

'Just look, Lizzie.' Mary held him out, but her heart flipped. His body was limp and chill in her hands. Her world stopped spinning. 'What have I done?'

Elizabeth closed her eyes and sat back. 'It's gone. It's all over, and I'm glad.'

Mary laid him on the floor and tried to stand, grabbing the wall for support whilst tears spilt down her cheeks. 'I didn't mean to do it.' Muscles tightened in her chest, and her heart knocked against her ribs. Murder. It was murder. And it felt like she was dying too; she couldn't catch her breath. She leant against the wall and took short, sharp breaths until her vision cleared and her breathing slowed.

Mary couldn't look at his lifeless body as she waited for the placenta to be expelled. Not bothering to cut the cord, knowing Elizabeth's body would discard it with the placenta, she left him attached to Elizabeth for now, little more than a child herself.

She had meant to spare him. She wiped away tears and dried her legs with her dress. They had to continue with their plan now, had to because she would be hanged if this was ever discovered, and so too would Elizabeth.

Mechanically, she bound him and the placenta in the muslin cloth, his body trussed like a mummy as if he was of no importance. But she felt the dead weight of him as she picked him up. She left Elizabeth, who bled profusely. Mary told her it was normal, but even so, she didn't expect so much blood. So much scarlet blood. It was done now; it could never be undone. She carried him to the open mine shaft, choking back tears.

'Please God, forgive me.' She whispered a short prayer over his body and held him motionless over the mine shaft, willing him to come back to life. It was useless. Her hands shook as they parted to let him drop into the dark abyss. With a heavy heart, she shoved the hefty slab back into place to hide the terrible secret. As she struggled with the stone, an echoing splash floated upwards when his body hit the water below.

She helped Elizabeth get up, and together they stumbled back towards the farmhouse. Mary pointed her feet in the right direction, hoping that would get them home, unable to think. Elizabeth needed to stop, to rest, and so Mary waited, trembling from top to toe, shaking her head in denial. She turned to look back, and a scream caught in her throat.

Did a shadow move out of the trees?

Was that dark shape a stealthy, crouched figure?

Were they being watched, followed?

If they'd been seen, they were as good as dead too.

***

WHEN MARY WENT to bed that night, she couldn't extinguish her candle, afraid to be enveloped in darkness. She held onto her soft blanket and clenched it tight, unable to let it go as tears streamed down her face. Images of a pale wrinkled body with small tight fists haunted her thoughts. She fought her dreams and instead focused on an evening five months before. When this nightmare first began. When Elizabeth came to her because she needed to talk.

They had retired to the shadows of their dark bedroom. A cold wind rattled the windows, moaning and sighing wantonly. They climbed into bed together to keep warm. Elizabeth's fair hair hung down to her waist like golden strands of silk, and Mary began to braid it whilst Elizabeth talked.

'You look like a ghost tonight, Lizzie.'

'I don't feel well.'

'You're sick?' Mary's voice rose in concern.

Elizabeth was silent.

'Are you?'

'Something happened, Mary. I did something.' Elizabeth's voice was barely a whisper.

'Lizzie?'

'I went to the woods one evening. Don't remember why—collecting wood? I just went. Why wouldn't I?'

'No reason not to.'

'So, I went. But someone was there, waiting. He grabbed me from behind. A hand over my mouth. He pushed me to the floor. Oh, I don't remember the details; it was quick, a blur.'

Elizabeth began to cry, and Mary stroked her hair while the pit of her stomach turned to ice.

'Are you telling me that he—?'

'Yes, yes, and now I'm having a bairn.'

Mary hugged her sister. 'Oh God, I feel sick. My poor dear, I have to do something, tell someone.'

'No, Mary. Never.'

'Yes, to make sure he pays for this. You did nothing wrong, Lizzie. Don't worry. Who was it?'

Elizabeth buried her head in her hands. 'I don't know. It was dark.'

'Someone we know?'

'I said I don't know.'

'Can't you remember anything about him? Tell me, please.'

'No, I can't. Stop it, stop asking. I'm scared. Promise you won't tell.'

'It's too late for that—the bairn.'

Elizabeth squeezed Mary's hands until they hurt. 'Promise.'

'But Lizzie . . .' Mary searched Elizabeth's pearl-grey eyes, normally so untroubled, and found terror and something else. Something she finally recognised as shame. She whispered, 'What about the bairn?'

'Just make it go away, please.'

How to make such shocking news go away? Elizabeth was only fourteen—a staunch Methodist, a good, dutiful daughter and beloved sister. But having a child at fifteen? The stigma would stick, no matter that it wasn't her fault.

So they disguised the pregnancy, and now they must conceal the birth, but it came with such a terrible sacrifice. A life had been taken. A life in exchange for her sister's, because she remained convinced Elizabeth would not survive the disgrace if this secret was revealed. After the loss of her mother, she could not, *would* not be parted from her sister or cause her father further suffering. She told herself over and over it was an accident; perhaps the child was not meant to be. But whenever she pictured him, so small and defenceless, a knife of pain twisted at her heart. She was part of a proud Methodist family, but now she had profound doubts about God. *How could he let this happen?*

Later that night, she woke drenched in sweat and clawed at the hangman's noose constricting her throat. She held a hand to her neck. Death would surely be her fate if anyone ever found out the truth, and she had another reason for wanting this secret to remain concealed.

She had a secret of her own.

Chapter 8

Mary lay in bed with her eyes wide open and stared at the dark ceiling. A cock crowed loud and clear from somewhere on the farm. The previous night's dreams surfaced, and her body tensed. She stifled an urge to scream, to run away and hide, to suspend time forever.

Images from the night would not leave her. *Would they ever*? But she had other lives to protect. She pushed back the bedcovers and sat up, glancing at Elizabeth. 'How are you feeling this morning, Lizzie?'

'Scared. I'm staying here today. I can't face anyone.'

'I'm scared too.' Her hand shook with the fear of what she'd done.

Mary forced herself out of bed and went to her little side table to pour cold water into a washbowl and splash it on her face. The cold morning air and water did not make her shiver like they usually did; her insides were already ice. She picked up a mirror to tidy her hair and peer at her reflection. She looked the same on the outside, but deep down she was changed forever.

And now to face the day as if it were the same as any other. She slipped downstairs into the cold dark kitchen, lit a lantern hanging from a ceiling beam, and waited until it threw light over the long wooden scrubbed tabletop. Furze and turf lay stacked beside the fire, at least

45

one job that didn't need doing today. Not that it mattered. Her mind and hands needed distractions.

Trying to ignore the family Bible that exerted some compelling force, she knelt and shovelled ash from the grate into a small barrow and wheeled it outside to dump into the ash pit, then returned to light the fire in the open hearth. She pulled at her bottom lip with her teeth. Elizabeth did not look well; a warm nourishing drink would help build up her strength and hasten recovery. *Was recovery even possible?*

She jumped when the kitchen door opened and her father and grandfather entered. Had either of them got up last night? Did they already know where she'd been, what she'd done?

'Morning, Mary.'

'Morning, Da. Morning, Gramfer.' Mary poured milk into a pan, but it spilt in a white puddle over the table. Taking a deep breath, she tried again.

'What are you doing with that? Where's our Lizzie this morning?'

'She's feeling unwell. I'm making her some lambswool.'

'Yer looking a bit pale yourself. Nothing serious, is it?'

'No, she's got a bad pain. Women's troubles, that's all.' That would end further questions. *Please, no more questions.*

'Could you make some of that for your old Gramfer? Smells so good.'

''Course I can. Sit yourself down. Won't be long.'

Her father looked at her without seeing and turned to leave, lines of grief crisscrossing his face. He forgot to close the kitchen door behind him as usual.

'You've left the door open again,' her grandfather shouted after him.

A draught of cold morning air crept into the kitchen along with three clucking hens.

'Them spickety hens wants their breakfast.' Her grandfather laughed as he shooed them outside and let the door bang shut, making Mary jump and drop the cups on the table.

'Just adding the sugar and nutmeg. It's nearly ready.'

'You doing all Elizabeth's chores for her today?'

'Yes, Gramfer.'

He smiled at her. 'Well, I'm going to help you today.'

Mary blinked back tears. 'Thank you, Gramfer. I'm grateful.'

Mary turned away from her grandfather, unworthy of such kindness. It made her want to cry.

'Are you all right, Mary?' He patted her shoulder.

She knocked pots and pans together, made a disturbance, looking busy to distract from the sobs jostling to escape and the tears on the brink of spilling down her cheeks. Did he hear her faint 'yes'? It took every ounce of her resolve not to break down and weep before him and tell him everything. To confess it all and unburden herself. Her grandfather had a way of getting the truth out and never judging. But this was different.

She picked up two cups, put one down on the table for him, and hurried away with the other one for Elizabeth.

47

Closing the kitchen door, she leant against it to wipe away tears with the back of her hand. The stairs creaked as she climbed them and tiptoed into her bedroom, placing the cup beside Elizabeth, who lay with her back towards her, facing the outside wall. 'I've some lambswool for you, Lizzie. You could sit in the kitchen later if you feel up to it. After breakfast when everyone will be out working.'

Elizabeth said nothing, so Mary backed out of the room. What else was there to say? What comfort could she offer? She had none to give, being empty and cold inside.

Back in the kitchen, Mary put the baking iron over the fire, rolled up her sleeves, and reached into the hutch containing the sack of flour. Never needing to weigh anything, she scooped out handfuls of flour into a bowl, added honey and whey, and began mixing the bread. It wasn't fair; it just wasn't fair. The man causing all this heartache should be suffering right now, not her and not Elizabeth. She pounded the dough hard with her fists until her hands ached, until her thoughts turned to Samuel with his warm, husky voice and strong hands. He was working on the farm today to help bring in the potato harvest. Her body craved to be with him, hungered for the comfort his touch would give. But what if he could tell something was wrong? What if the shocking truth burst out of her unrestrained? What would he think of her, a murderer? She shuddered and wiped away another tear. It would be best if they were not alone today.

With the bread proving, Mary turned to the porridge. Soon the delicious aroma of steaming milk and oatmeal filled the kitchen, but her appetite had gone. Her stomach churned with anxiety, leaving no room for food.

The kitchen door opened, and she rearranged her face into a smile as the farm labourers trudged in for their breakfast. Not meeting anyone's gaze, she concentrated on a stack of bowls and ladled out dollops of steaming porridge, trying not to spill a drop, then hunkered down by the fire, blocked from view to avoid being drawn into conversation.

Whilst no one looked, she darted for the larder and loitered there until the scrape of chairs signalled everyone was leaving.

Over at last. The first few hours, at least.

***

THE REST OF the morning, she skulked about the farm and made sure she saw no one. She returned to the kitchen at noon, when it was time to call everyone in from the fields once again.

She waited, twisting her apron round and round in her hands. They walked in laughing, chatty and hungry as usual. Each man hung his hat on nails fixed along the low oak beams as he passed into the kitchen. Then Samuel appeared, bent in conversation with her father and sat himself down at the table.

Mary stole a furtive glance at him. His flaxen hair had grown so long it curled thickly over his collar. He laughed, and she drank in the familiar sound. Raising his head, he gazed up at her with his deep blue eyes and smiled knowingly, sensuously. Her cheeks flushed with heat just as he intended, and her hands released their grip on the apron.

The last person to sit was Benjamin, as usual. He perched at the end of the long table with Jess at his feet, keeping himself very much to himself. He wouldn't speak; he wouldn't look up. He never did, and it didn't matter because he didn't matter.

The rest of the labourers' crammed food into their mouths, ate and talked at the same time. Everyone except Benjamin, who, unusually for him, stared at her. It was not like him to gaze so openly. She scowled at him, and he ducked his head low.

To sit down and join them would involve conversation, so she backed out of the kitchen and carried a plate of food up to Elizabeth instead, released from the threat of questions at last. Elizabeth still slept, curled up into a tight ball like a small child, but the cup stood empty.

Mary settled on the edge of her own bed and forced herself to eat the dinner, but it stuck in her throat no matter how much water she swallowed. Elizabeth's slow, even breathing calmed her, and she rubbed her tired eyes. The bed looked so inviting. Instead, she went downstairs and hid behind the kitchen door, listening as everyone rose from the table and filed out. She thanked God that was over and there wasn't much of the day left to suffer.

The kitchen door burst wide open, and she looked up to see Samuel standing in the doorway like a God, his broad chest filling the frame.

'Forgot my hat.' He smiled, reached up to the rafters, and snatched it. 'Haybarn at three, Mary.'

It wasn't a question. He would expect her to be there.

As the hour of three approached, Mary's body quivered like a taut wire. Her stomach churned as she paced around the kitchen. Only the thought of him holding her in his big arms calmed her. She walked to the hay barn, swinging a pail of food for the cows and hoping she looked nonchalant. He had to be distracted, so he didn't ask questions, didn't notice any difference. And surely it was time to let others know about their relationship. It had been fun keeping it private, having a secret just between the two of them, but now it was time to reveal the truth, and she needed him to agree. Perhaps today was not the day for that discussion. She couldn't trust herself to speak.

The warm, dusty barn welcomed her, all sweet hay, milky cows, and dry straw. The entrance by the big doors filled with soft afternoon light, revealing the dust motes that swirled in the air. As she moved towards the back of the barn, this natural light petered out. Even so, she knew he was there, waiting for her. Her flesh tingled, and she could smell the musky scent of his sweat. It filled her with desire.

She passed a stack of straw, and a muscular arm reached out for her and pulled her towards him. He gave a deep-throated chuckle, and the sound dampened the edges of her fear. She closed her eyes and pressed herself up against his chest, wrapped her arms around him, and clung on.

He kissed the top of her head. 'We don't have long, maid. The rest of the men are waiting for their afternoon drink in the field. I said I'd help you take it out to them.'

Mary held him even tighter, resting her head against his chest and listening to his constant heartbeat. She didn't want to ever let him go. He would always love and protect her, provided he never found out about last night. She sighed.

He laughed again. 'I hear the longing in that sigh. We'll find time to be together soon, I promise. We'll meet in the woods as usual.'

Unable to answer because a sob crawled up the walls of her throat, she gulped it down before it burst out.

'Mary, I'm going to be away for a few days. There's one more run with the boat before the weather turns. A ship is making its way to Bristol, and we're going to meet it out at sea. I'll just be gone for a few days, three or four. I need to get the boat ready. There's work to do when I get back, of course, but four of us is going, so should be easy.'

This time she managed to raise her head and look at him. His going might give her time to compose herself, for the pain inside her to subside. Yet to be without him, to be completely alone, the idea made her head swim. He was dependable, faithful, and his absence would leave her vulnerable and insecure. She fought back a rush of tears. His hand clutched her chin and stroked her hair, and he stared deep into her eyes.

Please don't find the horror hidden there.

'Don't be afraid for me. Don't worry; I won't be gone long, and it's an easy run, the last of the year. I'll be back before you know it. I'll bring you back some pretty French ribbons, and if I see any oranges, I'll get them for you. I know you loves them so.'

'We must talk when you get back.'

'We will, Mary. We will. I love you, maid.'

He leant against her, crushing his body to hers. Her mouth sought his, needing the familiarity of his warm lips.

The excitement of secrecy and the danger of being caught always aroused him. He gripped her hair, pulled back her head, and locked his lips on hers. So he wanted her now, but she couldn't. Could she? He grasped her, demanding, and thrust against her. God, he was so hard, it made her moan. He pinned her against the bales of straw, making it impossible to push him away. With his fingers, he hitched up her skirts.

'There isn't time,' she whispered.

'I'll be quick, but I want you so much. I want you now.'

He pulled her dress up higher, one hand expertly sneaking up the inside of her thighs, and she gasped.

'See, you want to just as much as me,' he murmured into her hair.

And she did. Unexpectedly overcome with desire, she reached for his breeches, undid the buttons, and pulled them down as he gave a low moan.

'Shh, no noise.'

He put his head by hers and gasped into her hair again. His strong hands clasped her waist, lifting her up. She threaded her fingers together around his neck and tilted her body towards him, wanting this as much as he did. He entered her, and her body quivered in response. His hips began thrusting in a demanding rhythm, and she cried out as he sank deep inside her. He groaned his approval. Her heartbeat increased as he plunged faster. He clenched his jaw, something he always did when he held himself back, trying to prolong the ecstasy for both of them.

'My God, that feels good, so good. I do love you.'

Panting for breath, she couldn't reply, her fingers rigid where they gripped him. Her whole body throbbed, lost in the sensation. For that wonderful brief few moments, nothing else mattered, and everything was forgotten.

Before he released her, he kissed her gently, then straightened himself out and strolled towards the door.

She stared at his retreating back, at the swirl of dust he kicked up in his wake. He stopped to turn and smile, framed in the barn entrance, tousle-haired and grinning. Holding that image in her mind would comfort her when he was away and she needed him but couldn't have him.

He hadn't guessed anything was wrong. Was she an expert at deceit now? When he returned from his trip, it was time to let everyone know about their relationship.

No more lies.

No more furtive meetings.

One secret was enough.

***

THAT EVENING MARY slumped on the old oak settle in front of a glowing fire. All the labourers had either gone to their own homes or to their own beds if they lived on the farm. This was usually her favourite time of day, relaxing, spellbound by the dancing flames, enjoying idle chat with her family.

The settle creaked as her grandfather and then her father sat down. They performed their nightly ritual of lighting pipes and supping homemade beer. The homely sweet smell of pipe tobacco drifted drowsily around the room.

'Going to be one more run, then,' her grandfather said.

Her father puffed at his pipe. 'Aye, Gramfer. One more.'

'What they getting this time?'

'I've heard it's ankers of brandy, bacca, tea, silks, and ribbons.'

'Well, they do likes their moonshine and bacca, and I'm partial myself.' Her grandfather raised his tankard as if in a toast.

'Let them take their pleasure where they will, and the money made will keep many families from starvation this winter.'

Mary let her head fall back against the top of the wooden trestle. The conversation flowed around her, and she spread out her dress like a butterfly's wings in the sun, enjoying the heat from the fire on her body.

Her father tapped his pipe on the settle. 'Should be an easy run; we don't see customs men on this coast very often.'

'No, no, they do like their firesides.' Her grandfather chuckled.

She cast her eyes to his face and smiled at his grey bristle-brush hair and beard, a curly mane of silver. He'd somehow managed to hold the family together after the death of her mother, and it couldn't have been easy for him. Her mother was his only daughter, his only child.

The trembling candlelight danced against the whitewashed walls, the yellow light spreading like melted butter. Her eyes grew heavy. Tomorrow was Sunday. They always went to church as a family on Sunday. Elizabeth had to go or someone might suspect her illness was serious, then the questions would be difficult to escape.

So, she'd got through the day. That should settle her, but it didn't; it disturbed her. Yes, she'd survived, but did that mean she could live with what she'd done? Live with the guilt and keep up the charade? Was she such an inhumane, wicked monster?

Her grandfather leant towards her. 'You be falling asleep, Mary. Go up to your chamber. Your da and me can riddle out the grate.'

'I will. Night, Gramfer. Night, Da.' She bent and kissed them in turn, keeping her eyes lowered, then picked up a flickering candle and carried it up the stairs to her bedroom. Elizabeth appeared to be asleep, so Mary undressed and slid under her own covers.

She tossed and turned, fighting sleep and the dreams it would bring, but the old house creaked and groaned like the timbers of an old ship and gently lulled her to sleep.

Chapter 9

Mary sat on the edge of her bed and gripped her knees. Sunday. A day to face yet more people, to act like nothing was different when so much had changed. Her eyes fell on her open hand lying palm up in her lap. That's how small he had been.

A wave of nausea gripped her. Mary squeezed her abdomen, but it didn't help. She grabbed the washbowl to retch until her stomach was empty. She wiped her clammy face with a cloth, sniffed and waited. One minute, she needed just one minute more. Taking a deep breath, she drew herself up, smoothed down her skirt, and headed for the kitchen.

Breakfast needed to be made, but Mary stood beside the table, unable to move. She shook herself to remove all thoughts, all images, and bustled about to prepare food, moving quickly, needing to return to Elizabeth, to get her ready for this day.

But back in the bedroom, Mary's heart sank. Elizabeth still lay in bed, her eyes closed and face pale. If Elizabeth refused to go, what could she do? She had no strength left to argue.

'Lizzie. Lizzie, are you awake?' Mary reached over and jiggled her shoulder.

'I'm awake.'

'Today's Sunday, church day. You have to go.'

57

'I can't do it, can't face everyone.'

'You must. If you don't go, Da will be worried. He'll send Grace over to check on you. I'll be right beside you. I'll help. Come on, please.' Mary pulled the covers off Elizabeth's face.

'Well, I don't want to, but I will.'

Relief flooded Mary, and she grabbed the back of her chair to steady herself whilst Elizabeth swung her legs out of bed to sit, looking like a ghost with dark rings under her eyes.

'Let me braid your hair for you.' Mary reached out for Elizabeth's long hair. 'Shall I tie a ribbon in it?'

'No, no ribbons.'

'I'll get a horse saddled for you after breakfast so you don't have to walk.'

'I'll have breakfast here and go down after.'

'Good idea. I'll bring it up now.' It was easier to agree, and anyway, Elizabeth would need gentle coaxing today, tomorrow, and probably for many days to come.

After breakfast, Mary stuck her head out of the kitchen door to test the weather and slumped against the doorpost. A spiteful breeze blew, and fat drops of rain exploded on the ground. But this was good; it meant they would need their cloaks today.

She grabbed two and returned to Elizabeth, fastening the bright scarlet cloak around Elizabeth's shoulders and tying it loosely over her stomach. The cloak was perfect for concealment, but the splash of colour only made Elizabeth's ashen face look like death. Mary pinched her sister's cheeks hard, expecting a cry of outrage. Instead, Elizabeth dragged her eyes upwards and smiled.

Mary stroked her face. 'You need colour. You look ill, so I must keep doing it.' Taking Elizabeth's delicate hand, she led her downstairs and pinched her cheeks once more before entering the kitchen with a bright smile fixed like a mask to her own face.

'There she be, then. How are you today, my Lizzie?' Her grandfather grinned at them both.

'Better, I think.'

'Did you have a nightmare last night? I heard you cry out once or twice.'

'It was nothing, Gramfer, just a dream.'

Her grandfather opened his mouth to speak again, so Mary threw Elizabeth's hood over her head and hustled her out the door towards the waiting horse. Mary's hands trembled and fumbled for the reins. The horse snorted, rippled his flanks, and shook his mane, sensing her tension.

Rough hands seized her own as her grandfather grabbed the reins and muttered, 'Kep, kep, kep.' The old horse butted his shoulder. 'Mary, don't annoy the horse.'

Mary edged away and let her grandfather lead the horse whilst she walked alongside. Her father took the opposite flank. She trudged towards the village of St Merryn and the parish church, her feet like dead weights. The wind caught and fluttered her cloak, driving the stinging rain into her face and icy fingers down her neck.

Her grandfather cleared his throat. She screwed up her eyes. He was about to sing; he always did. He loved Sundays and the chance to meet and exchange gossip, but the sound of his jaunty voice grated on her flayed nerves. She checked on Elizabeth, shrouded in her blood-red cloak that flapped in the cold wind.

At the village, her grandfather pulled the horse towards the big old oak tree standing in the middle of the square. At a loss of what to do, Mary joined him whilst he circled it with the horse and read the notices pinned to it.

Notices of farm sales, public meetings, lost and found. And wanted posters of sinners. Mary's heart raced, and the pictures swam in and out of focus to reveal her face. Wanted for murder. Her legs quivered and buckled, and she grabbed the horse for support.

'What are you staring at?' her grandfather asked. 'Ah, don't worry about him; he's been caught and hanged. Good thing too.'

Mary clung onto the horse, afraid to let go. Her grandfather led them to the parish church, calling out greetings to everyone as he went.

She had to get a grip. Mary stole a look at Elizabeth, who picked at a loose thread on her cloak, her face composed. Elizabeth slid from the horse before her father could help her down, and Mary grabbed her arm and guided her into the church vestibule. She shut the door and pushed Elizabeth's hood off her face to peer at her. Elizabeth raised her head and gave a half smile.

The dark, dank, musty vestibule carried the whiff of decay and transported her back to the old mine shaft in the woods. Mary shoved her hair off her forehead to push those unwanted thoughts away whilst Elizabeth watched from half-lidded eyes. The door swung open, and her father and grandfather swept in and led the way inside.

Mary sat on a hard, muscle-stiffening wooden pew with Elizabeth sandwiched between her and her father. She fought to relax, but her legs would not be still, quivering beneath her dress. Her hands plucked at her cloak, even though she strove to stop them. Elizabeth, she noticed, sat without moving.

The gloomy church bestowed little light, and the cloying smell of incense mixed with the nauseating aroma of unwashed bodies and clothes made Mary want to retch. She gulped and fought the urge. She needed a distraction.

She gazed around at the people surrounding her—Anglicans, Methodists, Baptists—they not only lived side by side, but shared the parish church for Sunday service. For all of them, this was just another Sunday, whilst she sat amongst them, impersonating her old self to disguise the wicked intruder she now was. Could any of them have secrets of their own?

In the front row, she found the bonesetter, Grace Partridge, sitting bolt upright with her thick arms crossed against her ample bosom. She acted as the local doctor, herbalist, midwife, and, of course, bonesetter. Never charging much and always in demand. Could she have secrets? Other peoples', certainly; she knew most of what went on in this village.

And there sat her uncle, John Landeryou, and his wife, Sarah. They got wed in this very church three years ago, but since that happy occasion, they rarely smiled and never touched each other. Even now, they sat with cavernous inches between them. Hardly a secret.

Directly in front of her sat old man Thomas Fox with his wispy smoke-grey hair curling about his head and a single front tooth standing like a headstone in his wide, grinning face. His little wife was beside him, simply called Granny because she was the oldest woman in the village. Mary liked them both—such simple, honest people. Could they have secrets? Not likely.

Beside them sat the Blewet family, William and Charity, with their only daughter, Jenny, her dear friend. She stared at Jenny's long copper hair and resisted the urge to reach out and let it run through her fingers. They were the same age, but Jenny looked so much younger due to her small frame and wide eyes. Everyone called her Little Jenny Wren. She gave a small smile. Her best friend was a little bird and someone she had always shared secrets with. Until now.

The vicar's voice fell like a gavel in the room, and Mary flinched. He loomed in the pulpit, menacing and crow black, and scowled down at his parishioners, hunched like a vulture.

'There are skeletons in your closets and monsters in your hearts.'

Mary listened, breathless, convinced his words were meant just for her. His piercing eyes bore down on her. The distance between them receded, and everything around her dimmed. He leant forwards and spoke directly to her, his red mottled face filling her vision.

'There is a God over mankind, and he has shown them clearly what they can and cannot do. You do not want to hear this, for you want to enjoy the pleasure of sin and don't want to know that what you have done brings displeasure to God. You need to acknowledge God and his rule book and live accordingly. Whosoever committeth sin transgresseth also the law, for sin is the transgression of the law.

'The God that holds you over the pit of hell, much as one would a spider or some loathsome insect over the fire, abhors you and is dreadfully provoked. His wrath towards you burns, and he looks upon you as worthy of nothing else but to be cast into the flames. He is of purer eyes than to bear to have you in his sight; you are ten thousand times so abominable in his eyes as the most venomous serpent is in ours. Blessed are the eyes that see the things ye see and which hear the things ye hear.'

Mary closed her eyes and stifled a cry. Of course God had witnessed what she'd done. God could not be deceived; he saw everything. There would be a penalty to pay and no mistake, but surely God would have some mercy and not punish the child she secretly carried. This child, her child, would not suffer the same fate as Elizabeth's. She would marry Samuel and keep her baby.

She would do anything to keep her baby safe.

The final words of the vicar rolled over her. 'Suffer little children to come unto me and forbid them not, for such is the Kingdom of Heaven.'

She dropped her head and dug her nails into her palms so she could focus on the pain she deserved, soundlessly begging for forgiveness.

***

ELIZABETH SAT BESIDE a fidgeting Mary whilst the vicar opened and closed his mouth. No words came out that she could hear. He slammed his fist down on the pulpit, but it made no noise. The ebb and flow of music and voices wafted around her, but Elizabeth heard nothing, saw no one but the strange ludicrous hunched figure in the pulpit. She was hollow, scooped out, empty.

Beside her, Mary fidgeted, twisting her hands like she could rinse the past away. But what would Mary do if she discovered the whole truth?

What if Mary found out that he had asked her to meet in the woods, promising coloured ribbons for her hair? That she went willingly not just for ribbons, but wanting him to kiss her. Never having been kissed by a man before, she had fantasised about it until it drove her to distraction, wanting his kisses to be the first.

Afterwards, he had told her it was her own fault for leading him on. Why agree to meet in the woods otherwise? He believed she wanted it. She was excited, he could tell, so he wasn't to blame; she was.

She hadn't fought him; she couldn't remember if she had even said no. She had meant to, but it had been a blur. She had frozen, gone rigid. So he was right. She was to blame.

She couldn't remember if he'd kissed her. She'd certainly never got any ribbons; all she had was an unwanted baby and the knowledge that she'd brought it on herself.

How could she tell all that to Mary and still expect her help and her love? It was an act of betrayal, and Mary would hate her for it. Elizabeth needed Mary. She'd rather die than lose her.

***

WITH THE SERVICE over, Mary grasped Elizabeth's hand and went outside to wait by the horse and escape the claustrophobic space. They left their father and grandfather to catch up with gossip.

Mary stood by the horse to shield Elizabeth. She kept her head down to avoid eye contact with anyone else but stole surreptitious glances to make sure no one approached them.

When Jenny Wren left the church with her parents and glanced around, looking for her, Mary raised her head, and their eyes found each other. Mary ran to her friend and wrapped her arms around her, wanting to whisper all her secrets in her ear. When Jenny hugged her back, she squeezed her eyes shut to close off the threat of tears.

Jenny murmured, 'Can I come over tomorrow? I need to talk.'

'Yes, come in the morning, after breakfast. I'll be free for a few hours.'

Jenny nodded. 'I'll be there.' She dropped her head to let her hair fall across her face, then drew her arms across her body and turned to join her parents.

Come back, Jenny. Come home with me now. I'll tell you everything if you do.

Instead, Mary saw the bonesetter striding towards their horse. Mary raced back to Elizabeth just before a booming voice called out behind her.

'How are you, Lizzie? Your da says you've been laid low.'

'I'm feeling better now.'

Grace crossed her arms as she studied Elizabeth. 'You still look pale. I can make you a potion to drink if you tell me what it was.'

'No need. Thank you, Grace.'

Mary glanced at the church. *Come on, stop your chatter. Come out so we can escape.*

'It isn't any trouble. I'll bet I know what it was.'

Mary choked, but before she could hear these words of wisdom, her grandfather's voice called out to them. 'Bring the horse over here. We're going home.'

65

Mary gladly grasped the reins, shouted a goodbye over her shoulder, and led the horse away.

On the slow walk home, her grandfather prodded her back. 'I said he's got a big nose, always sticking it where it's not wanted. He's always got to poke his nose in. Poke, poke, poke.'

But she wasn't concentrating on his chatter; there was too much to think about. What would her punishment be? She ran a hand over her belly and again prayed for God to spare her child.

She wanted this baby, and she would do anything to keep it safe.

Chapter 10

Mary waited outside the farmhouse, pacing up and down the track. She paused to fasten her cloak but let the hood drop back against her shoulders. Closing her eyes, she tilted her head towards the mellow sun, seeking its warmth.

She promised Elizabeth to never tell a soul, not even Jenny, but that would test her willpower to its limit. It was so easy to talk to Jenny; they always told each other everything, and now she had to keep a secret between them. Perhaps that was what happened to friendships once childhood was left behind. She kicked at a stone. Life was unfair.

When she looked up, she saw the sun glinting off burnished copper hair and rushed up the track to meet her friend, swamped by a wave of tenderness. She wrapped her arms around Jenny, crushed her to her chest, and rubbed a hand against Jenny's sharp shoulder blades. Mary's heart wanted to float away. 'C'mon, Jen, let's go to our special place. We can talk in private there.'

Linking arms, they ambled through the orchard in comfortable silence, stamping on the windfalls in the short grass to inhale the tart perfume of cider apples. There was no hurry. She wanted to keep Jenny beside her as long as possible.

At the end of the field, Mary swung her legs over the orchard fence, then waited for Jenny to climb over. They continued to walk hand in hand round a corner and collided with Benjamin, his arms overloaded with bits of salvaged rope. 'Sorry, Benjamin, I didn't see you.'

His eyes darted from her to Jenny and back again as he backed away from them, turned, and fled.

Mary shook her head. 'Now, don't tell me that wasn't strange.'

She drew Jenny on until they reached a small grassy paddock. Turning to her friend, she grinned. 'I only ever bring you here. Our field of dreams. When did we start calling it that?'

'We were just children when we did. I love it here.'

Mary pushed at a wooden gate that limped open on its hinges and squealed in torment. A flock of snow-white geese honked in disapproval and scurried with outstretched wings to the other side of the field. Two tree stumps, long-dead oaks, beckoned her like old friends beside the high hedge. The grass around their bases was scuffed bare. Mary slid into the worn curve of the wood, and Jenny sat beside her, her knees drawn up to her chin, her arms around her legs. Reaching across, Mary grasped one of Jenny's hands and brought it to her lips. It made her own appear clumsy.

'Jen—'

'Mary—'

They laughed together, and Jenny said, 'You first.'

Mary studied Jenny's hand. It was narrow and slender, but the skin was thick and hard across the palm. Purple bruises edged in yellow ran down the sides. She put her own hand around her friend's and lined her fingers up against the dark marks. 'Someone squeezed you tight.' She searched her friend's hazel eyes for the answer.

Jenny only replied, 'You first.'

'Well, I do have something to tell. I would've told you sooner, but he wanted it kept a secret. Only everyone will find out soon enough, and I want you to know before anyone else.'

Jenny's mouth stretched into a wide smile. 'A boy.'

'No, a man. I'm in love, Jen, and he loves me. It's the most wonderful feeling. I swear my heart actually flips when I catch sight of him. Like when I'm with him, there's nothing to fear. He's a light in the darkness.'

'What darkness? What man?'

'Samuel.'

Jenny squeezed her eyes shut. 'Not . . . the bailiff's son?'

'Yes.'

Jenny's smile faded, the colour in her cheeks draining away. One hand pulled free from Mary's grasp to clamp over her mouth, followed by her other hand whilst she shook her head.

Mary shrugged. 'What? You think he's too good for me, don't you?'

The silence between them grew until it became hard to lift aside, until Mary said, 'Dammit. Damn it all.'

Jenny moved her hands away and sat on them. Frowning, she kicked at the patch of bare earth. 'I think he's a lucky man to have your love, but my ma often hears his da telling everyone what a great catch Samuel is, how he's expected to marry well, to a maid who's da owns his own farm. To someone with money.'

'Well, too bad, 'cause Sam loves me.'

'It explains why he helps your da out so often when he should be working on his own da's farm, but even so.' Jenny stopped kicking. 'Has he asked you to marry him?'

'Not yet, but he will.'

Jenny said nothing.

'I *know* he will.'

'Be careful, Mary, his da is very powerful. I'm always worried my ma will lose her job, and then we'll lose the cottage. Mr Treleggan is a very hard man. He scares me.'

'Your ma is the best cook in the world; he'd never get rid of his cook. Why would you worry about that?'

Jenny dropped her head and gave it a shake. 'If he doesn't marry you, so what? You'll find someone better.'

'Oh, he'll marry me. He has to.'

Jenny's head shot up. 'Why?'

'I'm carrying his bairn.'

Jenny stared at Mary, her eyes filling with tears that slid down her smooth skin. Mary's bottom lip trembled.

Mary pushed herself off the tree. She knelt beside her friend and stroked her hair. 'Silly thing. Don't worry. You worry too much. Be happy for me. I am.' She brushed Jenny's hair off her face and tucked it behind her ear. Such a sweet face that she hid behind a curtain of hair, with freckles that swept across her cheeks and nose. Mary always wanted freckles like that.

Jenny sniffed. 'You really love him?'

Mary laughed. 'I wouldn't be having his bairn if I didn't.'

'Is he good to you?'

Mary paused. 'Are you asking me what it's like to have sex?'

70

Jenny's cheeks lit to a crimson blush that spread and disappeared below the collar of her dress. 'No.'

'When you're sweet on someone, I'll tell you all about it. Truth is, I love it. It's very special when you love the other person.' Mary expected Jenny to giggle, to ask questions, to want to know more. But she only wiped her eyes and stared into the distance.

'I still need you, Jenny Wren. No man can ever change that. I couldn't live without you.'

'Yes, you could. You're too full of life to ever be beaten by anything. Not like me. I'm a mouse.'

'Don't say that, little bird. You just worry too much, care too much what others think. But that's why I love you. And I'll always look out for you.'

Jenny's shoulders rose and dropped. She sighed long and low.

'What's wrong, dearest? You said you wanted to talk to me.'

Jenny opened her mouth to speak but paused and shook her head. 'No, I didn't.'

'Yes, outside the church, you said.'

'I said I wanted to see you. You looked so pale, I was worried.'

'Oh, it's just the morning sickness. It passes.' Mary sat back on her stump. 'Jen.'

'Hmm?'

'Don't tell anyone. No one knows about the bairn, only you.'

'And Samuel.'

Mary shook her head.

Jenny gasped. 'He doesn't know?'

'Not yet. When he's back, I'll tell him.'

'I'll pray for you, Mary, I will, and I'll never tell. I know how to keep a secret.'

'Yes, pray for me. I might need it.'

A bell clanged in the distance, and the sound carried across the fields.

Mary rose to her feet. 'Staying for milk and biscuits?'

'I can't. I have to help my ma in the kitchens.'

Mary helped Jenny to her feet, and they walked back hand in hand.

It was better if Jenny left now. The other secret inside her was clawing its way out, desperate to be free. She pressed her lips together, not sure she could contain the words if her friend stayed any longer.

Chapter 11

B enjamin poured himself a brandy, raised the glass to his nose, and took the time to inhale its smoky, woody odour. His mouth watered. Taking a sip, the rich taste of caramel and oak coated his tongue and burnt the back of his mouth. He swigged again. The warmth of the brandy trickled down his throat, and his body melted into his fireside chair. His eyes fluttered closed, his legs stretched out towards the fire, and the liquid heat of the brandy coursed through his body.

He licked his lips to savour the last of the drink. There was no point getting comfortable; the drink was for courage, not to make him sleep. No, he had to go out tonight to help the smugglers. He hated Samuel and didn't much like any of the other villagers, but that wasn't going to stop him. The money was good, far too good, and he needed it. But there would be about twenty men out tonight, and if any of them had been drinking, well, trouble might follow. His leg bounced up and down. He raised the tumbler to his right eye and watched the fire through the glass. Just like holding a ball of flames in his hand.

Now, what would that really feel like?

He slammed the glass down. Bad idea. This was not the time to get distracted. Besides, he could do this—keep his head down, keep out of trouble.

Rising, he went to the fireplace and pushed a shoulder against the protruding wall until it scraped open to reveal a dark cache. It was empty, but two ankers of brandy would sit there later. The wall grated shut. He rubbed his hands together. 'Come on, Jess. We have to go.' She stretched along the floor, scrambled to her feet, and leant her strong body against his legs. He smiled down at her, batted her ears, and went to the door, reaching for his hat and coat on the way.

Such a perfect night to transport goods—the moon waned, but there remained enough light to work in without the need for lanterns. He strode away from Treyarnon Bay towards Pepper Cove, following the cliff path. To his right, the rhythmic swell of the sea kept him company. Waves broke on the rocks below, and the exhilarating smell of seaweed drifted on the salty breeze. A dagger of moonlight pierced the surface of the black stretch of ocean.

The cliff above Pepper Cove sat quiet and empty. He must be early. He planted his legs apart, stood on the cliff edge, and looked down at the narrow entrance to the bay, fringed with the serrated jaws of black rocks. Once a vessel had slipped inside this cove, the towering cliffs concealed it, and cargo could be unloaded at leisure and unseen. The sandy beach had a gentle gradient; even a clipper could be beached here. The tip of nearby Will's Rock was just visible above the crashing waves. Smugglers once left a revenue man to drown on the rock in a rising tide. That was how much they were hated.

Others now stood behind him. He didn't have to turn to see; he knew from their sweaty odour, their heavy breathing, and the switch of mule's tails. His back prickled. *Relax.* They were not interested in him, not tonight.

A deep male voice behind him spoke, 'To the beach, men.'

Benjamin turned and made for a small track down to the cove, but the galloping hooves of a horse thundered towards him, making him pause.

Someone pushed him aside to have a look. 'Why, it's young Billy Bray.'

The horse and rider came to a stop. Billy slid from his horse and bent over, grasping his knees for support. He stared up at them, eyes wild and wide, the colour drained from his face. 'Oh hell, I saw a revenue boat coming round the headland, straight for Pepper Cove.'

'No, they can't be here.'

'I'm afraid they are. A cutter with pure white sails, can see it clearly in this moonlight.'

Benjamin turned back to the sea, and the ghostly white sails of the revenue boat glided swiftly and silently into view. He bit his lip to stop himself shouting it out.

Someone else gave the cry of alarm, and all heads turned to look. 'It's the revenue men, no doubt about it.'

'Call them what they are—gaugers. They'll be at the cove before Sam, waiting for him.'

'We have to warn him. Who's got a lantern?'

Benjamin trailed behind the men now moving away from Pepper Cove, along the coastal path in the direction of Samuel and his crew. He waited dry-mouthed for Samuel's vessel to appear. He raised a smile but dropped it before anyone else noticed. Samuel might get caught tonight. It would do the bastard good to fail for once. All the goods would be confiscated, so no money or brandy for him or anyone else. But still, the villagers would curse Samuel for it.

Samuel's fishing vessel rounded the headland, low in the water, torpid, hugging the coastline as closely as it dared.

'Light the lantern. Be quick. That's it, swing it; swing it so he sees the light move.'

The sails of Samuel's vessel lowered, and it came to a halt.

'Areeah! Them gaugers have seen the signal too. The cutter's on the move.'

The lantern swung in a wide arc of light, and the men about him stared, silent and grim faced. Benjamin stood amongst them, one of them tonight as they faced this crisis.

His head bent low, but his heart soared high and fast.

Chapter 12

In his fishing boat, Samuel rested his head against the back of his seat. Water sucked and slithered against the boat, and moonbeams floated on the waves. He wanted his bed. Nearly home with a good haul, well worth the effort. It would help to see the village through another winter, but most of all it would line his own pocket.

Wait, was that a light dancing on the cliff top? He strained his eyes and made out the dark silhouette of a line of men as a curve of light swung back and forth, back and forth. A voice from the clifftop shouted something, but what? It didn't matter, he knew. Gaugers. Had to be.

Samuel breathed fast and shallow, his field of vision narrowed. Focused on his boat, he sprang into action. 'Drop the sails, men. The gaugers are about.' He pointed to the warning light.

'Gaugers? No. What are they doing here?'

'I dunno, Jack, worry about that later. Drop anchor and heave the tubs overboard. They, at least, will come to no harm on the seabed for a few days. We'll come back and creep for them another day. Quick, men. Be quick.'

Samuel reached behind and grabbed a thick coil of rope. He tied it around a barrel, then moved off to tie the next, not stopping until they were all hitched together. He ignored his men's questions. *Focus. One job at a time.* It was faster that way. 'Right men, go.'

The barrels were hauled to the side of the boat and heaved overboard, and the vessel bounced with a buoyant spring that made Samuel stagger. He grabbed onto the boat and looked around. There it was—Will's Rock, an easy landmark. He'd find this spot again, no trouble. Dare he try to outrun the revenue boat, make it back to Treyarnon Bay?

'Raise the sails, men. Let's get out of here.' The boat set forth at a lively pace. They might just do it, beat the revenue men.

A loud boom made Samuel freeze. He didn't move until the water in front of his boat exploded in a spume of spray. He braced himself against the side of the rocking boat and wiped briny droplets off his face.

'Halt there! In the king's name, halt, or I will fire again.'

The shout made Samuel turn to see the cutter sweep into view, gaining on his fishing boat.

'I'm arresting you in the name of His Majesty, King George.'

Samuel sighed. 'Drop the sails again, men.' He raised his hands and waited for the cutter to draw close. It was pointless to get shot over silks and tea. But the corners of his mouth twitched as an intoxicating rush spread through his body. Fear could be debilitating or exhilarating; it could beat you and paralyse you, or it could make you feel alive. It was about time these runs became dangerous and the villagers understood the peril he constantly put himself in.

The revenue cutter drew alongside, and two gaugers boarded the fishing vessel with their flintlock pistols drawn. With a pistol aimed at his head, Samuel climbed aboard the cutter, and his men followed.

He stood on deck, hands on his head, and gazed back at his boat, now manned by gaugers. He'd get her back later. No point worrying now.

A pistol prodded his shoulder. 'You lot stay here. Make yourselves comfortable; it's going to be a long journey.'

He dropped his arms and shrugged. They must be going to Falmouth. That would be interesting; he'd never been. He found a wooden bench and sat, watching the dark Cornish coastline slip past. Watergate Bay, he knew that place, but now he passed places he'd never seen before, never been to. And this was only Cornwall. As darkness closed in, he reached underneath his bench and found an old sack, which he folded to use as a pillow. He lay back and closed his eyes.

He woke to the smell of coffee, stretched, yawned, and rubbed his stubbled chin. He needed some of that coffee, and he kicked his men awake. 'Morning, lads. Look about, this is what the south coast looks like.'

No one offered him anything to eat or drink, so with a pistol trained on his every move, he helped himself. He laughed. He'd been caught smuggling, that's all, and these revenue men acted like he was a criminal. He settled back in his seat to enjoy the view.

As daylight began to fade once more, he stood up and gazed around. That was a harbour ahead, had to be, busy with boats and big buildings lit up with lanterns. Falmouth. So that's what it looked like. He stretched his back and eased out his stiff shoulders. He could have some fun here before he returned home.

But the cutter didn't slow down; it sailed past the harbour entrance. Strange. He approached a revenue man. 'What harbour was that?'

'Falmouth.'

'Thought so. So, where are we headed?'

'You'll find that out when you get there.'

His men called him back. 'Where we going, Sam? Do you know?'

Samuel chewed over the question. Plymouth, it had to be. There was a navy base there, and he'd heard of men being taken by force, made to join. He took a deep breath and shrugged. 'I don't know, but I reckon they want my da's boat. It's going to Falmouth without us.'

'They can't do that, can they? That'll cost him dear.'

Samuel didn't answer, just watched his fishing boat until it disappeared from view. He loved that boat; he couldn't imagine his life without it. His father wanted him to be a farmer, but he would rather be at sea. A boat meant freedom. He sat back down, sure of what lay in store for him now, and he had plenty of time to mull it over. A tingle crept across his flesh, the thrill of excitement.

The evening settled in before they sailed into Plymouth harbour with just enough light to see. He stretched out his legs and rubbed his sore back again. Mildly amused, he watched the customs men draw their pistols and flick their wrists to indicate he had to leave. Did they really think he was stupid enough to make a run for it?

He marched off the cutter, and the revenue men pushed and jostled him into a small room. He stood his ground. He didn't appreciate being manhandled; there was no need for that. Nobody spoke. Samuel called out, 'What are we doing here? We've got a right to know.'

'You're joining the navy. Get used to it.'

His men circled him, beads of sweat clinging to their pale faces.

'It can't be true.'

'We wasn't doing wrong, just turning a penny.'

'I got a wife and baby at home; they'll starve without me.'

'Sam, do something. They can't do this.'

Samuel didn't answer. He couldn't. His body throbbed with anticipation. He lived in Cornwall, in St Merryn, had done all his life, and apart from a number of smuggling runs to Ireland and the Scilly Isles, he'd never ventured far from home. An unfulfilled curiosity about what lay beyond his village consumed him. So many uncharted discoveries beckoned. An urge to soar beyond his ordinary life gripped him. The navy needed more men, and for whatever reason, he was caught and this was his intended punishment. It was useless to argue. Anyway, the idea of an unpredictable, dangerous future at sea appealed to him. He moved towards a dirty window and used his fist to clean a round spy hole. Past the jumble of low buildings and boats, he glimpsed the sea stretching beyond his vision. In that instant he knew no road was forever. He had to adjust; he wanted to embrace it.

Mary. What about Mary? She would find another. Well, never anyone like him, certainly not in St Merryn. He shook his head and laughed at the idea. His old life had to go. It had become too easy, anyway. He exploited his good looks and charm just for fun because the small, narrow-minded villagers smothered him when all he wanted to do was feel the throb of life in his veins.

Samuel turned and eyed the revenue men preparing to leave. He walked over, his hands in front of him, palms up. He didn't want any violence. 'Can I talk with whoever's in charge? In private.'

A dark-skinned man approached and stared into his eyes. Samuel returned the stare, unblinking.

'Trying to wriggle out of it?'

'No.'

'So why should I bother with the likes of you?'

Samuel bent his head closer. 'Because I'll tell you where the ankers of brandy are.'

The man grinned and gestured for him to enter an adjoining room. Samuel opened the door with a pistol jammed between his shoulder blades. Round and hard. The room was windowless, airless. A box.

'What makes you think we don't know where they are?'

Samuel turned to face the pistol. 'Because you don't know when we hauled them over the side. You never saw us do it. Will be impossible to find without my help.'

The pistol was raised and pushed against his temple. 'So talk.'

Samuel searched the dark eyes of the man holding the weapon. 'Tell me what's going to happen to us first.'

The customs man dropped his hand, and Samuel let out a breath.

'Ah well, you're all going with Lord Exmouth's ships to Algeria to face their guns and free the Christian slaves, poor souls. You'll be joining Rear Admiral Milne aboard the HMS Impregnable.' He winked. 'I hope it lives up to its name. I've heard those Barbary pirates are partial to handsome young men.'

Algeria. Where was that? It sounded fancy enough, and he'd be a hero when he got back.

'So, tell us. The brandy.'

Samuel scratched his chin. He had to make him believe there were enough barrels for it to be worth his while. 'I want to do a deal.'

Hard metal hit him between his eyes, and the revenue man laughed.

'I knew it. Scared. You should be. No deal.'

'There's fifteen ankers waiting at the bottom of the sea. Yours in exchange for one of my men.'

'You're in no position to bargain. Tell or I shoot. One of your men will soon tell us.'

'They won't. They can't. Only I marked out a landmark, and only I can show you exactly where on a map.'

'Tell or I'll shoot one of them.'

Samuel gave him a slow smile. 'Now that would be murder.'

'Perhaps I'll just shoot you, say you tried to escape.'

Samuel glanced around the windowless room and shook his head. 'I don't think so.'

The man's face flushed, a vein in his neck bulged, and spittle gathered in the corner of his mouth.

The round barrel dug into Samuel's skull. He closed his eyes. A seagull called from somewhere. His heart missed a beat.

'Go and get one man. Just one.'

Samuel wiped the revenue man's saliva off his cheek with the back of one hand, pushed past the officer, and returned to his men.

'Jack, go home to your wife and child, quick. Go now before they change their minds. You'll have to make your own way, but go. When you get back, find Mary Landeryou. Tell her not to wait for me, to get on with her life.'

Jack twisted his hat in his hands, glanced at the others, then bolted for the door.

'What about us?'

'It's no good. We're bound for the fleet sailing to Algeria under Lord Exmouth.'

'No, that's not fair.' His men raised their fists towards the customs men and shouted. 'Bastards. Let us go, or we'll kill all of you.'

Samuel returned to his spy hole. Fists were no good against pistols. No, his fate was sealed.

He smiled, watching the winds of change blow across the vast stretch of sea.

Chapter 13

Benjamin watched Mary serve up lunch in the farmhouse kitchen, ladling out a thick stew that slopped down the sides of the bowls. She was distracted, miles away. He guessed she was thinking about Samuel, wondering where he was. Everyone knew he'd been caught smuggling, but so what? Smugglers were always acquitted and set free. It wasn't really a crime, not to the Cornish, and the magistrates liked their moonshine too. So everyone was asking the same question as Mary—where was he?

Mary looked pale today, lost and lonely. He knew how she felt, except he didn't want Samuel back.

A bowl of stew landed in front of him, and he reached for some of Mary's homemade bread, glancing quickly around at the other labourers. They were all talking, about Samuel of course, with mouths open and mashed up food on display. He gave Jess a pat. She had better manners then they did. The food smelt good, and he knew Mary had made it. He tore off a hunk of bread and dunked it into the bowl. He brought it to his lips when the man opposite him laughed and sprayed crumbs and spittle across the table. Benjamin dropped the bread. He'd just lost his appetite.

Everyone's heads jerked up when the kitchen door flew open and banged hard against the wall like a gust of wind had whirled in. But it wasn't the wind, it was the bonesetter. She bulged through the open doorway, filling the frame, then marched inside and swept away the quivering raindrops that had dared to perch on her coat. The door slammed shut with one swift blow from her hand, making it rattle in the frame.

'Listen up, everyone, I've got news.'

She bellowed out the words, but she didn't need to. They were all paying attention. This was the bonesetter, after all.

Benjamin noticed Mary sidle away and sit beside the fire, her back to the room, one hand rubbing her chest. No, her stomach. *Her stomach?*

'Jack has come home . . .'

A ripple of relief ran around the room, but Benjamin said nothing. He watched Mary.

'. . . with information about Sam, Billy, and Dick. They've all been taken by the navy, pressganged as punishment for smuggling. They're on their way to Algeria.'

Mary slumped in her chair and buried her face in her hands. He wanted to run to her, to hold her, to tell her it would all be all right—better even, now Samuel had gone. He sat still and said nothing whilst the questions flowed around him.

The bonesetter spoke again, 'Samuel was taken by surprise and taken quickly. Even his da knew nothing about it until Jack came back. He smells a rat, says we must have a traitor amongst us. No other reason for gaugers to be about that night. He thinks the navy paid someone well for that information. I don't know. We'll probably never know the truth; it could have just been bad luck.'

Mary slowly stood up at this information and swivelled to face the room, her eyes flitting from face to face, searching. Benjamin ducked his head and began eating. The thought of Samuel gone for good had just given him back his appetite.

***

WITH THE WORKDAY over at last, Benjamin had time to himself, time to think. He sat outside his cottage, his coat wrapped around him, his hat squashed down on his head and Jess curled up at his feet. Above him, a coal-black sky flecked with pinpricks of starlight, silent as a crypt. The steady pulse of the rolling ocean filled the air. A slight biting breeze lifted his hair and groped at his coat, prying it open.

He wouldn't sleep tonight, the excitement of knowing Samuel was gone keeping him awake, but instead of going for a walk, he wanted to sit and take time to think things over, to plan how to change his life. Jess raised her head to look at him, and he bent to rub her behind the ears.

Yes, he wanted to think and plan carefully just how to make changes to his lonely, miserable life. What did he want? Only what other men had—a wife and a family. Why not? He tickled Jess's ears again. This wasn't enough, just him and Jess, not anymore. He wanted to know what love was.

Surely that wasn't too much to ask? But he didn't want just any woman. He wanted beautiful, lovely Mary, even though she would never want him. He took a long deep breath of the fresh salty air. But things were changing; he could taste it on the wind. And Samuel had gone. The beginnings of an idea blew into his mind. A little seed that took root and grew and excited him. He gazed straight ahead at nothing as a fever built up inside him.

Mary was part of his plan. But what about Mary? She didn't like him very much. No, to be truthful, she probably loathed him, and if his plan worked, their life together would have one messy start. He just needed time to win her over. She needed his protection, and if he was right, so did the child she carried. He crossed his fingers, hoping she would do anything for her child. So, this was it—the time to change both their lives forever.

He got up from his seat, walked to the edge of the cliff, and peered down at the raging sea below him. He raised his arms and his head and shouted above the throb of the ocean, 'I have a fire inside me, and tomorrow, I make my move.'

***

BENJAMIN LEFT HIS cottage the next morning, reaching for his hat on the way out. He never went anywhere without it, and today it would help; he could hide behind it when he spoke to Mary.

On the clifftop, he battled with the wind that fought to hold him back. Clutching his hat with one hand, he bolted for the shelter of the fields and laughed as his coat billowed out behind him like a sail.

When he reached Upper Meadow, the wind came at him sideways, tried to topple him, snatching at his hat, so he rammed it on his head and ran again. He ran until he reached the five-bar gate, where he paused for breath and gazed down at the farm. It was too dark to make out any detail but the rain as it drove down the valley. Well, hell, he would never see Samuel walking down Sandy Lane ever again. Laughing out loud, his heart surged as he vaulted over the gate and sprinted towards the farm, unable to wait for this day to begin.

Benjamin was occupied with field work most of the day. What he wanted to do was drive the oxen and plough through the stubble field, a job that put a spring in his step, one he'd been doing since a boy of eight. So, when he passed the barn, he called in on the oxen and walked amongst them. Their warm breath filling the stalls with moist air mingled with the musty whiff of earth and grassy hay. As he ran a hand along the smooth oily back of one beast, its muscles rippled under his fingers. They were big, heavy cattle, yet gentle if treated with respect. He smacked a rump, but the huge beast never even noticed. If they got the upper hand, they were impossible to command, but he loved them. There would be no ploughing in this weather, though; rainfall had made the ground too heavy.

The barn was dry, quiet, and private. An idea popped into his head. He'd slipped into the barn alone and hadn't been missed, so what about here? It was the perfect place to talk to Mary with only the cattle for company. *Just go and get her. Get her. Now. Go.*

He paced back and forth. It was now or never. But what if she just laughed at him or refused to come? Everything went to plan in his head last night, but now the time had come for action, it was so much harder than he had imagined.

A trickle of cold sweat slid down his neck and between his shoulder blades. Concentrating on that slow descent, he walked to the barn entrance but couldn't go any farther. Courage had deserted him again, and he returned to

89

the comfort of the oxen. He'd rehearsed this over and over last night. *Come on, don't falter now; remember what you're fighting for. Just summon the words and let them roar.*

Taking a deep breath, he strode out.

Chapter 14

Mary sat by the warm fire quilting, seeking the cosy comfort of the kitchen to listen to the wind and rain beat against the windows. Despite the fire, she was cold and miserable. Her eyes smarted, and her heart ached. She cried every night, and once she started, she couldn't stop. This must be God's punishment, sending Samuel away. She was unlikely to ever see him again. His secret message to her from Jack was, 'Don't wait for me; get on with your life,' but how? She rocked with the pain of her life spinning out of control. Did she deserve this? She could only answer yes, but Samuel, poor Samuel, he didn't. And she'd never had a chance to tell him about their baby. Their poor child would never know its father. Which gave her another problem—to have a child without a father. Who would believe her now when she said it was Samuel's?

The kitchen door swung open, and for one brief moment of joy, she thought the tall figure in the doorway was Samuel, but her heart sank. It was only Benjamin.

Holding his hat, he inched his way towards her, and she rolled her eyes. What job was she wanted for now? Never getting a minute's peace or a moment to herself. He stood before her, holding his hat in front of his face. She sighed and packed up her quilt. When he didn't speak, she looked up at him. 'Well?'

'I need to talk to you, Mary. It's important.'

Not in the mood for talking, she heaved a sigh. 'So talk.'

'Not here. It's private. I don't want anyone else to hear. Can you come to the hay barn? Now?'

Mary frowned, about to refuse, to tell him *say it now or not at all*. But as she raised her head to look at him, as she opened her mouth to speak, he lowered his hat and stared straight at her, and there was something about the look of him that was different. His eyes. His eyes were on fire. Surely just the reflection from the flames, but his eyes—they blazed. She closed her mouth and nodded. In an instant, he was gone.

Mary heaved herself up and reached for her cloak. On opening the door she slumped against it. *Why did she say yes to him?* Bone-chilling rain drummed the ground relentlessly. It slapped her face as she slipped and skidded across the muddy courtyard to the barn. Why there? It held too many painful memories.

She ran into the dim barn and stopped at the entrance. There he was, pushed into a gloomy corner. A dark, unobtrusive, stooped figure. She marched over to stand in front of him, hands firmly on her hips. 'What's this all about, Benjamin?'

He wore his hat now and lowered his head so she couldn't see his face as he mumbled. She stamped her foot in frustration. He'd picked the wrong moment to speak to her; she wasn't in a good place right now. 'I can't hear you. Speak up.'

He dragged his head up. She stood only inches away from him and stared hard. It would make him squirm. A trickle of sweat slid down his neck already. His eyes blinked rapidly. He ran a hand across his face, cleared his throat, and stammered words she couldn't make sense of. He faltered. Was he going to turn and run? She didn't care.

Then he clenched his fists and stared up at the rafters like he was gathering himself, like he was preparing to do battle. Casting aside his hat, he straightened up and looked her directly in the eye. 'I know what you and Elizabeth did. In the woods. By the old mine shaft. I saw— I saw everything. I know what you did to the baby, Mary. And I know where you put it. I know it all. I'm the one person that knows everything.'

Mary's eyes grew wide. She covered her ears with her hands and shook her head in bewilderment. Dread gathered like a storm cloud in the back of her mind as the horror of his words sank in. She shuddered. He knew everything? He knew what she'd done, what she was? The room began to spin. She reached out to stop herself from falling but found nothing. Mary closed her eyes. His arms wrapped around her as he caught her, holding her briefly against his chest, then guiding her to a stool where he sat her down.

She wanted to cry, but the tears wouldn't come. His hand rested on her shoulder, and when she did at last open her eyes, he gazed at her with such concern it confused her. What did he want? What was he going to do with this knowledge?

He removed his hand, and she waited for him to speak again. She had nothing to say. He knelt down in front of her, going to hold her hand this time, but he changed his mind. Benjamin swallowed, took a deep breath, and spoke. 'Don't worry. I won't say anything to anyone. I love you. I can protect you. Always. I want to help you, and I can if you marry me. Please don't laugh at the idea. I know you

93

don't love me, and doing this won't make you. But I love you, Mary. And I want it so much. To be a husband . . .' He paused before he continued, 'and a father. I want a family. To be part of a family. I want to be normal, Mary. I don't expect you to understand. But it's all I want. All I've ever wanted. I don't care what you did.'

The pain in her head beat like a fist. He wanted to what? To marry her? He knew she'd killed a baby, yet he wanted her as his wife, to raise a family with her? It was too much; she couldn't take it all in. She stared at him, frowning, not understanding.

'Think about it,' he said. 'Let me know your decision soon. I can and I will protect you.' He stood up and used his hat to brush the dust off his knees, then walked away and left her.

Her head in her hands, she considered his words. Good God, a proposal of marriage! He was right about one thing—she didn't love him and never would; she would only ever love Samuel. She'd rather die than marry him and wouldn't do it; he could do what he liked. She wouldn't do it.

She stumbled to her feet, but her legs shuddered, unable to support her. She needed to talk to Elizabeth, to warn her, and she had to do it now. The rain continued to pound as she tramped across the yard back to the farmhouse to drag herself upstairs to her bedroom. 'Are you awake, Lizzie?'

'You know I am. I can't sleep anymore.'

'I've something important to tell you. It's serious.'

Elizabeth sprang up in bed. What little colour she had drained from her face, and her hand clawed at her throat. 'Oh no, what's happened now?'

94

'It's Benjamin, he's told me he saw everything, he knows everything. I said I heard a noise that night, and I was right; it was him. And he can't be lying. He could only know those things if he did see.'

'Oh, God. What's he doing creeping about at night? What are we going to do? I haven't gone through all this for nothing. It's too bad, Mary. What's he going to do?' Elizabeth cried and didn't bother to brush away her tears.

'I don't know. He says he won't tell, that he'll protect me, and it would be easier if we were married.'

'What! He never says anything to anyone.'

'He's saying something now.'

'And if you don't marry him?'

Mary shrugged. 'Nothing. Not if he does love me.'

Elizabeth rocked to-and-fro and pulled at strands of her hair, muttering to herself. Mary perched on her bed and brought Elizabeth towards her to hold her still, but Elizabeth's body trembled against her chest.

Elizabeth raised her head and clutched Mary's hands. 'I don't trust him. He never speaks, never lets anyone touch him. He's odd. He'll tell, I know it, then we'll both be hanged.'

Mary thought about him, about the way he'd held her, about the way he'd looked at her. 'He is odd, but he's not dangerous. I don't believe he will be.'

'No, no, we can't trust him,' Elizabeth sobbed. 'You have to do it. He can't tell if you're married, I heard Da say it one day. Husbands and wives can't give evidence against each other. So even if he wants to tell, he can't if you're married. It's the only way we'll be safe.' She rocked again in Mary's arms. 'Yes, then we'll be safe.'

'I can't do it, Lizzie. I don't even like him, and I think I might hate him for spying on us.'

'Please, Mary. I'm begging you, do it for us.'

Chapter 15

Mary hunkered down on a patch of grass with one shoulder leant against a makeshift wall, hiding, craving solitude. She didn't really want to think; she wanted to pretend nothing had happened as Elizabeth did, but it was too late for that. The sun's watery warmth spilt over the top of her head and down her back. She could feel it, and yet still she shivered.

It had been a week since she'd spoken to Benjamin. A whole week that felt like a lifetime. Samuel was gone, and yet life had not stopped just because her heart ached; no, it continued to grow inside her. Their baby, it was all she had left, and she had to protect it.

Boots clomped and scuffed along the path as someone approached on the other side of her wall. She froze. Metal scraped against the stone, and the rich, ripe smell of manure filled her nostrils. She shuffled forwards and watched through a chink in the brickwork.

Benjamin shovelled deep into a steaming heap of dung and threw another spadeful into a wheelbarrow. She was so close to him that if she could reach through the wall, her fingertips would graze his trousers. A small bead of sweat glinted on his neck before it slid and disappeared below his collar. She took her time to study this man who'd grow up on the farm with her yet remained a stranger, someone who had never mattered until now.

His shirt hung loosely about his body, but she could tell that simple living and hard work had pared away all excess fat and honed his muscles. He looked lean and strong like twisted wire. He paused to remove his hat and gloves and run his fingers through his unruly curly hair, then he leant on his spade and remained stock-still. What thoughts ran through his head? Thoughts of marriage and families? What was it he'd said to her? He wanted to be normal. *Well, it's not what you think it is, Benjamin, not at all.*

He cocked his head as if listening, and she panicked. Could he hear the thump of her heartbeat? Then he rammed his hat back on, pulled on his gloves, and continued to shovel just as the bonesetter rounded the corner.

Mary swivelled away, her back to the wall, not looking but listening.

Grace called out, 'Benjamin. I've been looking for you. We need to talk.'

A tingle started in Mary's chest and slithered to her feet like an icy fingernail had raked her body from the inside. She was afraid that Benjamin was going to tell the bonesetter everything. He wasn't just digging manure, he was digging beneath the facade, beneath the dirty lies and filthy secrets, digging to find the truth. She was afraid of the truth.

She scrambled away and headed for the refuge of her bedroom and her bed, curling up into a tight ball and running a hand across her belly. She spoke to her unborn child, 'I promise to do whatever it takes to keep you safe. You're all that matters now.' But if she had this baby as an unmarried mother, the parish could take it away. She knew of many such babies removed and given to rich but childless couples because the parish said they would have a better life. And because it was less likely the parish would be asked for poor relief, no doubt.

And if she told everyone the truth, that this was Samuel's baby, his father would try to silence her. As Jenny had said, his father was a hard man. If he didn't silence her, he would take the child, and she would be helpless to stop him; the bailiff had too much power. So, was marrying Benjamin the answer? It gave her a father for the child if she pretended the child was his. If Benjamin never knew the truth, he would believe it was his baby. The family he always wanted. *Be careful what you wish for, Benjamin.*

She got off the bed and paced the floor, crossing to the window, drawn to the liquid beat of raindrops drumming against the pane. She saw him again through the glass, walking in Lower Meadow, and a surge of panic swept through her. He wasn't the one she had planned to spend her life with. He wasn't the one she would have chosen. Not ever.

Behind her, Elizabeth ran into the room, her face flushed and eyes wild. 'Mary, you have to do it now. Marry him. He's going to tell, I know it; I've been watching him.'

'I've been watching him too. Who would he tell, and who would believe him?'

'The bonesetter, that's who. He was talking to Grace just now. Why? Why was she here? I interrupted them, pretended I needed her, and Benjamin ran off. She's gone now, but she'll be back and he'll tell her.'

Frowning, Mary watched Elizabeth. Her sister had changed, no surprise, but the change had altered their relationship. Did Elizabeth blame her for what had happened? Not only had she failed to protect her, but she'd killed Elizabeth's baby. Yes, Elizabeth had asked her to, but she hadn't know what she saying, it hadn't been what she really wanted. No mother would want that. When Elizabeth looked at her now, was it with disgust? If so, why would Elizabeth care if she had to marry Benjamin? 'I don't think he'll tell because he never willingly talks to anyone.'

Elizabeth stared at her, her hands on hips, then she reached for a canvas bag and began stuffing it with clothes.

Mary caught her sister's wrists and held on. 'What are you doing?'

'Leaving. I'm not waiting to be caught and hanged. You promised Ma you would always look after me, but you won't, so I'll look after myself.'

'Oh, Lizzie, sit down. I didn't say I wouldn't do it. I'm thinking about it because I agree with you; if I marry him, he can't tell anyone.'

Elizabeth wrapped her arms around Mary's neck and clung on. 'Thank you. It's the only way we'll be safe.'

Mary stroked Elizabeth's hair and held her tight. 'I agree it's better than hanging, so if I do it, I'm doing it for you. But wait—we haven't been courting. It'll cause a fuss. Da will refuse permission.'

'You can say you've been meeting in secret, and now you want to marry. Could you do it, Mary? Please say you'll do it.'

'It'll take more than that to convince Da and Gramfer.'

'I'll help you. We'll come up with a plan tonight.'

Mary shuddered. She didn't want anyone but Jenny to know about the baby and needed Elizabeth to believe she'd marry Benjamin simply to save them both. She was going to have a baby made of true love, the only part of Samuel she had left. She had to keep it. Benjamin's proposal was the right solution to her own plight—wasn't it?

'Will you let Benjamin know tonight? We have to let him know. It's been a week already, and I can't rest until he's been told.'

Mary sighed. 'I'll tell him. I'll go and find him now.'

Mary hurried away. The quicker this was settled, the better. She flew out of the kitchen door only to collide with her grandfather.

'Slow down. You're going like the clappers over a mill. What's up?'

'I need to find Benjamin. I've something to tell him.'

His eyebrows shot up, but she didn't offer an explanation. 'You'll need a lantern; it's getting dark. He's out by the gate fixing a hole in the hedge before he goes home. Here, take mine if you must go, and wear a cloak. It's started to rain again.'

Mary grabbed the light, giving his hand a gentle squeeze, then went outside, crossed the yard, and made her way to Lower Meadow. Raising the lantern, she scanned the field. There he was, grappling with an old bedstead to plug a hole in the hedge. She watched him finish and get ready to leave. 'Benjamin, wait. It's me,' she called out.

He turned and walked towards her without a coat. He was soaked through by the rain, but he didn't seem to care or feel the cold. She stood opposite him, the silent

101

tension between them thick as if it was a solid thing. Darkness closed in around them, closed in around her.

'Tell me, Benjamin, I need to know—did you tell the gaugers about Samuel?'

'No! Wasn't me. Why would I?'

'I don't think you'd be able to ask me to marry you if Samuel was here.'

'But he's not here, is he? What good would he be to you, anyway?'

She stopped herself from replying, not wanting to give too much away about her and Samuel. Did she believe him? No, not really; he was the obvious choice. 'You say you love me, but you don't know what love is.'

'And you do?'

She hesitated, not wanting to admit she was in love. But yes, she knew what real love was, and this wasn't it. 'I've told Elizabeth. She needed to know.'

He didn't reply, just stood there, his dark eyes staring from under his dripping hat.

'Anyway, I've made a decision. It's yes. It has to be yes. What choice do I have?'

Benjamin sprang into life at her words. He reached out to touch her but missed. 'You'll not be sorry, Mary.' He laughed, shook off his hat, and tipped his face towards the rain. He closed his eyes and let the water run like rivers down his skin.

'I'll tell Da and Gramfer tomorrow night. Won't be easy convincing them about it.'

'No, Mary. I must ask your da if I can marry you. I have to do it properly.'

'If you ask, my da will likely say no.'

102

'Likely. But not after he talks to you. Once he knows you want to be married, your da will do whatever you want.'

'It won't be so easy, but tomorrow night, then?'

'Yes, Mary. And we'll be married as soon as.'

'Yes.'

Benjamin threw his hat up into the air, the raindrops spinning off before he caught it. He called Jess, who sheltered under the hedge, and turned to walk home.

Mary wrapped her arms around her body in a hug. She'd walked into a trap, the cage door had slammed shut, and now there was no escape.

She held her lantern up high and peered through the gloom as he walked away. What was he doing? Oh, dancing, dancing in the rain! He was a very strange boy.

***

MARY DREADED THIS, to tell yet another lie. Once started, this lie had spread to involve more people. Where would it end? She sat by the kitchen fire with her father, grandfather, and Elizabeth, her head bent low, grateful to have Elizabeth beside her, her ally tonight. All day, her stomach had churned nonstop, and she'd spent her time gulping down nausea or running for the privy. From worry or because she was pregnant? Probably both. She fought to keep calm and sat on her hands so no one would notice them shaking.

The kitchen door opened, and her stomach twisted into a tight ball. She turned to look.

'Benjamin, come in and sit by the fire,' her grandfather called out.

Removing his hat to hang it from a rafter, he walked towards them and stood beside Mary's seat. He smiled down at her.

She frowned. He didn't look nervous at all; he looked poised, and when he put a hand on her shoulder, it was steady.

He cleared his throat. 'I've come this evening to ask you, Mr Landeryou, for permission to marry your daughter. Mary.'

Her grandfather choked and spluttered on his beer, and her father let out a burst of staccato laughter that ricocheted around the room. A rare sound from him these days. He replied, 'Get along with you. It's not a thing to make a joke of.'

Benjamin drew himself up tall. 'It's no joke, Mr Landeryou. It's serious. I mean to marry Mary.'

'Well, you're bold for asking, but the answer's no.' Her father glanced at her, raised his eyebrows, and shook his head. 'Go home, Benjamin. We'll say no more about it.'

Oh God, she had to intervene. What would their reaction have been if Samuel had stood there and asked them? Not this, surely. She had always imagined it would be him and held that thought—*pretend this is Samuel. Put on a performance, an act. Do it for the baby.* 'I want to marry him, Father.'

Her grandfather put down his beer and peered from one to the other. 'But you haven't even been courting.'

'We've been meeting secretly, Gramfer, for many, many months.'

'Jimmery-Chry! Impossible. Benjamin is one of our hardest workers. He's never missing, never.'

'We found time, Gramfer, we did, and now we want to marry.'

Her father hoisted himself off his seat and spoke. 'I'll not agree to your marrying, not yet. But if you keep company and it's no secret anymore, you can ask me again in one year.' He sat back down with a firm, short nod, and her grandfather slapped him on the back.

Mary's heart skipped a beat. Benjamin might be willing to accept that offer, but she couldn't. It was now or never. She had a baby to think about. She took a gulp of air. 'No, Da, I love him. I don't want to wait.' Her voice trembled with emotion, and Benjamin's hand squeezed her shoulder.

'I don't want to wait either. We both want to marry. Quickly.'

Her father's eyes narrowed, his face crimson as he stared at them. Mary's face flushed. He probably thought she was pregnant. He was right, of course.

'What? Are you two in some kind of trouble?'

Before Benjamin could speak, Mary whispered, 'Yes, Da. We are, and so we have to get married.'

Benjamin exhaled beside her, and Elizabeth grasped her hand and squeezed it. The silence that followed was shattering. She'd fallen from grace. She lowered her head and wept. It was all too much to bear. How low would God make her sink? As her tears flowed, she scolded herself. It was only self-pity. She had no one but herself to blame, throwing another damned lie into the stew. What brewed now was chaos. She wiped at her eyes with her free hand, but the tears refused to stop.

'I can't pretend I'm not angry.'

Mary raised her eyes to look at the glaring face of her dear father. His hands clenched into tight fists, and his jaw moved as he ground his teeth. He only ever did that when he was furious.

'You have to marry now, have to, so it's a good job that both of you want it.'

'We do, Mr Landeryou.'

'Sit, Benjamin. We have things to talk over.'

Mary shifted along the oak settle to make room. Benjamin squeezed in, pressed up against her side. It was the closest contact they'd ever had. She wanted to laugh like a lunatic. He reached across, seized her hand and held it. His hand was warm and firm, and she could smell him. Not the musky, sweaty scent of Samuel that aroused her, no. He smelt clean, neutral. Even wholesome.

'You have to marry quickly, but the banns need to be read first, so three weeks is the earliest. Let's say three weeks' time.'

Mary calculated when her baby was going to be born. If they married in three weeks, it would be at least two months earlier than expected. Could she get away with that? She certainly dared not leave the marriage any later. She managed to nod in agreement with her father, but it was all so unreal, dreamlike, a nightmare she would wake from. She gazed at the fire and let her thoughts drift with the rising smoke. If only Samuel was here. Her throat constricted, and she ran a hand across her belly.

'No, we'll live at Treyarnon Cottage. At least for a while. At least for our first year.'

What? Did Benjamin just say they'd live at the cottage?

'No, no, no, what's wrong with living here? We can make room. The family has always stayed here,' her grandfather cried out.

'Not for our first year. We won't be far away. And we'll both be here every day,' Benjamin replied.

'Well, 'tedn right and proper.'

'Stop that there grumbling, Gramfer. They're going, and that's that. It's a good idea, I think.' Her father rose and stormed out of the room. In the silence left behind, he stomped up the stairs and banged the bedroom door shut.

Her grandfather leant towards her. 'Don't you worry, Mary, love, he'll come round; it's a shock, that's all.'

'It's best we live at the cottage for a while, Gramfer, until he forgets he's angry.'

Her grandfather mumbled words of disapproval, but after seeing how enraged her father was, living at Treyarnon Cottage would be a welcome escape.

Later, when Benjamin rose to leave, she followed him outside and closed the door behind her. He stood in the darkness with his hands in his pockets, watching and waiting.

'You know what I said in there about being in love and being in trouble was all lies, don't you, Benjamin?'

He searched her eyes like he was digging out the truth. 'Just remember, I'll protect you.'

They stood in silence and looked at each other. Just strangers, two strangers about to get married. Then he simply turned around and walked away. She shook her head at his retreating back. What would she find to talk about with a man of so few words? Shrugging, she went back inside and found only Elizabeth in the kitchen.

'Well, you've done it now.' Elizabeth pushed empty mugs around the table.

'Yes, I have, and now they think I have to get married.' Mary slumped on a chair and gripped the edge with her hands.

'Don't you worry. When you're married, no one will care either way.'

Mary studied Elizabeth and frowned. 'But it's a lie, Lizzie. Another lie.'

'There's so many, Mary, I'm getting them confused with the truth.'

Mary rubbed her face and closed her eyes.

Had Elizabeth guessed about her baby? 'Go to bed. I'll clear up. I need some time to think on my own.'

***

ELIZABETH DETOURED THROUGH the kitchen on her way to bed, reached out a hand, and closed her fingers around cold metal. She tucked her confidante inside the sleeve of her dress and made her way upstairs.

In her dark bedroom, she withdrew it from her dress and caressed the metal before placing it on the table beside her bed. She reached for her tinderbox and prepared to light her candle. Her hand shook as the tinder caught, her pulse quickening.

She undressed, got into bed, and pushed back the covers. Reaching under her pillow, she withdrew a cotton rag and placed it under her left wrist. A wrist scored by red lines where cuts had been made and left to heal. Elizabeth gazed at the table. She smiled. She could take her time; Mary would be a while. This had to be savoured.

Pushing lank hair off her face, she picked up the knife and turned it this way and that in the candlelight. Her conspirator, her salvation. She licked her lips, lay her head back on the pillow, and gripped the knife in her right hand. In slow motion, she drew it across her left wrist, slicing deep so blood gushed from the wound.

She opened her mouth and drew in a long breath. A fierce, stabbing pain ripped through her arm, slashed through her body. This was good, so good—the thrill of pain; the heady, sweet, metallic smell; the pounding of her own heartbeat. She released her breath to watch her bad thoughts escape with the blood.

Closing her eyes, she abandoned herself to the sensation, letting the knife drop to the floor. Her body swept up in bliss, her pain replaced by euphoria, she drifted away, floated free.

Chapter 16

Mary trailed behind her family on the slow walk towards St Merryn. Her legs dragged, reluctant and heavy. It was time for the wedding banns to be read out in church, and she dreaded what the villagers would say. She wanted to curl up in bed and never leave, but hiding was no solution because there would always be a next day, and a next and a next.

At least Benjamin wouldn't be there; he never went to church, another thing her father disapproved of. She must have sighed because Elizabeth turned and waited for her, holding out an outstretched hand, which Mary clasped hungrily.

Once inside the cold church, Mary sat straight and rigid on a hard pew and glanced at her sister. At least the wedding meant no one was taking much notice of Elizabeth, and good job too. When had she last washed? Her hair hung lank and greasy, and her pallid skin was waxy.

The vicar's fist pounded the pulpit, thump, thump, thump, and she jolted to attention. He leant forwards, focused his brittle eyes on her, and with great relish threw the news out into the congregation with his loud penetrating voice, where it dropped like a boulder, causing a ripple of whispers to wash over her.

'I publish the Banns of Marriage between Benjamin Carnarton of this parish and Mary Landeryou of this parish. If any of you know cause or just impediment why these two persons should not be joined together in Holy Matrimony, ye are to declare it. This is the first time of asking.'

Heads turned in her direction, and she dropped hers, squeezing her eyes shut. She wanted to run or to become invisible, she willed it, but she sat on a hard seat with nowhere to hide. Keeping her eyes closed, she retreated like a snail into the protection of its shell. She closed her mind to those around her and let the service crawl by in a blur. Only when her grandfather leant down to whisper in her ear, 'Leave them to me,' did she realise it was over. But on leaving the church, a swarming throng surrounded her with question after question.

'Didn't know you'd been courting, maid.'

'How long have you two been keeping company?'

'How come we didn't know anything until now?'

'Benjamin! You must be mad to marry that one or in some trouble.'

A small hand grabbed her own and held it. Jenny's hand rested on her shoulder, and Mary whimpered. 'Mary, hush now, what's going on?'

Mary gulped and wiped at her eyes. 'Not here. I'll come over and see you soon.'

'Are you all right? Are you really getting married?'

'Yes and yes.'

'To Benjamin?'

'Yes, I must.'

'But to Benjamin? I don't understand.'

'No, I don't either. Later, Jenny, later.'

Her grandfather seized her arm and pulled her through the crowd, guiding her towards her father and Elizabeth, who waited for them up ahead. Mary clung onto Jenny, but she slipped through her fingers and out of sight.

Her grandfather laughed. 'They loves every lil diddle. Don't you worry, Mary, love, it's just gossip.'

Mary took a deep breath. 'Da is still angry with me.'

'Oh, he'll be fine. He'll give you away on the day with a smile.'

'Gramfer, will you be a witness with Da?'

'*Awmylor,* Mary, I'll be glad to. I s'pose Benjamin doesn't have anyone?'

'No, Gramfer.'

Her grandfather patted her arm and whistled a jovial tune. She raised an eyebrow at him. *Why was he always so damned happy?*

In the weeks that passed, drawing her ever nearer to her wedding day, she sensed her body changing with the new life she carried. It was all that kept her going; she wanted this child so much, nothing else mattered. Nothing else carried the same weight of importance.

She locked all other secrets securely away, never intending to reveal them to anyone. Only Jenny held a key that could lay them all bare. She longed to go and see her friend, but she was afraid that if she did, she would tell her everything. She needed more time to fasten more bolts across her heart.

So she stayed away from Jenny Wren.

***

MARY USUALLY HAD trouble sleeping, but this particular morning, she couldn't wake. She flailed and writhed in bed, unable to surface from a dark dream where a faceless mob yelled for her baby. She gripped her child to her breast, but they ripped it from her grasp and screamed at her, 'Child killer. You don't deserve it.'

She tried to wake and breathe, but her chest was tight like a hand squeezed it shut, making her gasp at pockets of air. She wanted to call out for help, but the words wouldn't come. She couldn't speak, couldn't move, and a terrible feeling of dread weighed her down. She couldn't remember. She had to remember something, there was a reason for this sense of panic, but what was it?

And then it hit her like a punch to her stomach. Married, she was getting married today. Praying every night for a miracle, that Samuel would return to rescue her, had been futile.

The day had arrived.

Dragging herself out of her warm bed and wrapping a shawl around her shoulders, she went to the window and opened the shutters to a dark, frigid morning. Mary gazed through the window at her ghostly reflection and reached out a hand. The girl gazing back at her looked how she felt, helpless and defeated. This was her life now. She turned to trudge downstairs.

Once the fire in the kitchen blazed, Mary spent a moment warming herself in front of it. 'I'm doing this for you,' she whispered and ran her hands over her belly. 'It's only the thought of you that keeps me going.'

The kitchen door creaked open, and Elizabeth entered.

'You're early, Lizzie.'

'Thought I'd help you today, the wedding being so early. Give you time to get ready.'

'It's only a simple wedding breakfast, and we're all back to work straight after.'

'I know, but Da said you and Benjamin can leave before supper today. Are you packed?'

'I don't have much to take, and I'm leaving some things here.'

'Oh?'

'I will be back, Lizzie. I can't live at that cottage forever.'

Mary made the bread, hoping it would stop her thinking, but it failed to even stop her hands shaking.

'Mary!'

Elizabeth's shout broke into her thoughts.

'Leave that now, it's finished. You must get ready. We have to go soon, and you can't be late.'

Mary shoved the dough aside to let it prove, closed her eyes, and took a deep breath. This was it, then. This was it. In slow motion, she turned and headed for the stairs. Wandering into the bedroom, she selected her best Sunday dress and bonnet and stared at her hat, the ribbons coated with a thin layer of dust. The last time she'd worn this had been to winnow the corn with Samuel. She should tie new ribbons on it, ribbons in her favourite colour, perhaps. She picked up the hat and turned it round and round in her hands. But all the ribbons she owned were given to her by Samuel. She tore them off the hat one by one. No ribbons today. They would only remind her of the man she should be marrying.

She would wear her sensible work boots. It would be muddy on the walk to the church and back. It didn't

114

matter what she looked like, and Benjamin wouldn't worry; he didn't have a Sunday best to wear. She brushed out her long dark hair and tried to plait it, but the strands twisted and fought her fumbled attempt. 'Lizzie, I need your help.'

'Are you nervous?'

'I'm marrying a man I don't love and never will. I don't even know him very well, so yes, I am.'

'Well, yes, but you do know him. You've known Benjamin from a child.'

'But it's hard when that person doesn't speak.'

'Perhaps he will when you get to know him. This wedding is for the best.'

'The best? The best of a bad situation. You know I love Samuel and wanted to marry him. This feels like a betrayal.'

'He's not here, is he? He wanted you to move on.' Elizabeth put an arm around Mary's shoulders. 'You know I love you for doing this for us, don't you?'

'I wish I could love myself for it, but I don't.'

'Don't cry. Let me plait your braid. You never know, one day you might be glad you married Benjamin instead.'

Chapter 17

Benjamin paced up and down his cottage floor. It didn't take many strides. He was ready far too early, and now the slow passage of time seemed endless. *The ring*? Yes, the ring was safe, safe in his pocket.

He brushed imaginary dust off his new jacket. Second-hand it might be, but it had years of wear in it, it fit, and it was clean and tidy. So were his breeches. The boots were old and worn and too small for him, but clean. All last night he'd scrubbed the mud off them.

A wet nose nudged his hand, and he laughed at bright curious eyes and a lustrous coat. 'Jess, you look as handsome as me. Quite right. It's a special day. Very special.' His hand shook as he stroked her gleaming inky black coat, and his stomach turned over with nerves. He reached into his jacket pocket and tapped the ring. Still there where it was when he'd checked a moment ago.

He glanced around the cottage. Was there anything left to do? The fire waited, ready to be lit. The floor was swept clean, every surface wiped, the sea salt removed from the windows, and the bed made with fresh, clean bedding. *Oh God, the bed*. It was thinking of the bed that made him start pacing in the first place, to stop the tremors. There wasn't enough room. The cottage was driving him crazy; he needed a longer walk. 'Come on, Jess. We'll take the long way. Wait for her in the church.'

116

He picked up his work clothes to change into later and opened the cottage door. A bitter cold, frosty morning welcomed him. He exhaled and released his warm breath in a white mist, stuffed his hands into his pockets, and set off, listening to his boots crunch on the crisp grass. He tried to stroll, but his legs wanted to run with the thrill of being alive. Like a snake, he was about to shed his old skin, and he could not wait.

He took the longest route possible to the church, desperate to walk off his nervous energy, while Jess bounded around him, circling, darting, and racing away only to charge straight at him before veering off at the last minute. He whooped at her and joined in, chasing her, cavorting in an unrestrained frenzy, but he skidded to a stop on nearing the church.

A crowd of noisy onlookers had gathered, waiting to enjoy the spectacle. He narrowed his eyes and rubbed the back of his neck with one hand. Now he had to walk past them all. He reached up to pull down his hat, but it wasn't there. *Damn, how did he forget that?* He took a gulp of air. They didn't matter, were nothing. They couldn't hurt him now. He placed his bundle of work clothes under a bush. 'Wait here, Jess. Wait,' he whispered. Patting the ring once more, he puffed out his cheeks, straightened his jacket, and strode towards the church, forcing his head up high.

Their eyes bore into him, but he focused only on the church door ahead. Their whispering chatter sank to a low murmur when he passed, only to rise up boisterously again behind his back. He smiled. He was certainly giving them something to talk about. Let them talk.

He reached the south porch and pushed open the first heavy oak door, stepped inside, and let it close with a thud behind him. He tugged down the sleeves of his jacket and swallowed, then he opened the next door and walked down the stone steps.

Such light. He stared around him, dazed. Even on a cold dull morning, the church was full of light. In front of him were pillars and arches of stone. Seven, he counted seven of them. He spun around to face the same direction as the pews. Up ahead was a carved stone font and a raised platform dominated by a pulpit, all framed by a multicoloured window of fractured light, the panes like exquisite jewels. He tilted back his head to see the arched wagon-roof ceiling. *Well, damn, what a sight.* He hadn't expected anything quite so beautiful or to find such peace.

He took a step and hesitated, his tread echoing around him. Someone sat in one of the pews up ahead, and they gestured at him to come forwards. He walked down the aisle towards the bonesetter and groaned. Actually, he liked Grace, but she asked too many questions. She was very fond of Mary, so she probably thought she could do better. Do better? By what, marrying Samuel? The very idea made his hands clench into fists.

Grace called out to him. 'You have to sit just there and wait. I'll sit behind you, don't suppose anyone else will. Have you got a ring?'

He patted his pocket, assuming this gesture was telling enough, and sat down with his back to her, hoping the questions were over. One of her big hands prodded at his shoulder. He heaved a sigh and swivelled in his seat to look at her.

She stared at him. He squirmed, but just as he was about to turn away, she simply said, 'Well done.'

His mouth fell open. He snapped it shut and nodded, grinning as he turned from her.

Benjamin waited as the minutes unhurriedly slipped by, rechecking the ring in his pocket, drumming his fingers against the wooden pew. He whirled around when the oak door gave an unmistakable creak. Mary's uncle, John Landeryou, walked in with his wife, Sarah, following diffidently behind.

Grace leant towards him and muttered, 'Full of happiness as always.' But her words drifted past him.

The door moaned its protest once more, but when he turned to look, William Blewet ushered Charity and Jenny inside with a protective arm around them both, all of them dressed in their Sunday best. Benjamin wasn't expecting anyone else to come, not to see him married, not even for Mary.

He toyed with the ring, but his hands shook too much. How was he going to stop his hands from trembling? The door groaned open once more, but this time he sat transfixed, unable to look. It was her; this time it was her. He tensed as footsteps drew nearer and jolted back to life when the vicar said, 'Please stand.' Where had he come from? He hadn't noticed him arrive. He managed a sideways glance at Mary but saw only her bonnet, then the bonesetter's hands clamped on his shoulders to raise him up beside Mary.

The vicar opened his Bible and bellowed, 'Dearly beloved, we are gathered together in the sight of God, and in the face of this congregation, to join together this man and this woman in Holy Matrimony . . .'

119

Benjamin lost the thread of words, unable to concentrate, and stole another look at Mary as she closed her eyes.

'Therefore, if any man can show any just cause why they may not lawfully be joined together, let him now speak or else hereafter forever hold his peace.'

Silence.

Mary's eyes were still closed. She was probably praying Samuel would throw open the doors and rescue her. He closed his own eyes and prayed he wouldn't. More meaningless words fell about his ears until his own name was spoken.

'Benjamin Carnarton, wilt thou have this woman to thy wedded wife, to live together after God's ordinance in the holy estate of Matrimony? Wilt thou love her, comfort her, honour her, and keep her in sickness and in health, and forsaking all others as long as ye both shall live?'

He turned to face Mary and couldn't stop himself saying, 'Oh yes. I will. Gladly. I will.' Titters of laughter filled the silence. The vicar raised his eyebrows, but Benjamin didn't care.

'Mary Landeryou, wilt thou have this man for thy wedded husband, to live together after God's ordinance in the holy estate of Matrimony? Wilt thou obey him and serve him, love, honour, and keep him in sickness and in health, and forsaking all others, keep thee only unto him, so long as ye both shall live?'

Mary stood motionless with her head bowed. Silent.

His heart raced, pounding through his veins, and the tremors in his hands spread to his legs. *Say yes, Mary, say yes*. He couldn't take his eyes off her and caught his breath. Was she raising her head? *Come on, Mary, do it. Please.*

She took her time but spoke the words he was desperate to hear. 'I will.'

He staggered backwards, flooded with relief. The bonesetter's strong hands held him steady.

'Who giveth this woman to be married to this man?'

Benjamin watched Mary's father grasp and squeeze her shaking hand and give it to the vicar. So, she was shaking too. She was vulnerable and scared, and his heart went out to her. The vicar leant forwards and plucked Benjamin's right hand, then placed Mary's in it. Two hands trembling together, his from joy. But hers?

Taking his cue from the vicar, Benjamin looked straight at Mary, raised his voice, and deliberately pronounced each word. 'I, Benjamin Carnarton, take thee, Mary Landeryou, to my wedded wife, to have and to hold from this day forwards, for better, for worse, for richer, for poorer, in sickness and in health, to love and to cherish, till death us do part, according to God's holy ordinance; and thereto I plight thee my troth.' He'd never before said so much in one stretch.

Mary did not look at him. She kept her eyes and head down, and when it was her turn to speak, she was so quiet, he strained to hear her, her voice a long, anguished sigh. 'I, Mary Landeryou, take thee, Benjamin Carnarton, to my wedded husband, to have and to hold from this day forwards, for better, for worse, for richer, for poorer, in sickness and in health, to love, cherish, and to obey, till death us do part, according to God's holy ordinance, and thereto I give thee my troth.'

It was too painful, but he was nearly there, nearly, and he cared about nothing else. The vicar asked for the ring, and he reached into his pocket to retrieve the precious golden band with an intricate engraved design of roses twisted around the outside. Mary would recognise it, for it had belonged to her mother. Her father had given it to him one cold afternoon, pressing the warm yellow metal into his icy hands. He had awkwardly and gruffly told him to keep it safe, and that his late wife, Jane, had made him promise he would give it to Mary when she married. He always kept his promise.

Benjamin placed the ring upon the Bible, and this time, Mary did raise her head and look at him with wide, astonished eyes, then she turned and stared at her father, who nodded at her. Benjamin slipped the ring onto her unsteady finger and repeated after the vicar. 'With this ring, I thee wed, with my body, I thee worship, and with all my worldly goods, I thee endow, in the name of the Father, and of the Son, and of the Holy Ghost. Amen.'

Mary's eyes filled with tears, and he pretended the gift of the ring had caused them and not this marriage. Benjamin knelt down when told to do so, and the vicar said a prayer before finally saying the words Benjamin wanted to hear.

'Forsomuch as Benjamin Carnarton and Mary Landeryou have consented together in Holy Wedlock, and have witnessed the same before God and this company, and thereto have given and pledged their troth either to other, and have declared the same by giving and receiving of a ring, and by joining of hands, I pronounce that they be man and wife together, in the name of the Father, and of the Son, and of the Holy Ghost. Amen.'

The service wasn't over yet, but Benjamin was deaf to the rest. He'd done it, achieved the unthinkable because he'd dared to dream. He pressed one hand down on the top of his head to stop it floating away, held his other hand to his mouth to contain a shriek, and shuffled his legs to disguise a dance. This was all he'd wanted for so long, and now it was his.

He signed the register with a cross, never having learnt to read or write, but he watched Mary and her father sign with their names. Hell, he would learn his letters, and why not? He could do anything he wanted; he was as good as anybody now.

Benjamin turned to walk out of the church and reached for Mary's hand to thread her fingers through his. She'd stopped trembling, her velvet skin milky white, but she refused to look at him. She clenched her teeth as if to stop the tears, but he wanted to whoop and jump with joy. He would win her over one day. That was his next challenge, and he would never give up trying.

The waiting group of villagers gave a subdued cheer and, as was the custom, threw shoes after them for luck. Mary's grandfather slapped him on the back, but otherwise he was ignored.

He didn't care, not now that he had Mary.

Chapter 18

Once back at the farmhouse, Mary just wanted to be alone to make sense of her life. She didn't feel any different, didn't feel married. She couldn't do that, of course, be alone, not with the wedding breakfast about to start, so she put the bacon in the smoke chamber over the flue whilst Elizabeth cooked the eggs in a pan over the fire.

At first, no one said a word. Everyone kept their own thoughts private and unspoken. The silence hung in the air like a tangible thing, to mingle and fuse with the drift of smoke and waft of cooking bacon, until the clatter of plates on the table broke the spell, until chatter replaced the hush.

Mary sat next to Benjamin but didn't speak and couldn't bring herself to even look at him. She knew it wasn't his fault. He'd saved her, but right now it didn't feel like it, so she let herself devour her resentment of him, and like a poison, it filled her veins.

Once the breakfast was over, Jenny's mother, Charity, collected the teacups together and lined them up on the table. It wasn't until Charity spoke that Mary understood the awful truth of what she intended to do.

'I'm going to read the tea leaves, see what the future holds for everyone.'

Mary cried out, 'No!' at the same time as Elizabeth and Jenny. *The future?* She didn't want to know, and she didn't want anyone else to know.

'Don't make such a fuss. I always do it, and it's right and proper to do it now. I'm starting with the bride.'

Mary closed her eyes. How could she have forgotten that Charity believed she had a gift for seeing into the future? Charity always did this at a gathering. Mary wanted to argue, to tell her she didn't want to know, but fear hampered her tongue. *Oh God, what would she see?* She could only watch mesmerised as Charity performed her ritual.

Charity picked Mary's teacup up in her left hand and turned it three times from the left with a quick flourish. Then with great care, she turned the cup upside down on the saucer and left it until all the moisture drained away.

Hushed, everyone waited until Charity picked the cup up and turned it around, peering inside before she spoke in a soft, low voice. 'I see . . . I see a curtain, yes, yes, someone is hiding something from you.' She paused. 'Something else. There's a creature, an animal of some such. I know it; it's a cat. A cat means treachery. Someone will betray you, or maybe they already have. And a cup— no, no handle, and it's small. I know—an egg cup. Let me see . . . you will escape disaster.' Charity put the cup down and gazed around, smiling.

Mary heaved a sigh of relief. All nonsense. She saw nothing. Nothing.

Charity moved on to Elizabeth's cup and took her time to study it. 'Well, well. I see an altar, and it's big, so it's important. It means sorrow and distress. And there's a stick . . . no, not a stick, a candle. Oh, a candle, now that's problems, worry, and illness.'

Mary cast a sidelong glance at Elizabeth, but she'd withdrawn into the protection of her own world.

'I see a ball . . . no, no, not that.' Charity paused, frowning for a moment before raising her eyebrows. 'Of course. It's an onion.'

'It's enough to bring tears to my own eyes,' her grandfather muttered.

'You have a secret, and it will be discovered, but not until later in life.'

Elizabeth dropped the knife she toyed with. It clattered to the floor, and as she bent down to pick it up, her hands trembled.

Mary twirled her wedding band round and round her finger again. *None of this could possibly be true, could it?*

Charity picked up Jenny's cup and let out an exasperated cry. 'Jenny, you didn't leave enough in the bottom. It's just a muddle and of no use.'

'I didn't know you were going to do it.'

'I always do it.'

Jenny shrugged and dropped her head down low, keeping her eyes firmly fixed on the table.

'Come on, woman, look at my cup,' her grandfather said, leaning over the table towards her.

'All right, I'll do you now. Well, well, I see lots of bees all over, and I think some are bumblebees.'

'Bees?'

'Oh yes. You have many friends, you love life, and you're always happy and easily pleased. And I see a jug;

you will have good health. And you will have good luck, 'cause I see a three-sided shape.'

Her grandfather gave a wrinkled grin and laughed. 'It's all true, these tea leaves.'

'Benjamin next, I s'pose.'

'Don't bother.'

'No bother. So, what do I see? I see a dog, a large dog.'

'I bet even I could see that,' her grandfather mumbled.

'A large dog, a protector.'

Benjamin bent and patted Jess on the head.

'I can see an arch. That stands for hope. Oh look, I see a hat. Now, what does that mean again? Oh, I know, success. And I see a knife . . . no, it's bigger, a sword. I believe that means trouble, trouble and pain. Near the bottom of the cup is a cross, a big one. *Awmylor,* it's more trouble, even death.'

Benjamin shook his head and said nothing.

'The next cup I have belongs to Grace.'

'Oh good, tell us everything.' Her grandfather chuckled, rubbing his hands together.

The bonesetter unfolded her chunky arms, shook her head, and grinned. 'I won't say I don't believe; I've seen enough strange things to know better. Let's have it, then.'

'Good, 'cause the first thing I see is a bracelet, and I know what it means—you'll make a discovery too late. And I've seen this sign often enough—an ear, and it's large. You'll be shocked when you hears about some scandal or abuse. And finally, a finger, so you'd better pay attention.'

Grace said, 'Pfft,' and flapped her hand dismissively at Charity. Mary rested her head on her hand and watched the bonesetter through her open fingers. *Did a shadow of pain just cross her face?*

Attention moved on to Sarah Landeryou.

'Hmm, not much to see in Sarah's tea leaves either, but I do have something. A chain, but it's broken.' She looked up at Sarah as she spoke. 'There's something in store for you in the shape of a stranger. And I see another animal, another dog? No, not that. I can't think . . . oh wait, yes, yes, I know. It's a badger. A badger, eh? Oh, Sarah, you do regret getting married.'

Elizabeth and Jenny let out giggles of laughter, and her grandfather snorted, trying to stifle a laugh, but not very hard.

Mary's uncle thumped his hands down on the table, making the cups rattle, then he rose to his feet. 'We have to go home now. Work to do.' With that, he walked to the door, reached up for his hat, and left, banging the door behind him.

Sarah also rose and nodded at them all but said nothing. Her face expressionless, she hurried out after her husband.

'Well, he had a face like a wet weekend,' her grandfather said.

'I don't know what their problem is,' said Charity. 'They don't have chick nor child to worry about.'

'And maybe that's their problem,' said Grace, shaking her head. 'More belongs to a marriage than four bare legs in a bed.'

'Leave them be. It's back to work for all of us, I think,' her father said, glancing around the table. 'And I have to say, you were well dressed today, Benjamin.'

Benjamin's eyes grew wide in surprise, and Mary didn't blame him; her father never normally noticed anything. Mary took a longer look at Benjamin and regarded the new jacket. It didn't impress her.

Everyone rose to leave. Mary shooed them out and refused offers of help to clear up, wanting, *needing* to be left alone. Jenny crossed the room, wrapped her arms around her, and clung on. Mary prised her arms apart. 'Don't worry, Jen, I'm fine.'

'If you're sure. Goodbye, Mary. I do love you.'

'I love you too, Jenny Wren.'

Jenny looked up at her and smiled, but was that sadness in her eyes? Worrying too much again, worrying about her and Benjamin, probably. Jenny turned and left.

Mary shut the door behind her and returned to the table, using her fingertips to pick a teacup up by the handle and peer inside. An erratic brown smear of tea leaves splattered the inside. Did it mean anything? She twisted and turned the cup. 'Nothing. There's nothing here but a mess. It has to be just rubbish,' she muttered.

Letting the cup drop onto the table, she gathered up the dishes as Charity's words ran through her head.

Chapter 19

B enjamin changed into his work clothes and carefully folded his new jacket. Giving it a pat, he imagined time off with Mary when the jacket could be worn—market days, fair days. He'd never had a day off in his life; what would that be like? To go to a fair, where there would be people, crowds of people? He shivered, but maybe going with Mary, it would be different. He continued to daydream, and the endless day full of inexhaustible hours plodded on. He'd never wanted to get home so badly.

At suppertime he entered the kitchen, hoping to find Mary ready to go. She wasn't there, but it was full of the labourers, all sat enjoying slices of wedding cake and glasses of beer, which they raised in a silent toast to him. He ignored them all.

'Come in and wait, Benjamin. Elizabeth, go and get Mary. She must be ready by now; she's been up there ages. Do you want a beer?' Mary's father asked him.

He shook his head. He just wanted to leave, leave with his new wife. *Wife!* Mary's father was completely unconcerned about sending his daughter away with him, but then he didn't know this was all brand new, fresh, unfamiliar territory. He wiped his hands down his trousers. *Where was she?*

At last, she entered the kitchen. He waited impatiently, his arms crossed, tapping his foot as she gave out hugs and kisses to her family. Finally, she turned to leave, picking up her box of belongings. He sprang into action and took the box out of her hands. She didn't look at him or thank him. It didn't matter. They were leaving at last.

With Jess beside him, he sprinted down the farm track and reached the end before he realised Mary wasn't beside him. He turned to look for her. There she was, taking her time. He waited for her, falling into step beside her when she approached. 'We need to go faster, so I can get home. Light the fire. Warm up the cottage.'

She didn't look up but did give in and lengthened her stride.

Jess ran up ahead and stopped to bark at a curiosity on the track, waiting for them to catch up with her.

Mary got there first and gave a small cry. Benjamin looked over the top of the box at a small bird, its wings spread out as if in flight, still soaring free. 'It's just a little bird. A wren. Broke its neck, I reckon.' He stepped over it and walked on, breathing in the evening air and waiting for the smell of manure, hay, and drifting woodsmoke to give way to the briny, fresh smell of the sea, telling him he was nearly home.

Jess arrived at the cottage ahead of them, pawing at the door. Benjamin laughed, lifted the latch, and made straight for the bedroom to put Mary's box in a safe place.

***

MARY STOOPED, STEPPED inside, and closed the door quickly to keep out the raw chill wind. She shivered. It was so much colder on the cliff top, so close to the sea. It sounded different too, with seagulls screaming to be heard above the pounding waves. It smelt . . . alien.

The scratch and scrape of flint on steel drew her eyes to leaping flames. A warm glow spread out from the hearth, but the rest of the room remained in shadow. While Benjamin lit candles, she picked up a holder and strolled around the living area.

With the candle raised in front of her, the dark, gloomy corners of the room revealed wooden cupboards that looked skilfully homemade. She brushed against a table and released a heady, sweet scent from a jar containing pale yellow winter jasmine. At a windowsill, she ran a finger along the edge. Spotlessly clean but littered with a curious collection of seashells. She picked up a small cone-shaped shell, brought it to her nose, and wrinkled it in disapproval. It still smelt of the sea.

At the back of the room, she found a closed door and hesitated for a second before pushing on the handle so it swung open. The interior revealed cupboards, chairs. A double bed. She reached for the door handle to pull it shut, being careful not to step across the threshold. That could wait. Next to this room was another, full of clutter but perfect for a child's bedroom.

Walking around the room's perimeter, it didn't take many steps before she arrived back at the fireplace. Two homemade sweetheart chairs were arranged on either side, their smooth polished wood of holly and ash gleaming in the firelight. A small table sat between them with the evening's supper laid out with glinting glasses of amber liquid. Jess sprawled out as close to the warm fire as possible, her eyes shut and her legs twitching.

Taking a seat opposite Benjamin, she reached for a plate of food. She guessed the honey-coloured drink was brandy and took a sip. She didn't usually drink, but the fiery liquid flooded her. As the heat surged through her body, it gave her confidence. She picked up the glass again, drank it down in one, and spluttered and coughed.

Benjamin drained his own, then reached across and refilled them both.

She wiped her mouth with the back of her hand. It worked; the alcohol made her fearless. She wasn't hungry but ate some food to steady her stomach. This time she sipped the brandy, enjoying the warmth of it coursing through her body. Now she was bold enough to look at him. Her eyes narrowed. They had to sleep together tonight and many nights to come if she was to convince him this child was his. She ran a finger around the rim of her glass. She wanted it over and done with quickly, whilst numbed and drowsy from the drink.

Benjamin poured himself another and tilted the bottle towards her. She nodded. One more would be enough. She gulped it down. Was he going to sit there in silence and drink all night? Surely not. If the brandy affected her, what was it doing to him? If she got up to leave, would he follow, or was she going to have to seduce him? She giggled and raised herself unsteadily, took up a candle, and walked around the back of her chair. When she looked up, he stood in front of her. Close.

He said nothing, but a charged current ran between them, the tingle starting in her scalp and sliding down to her feet. He desperately wanted her; everything about him shouted desire. If she reached out to touch him, would he feel hot, like a violent storm about to erupt? This was

133

different, to possess power over him. This was new. She never dominated Samuel—quite the opposite.

She didn't move, would make him wait. He stood not quite motionless, like a quivering wire, then dropped his head and stepped aside to let her pass. She brushed against his shoulder and smiled in the darkness when he vibrated at her touch.

In the bedroom, Mary held the candle aloft. Which side of the bed did he usually have? It didn't matter. She would decide, and he could make do. She found her box of possessions at the foot of the bed and rummaged around for her nightdress and hairbrush. In her haste to pull her dress over her head, she stumbled against the bed and giggled. She tried to fold her clothes, then gave up and threw them on the floor.

Mary pushed down on the wooden bed to test the ropes and wasn't surprised to find them as tight as they could possibly be—this was Benjamin's house after all— and she slid into bed, shivering. She untied her braid, then grabbed her brush and ran it through her hair until it flowed down her back satiny smooth. Whenever her hair flowed loosely about her shoulders, Samuel would run his fingers through it, bury his face in it, stroke her, caress her, kiss her. *Oh God.* She squeezed her legs together. That was Sam; why should Benjamin be any different?

All she had to do now was wait.

Chapter 20

Benjamin returned to his chair and took up his drink. He so wanted to run his hands down her slender neck, to caress her cheek, but when she raised her candle and stared hard at him beneath those long dark eyelashes, his muscles froze.

She must know how desperate he was for her, but she wasn't going to make this easy. God, how her lustrous hair gleamed in the firelight, the colour of nutmeg. He wanted, he needed to explore her body, stroke her velvet skin. The pit of his stomach ached for her. He gripped the arm of his chair to try to contain his growing erection. It was no good; he was beyond control. But he did not want to force himself on her or to feel her flinch from his touch. If she was lifeless beneath him, he would stop, even if it tore him apart.

He grabbed a candle and scrambled towards the bedroom, tripping over his feet. Once in the dark, he would have more confidence to reach out to her. In the dark, he could be anybody.

At the bedroom door he paused, pushed it open, and held up the flickering flame. She'd taken the far side of the bed, and her burnished dark hair was splayed across the pillow. The sight of it ripped him open. Hot candle grease ran over his hand, but he ignored it. He crept into the room and closed the door with a click behind him. Blowing out the candle, he set himself free.

He undressed in the hope his hot, naked body would melt her, then pulled back the covers and climbed into bed. At first, he reached for her hair. It ran like silk through his fingers. Inching nearer to her body he stroked the side of her face and with his fingertips, tracing across her eyelids, across her mouth.

She didn't move.

He inched closer.

Benjamin ran his hand over her cotton nightdress, across her breasts, down her stomach, down her thighs. Her muscles were rigid, her legs clamped together, but the ache in his belly turned to fire. He shivered. He needed, wanted more.

He pressed his bare flesh against her flimsy garment. If only his inflamed skin would scorch it. Thrusting his erection up hard against her thigh, he put his mouth to her ear. Could she hear him panting? Slowly, cautiously, he pulled open the ties of her nightdress to expose her body. His hand grazed her bare skin. Her nipples rubbed against his palm. He flicked his fingers over them, felt their reaction. Hard, rigid—a response at last. He cupped a breast and caressed her soft curves, trailed a hand down the side of her body, and stroked the indent of her waist, over her hips towards her thighs.

Nothing. She didn't move.

Please move. I want you, need you. His hand brushed her thighs and pushed her legs apart. His fingers danced over her. God, she was beautiful everywhere.

But she didn't move.

He buried his face in her hair and stifled a cry. He couldn't take her like this.

Slowly, cautiously, her legs thrust against his, opening. *Did she mean it?* He had to be sure, or she'd hate him forever.

Her hand crawled across his chest, trailed through fine hair, down to his stomach. Exploring his firm muscles, tight flesh. Her hand slid down his side, down one leg, and his breath burst from him in a cry. Fingers curled around his erection and squeezed, then moved. Up and down. He bit down on his thumb, but she'd pulled a trigger, and he exploded in a pent-up rush of heat and fluid.

'Sorry, Mary. Was your touch. Just too much.'

'Don't worry.'

'We can try again later.'

He rolled onto his back and stared into the darkness.

She got out of bed, and his china bowl clanged when she knocked into the dresser in the dark. Water splashed as she washed her hands. 'Tomorrow. We'll try again tomorrow night,' she said.

He smiled and waited for her warmth to return next to his body, her hair falling across his face.

They had a lifetime of this. It could only get better.

***

THE NEXT MORNING Mary woke to the screech of seagulls and yawned, her limbs weightless. She must have slept well for once. She couldn't even remember her dreams.

Wait, something wasn't right. The bed was different. Her arm skimmed across the sheet. Empty and

137

cold. And big. She sat up. Of course. Married and at the cottage, not at home. How could she forget? A dog barked outside, and a man laughed. Benjamin.

She rubbed at the goosebumps on her arms and got out of bed. Clean water in a chipped china bowl stood on the dresser. She reached for the cloth beside it, screwed up her face, and danced on tiptoes, gathering courage. She hated freezing cold water in the mornings. She dipped the cloth into the bowl and let out a sigh. It was warm. He'd done this?

Using the cloth, she wiped her body clean. He'd run his hands over every inch of her last night; no wonder he couldn't control himself. She smiled but changed it to a frown. She'd expected to be repulsed by him, but somehow he'd excited her, made her want him. Or was that just the brandy? No wonder the Methodists wanted everyone teetotal if that's what drink did to you. He hadn't tried again.

Had she wanted him to? Yes, she had. What sort of woman was she becoming?

She reached for her clothes, neatly folded on a chair, and stopped. Looked at the floor. That's where she'd left them, so he'd done this too. She dressed and left the room, stretching her arms above her head, then walked to the fireplace. Gone, the dishes from last night, washed and stacked away. He was trying to impress or make up for last night. It would never last; he was a man, for God's sake. This wasn't what men did.

The cottage door opened, and Benjamin and Jess entered. He gave her a smile that stretched across his face and reached his eyes. She'd never seen him smile before— not like that, anyway. Not with abandon.

'We'd best get off to work. When you're ready.'

She nodded at him. She nearly smiled back.

'Mary.'

She said nothing. Held her breath. *Please don't talk about last night.*

'Can you teach me my letters?'

She exhaled. 'Why?'

'You can read and write. I've never had the chance.'

She chewed on a fingernail. It would give them something to do in the evenings. Better than trying to make conversation with a man of so few words. 'I will. Do you know how to make slate pencils from the slate in the ground?'

He shrugged. 'Seen it done.'

'Good. I'll bring my old school slate home tonight and we'll start.'

They left the cottage together, in silence as usual. She couldn't think of anything to say, and anyway, the silence was comfortable. Instead, a chorus of crashing waves accompanied them as they walked along the clifftop. She hurried to keep up with his long, powerful strides, hugging her cloak about her as they crossed Upper Meadow, reaching the five-bar gate leading to Sandy Lane, where they stopped. Benjamin leant on the gate, his arms folded across the top bar. He didn't move.

She huffed. 'What have you stopped here for?'

'We like to look.'

Mary glanced down at Jess, who sat staring through the bars, so she turned and also took a long look. She must have sounded annoyed when she said, 'It's only the farm,' but she didn't mean to. She'd never viewed it from here before, and it caught her breath to see it spread out below her. Mary drank in the sight of home, of love. A curl of smoke poured from the farmhouse chimney, and squares of flickering yellow light nodded at her, beckoning in warm welcome. Her heart surged at the familiarity, and she clambered over the gate, desperate to be home.

She left Benjamin and Jess at the edge of Lower Meadow, where he joined the potato pickers. He opened his mouth to speak, then closed it again, saying nothing, so she turned and dashed for the farmhouse.

The delicious sweet, nutty smell of baked barley bread greeted her in the kitchen, where Elizabeth had control of the breakfast. 'You're up early, Lizzie, what can I do?'

'Nought in here, but Gramfer could do with help outside.'

Mary stopped pulling at the ties of her cloak and turned to leave.

'Mary?'

'Yes?'

'How are you?'

She stared at Elizabeth, thinking. Such a simple question. Why was the answer so complicated? In the end, she said, 'I'm fine, Lizzie. Fine.' Because she was. Life could be worse, so much worse.

She could be waiting for the hangman's noose.

***

THAT EVENING MARY ate supper at the farmhouse with Benjamin next to her at the end of the table, silent. When Elizabeth leant over him to put food on his plate, she saw him flinch. He waited for everyone else to start eating and for the conversation to flow before he picked up his own fork. He was strange; Elizabeth was right. Perhaps she shouldn't trust him, but for some reason she did.

After eating with her family, they walked back to the cottage. She sat in one of the chairs and waited for him to light the fire and candles whilst she wrote the alphabet out on the slate. He put the table in front of her and pulled his chair next to hers.

'I've written down the alphabet. See?'

He leant close to look at the slate, his shoulder against hers, their legs touching.

'Repeat each letter after me. A.'

Silence. Perhaps this was too hard for someone who rarely spoke. 'Benjamin?'

'A.'

He placed his hand over hers and followed the letters with her. Warm, strong, clean. His hair tickled the side of her face, and she sucked in the soapy smell of him.

Her head bumped his. Her body was angled across his chest so he could reach the slate. The top buttons of his shirt were open. Dark curls of hair escaped. His skin beneath, pale. She had run her fingers down that chest last night, to his stomach, to. . .

He turned to look at her.

'Oh, H. That's an H,' she said.

They continued to read. His voice was low and clear. It didn't enter her ears; it melted into her pores. He should use it more often. He laughed at the letter Q, and she tingled, his breath warm over her face. They read through the letters a second time, but he went first. She helped only when he stumbled. He was quick; this was going to be easy.

141

At the end, she said, 'That's enough. There's always tomorrow.'

Benjamin nodded but didn't move his chair away. He rose and put the slate and pencils in a cupboard, then brought out two glasses and the brandy.

Good idea. She needed that brandy; it could be responsible for her actions tonight. 'Where did all this brandy come from?'

'Smuggling runs. I get paid in cash and brandy.'

Her swallow caught in her throat. *Samuel.* She raised her glass and took a sip. He always tasted of rum. She rubbed a hand across her left breast to ease the pain.

They finished their drinks in silence.

When he lifted the bottle again, she shook her head. *Might as well get this over with.* Or was the truth that she wanted this, was excited again?

Mary rose and went into the bedroom and undressed, but she didn't bother with her nightdress this time. What was the point? She climbed in, shivered, and pulled the covers up to her chin.

The door opened, and in the flame of the candle, his face was flushed. He held it up high for one long moment, staring at her, then blew it out.

Darkness again. She preferred it that way too.

The covers stirred and he was at her side, naked and warm. She stopped shivering.

His hand crept between her breasts, over her stomach. His fingers found her.

She closed her eyes and tried to think of Samuel.

He moved on top of her and his knee thrust her legs open. He took the weight of his body with his arms.

She didn't move, still trying to think of Samuel.

She dared not reach for him again, but she didn't need to guide him. He nudged inside her, moved inside her, thick and hot. She gripped his shoulders and moved with him, closed her eyes and moaned and forgot herself.

He juddered and collapsed. 'Sorry, Mary.'

She sighed. 'Never mind. There's always tomorrow.'

***

MARY LAY IN bed only half awake and let sleep drag her back into its clutches without a fight. A delicious dreamy languor stole over her body. It was early, and she didn't have to get up yet. She didn't want to either. A noise filtered into her dreams—just Jess, chasing rabbits in her sleep again, her legs scrabbling at the floor.

She'd been married a week now, her first week as a married woman. She had a ritual of reading with Benjamin every night. Their bodies touching. His voice and smell rolling over her in waves. A glass of brandy, always, then bed. They never kissed. She'd tried once, but he'd jerked his head away. She wouldn't try again. He wasn't Samuel. And he never lasted long. Oh no, he wasn't Samuel. But even so.

Thank goodness today was Sunday. She could at last go to church and repent for her many sins. She exhaled quietly. It was time to get up, and she didn't want to wake Benjamin. He had no reason to rise early today; he never went to church.

She hummed to herself on the walk to St Merryn and talked endlessly to her baby. Would it be a boy or a girl? A boy, that would be best; a boy who would grow up the image of his father.

Perhaps not. Perhaps he'd just have his eyes.

Once at church, she found the service deeply dissatisfying. Mary wanted to confess her sins to God and ask him to forgive her for the sake of her innocent baby, but the Vicar's thundering voice crashed in on her thoughts and pounded at her concentration.

On her way back to Treyarnon Cottage, she lingered in the lanes and found it easier to talk to God amongst the high hedges and overgrown brambles. She neared the cottage but stopped and ambled to the cliff edge to watch the raging waves and float her restless troubled mind out to sea. Better. It felt better being here. Turning back to the cottage, she opened the door and stooped to enter. Once inside her eyes were drawn to a tin bath glowing in front of a roaring fire. A white mist of steam billowed and eddied from the bath, and she stared open-mouthed.

The door opened behind her and let in an unwelcome blast of cold air. Vaguely aware of Benjamin apologising as he swerved to avoid colliding with her back, she didn't, couldn't move. He shuffled across the room, carrying a bucket heavy with water, and placed it over the fire. He said words to her, but she couldn't hear; all her senses were drawn to the bath.

In a trance, she wafted over to it and looked in. She'd never bathed this way before or immersed herself in water. Once when she was small, she'd climbed into a cattle trough, but that didn't count; she'd been fully clothed, and the water was icy cold. There wasn't the privacy for such a luxury at the farmhouse. A hot bath was unheard of.

'Mary.' He touched her arm. 'I've drawn a bath for you. I always have one Sunday morning. I thought you could go first. I'll get in after. I've bolted the door and closed the shutters. Get in quick, whilst it's hot. Go on.'

She stared at him, bit her lip, and brought her hands together as if in prayer. Wa*s this real? Oh, please let it be true.*

He glanced at her again. 'Hurry up. It's getting cold waiting for you.'

She shrank back, wrapped her arms around her body, dropped her head, and flushed at the idea of undressing in front of him in the cold light of day. When she looked up again, he'd gone.

After pausing for a long moment, she tiptoed to the bath, held a hand over the swirl of mist, and smiled. Checking she was alone, she stripped off her clothes and abandoned them on one of the chairs he'd pushed to the side. Clutching her hands to her breasts, she dipped a toe into the water and snatched it back again, gasping at the shock of scalding hot water touching her flesh. She tried again, and this time let her foot dangle and her skin adjust to the heat. Stepping in, she watched the hot water lapping around her knees. Holding the sides of the tub, she sank with a moan of delight into the steaming water and immersed herself in bliss.

She couldn't get her whole body underwater, but with her knees bent, she could slide her shoulders down until the water sloshed against her chin. Benjamin had sprinkled dried rosemary in the bath, and she closed her eyes and breathed in the aromatic scent. She could stay like this forever. *Did he really say he did this every Sunday?* She cupped the water in her hands. It cascaded over her knees as she rubbed at a spot of grime on her leg until it dissolved. Catching sprigs of green rosemary as they drifted by, she trickled water over her face. It ran in hot rivulets across her closed eyelids, her nose, her lips. Unbraiding her long dark hair, she set it free to trail in the water.

She closed her eyes and took a deep breath. Holding her nose she plunged her head below the surface. In the silence of her underwater world, she forgot where she was. Only when she surfaced again could she hear the fiery sputter and crackle of burning furze and peat. And the footsteps behind her.

'I've brought a linen sheet for you. To dry yourself with. And I forgot to give you the soap.' He dropped the sheet on the floor, then knelt down beside her. 'Lean forwards. I'll wash your back.'

She closed her eyes and did as she was told, wrapping her arms around her legs and letting her head drop towards her knees. She exhaled as a cloth was drawn across her back, brushing against her neck. Water streamed over her head as he washed her hair. *When had she ever been so clean, so pampered, so relaxed?* Never. If the tub were bigger, her body would unfurl and float on the surface of the water like the tendrils of her hair.

He left her then and sat on a chair near the fire. She found the cloth and dipped, squeezed, and glided it over the rest of her body. 'Can you open your eyes underwater?' She hadn't meant to say her thoughts out loud.

''Course you can.'

She took another breath, closed her eyes, and ducked under once again. But doubt crept under with her and held her eyes shut.

When she surfaced, he murmured, 'You should trust me, Mary. I do know how to swim.'

'How? Where?'

'At Treyarnon Beach. In the rock pools. Even in the sea. I'll teach you one day.'

'Shall I get out now?'

'No, no. Stay put until the water goes cold.'

'What about you?'

'I've got more water on the boil.'

'Benjamin.'

He said nothing, but he turned his head to look at her.

'I've never had a bath before. It's a marvel.'

'Well, we'll do it every Sunday.'

'Why? I don't know anyone else that does.'

'I like to be clean.'

'Why?'

'Just do. I hate the stench of sweat and dirt. Of other bodies. Except yours.'

'And you don't like to be touched. Why?'

He shrugged. 'It reminds me.'

'Of what?'

'I went to watch my da hang. Changed my mind but couldn't get out of the crowd. They pushed, shoved, stank.' He turned his head away, but she caught his whisper. 'I couldn't get out.'

She lay back in the water and sighed. She should thank him for this; this was beyond words. But she couldn't bring herself to say more—he might get the wrong idea, he might think she liked him. She couldn't allow that to happen, could she?

She wanted to stay until the water was so cold it made her shiver, but that wouldn't be fair, so she hoisted herself up, giving the bath one last lingering look. She reached for the sheet, wrapped it about her body, and stepped out.

'Come and sit here. Dry yourself.' He got up, reached for the bucket of bubbling water, and tipped it all into the bath, then stood in front of the fire and undressed.

She lowered her head but raised her eyes to watch. He had no inhibitions, no embarrassment at being naked before her. She knew his body in the dark; she'd explored it. She admired it now. He was muscular, lean, long-limbed. Dark hair curled across his chest and down his body, his firm stomach muscles, his skin stretched tight. And scars. They were dark and raised, about an inch long, scattered about his torso. The scar on his face was long and thin and red.

He turned his back to her as he stepped into the bath, and she sucked in a quick breath. A black snake curled along the base of his spine. She bent forwards to have a closer look. It rippled and writhed as he moved, and she longed to reach out and stroke it.

He peered over his shoulder at her. 'It's a tattoo.'

'I've never seen one before.'

'Had it done in Padstow.'

'Why a snake?'

'They shed their skin. Start new.'

'It's beautiful.'

'Is it? I've never actually seen it.'

'Well, you don't have any mirrors in the cottage.'

She stopped when his face darkened and he scowled. She should have realised he never wanted to look at himself, at his face. He turned around again and sat down in the hot water. She opened her mouth to speak but closed it again. She could tell him it wasn't that bad; scars didn't bother her. He didn't have missing or black teeth like many, and he didn't have a pockmarked face like many, but perhaps that was part of the problem. He didn't have a face like many. Actually, she liked his face. Even so, the truth was that she wished he looked like Samuel. She dared not tell him that, so what could she possibly say to make it better?

She dried herself off with the sheet and continued to sit in front of the warm fire, her head resting on the back of the chair. Eyes half-closed, she watched him as he vigorously soaped and scrubbed his body. He ran the cloth over his head, and streams of water slithered and slinked down his back. Down towards the coiled black snake. It flickered.

It was embedded in his flesh; it was part of his body, but it had a vitality of its own.

***

BENJAMIN GOT OUT of the water and dried himself off in front of the fire, his back to her. She was watching him; he didn't have to look to know that. His skin prickled, and his body responded. The fire in his belly was back.

He turned to face her and let his sheet drop to the floor with a whoosh. Her eyes slowly travelled the length of him. He bent and picked up her hand and pulled her to her feet, walking backwards towards the bedroom, watching her face. She clutched her own sheet to her breast.

In the bedroom, he let go of her and sprawled across the bed, on top of the sheets, and waited. He wanted her to come willingly.

She dropped her sheet and came to the edge of the bed so he could see her, then climbed on like a cat. She ran her tongue down his neck, her breasts brushing against his chest.

He opened his arms wide and surrendered to her touch.

She licked across his damp, gasping chest and continued down his stomach, her eyelashes skimming his goosefleshed skin. She continued her descent, and his whole body jolted and bucked at her touch.

Benjamin wound his hands in her hair and dragged her up against his chest, shaking, clinging onto control by his fingertips. He wanted to get it right this time, for her to come first. He grasped her shoulders, thrust her back against the bed, and opened her legs with his knee. He kissed her neck but avoided her mouth. She would hate the touch of his scarred lips on hers.

Gripping the bedclothes in his hands, he moved his mouth over her body. She smelt of rosemary. He moved across her nipples, taking in the sight of her, down her breasts, down her tensed stomach. She sighed rapidly and raised herself to meet him, so he ran his tongue over her and lost himself in the taste of her. Taking his time, he nudged and guided himself inside, clenching his jaw to hold himself back, to halt the rhythm of his strokes. He watched her eyes close, her fingernails digging into his shoulders. She wrapped her legs around him, arched her back, and cried out, then he could not stop, thrusting, thrusting until he came with a frenzied, wild, guttural howl.

***

MARY LAY IN bed in the early hours of the morning and listened to Benjamin's steady breathing as he slept beside her. She mulled over last night, trying to unravel, to understand the stranger she had become. She'd betrayed Samuel yesterday, and the guilt clawed at her heart.

Benjamin had reached for her again that afternoon and again last night, and she'd wanted him, craved him. Running her hands over his firm body, his unfamiliar body, thrilled her. He gave himself up to her, gave her complete control. The power she held over him was potent, and she couldn't resist. But she despised him, didn't she? He was supposed to be just a convenient refuge for her baby. He had quietly become so much more.

She ran her hand down her body. Would he want her the same way this morning? She shivered. Her body wanted to find out, wanted his callused hands to possess her, but her heart cried out for Samuel. She was a traitor. She had to listen to her heart. Before she could change her mind, she slipped out of bed and splashed water on her face, turning to check she hadn't woken Benjamin.

Mary hurled on her clothes and tiptoed towards the door in the semi-darkness, tripping over Jess curled up asleep at the foot of the bed. Cursing when Benjamin stirred, she frantically leapt for the door and closed it behind her, her heart hammering with apprehension. *What was she so nervous about*? Was it because if he called her back, she would go willingly?

She needed the privy. Mary opened the front door but flinched as a gust of bracing wind slapped her face. She could hear Benjamin moving in the bedroom, so she grabbed her cloak and launched herself into the raw morning. When she returned to the cottage, she found him cleaning out the ashes.

He turned to face her, and his beaming smile slid off his face as she scowled at him. She didn't mean to; she was just so confused. How could she say she loved Samuel when she wanted to make love to Benjamin?

He heaved a sigh. 'I'll take out the ash. When I'm back, we should leave for work. Come on, Jess.'

She returned to the bedroom to make the bed, but he'd already done it. She reached for his pillow, picked it up, and compulsively buried her face in it. A lingering scent of him clung to the cloth, and her body quivered.

She thumped it hard and put it back.

Chapter 21

The bonesetter stomped through St Merryn, using her powerful arms to make her legs go faster, having woken that morning with a desperate foreboding that made her stomach churn. She always listened to her stomach, obeyed it at all times. She had a destination in mind, but when she passed Ladybird Cottage, a thin voice called out from the doorway.

'Help, we need help.'

She closed her eyes and groaned. She didn't want to stop. Perhaps she could come back later? Turning, she found Granny Fox at the front door of the cottage. Grace called out, 'Can it wait?'

The old lady just held out her bloodstained hands and shook her head.

Grace pressed her lips together. There was an external force at work today, trying to slow her down. She marched up to the cottage and ducked inside.

Thomas Fox sat in the parlour, a blood-soaked rag wrapped around his hand.

She squeezed inside the cubbyhole of a room, knocking chairs aside with her hips. She couldn't sit on them anyway—surely they weren't full size?—and found what she presumed was a cupboard, pulling it across and using it as a stool.

Grace concentrated on the wound, not bothering with small talk today. It was obvious the slip of a knife had gouged a deep gash. Was his eyesight failing? She peered into his watery blue eyes, and Death leered back at her. Thomas nodded and smiled. So, he knew he was dying. Perhaps Death wasn't an unwanted guest.

She reached for her overstuffed, scruffy leather bag and removed an assortment of bottles and implements, placing them beside her until she found what she was looking for. A glass jar of comfrey, elder, marigold, and beeswax. She smothered the wound in the mixture. That would help cleanse the gash and stop the bleeding. No need for stitches, thank God. She patted his leg, noting the absence of flesh over bone. 'Are you eating enough?'

'Enough for a horse.'

He wouldn't last long like this, not without fat. She opened her bag, and with one wide sweep of her arm, whisked everything back inside, eager to be gone. She rose and bumped her head on the ceiling. Bending double, she backed out the way she'd come in. Once outside, she turned to leave, but Granny shouted from the doorway. 'Grace. You've left the jar behind.'

'Keep it,' she said, throwing back her shoulders, lowering her head, and marching on. Nothing else was going to stop her. Nothing. Never a fast walker, she paced herself and concentrated on putting one foot in front of the other, enjoying the sensation of her thighs rubbing against her wool stockings.

When she reached Harmony Cottage, she didn't miss a beat. She shoved open the front door, stomped inside without knocking, and was struck by an eerie silence, which she broke by calling out, 'Anyone home?' She didn't

154

wait for an answer and walked through the cottage. Leaving by the back door, she headed across the grass towards a humble wooden barn, driven by an instinct she couldn't ignore or explain.

The open barn door swung open and creaked on its hinges, so Grace stepped inside. The light at this time of year was weak, and she peered into the gloom at something ahead. Could that be the shape of a figure knelt in the dirt?

Grace shuffled towards it, and the shape revealed itself as the hunched form of Jenny's mother, Charity Blewet. Her hands were over her face, her frame shaking as dry, silent sobs racked her body. Grace paused and rubbed a hand across her stomach. This was not good, not good at all. She rubbed her belly again. *Come on, old girl, keep going.* She stepped around Charity and stumbled further into the semi-darkness of the barn.

She ducked under a low hanging cobweb swaying in a non-existent breeze and found Jenny's father, William. He knelt down on one knee, his head bent. One hand clawed at his heart, and the other arm was raised up high, stretched taut, his hand clutching a foot. His wheezing gasps were the only sound to fill the barn. He fought to suck in air through his pursed lips, his face beetroot.

She dragged her head away from him and let her eyes travel from the foot, up the leg, and to the rest of the slender body. Grace staggered backwards, closed her eyes, and moaned as shock sent a painful jolt to her heart.

Jenny Wren hung by a noose around her neck, the rope suspended from a low beam. Her head lolled sideways, lifeless, her sweet elfin face engorged and contorted in agony. Swollen tongue protruding, eyes bulging, lips blue.

Jenny had come to her for help, and she obviously hadn't done enough. If she'd got here sooner, could she have saved her? Could you save someone determined to take their own life, to end their own suffering? *Oh, Jenny, there is always another way.*

Grace reached out for a rusty old billhook fastened to the side of the barn, picked up an overturned stool, and stood on it. She pulled Jenny towards her, supporting the body while she hacked and sawed at the rope, forcing it to release its snared prey.

As Grace brought Jenny's stiffening body down, William released his hold and gazed at her, his eyes flickering with hope. She shook her head at him. Jenny was gone, a slow death by asphyxiation, but he didn't need the details.

She laid her body down, careful to place her in a clean, dry spot, then went to William, whose rasping breath was louder, strained.

'Let me go. Let me go too,' he wheezed.

She shook her head. 'No, William. Charity needs you.' She rummaged in her bag, produced a jar, and wafted it under his nose. He gasped and spluttered, and she waited for him to recover. Stroking his back, she told him, 'Breathe, slowly. Breathe.' She helped him to his feet. How could she support him through such a terrible loss? He would never get over it. His only daughter was his world, his reason for being.

Grace gathered Jenny up, her body as light as a cluster of feathers, then hoisted Charity onto her other shoulder on her way out of the barn, taking them inside the cottage to the stairs. But there was no way could she get up the stairs with both of them, so she passed Charity to

William and carried Jenny, squashing herself up the narrow, winding staircase, careful not to damage the body.

At the top, she kicked open the door to Jenny's room and laid her on the bed, putting Jenny's arms over her stomach as if she was only sleeping. As if. Leaning over the rigid body, she saw droplets of tears coursing down Jenny's cheek. Grace jumped. *How could a corpse cry*? Another droplet rolled like a glass bead down Jenny's smooth skin, and then she understood—they were her own silent tears. She brushed them away.

Finding a sheet in the cupboard, she threw it over the body, but it was pulled off by William and Charity, who sat beside the bed, arms wrapped around each other, absently rocking to-and-fro, tears and sobs erupting from their shaking, trembling bodies.

Grace gulped down her own sobs. She knew as well as anyone that death was rarely easy. Many years before, when typhus had swept through this village, she'd lost her mother, then her father. She had promised both to continue with all they'd taught her, especially the family tradition of bonesetting. Then the sickness took her husband. Those deaths had left a hole in her heart that she tried to fill—with work, with food. It was still there. She was still trying to fill it.

***

IT WAS THE end of a long day, and Grace wanted to sleep, to rest her aching legs, her throbbing head. She'd had done all she could to take care of William and Charity, and now the villagers would rally round. Gossip was rife, of course, escaping like a pandemic, but it was all guesswork; only she knew the real reason for Jenny's suicide, and she would never tell.

She had one more task to perform. Mary and her family had to be told before the whispers reached them. Mary and Jenny were such close friends; Mary deserved to know, and even if the news was going to inflict grief and heartache, she had to be the messenger. It was just her way of taking care of the villagers, and sometimes it was painful to do.

It was evening before she reached the farm. Not bothering to knock, as usual, she threw open the heavy oak door, stepped inside, and took a moment to take in the scene. The family sat around the kitchen table having supper, chatting and laughing. A lantern hung over the table on a ceiling beam. It cast a dancing buttery light over the smiling faces below.

'Watch-eer, it's Grace. Come and sit down, maid. What brings you out so late? Not that you aren't welcome.'

Grace choked back a sigh. 'I've come to bring you news. Bad news, I'm afraid. Very bad.'

The room fell silent. All eyes turned in her direction, forks raised, mouths left open, suspended in that moment between not knowing and knowing. She paused to let them stay in limbo before she sent them to hell. She tried to swallow, but her mouth was dry. 'It's little Jenny Wren. I'm so, so sorry to tell you—she has died.'

The deathly silence continued until Mary's grandfather softly asked, 'How did it happen?'

How indeed. How could she tell them she was assaulted, violated by someone she knew, and then she discovered she was pregnant? The baby was taken care of, but that only made it worse. The nightmares, the disgrace, the guilt, the loneliness, and the sin were all too much to live with. There was no gentle way to say it. 'Was a suicide by hanging.'

A knife clattered to the floor. Mary stood up, shaking her head. 'It can't be true. I'd know, so it can't be true.' Mary walked right up to her face and said, 'It's a lie—a stupid, stupid joke.' Mary turned and ran upstairs, followed by Elizabeth.

Benjamin rose to follow, but Grace blocked his way. 'Let them be. They need time to make sense of it, and then time to grieve.'

'Jimmery-Chry! She wasn't melancholy, was she?' The old man sniffed.

'These young women hide so much, old man, but no one knows why, and now we never will.'

Grace wiped at her eyes with her fingers, her gaze following Mary's father, who left the table to sit by the fire, his back to her. The old man dabbed at his own eyes, trying to stem the flow of tears. 'It will hit Mary hard; they were true friends.'

'I know. I've brought something to help her sleep, and Elizabeth too.'

'How are William and Charity? Not on their own, are they?' Mary's father spoke between sobs whilst staring into the fire.

'No, no, they're being cared for.'

'Well, I don't believe it myself. And no funeral, not for suicide.'

'No, there won't be.' Grace agreed.

'Who found her?'

'Her father.'

'Oh my God, the poor man.'

159

Grace now craved a drink, could almost taste the sweetness in her mouth, and she wanted the warm embrace of her own cottage. She didn't drink as a rule, but today broke all the rules. 'I'll leave you now. I have to go.'

She hurriedly turned and left, moving as fast as she was able, wanting to immerse herself in her own company, her own thoughts, and that large drink.

Out on the track in the dark, she heard running feet crunch up the path behind her. Not wanting to, she stopped and waited to find out who they belonged to.

Benjamin appeared out of the darkness, swinging an arc of light beside him. 'You need a lantern. Gramfer has decided, so don't argue.'

He held the lantern up and out to her. She didn't take it straight away, deciding to hold him there, to search his face. 'I can think of only one reason why Jenny would take her own life.'

He dropped his arm so the light puddled their feet and left his face obscured, shrouded in darkness.

'Can you?' She gave him time to reply.

He shuffled his feet and cleared his throat. His feet scuffed the track some more, then he gave a muffled reply. 'Aye, I can.'

'Hmm. I knew it.'

Taking the lantern from him, she turned and marched home.

***

BENJAMIN STOOD OUTSIDE the vicarage and stared at the door. *Just knock. Say it and go.* He dropped his head

160

and sighed, then turned to leave. He couldn't do it. Say what? Where were the words?

Walking away, he shook his head. *Wait a minute.* What about poor Mary, poor Jenny? This wasn't about him; he owed it to both of them to get over his own fears. Clenching his fists, he turned back and rapped on the door before his courage deserted him. The dark wood swallowed up the thud. The clang of bolts being drawn back made him ram his shaking hands into his pockets.

The door creaked open, and the vicar stood over him, looking down his beaked nose, his hands on his hips. 'What do you want?'

'A word. Or two. Inside.'

'No.'

The vicar tried to slam the door, but Benjamin wedged his foot inside. He'd come this far and wasn't leaving now. He took his shaking hands out of his pockets and held one firmly against the door. 'I said a word.' He would not say please. Not to him.

'If you don't leave now, I'll call for help. Have you arrested.'

'Benjamin!' A booming voice called out his name, and feet thudded towards him. 'Good for you.' Grace gave his back a thump, and he tumbled inside the vicarage, throwing the vicar against a wall.

The vicar grumbled, straightened his jacket, and turned to walk down a passageway. Benjamin followed the man's hunched back into a cold room. He pulled the collar of his jacket up and shivered. He squinted to see. The curtains were open, but no light came through the window because a leafless bush outside grew against the pane, its thorns scratching like nails against the glass. Large furniture dominated the room, all dark, heavy wood, no soft edges, no carvings to add beauty. He wasn't asked to sit, and he didn't want to.

'Well?' The vicar addressed the bonesetter.

Grace turned and raised her eyebrows at Benjamin.

He removed his hat, wringing it in his hands. 'It's about Jenny. Mary wants her buried in the churchyard.'

The vicar's eyes were hard, a chilling blue. Just like Samuel's. 'The law of the Church stands firm; suicides cannot be buried within the grounds of a church. She must be buried at night, at the crossroads, where the four roads meet. Don't you know this?'

Benjamin cleared his throat. 'Yes, but it's Jenny, a young woman who's done nothing wrong. She can't be buried with the murderers and thieves.'

'With your father, you mean.'

'My father was a murderer, nothing like Jenny.'

'And you're the son of a murderer.'

The bonesetter took a step forwards, and the vicar backed away, sinking into a chair. He cleared his throat, then spoke again. 'She took her own life; her death is a *felo-de-se*. I cannot make exceptions. A stake must be driven through her heart, and then she must be buried without ceremony. It is the law of the Church.'

Benjamin was sure he stressed the word *driven*. He turned his head away at the brutal statement. This was pointless. The man just didn't give a damn.

The bonesetter stamped her foot and leant her massive body over the vicar's chair, casting him in even darker shadow. 'Once fourteen years have passed, then her body can be moved and buried in the churchyard, it's true, isn't it?'

The vicar glared and said nothing. Grace bent her head close to his thin, angular face and gripped the arms of his chair, her knuckles white. She never took her eyes off him.

The vicar pushed his head back into his seat to put distance between them, then dropped his eyes, breaking contact first, and muttered, 'Yes, yes. The family can move her after fourteen years have passed.'

Benjamin watched her. She wasn't afraid of anybody. He needed some of whatever it was she had, because when she spoke, everyone always listened. And she always won, especially now.

He could see the fear in the fool's eyes.

Chapter 22

Wedged into a dark corner of a room crammed full of people, Benjamin braced his legs and pushed himself against the wall. So many people, they sucked all the air out. He was going to suffocate; he wasn't sure how much longer he could stand it. All the windows and shutters were closed to ensure no light could escape and be seen from outside, and the only ventilation was an open door leading upstairs. It wasn't enough.

Tallow candles filled the room with rancid smoke but little light, and lanterns filled with pilchard oil hung from the dark beams. The room reeked of fish. But he could still smell them, the unwashed bodies and clothes. He shouldn't be here, didn't belong. He was only here because of Mary. He screwed up his eyes against the smoke and peered about the room through slits. Dark shapes passed around brandy whilst he went unnoticed or was ignored.

Benjamin clenched his sweaty palms and closed his eyes. He tried to breathe, but the noise of sobbing, weeping, and sighing intensified. His skin crawled. Filth, so much filth. He had to get out before it smothered him.

When he opened his eyes again, a vast shadow rose from the middle of the dark and wretched room. It raised a lantern in one hand and swept the light across each of the gloomy corners until it found him, then it shoved bodies aside and came for him.

Benjamin winced as the light was brought up to his face. Shielding his eyes with one hand, he turned his head away until the light dropped down low again, then he looked up to face the phantom before him.

Grace spoke. 'I needs your help. Can you go to the crossroads and watch where they bury her, then come and tell us when the coast is clear? You mustn't be seen, so you can't take a lantern. It's terribly dark, but I'm guessing Jess can help you.'

It was just the excuse he needed. He nodded at the bonesetter but paused and stared at the stairs. *Mary. He should go up and check on her first.*

'You can't go up. Women only. Don't even try,' Grace said, blocking his way with her body.

He had to escape, had to get out, so he gratefully bolted for the front door and closed it behind him, leaning against it and gulping down lungfuls of the clean night air. His hands swept his body, trying to brush it clean. He walked down the path, away from the Blewets' cottage, and whistled to Jess, who left the sanctuary of her hedge to join him. He pulled the collar of his jacket up and shivered. Such a raw night, painfully dark with a wicked wind.

In the pitch black, it was hard to even make out the shape of the roadside hedge. This wasn't going to be easy because Jess didn't know the way to the crossroads. It was the one place he never went. Benjamin paused to consider his next move. How was he going to get there in the dark?

Just then a muted noise behind him made him jump. Someone was coming. He needed to hide and fast. He groped his way along the hedge, his heart pounding, until he found a gap. Without a second to lose, he pushed himself inside and lay down flat with Jess beside him. A rumble of cart wheels and the slow clip-clop of horses' hooves drew near. The soft weary whisper of men's feet passed by his head. They were all carrying lanterns to guide the way. He guessed who they were—officials of the parish, church wardens, and their helpers taking Jenny's body to the crossroads.

Once they'd tramped by, he crawled out from under the hedge and crept after them. Using their receding pinpricks of light to shepherd him, he followed, stumbling along the rutted track leading to the crossroads, the gibbet, and the graves of the dead. It was a dark and barren heath where the gibbet rope hung. It was unhallowed.

The procession stopped when they reached their goal. Benjamin circled around them to spy from the safety of the dismal darkness, flattening his body against the cold, hard earth. With one arm wrapped around Jess for warmth, he kept a furtive watch.

A pit was dug but not without difficulty. The ground here was stony and unyielding, the men taking it in turns until it was deep enough. Benjamin frowned. It might be deep, but it wasn't big, more like a child's grave. Jenny's body was roughly hauled from the cart, then she was stripped and thrown naked into the waiting pit. Her clothes would be handed out to the poor. A church warden jumped into the hole, his feet astride the body. In the deathly quiet of the night came a thump, thump, thump as he hammered a wooden stake through her flesh, her muscles, her bones, lashing her to the grave. The hole was filled in, pounded flat, and without a word, they all departed. No prayers, no minister, no mourners.

Benjamin shook his head. *This wasn't right*. It might be the law to treat suicides like common criminals, but they were just desperate people. And the stake! As if they really could rise up from the dead. No, this wasn't right.

Benjamin raised himself. Brushing his jacket down, he picked his way over to the grave. He knelt down and laid a hand on top of it. 'Sorry, Jenny. I'm truly sorry.' Something caught his eye. The light wind had found and plucked at the edges of a green ribbon, drawing it towards him. He picked it up and kissed it. 'Something of yours they missed.' He tucked it into his jacket pocket.

Benjamin surveyed the area, scowling. He wasn't afraid of the dead, but memories long submerged now surfaced and refused to be buried. A cold shudder ran through him. He walked around the graves until he stood, his feet apart, at a spot that was no more than a slight hump in the soil. It was the right place, he just knew; he could feel the evil below his feet.

He raised a hand to his face and traced the jagged scar running from his forehead to his jaw. It missed his eyes but caught his mouth, leaving it puckered, distorted. It was all because of him, the bastard in the ground.

It was possible that the brute was his father, but Benjamin would not, could not believe that. What man would take a knife to his child, even if in a drunken rage? His poor mother had fought to protect him, and he'd beaten her to death in front of him, just a boy. No, Benjamin did not believe he was his father; his mother may have lived with this poor excuse for a man, but she'd never taken his name. Remembering the man's face made Benjamin's body rigid with rage. His fists clenched.

Now his dreams were haunted by his mother's screams. He was damaged beyond his physical scars, he knew it, and he spent his life being passive, taking jibes and taunts without retaliation just to prove he was nothing like that monster. Nothing.

Chapter 23

The room was in darkness. The women preferred it that way. Just a few scattered candles bobbed like kitchen maids in the gloom.

The ebb and flow of murmuring female voices filled the room and swirled around her, but Mary sat on Jenny's old bed, lost in her own thoughts. She ran her hand across the top of the rough bedsheet, remembering their girlish conversations when they'd unburdened their hearts and their heads freely, intimately. A gentle hand reached out and stroked Mary's hair.

Mary reached for Jenny's pillow and smiled in the darkness at the memory of them collecting the goose feathers one cold December morning. They'd laughed and shrieked together whilst the men plucked and the goose down fell like a blizzard about them, sticking like unmelted snow to their hair, their eyelashes, their clothes.

Mary sighed, and one of the women reached out and brushed her fingers down Mary's cheek. They'd shared so much in this room—private thoughts, desires, plans for the future. This had not been one of them. This had never been one of them.

She brought the pillow up to her face and buried her head in it. *Why, Jenny, why?* No matter how many times she asked the question, it was never answered. She'd been too wrapped up in her own secrets to hear her friend's call for help. Friend? She had no right to call herself that. A friend would have visited. A friend would have talked. A friend would have known, would have helped, would have . . . saved her.

A hand stroked her numb back, but Mary was unaware of who it belonged to. She didn't deserve their sympathy, but she gave herself up to them anyway, yielded to their comforting arms, hoping their warmth would thaw her frozen insides.

Female hands reached for her, pulled her to her feet, and guided her out of the room, down the stairs. She submitted to wherever they propelled her, too dazed to resist, unable to take anything in, not understanding.

Once outside, the bitter cold and bleak darkness wrapped itself around her. As she took a breath, a shard of icy cold air entered her and stabbed at her heart. She let out a thin wail, but it was lost in the night.

Silently, with heads bowed, figures ushered her on. She surrendered, shuffling along with them. Mary came to a stop, aware of a circle of light that she became a fragment of, a wreath of candles in the dark. She wavered, swayed on her feet, and Benjamin's strong arm circled her waist and drew her close. He took her hand and wound a green ribbon through her fingers. 'It belonged to Jenny,' he whispered in her ear.

And that was when she fell. Fell into a dark abyss until she slammed into reality and the ice in her veins fractured and spilt from her eyes in a never-ending flow of tears. A howl of grief rose in her throat and escaped into the starless night. Benjamin deftly turned her head towards his chest to muffle her cries. 'Sorry, Jenny, I'm so sorry,' she sobbed.

***

A FEW WEEKS later, Mary stood in the farmhouse kitchen doorway watching Benjamin and Jess walk off into the gathering darkness, back to their cottage. She couldn't wrench herself away, staring until the night engulfed them. She wanted to go with them. It was time to go home. She'd been staying at the farmhouse since Jenny's death, and now it was time she left.

Mary turned and closed the door, leant against it, and listened to the silence. Lately, the house had overflowed with a melancholy vibration of heartbreaking sobs, but tonight it was quiet. She picked up the milky drink she'd prepared for Elizabeth—it contained something given to her by the bonesetter, something that would help her sister sleep, but Mary dared not take it. She had no idea what was in it. What if it harmed her baby? So Mary didn't take it, and she stayed awake at night. Now exhaustion seeped through her and she was bone tired, so tired she had difficulty thinking or moving. She crawled upstairs to her old room, where nothing had changed yet everything was different. 'I've your drink for you, Lizzie, but before you drink it, I need to talk.'

'I need to talk too.'

'I'm going home with Benjamin tomorrow. If I don't go now, I'm afraid I never will.'

'Is it that bad?'

Mary hesitated. 'Yes—I mean, no. I want to go with him.'

Elizabeth kept her head down, twisting the bedclothes round and round in her hands. 'I've been

171

thinking. What if Jenny was with child, what if she was the same as me? If you hadn't helped me, I would've done what she did, I know it. I thought about it.'

Mary slumped on the bed and rubbed at her tired eyes. 'I've had the same thought. It's the only answer.' She heaved a great sigh and groaned. 'I know I failed her as a friend. I should've helped her.'

'But you didn't know. She never told anyone.'

'Only because I didn't ask. If I'd spoken to her, she'd have told me everything.'

'Maybe she didn't want to talk about it. Maybe she couldn't.'

Mary dropped her face into her hands. 'No, I failed her. I could've helped, but I did nothing.'

Elizabeth reached for her drink, shaking her head at Mary. 'Those closest to us are often the very people we can't tell.' She gulped the milk down. 'It is easier by far not to think at all.'

***

MARY WALKED HOME with Benjamin the next evening. They didn't talk, and she was grateful. Like him, she had nothing to say. So much had happened in such little time, and she was tired, so tired. On leaden feet, she dragged herself home.

Once inside, she aimed for the fireside chair and sank down so it cradled her weary body. She waited while Benjamin lit the fire and poured a brandy. She needed the rhythm of their life to restart, to feel the expected beat of routine.

Mary prayed the brandy would give her a dreamless sleep but didn't have faith it would. Sleep eluded her, had done for weeks now. No matter how exhausted she was, it remained out of reach. *Perhaps she was afraid of what her dreams would reveal*. She gulped down the drink, but it rippled through her body like a spent wave, then it was gone. She nodded for another.

She rested her head on the back of the chair and tried closing her eyes. But it was hopeless. She still felt wide awake. Perhaps going to bed would help. Gripping the sides of her chair, she heaved herself up, lurched towards the bedroom, and discarded her clothes, let them drop, left them where they fell. Naked, she climbed into bed and lay with her eyes open for another night of torture, of tossing and turning and begging for respite.

Still awake, she saw the door open and Benjamin tiptoe into the room. He held his candle aloft and stared at her, frowning.

Sighing, she ignored him. He could do what he liked with her tonight; she was too worn out to care.

He climbed into bed beside her and gathered her up in his arms.

She did not resist.

He laid her across his bare chest, and the steady pulse of his heart reached her ears. He was warm, and his warmth wrapped itself around her. He pulled back her hair, and his hand stroked her back, delicately, oh, so tenderly, up and down, up and down.

Her eyes grew heavy. She closed them tight.

As his chest rose and fell, so she drew breath, drawn into his ebb and flow. Lulled by the rhythmic drumming of his heart. Breathing in and breathing out. Rising and falling. Floating and sinking. Drifting, drifting, drifting.

***

MARY WALKED ALONG the cliffs in the pitch dark. Waves crashed into the rocks below her, but there was nothing else—no screech of gulls, no wind, just pounding waves. Short tufts of grass bounced beneath her bare feet. Her nightdress billowed around her ankles, but to what breeze? She couldn't feel any current of air, and she wasn't even chilled. What madness had brought her out here? She couldn't recall.

A rush of air poured into her ear, moaning her name, 'Mary. Mary.' It sputtered and spewed it again and again. She hesitated. It was surely her imagination. But no, there it was again. She stepped towards the cliff edge, her heart hammering. Up through the mist of water, her name spurted once more. She leant over the cliff edge in confusion. *Surely no one could be down there*? This time, when her name bubbled up, her legs buckled in shock. It was Jenny's voice calling for her. 'Mary. Mary.'

Leaning as far as she dared, she leant over the edge to look and tipped forwards when her legs gave way. Her hands grappled for something, anything to hold onto. Her fingers curled around some bracken, and for a split second, she hung, suspended over the edge. The bracken snapped and sent her hurtling, screaming, plummeting downwards into blackness. A rush of air swept past her, the salty sea sprayed her face, and the jagged rocks opened their arms to meet her. She cried out once more as her heartbeat pounded in her head.

She was going to die. To join Jenny.
It was what she deserved.

***

MARY'S EYES SNAPPED open. Where was she? As her nightmare melted away, she became aware of her surroundings. She lay draped across Benjamin's chest, the steady beat of his heart against her ear. The beautiful melody of a blackbird startled her. Morning had broken. Somehow she'd slept through the night, the first time for weeks. Sleep didn't weigh down her eyelids. Her limbs were so light, she felt as if she could float, refreshed at last.

Except for the dream. That dream had disturbed her. It left her wanting to take control of at least one thing in her life, and that one thing lay naked beneath her. He would let her do whatever she wanted with him. Besides, they hadn't slept together for weeks, and now was the time to rectify that. She narrowed her eyes. Was he awake, and would he be shocked by her actions? Let him; he had to learn that she wasn't the woman he thought she was. He wrapped her up in someone else's skin, and her true self needed to be revealed. Her wicked self.

She angled her head to face him in the semi-darkness and could make out his features, his dark eyes staring sleepily at her. She raised her body, her head level with his, and watched him, examined him.

He never took his eyes off her. He swallowed, and his Adam's apple flickered, his sweet breath quivering.

She closed her eyes and inhaled the warm smell of him. When she opened them again, he still stared expectantly. Taking her time, she slid her hips and legs

175

across his body until she lay prostrate on top of him. She smiled, registering his surprise. He was hard beneath her, his breath fast and shallow to match her own. She dropped her head close to his but did not touch. They never kissed; their mouths never met in intimacy.

His hands gripped her waist. With eyes half-closed, she straddled him and let out a groan of pleasure as he entered her. She forgot about him then, gripping his shoulders to rock her hips up and down, relentlessly up and down, crying out with sheer pleasure as her climax swept her away.

It wasn't enough. She wanted more. Seizing her hair in one hand, she wound it over her head, arched her back, and let him see the whole of her while her hips continued their steady rhythm.

His jaw clenched and his fingers squeezed her tight, but he kept his eyes open. She wouldn't let him come, not yet, and shook her head at him. Made him wait until she was finished with him and cried out as another explosion ripped through her. His arms tightened their hold as she clung to him. Her legs trembled, and her bones dissolved. He gave a long drawn-out groan and shudder.

She collapsed onto his chest. Stupid tears sprang to her eyes, which she shut tight to stop the tears from falling. *Why cry now?* Mary muttered into his chest, 'I think I'm broken.'

He gave a short laugh. 'I am too. And if that's broken, I don't mind.'

'I'm serious.'

He stroked her hair. 'So am I.'

Now was a perfect time to tell him she was pregnant, but for some reason, the lies that came with that information, held fast in her throat. *Why was this so hard?*

He continued to stroke her hair and hold her tight as she put her deceit to one side, unable to break the spell he created.

Chapter 24

Mary's fingers traced the swirls and grains in the wood of the old oak kitchen table as she looked around at her family. They all acted relaxed and carefree, but if she'd learnt one thing, it was that appearances could deceive. Her gaze flickered to Elizabeth, her hair lank across her vacant eyes, relying too much on the bonesetter's potion to get through each night. Mary needed to keep a close eye on Elizabeth.

Benjamin coughed beside her. God, she had to tell him she was pregnant soon, had to release this news because keeping it locked up inside her was making her sick. Knowing she was going to tell him made her stomach hurt, but by telling him, she could set herself free. A loud knock on the kitchen door startled her.

'Come in, come in, the door's abroad,' her grandfather called out in a singsong voice.

The door opened to a clamour of pans clanging and clinking together.

A wide smile spread across her grandfather's face. 'Why, it's Johnny Fortnight, come to sell his pots and pans. Drop them by the door, and come and have some bread-an-dippy and a beer.'

Mary turned in her seat to watch the peddler transform from a clanking, swaying silver mountain to a tall, raw-boned, hollow-cheeked man wrapped in an

178

overlarge black coat, which he also removed and hung on the back door.

'You're just a cage of bones. Come and eat and tell me everything; I'm dying to know it all,' her grandfather called out.

Mary held a hand to her nose. The other gripped her stomach because the reek of sweat he brought into the room was sickening. Benjamin edged away, and Mary sidled up the kitchen table with him, sneaking a look at Benjamin's face screwed up in disgust, his plate of uneaten food pushed away. Ah well, her grandfather always made everyone welcome. There was no stopping him, so she poured some homemade beer into a tankard and passed it down the table.

The peddler picked up the tankard and swigged it, nodding at her as he thumped it back down on the table. Mary refilled it but wrinkled her nose at the sight of his black grubby fingernails and dirt-ingrained hands. She ran her fingertips over her own clean skin. Washing was a joy she did not take for granted. She glanced at Benjamin.

'How are you, Johnny Fortnight?' her grandfather asked.

'Middling, middling, old man.'

'What's the gossip?'

'Ah well, now, let me see. A newcomer has moved into St Merryn, in Fiddlers Green Cottage, one next to the inn.'

'A newcomer? When? Who?'

The peddler didn't reply. He finished his beer, wiped his mouth with the back of his hand, and belched long and loud. Mary's lip curled in disgust, and even her grandfather turned his head away from the stinking breath that escaped into the room. When the peddler knocked his tankard against the table, Mary took the hint and refilled it while her grandfather tapped his fingers in an impatient rhythm.

The peddler pushed his chair back, stretched out his long scrawny legs, and began to spin his yarn. 'A man has moved into Fiddlers Green. A strange man, odd man. Middle-aged, I believe, but hard to tell; he won't look at anyone for long. Wouldn't let me past the front door when I called on him.'

Her grandfather gasped and shook his head. 'That just ain't playing fair,' he muttered.

'I held the door open with me foot to keep him talking. He hasn't got a name. If he has, he won't tell it, says he's a doctor. He speaks funny, like he can't say the words. The villagers have decided to call him the French doctor.'

'A foreigner?'

'Aye, a foreigner. A short man with a big red nose, always wearing a hat. He's got a hippety-hoppety walk.'

'Does he treat people, this French doctor?'

The peddler threw back his head, laughed out loud, and sent spittle flying to land on the table. Mary flinched and made a mental note to wipe it down later. The peddler wiped tears of laughter from his eyes, then he replied, 'He has been treating the villagers, and the bonesetter, Grace, isn't happy.'

Her grandfather thumped the table with his fist. 'Ooh, I bet she's pounding around in a rage.'

'She is, she is, telling everyone he's a fraud.'

'Who's he treated, then?'

'He tells a tale 'bout treating a man from St Agnes.'

'St Agnes? He likes to travel, then.'

'This man could eat but never get fat, always grumbling about his stomach. He gave him some medicine in a bottle, called Doctor Lamb's medicine. Says he passed a worm seven foot long and has never been better.'

'Hmm. Doctor Lamb's medicine . . . don't sound foreign, does it? Is that his name then, Dr Lamb?'

'No idea what it is. He won't say.' The peddler fell silent, a frown creasing his forehead as if he was deciding something. Then he spoke. 'I did hear something else, something I wasn't supposed to, but since you're always making me so welcome, I'll tell you. It isn't much, but it's something.'

'Where'd you hear it?'

'Tresillian Farm, I was there backalong. They's teetotal and don't give me nought but tea to drink, so I don't mind telling you that gives me beer. I heard them say they have a new machine for the farm.'

'New machine? What's it do?'

'I dunno. I'm no farmer, but I heard them say something about seeds. Sowing seeds by machine.'

Out of the corner of her eye, Mary caught sight of Benjamin leaning forwards to catch every word.

Her grandfather passed a hand through his hair. 'How can they afford that and why? The harvest this year was a failure, weren't no crops to harvest. Was a year without a summer.'

'Aye,' replied her father, 'but because of that and the Corn Laws, the price of grain is the highest I've ever known.'

'It's terrible,' the peddler broke in. 'There were food riots. I saw them myself. Poor can't afford to buy grain. On market day, I saw a corn store broken into and looted, I did.'

'It's true, and now the war with Boney is over, there's many soldiers and sailors returned and looking for work. Labour is plentiful and cheap, so who needs to waste money on newfangled machines?'

'It's the way to go, Gramfer. If farmers want to survive,' Benjamin said.

Mary turned to stare at Benjamin along with everyone else. He so rarely spoke, and now he joined in a conversation? Not only that, but he had views on farming, ideas differing from her father's or grandfather's. She shook her head. What did he know about machinery?

'We don't have the money for such things, so don't be getting fanciful ideas.'

Benjamin didn't answer, just smiled to himself, lost in his own thoughts. Mary frowned. She would speak to him about it one evening, and he could explain it to her, tell her what he knew.

Once the beer was drunk, the peddler got up to leave. He had other households to visit, and money had to be made. The instant he left, Mary reached for a cloth from the kitchen and wiped down the table where his spittle had dried to a white smear. She pinched her nose because the filthy stench of him lingered. She and Benjamin decided to leave too, rushing her goodbyes. Benjamin reached the door before her and was gone. She found him leant against the farmhouse wall, gulping down the clean night air.

A thick mist had gathered in the valley whilst they'd been eating, creeping and rolling towards the house. She raised her lantern. Where was the path? It was obscured by a murky veil. She stepped forwards to enter this ghostly world, but when she turned to look back, the fog had already swallowed the farmhouse. Benjamin and Jess materialised out of the haze in front of her. As she drifted to join him, the knowledge imprisoned inside her squirmed in the pit of her stomach, demanding to be released, to be known. Benjamin reached for her hand, and she let out a slow breath. It was now or never. 'Benjamin.'

He didn't reply.

'I'm pregnant.'

He stopped dead. She took a few paces and waited for him, but he disappeared into the swirl of fog, leaving her alone. She held her lantern up, and her bottom lip trembled. She didn't want to be abandoned; she needed him. *Come back. Oh, please come back.*

He emerged from the billowing gloom with a crooked, boyish grin on his face. Snatching the lantern from her and dropping it on the ground, he grabbed her waist, lifted her off her feet, and spun her round and round. She held onto his shoulders but couldn't look at his bright smile and glowing eyes.

Breathless, he placed her back down to face him, and the unearthly mist drifted dreamlike into the space between them. 'Truly?'

'Yes.'

Shaking his head at her, he smiled and reached out to brush her damp hair off her face. 'I do love you, Mary. My lovely wife.'

She wished he wouldn't say that. He was only just discovering who she was, and he was never going to find out everything about her. *You can't love someone you don't know, someone wicked.* He was such a fool.

183

As they walked on in silence, they climbed out of the valley towards the cliffs, where the mist dissolved and melted. With Benjamin gripping her hand, they ambled home in the still and dark night.

Chapter 25

The bonesetter opened her front door, and a fierce gust of wind tore at her voluminous brown coat and made it billow out behind her. She grabbed it and wrapped it snugly around her body. Picking up her leather bag, she went out to meet the squall head on. She walked to the bottom of her path, planted her sturdy legs apart, and took the full force of the wind. Daring it to push her backwards, she laughed as it slapped at her face and brought tears to her eyes and a flush to her cheeks.

She had an uninterrupted view of Constantine Bay from her cottage and loved its untamed beauty. The sculpted sand dunes were the colour of wheat fields in the morning light, topped with dark rippling grasses, rising up from the wide sweeping crescent of pale golden sand.

The bonesetter turned and let the wind propel her towards St Merryn. As she arrived in the village, a young child ran towards her. Between gasps for breath, he burst out, 'Jack's boy—has broke—his leg.'

She nodded at him. 'At Jack's cottage?'

'Yes.'

'Run back and tell them I'm coming.'

She arrived at a small whitewashed cob cottage to the pitiful sounds of a young child wailing in pain, followed by shouts of, 'Grace is here, she's here.' Since the door was wide open, Grace ducked inside the doorway and stopped

185

to take in the scene. There was a single room downstairs and probably one up, and it had a dirt floor. It was poorly lit, drab, and stank of fish. Like every other cottage in the row. The top of her head brushed against the low ceiling. A boy sat on the floor, clinging onto his mother with one hand and one of his legs with the other, his small face screwed up in agony as he howled. She walked across and stood over him, hands on hips, weighing up the situation. 'How did he do it?'

'Climbing the bloody oak tree. Fell out, didn't he? French doctor was here. Said he could fix it, but he made it worse. Leg is more crooked than ever. I don't trust him.'

Grace bent down for a closer look, gave a curt nod, then straightened up and took another look around her, knowing there was no time to lose. 'We need to get him on the table.' Pointing at his heavily pregnant mother, she barked out orders. 'I need a bucket of cold water to soak the strips of material I'm going to give you. Jack, cut me two pieces of wood. Let's get on with it.'

The boy screamed out, 'No!' But she knew this was nothing; his screams would be for real soon enough. She couldn't think about that. If she wanted to save his leg, she had to get on with it. Grace helped his father lift the shrieking boy onto the table. It wasn't difficult. He made a great deal of noise, but his leg was too painful for him to fight back, and he was such a puny little thing.

'Hold him down, Jack, I need him to be as still as possible.' Grace reached across the wooden table and probed his leg with her strong hands—man's hands, she'd often been told, but she didn't care. Their strength was useful. She gently ran her hands down the boy's shin until she found the exact position of the break and breathed a sigh of relief. 'It's a clean break, will be easy to fix. I need you to be brave, little 'un. I've got to get the bone in.'

Amidst the boy's screams, she cracked her fingers, then inhaled through her nose and exhaled through her mouth. She placed one firm hand on his thigh, the other around his ankle, and pulled and wrenched his leg muscles downwards to free the bone. Keeping a hold on his ankle, she used her other hand to squeeze and push the bone back into place, then released his leg and placed it alongside his undamaged one. 'Just making sure they're the same length.' She winked at him. 'All done.' She bound his leg in a splint using the wet strips of cloth that would tighten as they dried.

His father clapped the bonesetter on the back. 'Good job, Grace, good job.'

She nodded. It was, and she knew it. This was what she excelled at.

He walked her to the door and saw her out, placed a hand on her shoulder that he removed and then put back. She waited patiently. He had something to say but obviously couldn't find the words.

He cleared his throat. 'Some villagers have been saying that I was the traitor 'cause I'm the only one that came back from that smuggling run, but it wasn't like that. Sam knew my Annie was pregnant and my family would starve without me or end up in the workhouse, so he got me released. I didn't have nothing to do with it; I would never have told anyone, but if his da believes the lies, we could lose our cottage.'

Grace patted his hand. 'Don't worry, I know you didn't do it. I'll spread the word.'

He let out a sigh of relief. 'I'm that grateful to you.' He shuffled his feet. 'Sorry, Grace, I don't have any money. Will you take rabbits?'

Grace smiled. Of course she would.

On her way home, a villager chased her up the road, calling out, 'Grace, stop, wait, we need you.'

She stared at his blood-spattered shirt.

'T'ain't mine,' he muttered, following her gaze. 'It's old man Bartill's.'

She pursed her lips and followed him to Bartill's cottage.

A makeshift bed of straw and blankets sat in the cramped downstairs room, and the old man lay prostrate on it whilst his wife held a blood-soaked rag to his mouth. Dark dried blood covered his chin and clothes, and fresh blood seeped from between his wife's fingers, drip, drip, dripping onto the floor. 'Tell me,' Grace commanded.

'He met the French doctor today and showed him the lump he has on his lip, the one he's had forever, the one minding its own business, doing no harm. Frenchie says he'll take it off, will be easy. Said he'd do it just for a pint of ale.'

The old man mumbled a response, but his wife clamped the rag even tighter against his mouth.

'Frenchie came over and cut it off, just like that. Oh, it's gone, to be sure, but it won't stop bleeding. My poor Charlie fainted, he did. He can't bleed all night; he hasn't got that much blood to spare.'

Grace threw her bag on the floor and punched the wall with her clenched fist, leaving a dent. 'He's always making mistakes.' She took a deep breath and a moment to recover, then grabbed the bed to help her kneel beside the old man. Getting down was one thing, but getting herself up again—that would be a fight. She opened her bag and removed an amber bottle containing beeswax, marigold, and goldenseal and a honeyed yellow buckskin cloth, which she positioned on the bed and opened to reveal a suture kit. 'Let me have a look.'

She worked quickly and deftly, using silk thread to close the gap on his mouth, blotting the blood with a clean cotton rag, and finishing with a liberal coating of the beeswax mixture.

'You do have a light touch, considering your fingers are so fat.' The old lady nodded at her.

Grace sat back to examine her handiwork. Blood still oozed from the wound, trickling down the side of his chin. She moped it up and told him to hold the rag against it. 'Will stop bleeding soon.'

She shook her head. 'But I keep trying to tell everyone, that man isn't French, he's Cornish. And he isn't a doctor. If he isn't stopped soon, he'll kill someone.'

Chapter 26

Rain pattered against the bedroom window whilst Mary lay in bed, staring up at the dark ceiling, waiting for fingers of morning light to stealthily creep across the room. She squirmed, trying to get comfortable. A flush of heat charged through her body and made her throw the bedclothes off. The baby kicked again, kicked hard against her ribs. She peered down at her bulging stomach rising up in front of her, a great protruding mound. *How did her skin stretch so far?* She wriggled her toes but couldn't see them

Benjamin lay fast asleep beside her, his steady breathing a comforting tempo, one of his arms thrown across her swollen, tender breasts. It pinned her to the bed like a protective shield, just what she needed.

Running a hand across the taut skin of her bare distended belly, she smiled as another punch smacked her. Her body was possessed, occupied by a child created with Samuel. Her smile faded as a dull ache pulsed through her, gripping her muscles, the same ache that had woken her earlier. She closed her eyes. Where had the time gone? Seven months had passed since she'd last seen Samuel. It was May, and her child was due, but surely not now. 'Go to sleep,' she softly murmured. 'You have to be late because everyone thinks you're due in July.' What would they think when it came early? She sighed. Right now she was past caring because her swollen feet ached, she couldn't take a deep breath anymore, there wasn't any room, and her stomach was going to explode. Now she desperately wanted to pee. She gently lifted Benjamin's hand and raised herself, but he woke instantly.

'It's early, Benjamin, go back to sleep. I'm just going outside.'

'Baby keeping you awake again?'

'Yes, but I don't mind.'

'I'll make you a cup of tea. I'm awake now.'

She heaved herself out of bed, supporting her stomach with one hand, and struggled into her clothes. Her boots were another matter. She couldn't reach them, even when sitting on the side of the bed. 'I need help with my boots.'

Benjamin stumbled out of bed and staggered to her side, pulling his trousers up with one hand. He eased her feet into her boots and tied up the laces. He was agile, supple, and muscular, and she couldn't even bend over to put her own boots on. She hauled herself off the bed and braced her back with her right hand but stopped to grip the bedpost as a mild pain rippled through her. She bit her lip and waited, then breathed a sigh of relief. It was nothing. Like a duck, she waddled to the door.

When she returned to the cottage, Benjamin sat her down in a chair and handed her a steaming hot cup of tea. She blew across the rim to cool it.

'I'll do your work for you today. You need to rest.'

He'd been doing all her outside work for months now. Milking, collecting eggs, hoeing, and hand sowing seeds. She opened her mouth, intending to thank him but moaned instead, her face twisted in pain. Benjamin watched her, biting his nails.

191

'Don't worry. I just need the privy again.'

They set off early for the farm. They had to because she could only plod. A light drizzle kept them company. Even though her feet ached again and walking was hard for her, she enjoyed it. It gave her time to think and plan. There was no better way to waste time. Today she thought of names for the baby.

But for the rest of the morning, Mary couldn't relax because the spasmodic pain kept returning. 'Not yet, not yet,' she whispered to her baby, but it wasn't listening, impatient to be born. As another cramp gripped her, harder this time, she accidentally knocked over a flagon of homemade beer in her clumsy rush to be seated at the kitchen table. The loud crash made her jump as it fell and struck the tabletop, disgorging its contents in a surge of caramel liquid that flowed down the oak table and cascaded over the edge to form a messy, sloppy pool on the flagstone floor. She sat impassively and watched it, then puffed out her cheeks and released her breath to control her beating heart. *There was plenty of time, no reason to panic, just find Elizabeth.* She heaved herself up and shuffled towards the door. Not bothering to clean the mess or even right the flagon, she lumbered outside.

It still spat with rain, and a cold blustery wind flattened her skirts against her legs. She reached the chicken run, stopped to lean on it, and looked around for someone, anyone to help. Where were they when she needed them? Where was Benjamin? He never left her side these days, and now she couldn't find him anywhere. Droplets of rain thrummed against the wooden run as she strained to hear any sound of human voices. A young farm boy rounded the corner, and she called out with a slight quiver in her voice. 'Come here, I need help.'

'What's to do, missus?'

'Go and find Elizabeth and tell her I'm going home; my baby's coming. And then run and fetch the bonesetter.'

He gawped at her with wide round eyes.

'Go on, then.'

He was off, running like a hare.

That should do it. She laughed and turned to begin her ponderous trudge home.

The haze of drizzle turned the afternoon monochrome with black clouds stalking her. The relentless drizzle sent beads of rain coursing down her face, her hair, and her clothes, all now sodden. She'd forgotten her cloak and stopped to gaze back. Too far. She might as well continue home. Even her feet were soggy and cold because she couldn't sidestep the puddles, splashing through them and wincing as water sprayed up her skirt against her numb bare legs. *Oh, to be in her warm bed with someone taking care of her.*

She reached the cliff path, and her dull pain turned into a searing ache that brought her to her knees.

'What ails you?'

Someone to help her at last. She raised her head, her eyes full of tears that mingled with the beads of rain tracking down her face. She couldn't see all his features because his hat was crammed down low on his head, but she recognized his plump ruby nose protruding into the rain. Fat wet missiles bounced off it and continued to run down his chin—the French doctor. 'I need to get home. I need help; my baby's coming.'

'Mary, is it? Mary Carnarton?'

She nodded.

'Baby's not due yet, is it?'

She shrugged. 'It isn't waiting.'

'Well, now, don't worry. I'm here to help you.'

Mary gripped her swollen stomach with one hand as if to keep the child inside, holding his arm with the other. He walked with a limp that made one shoulder rise and fall, pulling her awkwardly up and down with him. *Where was his French accent?* As another contraction swept through her body, it took with it all questions in her mind.

They entered the cottage, and Mary pointed towards the bedroom door, shuffled inside, and collapsed on the bed.

'You get into bed. I'll be back shortly, need to prepare a few things first.'

'My boots, can you take off my boots?'

He bent down to untie her laces, and his callused hands trembled. He slid her boot off her foot, and his twitching grubby fingers rose a fraction too high up her leg, lingered a fraction too long on her skin. She recoiled at his touch. He stank of stale beer and greasy clothes. She didn't want him with her, not this grimy stranger. She wanted Elizabeth and Grace. Not trusting him, she wouldn't remove her wet clothes. Instead, she lay on top of the bed, shivering and drained. Another pain racked her back, belly, legs, and groin. She squeezed her eyes shut and clenched the bedsheets. There was nothing she could do now; her child was on its way.

The French doctor returned. He brandished two strips of linen and carried a white bowl. 'I need to bleed you to stop any inflammation.'

Mary wanted to scream. A cold, clammy sweat crept over her body. 'N-n-no, please, n-no,' she stuttered.

'Don't argue. It's always done this way.' He patted her arm, but again his dirty hands fluttered.

He reached for her right arm, but she wrenched it away, shaking her head. 'I said no.'

His hand shot out and slapped her face, the sting bringing tears to her eyes. He grabbed her firmly and rolled up the sleeve of her dress, his fingers pinching her flesh, his tongue flicking across his lips. He tied a piece of cloth tightly around her upper arm then he withdrew a small, slender knife from his breast pocket and waved it in the air before her face.

'Always carry it around with me.' He gave a sly grin and dropped the empty tin bowl. It chimed like a bell when it hit the floor.

She wanted to scream, but no sound would come. She wanted to fight, but another spasm of pain paralysed her body.

'Just going to open a vein.'

He advanced towards her, and the knife glinted in his hands. She closed her eyes and cried out at a sharp stab as the knife slit open her flesh and punctured her vein, then her tense body became slack. The spasm and the pain subsided, and she was left with only the soft splashing of her blood as it splattered into the bowl.

'You'll thank me for this later.'

She kept her eyes closed, refusing to look at him, and concentrated on her baby. There was something wrong, wrong with the baby. It struggled. She instinctively knew it, but she dared not tell him. *What else would this monster do to her?*

He disappeared, but where? What was he doing in the cottage? She opened her eyes, but the room swung and swayed crazily, and the doctor swam in and out of focus. She would pray. She needed protecting from this evil. She would give herself completely up to God, let Him decide her fate.

'I am no longer my own but thine. Put me to what thou wilt, rank me with whom thou wilt. Put me to doing, put me to suffering. Let me be employed for thee or laid aside for thee, exalted for thee or brought low for thee. Let me be full, let me be empty. Let me have all things, let me have nothing. I freely and heartily yield all things to thy pleasure and disposal. And now, O glorious and blessed God, Father, Son, and Holy Spirit, thou art mine, and I am thine. So be it.'

A door banged open, and footsteps ran in her direction. She opened her eyes but shut them again because it made her dizzy. *Was that Benjamin or was she dreaming?*

'Mary, what's he doing to you?'

'She has to be bled; it's the way.'

'Not here, it isn't. If you've hurt her, I'll kill you, I swear.'

The French doctor just laughed, and that's when Mary heard boots scrape along the wooden floor like a weight being dragged from the room.

The French doctor pleaded, 'Don't, I'm begging you, don't—' His words were cut short. The only sounds were his screams. Mary clenched her fists and cried, 'May he rot in hell.'

Benjamin stood beside her, untying the binding on her upper arm and using it as a tourniquet over her wound.

She opened her eyes a fraction. His knuckles looked sore and grazed, his eyes narrowed to mere slits. A vein in his neck pulsed to an unrestrained beat. He looked up at her, and his expression melted into a strained smile. This was the Benjamin she knew, passive; she'd never met the other before, would never have guessed he could be so ferocious.

'Bonesetter's on her way. Won't be long. My God, Mary, you're wet through. You can't stay like this. Let me help you out of these clothes and into bed.'

She shook her head weakly. 'My baby, something's wrong. I'm afraid.' She grabbed his hand and cried.

He gulped and stroked her hair. 'Hold on, my love. She'll be here soon.'

A loud clumping of boots reverberated through the wooden floor, and a buxom, stout figure filled the bedroom door, hands on her hips, followed by two ruddy-faced women from the village.

Mary laughed through her tears. God had answered her prayers at last.

***

'OUT, BENJAMIN I'M here now. Out, leave us to it.'

'She's wet through. I can help undress her.'

A firm hand thrust up hard against his chest and pushed him back towards the door. 'We'll do it.'

'She's afraid for the baby.'

The bonesetter pushed him steadily backwards.

'She's sick. I'm afraid for her.' He was nearly at the bedroom door now. 'The French doctor was here.'

The bonesetter paused, and her eyes flashed with anger. 'He's not French and not a doctor. Wanted, that's what he is. Where's he now?'

Benjamin absently rubbed his swollen knuckles. 'Out back. I'll make sure he goes when he wakes.'

'Good. Now scoot.' She gave him one final push out of the room and slammed the door hard in his face. 'Harken!' she shouted from the other side. 'Light the fire and boil up plenty of water. Tell me when it's done.'

He leant his head against the door and screwed up his eyes. They'd never let him in; it was useless to try, so he turned to do as he was told.

And then he waited.

He paced the floor in short, quick strides, then froze when Mary screamed. The sound tore into him, wrenched him apart. He gripped the back of a chair, his knuckles white. Silence. He clutched his chest, couldn't swallow. Mary moaned long and low. Damn, he couldn't stand this. Her cries of pain were torture, but in the silences that followed, his heart stopped beating.

He prowled around the cottage, unable to keep still. He padded up to the bedroom door, and with hands outstretched, grasped each corner of the doorpost and waited, trying to listen for clues. He banged his head in frustration against the door, unable to decipher the sounds. *How much longer?*

The bedroom door opened, and one of the women from the village emerged, red-faced and sweaty, her hair plastered to her face, fatigue etched around her eyes. A farrago of spicy, sweet scents wafted around her. 'More hot water needed, and we want duck fat.'

Benjamin stared down at the top of her tousled hair. 'Please tell me something. How much longer?'

She threw back her head, but the scowl on her face melted at the sight of him. 'Baby's coming feet first. It's common when early, but it's stuck, probably the cord stopping it. Do you have duck fat? It's needed, and quick.'

He moved like lightning, bolting for a cupboard and returning to place the bowl of cold, greasy fat into her hot hands. He watched her retreat towards the open bedroom door. Benjamin ran his fingers through his wayward hair, not daring to follow. What would he witness?

He stalked the room again until the wail of a baby broke the silence. He laughed, rushed up to the door, and planted his feet wide apart, slumping against the door with a smile. Mary's voice reached his ears.

At long last, the door opened, and the women came out carrying an assortment of bloody sheets and rags. They nodded to him as they made way for him to enter.

Creeping inside, he knelt beside the bed, beside Mary, who cradled her swaddled baby. She looked up at him, her face dazed by exertion and awe. His heart knocked hard against his ribs, and he sat for a minute without breathing, just looking. Could he possibly ever love her more than he did right now?

'We have a beautiful, perfect daughter. Come and meet Eliza Ann.'

She held her out to him with tears streaming down her face. He reached for the child and fought back his own tears. This tiny bundle of pink wrinkled flesh was the start of his new family, of everything he'd ever wanted.

Mary tugged at his sleeve. 'I was so scared when that French doctor was here, but I prayed to God and He answered.'

'I thought that was me.'

'Yes, and you. But God could've punished me, and he didn't. I think God has something else in mind for me.'

'Still think God wants to punish you?' He shook his head. 'We do that to ourselves.'

He watched her smile and force her eyes open to watch him cradle and rock the baby. He wanted this tender image to burrow deep into her memory and nestle there. Then she frowned. 'Oh no. We don't have a crib yet because this one is so early.'

'Yes, we do. I made one weeks ago. I'll fetch it later.'

'You kept that quiet.' She stroked his hand. 'Thank you. I know I may not say it, but I am grateful.'

He looked at her and smiled. 'I don't need words. I just need this.'

Chapter 27

B enjamin sat in a soft margin of grass surrounding a field of tall ripe wheat, and Jess lay in the shelter of a hedgerow full of plump, juicy blackberries. He reached out to grab a handful and stuff them into his mouth. A burst of sharp, tart liquid hit the back of his throat, making him screw up his eyes. He raised his head to squint at the early morning sun as it laid a gentle hand over the golden field, drying the glistening droplets of dew clinging to the wheat stalks. It grew hotter with every passing minute and would be scorching by the afternoon, drugging his body with lethargy but clearing that field of its rich harvest—he smiled, there was nothing quite like it.

Bent in concentration, he carefully ran his whetstone against the blade of his sickle. The metallic clink and scrape of stone against metal competed with the dry chirping of crickets in the grass. He held his sickle up to glint in the sun. Hanging it in the apple orchard all winter so the blade went rusty was a good move; it was now ground to a thin, sharp edge. It made a backbreaking job that bit easier, and there couldn't be a job more backbreaking than this. Just one more thing to do. He reached into his pocket, pulled out a soft strip of tan leather, wound it around his right hand, and used his teeth to pull it into a knot. That should keep blisters at bay.

He stood and tied the whetstone to the leather strap holding up his pale blue linen trousers, leaving his white cotton shirt to hang loose. He pulled his wide-brimmed hat down low, picked up his gloves and sickle, and was ready. Ready for the final day of reaping.

A low murmur of voices floated across the field and caught his attention. Other reapers filed into the open field gate. Besides the usual field hands, they included villagers and half a dozen miners. All here to help bring in the harvest for nothing more than the food and drink.

Following behind the men were the women and children, streaming through the gate. The women stopped to gossip as the children ran on ahead, and his eyes roved over them, searching for Mary until he found her tall, slender frame. The yellow ribbons on her bonnet hung loosely in the breathless air, her thin cotton dress moulded to her graceful body.

He narrowed his eyes and watched her weave in and out of the huddle. She'd been distant during the harvest, just when he believed he could reach her. This was an exhausting time for everyone, but it was especially hard for her. Eliza was only three months old, but that wasn't it. They stayed at the farmhouse now. He only intended to stay until the harvest was in. It made sense since he never finished work until it was dark. They were never alone, God how he hated it, but that wasn't it. They shared a bed but weren't intimate. Hadn't been since the birth of Eliza, no, not for at least a few months before that. He wanted her badly—but he could be patient and wait; it had to be her move—but that wasn't it either.

Scuffing his leather boots in the grass to wipe the dust off them, he watched the men approach. Who was he fooling? He knew exactly what it was. Ever since Mary had been old enough to gather up the sheaves, she had always followed Samuel in the wheat field. The harvest made her think of Samuel. She missed him and resented anyone who took his place. He tapped his sickle against his worn boots. He had to make her notice him and forget that bastard, but how?

The trickle of men flanked the edge of the field, exchanging insults and challenging each other. There was always a competition between the men as to who could finish reaping first. They saw it as a sign of virility. *That was it!* It was the only way. He needed to join in the rivalry and be the first to get to the other end of the field, but he usually made sure he went unnoticed, was unremarkable. Hell, today would be different. He'd show them what he was capable of. Show Mary.

No one ever matched the miners' strength, speed, and stamina, though, and one miner in particular set a heart-stopping pace. Benjamin positioned himself next to the tallest, broadest, most powerful of them and gave him a sidelong glance, taking in his strapping, sinewy strength. Benjamin gulped, then turned to look for Mary.

The women strolled up the field together, their straw bonnets bobbing up and down in time with their musical laughter as they chatted happily. He quickly turned his back on them. A crowd of mocking, sneering women, they petrified him.

Mary's voice called out to him. 'Do you mean to be next to the miners? You'll get left behind.'

The women tittered, and his back stiffened. He made himself face her. Oh, Mary, such a beauty. Her dark hair fell in a neat braid down her back, her straight fringe skimming her eyelashes. Her dress clung to her long, slender legs as she moved with feline grace. She was his, and he had a child now; he was as good as any man. 'I'm fine here.'

She dropped her head and did not meet his gaze. Passing Eliza to one of the older women, she pulled on her gloves and shrugged at him.

So be it. Now he must prove it to her.

With a gin-clear sky above him, he began reaping. He bent to grasp a handful of ochre wheat in his left hand, cut the stalks in one swift movement using the sickle in his right, and stayed down to reach for another handful, to cut and grab until he couldn't hold any more, then drop the sheaves for Mary to pick up and bind. He shuffled forwards, bent over in his stroke in the timeless rhythm of rural life.

With the sun arcing higher in the gloriously blue sky, he continued reaping. The warm rays played down on his back and penetrated his cotton shirt. Mice scuttled ahead and away from him, and insects whirred about his head. The wheat rustled and whispered, and the dry, parched dust settled on his exposed skin, itchy and uncomfortable. He concentrated solely on cutting, cutting, cutting. The hours melted away.

Bent double under the dazzling sun, he seized, sliced, and moved ever forwards. The ache in his back let him know this stance wasn't natural. He fought the urge to stop, straighten up, and ease out his back, to rub the irritating dirt off his skin. *Mary.* The thought of Mary would keep him going until the welcome call for dinner.

At the sound of the bell, he marked his place in the field, raised his arms above his head, and stretched out his body, smiling. *Oh, the relief.* He took off his hat and wiped his face, leaving a brown smear of dirt on his white shirt sleeve. Hanging back until last, he trudged towards the farmhouse and called Jess to keep him company.

At the farmhouse door, he hesitated. The pungent smell of sweat made him hold a hand to his nose. How come no one else noticed? A crowd of hot, clammy bodies thronged inside the kitchen, all the men, women, and children from the fields. The smell of fresh-baked bread and roasted meats tempting him inside. He was starving and didn't care what he ate. Taking off his hat, he tucked it under his arm and pushed his way towards the table laden with food and drink. He grabbed two rabbit pasties and a mug of buttermilk and backed out the way he came in, trying not to touch the wet, perspiring bodies.

Once outside, he leant his back against the farmhouse wall and slid to the floor beside an open window. He bit into the pasty, shared it with Jess, and listened to the banter erupt from the window.

'Well, the miners are taking the lead again.' A fist thumped the table, and a cheer swept the room.

Mary's grandfather piped up. 'It's a long way to go yet. It's a good crop this year, and one of our own is splitting along with them.'

Someone replied, 'He won't keep up for long, old man. No one will.'

Her grandfather laughed. 'We farm labourers are fitter than you know. Take me, I could still jump a five-bar gate.' A roar of laughter and whistles burst from the room.

'I could. If it was laid flat, that is.'

'Not even then, old man, not even then.'

Benjamin leant back against the warm farmhouse wall, eased and stretched his sore back, and flexed his painful hands. Only another five hours to go.

Under a broiling sun, Benjamin dragged himself back to the field, his eyelids already weighted down by tiredness. The afternoon was punishing because of the blistering heat. The scalding sun burnt through his cotton shirt, which stuck to his slick, damp body. The dust and grime glued to his skin in a thick brown layer as it mixed with his trickling sweat. He desperately wanted to claw the irritating, prickly dirt off his skin, but he didn't have time to stop. He kept his head down and focused on the stalks of wheat, his eyes burning if he dared to look up at the ball of shimmering fire flaming like a furnace and beating down on the sun-stained bodies below.

At four o'clock, the distant ring of a bell shattered the silence. He slowly straightened his back but held onto it with one hand as it creaked upright, then winced as he turned to look back. A ragged line of reapers stretched out across the field, leaving short golden stubble in their wake. The women and children who followed picked up the sheaves left on the ground. Older women were passing glasses of cider out to everyone, and Benjamin waited in the field for his drink. He glanced across at the other miners, but there was only one ahead of him. So, it was just the two of them in a race to finish. He had to push himself on. To fail now would just leave everyone laughing at him.

The miner ahead stared down at him, his face smeared nut-brown with grime. His cool cornflower-blue eyes appraised him. 'Think you can keep up, do you, lad?'

Benjamin tried to speak, but his parched tongue stuck to the roof of his mouth. He managed to open his cracked lips to drink some cider. The crisp bubbling liquid seeped through his sun-baked body to replenish and recharge. 'I do.'

'We'll see.'

He drank more cider. He needed it before he could even think about swallowing food. Could he keep this up for another three hours? Was he mad? His eyes shifted to Mary, still working, picking up the sheaves. *No, just madly in love*.

The heat closed in on him, suffocating and choking. He stooped again and seized the dry, resilient stalks, slashing at their bases to set them free. His muscles begged, screamed for mercy, pleaded with him to stop, but he couldn't, wouldn't. Panting, he forced himself on. He raised his head to gauge where the field ended, but the wheat turned fluid before his eyes, a wavering, watery mirage as the heat bounced off the soil. The trees edging the field looked wilted and hung their drooping heads. Nothing stirred, nothing. Even the birds were quiet. Only the soft swoosh of sickles through stalks broke the silence.

Sweat drenched him, and his head throbbed, pounding like a drumbeat. He stopped to take a breath, and the searing heat burnt his throat, scorched his lungs. The relentless sun beat on his head and back and bit into his flesh. It didn't matter. He was nearly there.

The miner in the lead caught his eye and grinned. Benjamin didn't have any strength spare to grin back. With a surge of speed, the miner aimed for the end of the field, the stalks of wheat falling to the ground around him. Benjamin's body cried out as he tried to follow, but a voice bellowed out above him, 'I win again.' The miner stood with his feet apart, his great arms raised high above his head, brandishing his sickle like a weapon. A cheer went up in the field.

Benjamin forced himself to finish. Not far behind, but he hadn't won. He rested his hands on his thighs, gasping for breath. The miner's great paw of a hand reached out for him and hauled him upright, grabbed his shoulders, and spun him around.

The field of men, women, and children stopped their work, and their eyes quietly focused on him. Benjamin squirmed under their gaze. He'd failed. He dropped his head in shame. The silence was broken with claps and shouts from all the workers. 'Hurrah!'

All except one.

He walked towards Mary and stood before her. He'd done his best; he could do no more. She must know this was all for her.

Mary reached out and pulled off his glove, undid his leather strap, and turned his hand over, palm up. She brushed her lips against his sore, hard skin and raised her eyes to look at him.

He tried but failed to fathom the thoughts that lay behind them. It wasn't love; it was never love with Mary. Maybe approval? Approval would do.

Benjamin helped her gather in the sheaves. The aches in his body didn't matter anymore.

He was floating.

He was worthy.

Chapter 28

The muscles in Mary's legs quivered as she bent down to tie up her final sheaves of wheat. She groaned. Her body felt like that bundle—tight, taut, trussed. It had to be time for another break. She couldn't bend any more. Hands on her hips, she gazed about her, at the precious sheaves of bound wheat scattered around the field waiting to be gathered up, to be protected. Another harvest secured. Well, nearly.

Her cotton dress clung uncomfortably to her body in the heat, brown, grimy, and dirt covered from top to toe. Well, it would make her next bath all the sweeter. Under a warm and mellow slanting evening sun, she brushed the hair from her eyes and looked around for Benjamin. She wanted to rescue him, to take him away from the swarm of workers, to have some quiet time with him before making the hand-mows.

He stood alone as usual, except any passing labourer gave him a slap on the back or a nod. He wouldn't be used to it; it would unnerve him. She sauntered up to him and clasped his hand, then walked backwards to pull him towards an escape route.

'Where we going?'

'Somewhere quiet, just us two.'

'Can I wash under the pump first?'

'No, no time. Don't argue; just come.'

She led him by the hand, and he came willingly out of the wheat field and into another field of long, lush grass. She trailed her spare hand languidly through the meadow. It rippled through her fingers, caressing her tired hands.

Mary drew him onwards until they arrived at the small meadow where the pristine white geese kept the grass short and springy. She gazed at it over an old makeshift gate where a single green ribbon trailed through the slats. No one would ever guess it held a magical secret, because you had to enter, not skirt around the edges, but plunge right into it to discover nature's breathtaking gift. Turning, she smiled at him. 'We're here, my special place. Well, mine and Jenny's, particularly at this time of year. I haven't been able to come here for a while, though. Too many memories.'

He arched his eyebrows at her. 'Let me lean on the gate, then. I'm that weary.'

'Oh no, we have to go in.'

She opened the rickety gate, and the huddle of honking geese dashed away. Still holding his hand, she ambled towards the middle, inched towards it, waiting until an explosion of small brown butterflies erupted from the ground and flew into the air with each delicate step she took. Mary laughed as a cloud of the dainty creatures floated about them, sailing on gossamer wings. Opening her arms wide, she spun around and around as the butterflies soared and quivered about her. 'I don't believe they have any thoughts, any worries. They live for today. Come and sit for a while. We've got time.' She sat and patted the grass beside her.

He pulled off his hat, dropped it, and sprawled on the ground.

Copying him, she lay back in the sweet grass and watched the butterflies settle around them, listening to the constant rattle of crickets.

Benjamin let out a groan. 'I'm afraid to close my eyes. If I do, I'll fall fast asleep.'

A small speck in the sky caught her attention, then a glorious babbling, rolling trill showered down on them as a skylark plummeted back to earth, singing and warbling before it climbed back up.

'He's showing off, trying to impress a female.' She rolled onto her side and studied him. 'It always works.'

He lay with his arms behind his head, the sun striking lights in his hair, a faint smile playing on his cracked lips. She reached across to push open his shirt and pressed her hand down on his damp, burning chest, then lightly drew her fingers through his fine dark hair towards his stomach. His flinty muscles bunched and shuddered beneath her touch.

He trapped her hand beneath his own. 'I'm caked in dirt and grime. I stink of sweat.'

'So do I.'

'I ache.'

She paused and took her time to stare into his eyes before she replied softly, 'So do I.'

He gave her a long, intense look, searching the depths of her eyes, then he released her hand.

She continued her descent. She slid her hand under his belt until her fingers stroked him, rigid and stiff. She gripped him tight, and he moaned. As she withdrew, she dug her nails into his tender flesh, and he cried out. Reaching for his belt, she grappled to untie it, to release him. Her own hands shook too much, and Benjamin's dirt-encrusted fingers took over. She lay back as his hands travelled up her thighs, pushing her damp dress higher. A judder rippling through her, the weight of his thighs thrusting her back into the soft grass. 'Gently, please.'

'Of course.'

He rocked, steady and regular, drew her into his insistent rhythm. Her eyelids fluttered and closed as she clung to his trembling, twitching body.

She'd been afraid, so afraid that Eliza's birth had changed her, that she'd feel nothing or worse, feel pain, so she'd withdrawn to protect herself. Sometimes, when she remembered that day, it made her cry, but she kept that to herself. Now she floated free, unbound, the pent-up tension exploding through her body, and she cried out in pleasure and relief.

Benjamin rested his elbows either side of her head. When she opened her eyes, he stared at her, then his mud-caked face cracked, his shoulders shook, and he started to laugh. She joined in, but the butterflies had taken possession of her body, and her insides continued to flutter and tingle.

Benjamin staggered to his feet and offered Mary his hand. She gazed at it, pulling a face before she clasped it and let him haul her up from the grass. She could quite happily stay there for hours, but work called. He didn't let go of her hand, and she let him steer her back to the wheat field. He held on tight as they walked through the open gate to join the other labourers, and she didn't pull away, only dropping his hand so they could return to work.

She saw her father and joined him at the edge of the field.

'Pass me the bundles, Mary, love, it's time to start making the hand-mows.'

She bent to gather an armful of the bound sheaves and watched her father whilst he hummed to himself, building up layer after layer into a solid, massive cone.

'Ladder now, Mary, love.'

She passed him their old wooden ladder, which he leant against the mow. He clambered up and waited for more sheaves. She stood on tiptoes and stretched her arms high so he could take them from her. Once finished, he climbed down, brushed himself off, and said, 'He's done well today, that lad of yours.'

'Yes, Da, he has.' She scanned the field until she found Benjamin bent double, his once white shirt flapping open. It was time to take him home for privacy, for that longed-for bath. Wait—she just called the cottage home and meant it. When had it become more than just the cottage?

'You work well together. Good job too,' her father said. 'One day it will be you two running this place.' He ran his hand down her hair. 'Just like your mother.'

She pushed her cheek into his palm and kissed it, watching his eyes mist over. He nodded at her and moved up the field, calling out, 'Pass me the bundles, Mary, love.' She laughed and gathered another armful.

They worked until the evening shadows crept across the field and the casual labour gradually drifted back to their own beds. Mary sucked deeply at the cool night air, rubbed her back, and rolled her shoulders. Exhausted but somehow relaxed, all the knots inside her unwound. As darkness closed in, a fingernail of moon hovered over the top of the hand-mows, dark shapes rustled past her through the stubble, and the sweet smell of thyme scattered its perfume through the still night air.

With the final hand-mow finished, her father walked to the top of the field, and in the fading light, he stood straight and erect by a bunch of wheat that had been left standing. He called out, 'Everyone gather round.'

The workers made their weary way up the field, and Mary turned to collect Eliza from one of the women. Her daughter gave a yawn. Her hand grasped at a ribbon from Mary's hat and held on, and her blue eyes fluttered closed. Mary rested her cheek on Eliza's sleepy head, inhaling the warm milky smell of her. Now she could think of Samuel. She'd put it off, afraid it would break her. She'd been afraid of too much lately. Every time she gazed into Eliza's blue eyes, she saw him, and now he would always be with her.

Benjamin's hand rested across her shoulders. 'Come on, you two, your da's waiting.'

Together they joined the others to gather around her father, when a shout in the distance drew their attention. It came from far off, but in the still of the night, the sound carried out of the valley.

'Tresillian Farm,' Benjamin muttered.

'How come they're always first?' her grandfather grumbled.

'It's the seed drill. They plant their crops in straight rows, not scattered about like we do. The wheat is easier by far to harvest. And to weed,' Benjamin replied.

Mary's lips twitched at the sight of her grandfather's open mouth. Benjamin's knowledge didn't surprise her anymore.

Her father bent and cut the standing wheat, raised it high in the air, and in the time-honoured tradition, shouted, 'I have them, I have them, I have them.'

Smiling, she joined everyone else and shouted back, 'What have you? What have you? What have you?'

'Have a neck. Have a neck. Have a neck.'

'Hurrah. Hurrah. Hurrah.'

Mary turned and made the slow walk back to the farmhouse, following the trail of workers who slid arms around shoulders or waists. They all meandered back together. Benjamin's arm linked through hers, Eliza limp and heavy against her chest. Cries continued to float up the valley from other farms finished with their own harvests, and Mary tried to identify the disembodied voices. Then the labourers sang soft and sweet.

'Here's a health to the barley-mow, my brave boys,
Here's a health to the barley-mow!
We'll drink it out of the jolly brown bowl,
Here's a health to the barley-mow!
We'll drink it out of the nipperkin, boys,
Here's a health to the barley-mow!
The nipperkin and the jolly brown bowl,
Here's a health to the barley-mow, my brave boys.'

She hugged Eliza securely to her chest, joined in, and caught herself smiling.

Happy? She was happy. Life wasn't perfect; she still missed Samuel, but now she had Benjamin and Eliza, so happy? Yes.

Chapter 29

Benjamin set off for work with Mary, carrying Eliza in her basket as usual. Four months old now and getting heavier every day, but he found the weight of her reassuring.

It was the worn-out end of September, and the morning had a freshness that invigorated him. The indolent heat of the summer had gone, replaced by mild, mellow sunshine.

When they arrived at the farmhouse, Mary's grandfather ran out to greet them. 'I'm overgone, overgone.' He jumped about as if the ground was made of red-hot coals.

'What's the matter, Gramfer?' Mary asked.

'There wasn't dew on the grass this morning, which means it's going to rain. We have to get the hand-mows into the mowey today.'

'Corn carrying today? Can't it wait till tomorrow?'

'No, no, the sheep have crowded together around a furze bush; they know it's going to rain. My chickchakers are unprotected, and I want them safe. Everyone must help, the whole boiling lot of them.' He danced around them, pointing to the sky with both hands.

Benjamin nodded in agreement. The old man was never wrong about the weather. If he said it was gathering to rain, then it was. The wheat sheaves stacked in the field were easily damaged by heavy rains, so they had to be brought into the rickyard and protected. It would take all hands. It would take all day. It might even take all night.

Benjamin stared hard at Mary. She'd not been well that morning, had been sick again, and she still looked chalk white. He strode up to her and brushed her pallid face with the back of his hand. 'Swap with Elizabeth today.'

'Perhaps I will. I'd rather stay inside and work in the kitchen. I can do the baking standing on my head, but I'm not sure I can manage the hand-mows, not today.'

'So swap.'

'I'll try. She never leaves the farmhouse these days; it will do her good. I'll get her.'

Mary disappeared inside, and Benjamin waited in the rickyard for the rest of the labourers to gather. He gazed up at the early morning sky. The old man was right; menacing dark clouds flocked together on the horizon. At a guess, they just had today before the rain came. His gaze drifted downwards to the farm track and the tall, stout figure of a man in a billowing black coat walking towards him. Benjamin didn't know him, but he'd seen his type before. The tanned, swarthy skin the colour of mahogany; his face a crisscross of deep wrinkles; a long razor cut, the scar thin and white, slashed across one cheek.

'Watch eer,' Mary's grandfather called out, always the first to greet strangers and make them welcome.

The newcomer tipped an imaginary hat. 'I'm wanting work if there's any to be had.'

'I'd say, looking at you, that you'd be happier at sea. A sailor, I believe.'

'Yes, but now the war with Boney is over, I have to find work wherever I can get it.'

217

'Yer in luck. We're corn carrying today.'

'Good.'

Benjamin narrowed his eyes at the stranger, who replied to the old man without looking at him, his gaze fixed elsewhere. Benjamin turned his head to follow his line of sight. *Just what was it he found so fascinating?* He sucked in a deep breath when he realised. Mary and Elizabeth stood together in the kitchen doorway, and the sailor—the intruder—couldn't take his eyes off them.

Benjamin prowled over to Mary, reached a hand around her waist, drew her towards him, and kissed her hard on the top of her head. Glancing at him, she raised her eyebrows and pushed him away, but he'd laid claim to her. He turned to the newcomer and glowered to make sure he understood.

The sailor returned his stare, unflinching, a hefty, grizzled bear of a man with greasy limp hair and close-set piggy eyes.

Benjamin strode towards him but caught a foul smell from the man's soiled clothes and flinched. 'What are you staring at?'

The sailor turned his back and walked away, saying nothing. *So, that's the way it was.* Well, he would watch him, watch him closely. Benjamin peered up at the sky again. The intruder reminded him of those brooding clouds, ominous and threatening, and Mary and Elizabeth, like the hand-mows, needed protection. His protection.

The workers trailed into the field, and Benjamin followed. They all began dismantling the hand-mows and stacking the shocks onto the wain, and Elizabeth joined in the work. Maybe the fresh air and gentle sun would bring some colour to her deathly pale cheeks? Her flaxen hair, usually so silky soft—that Eliza also had in abundance—drooped, tangled and unkempt. She spoke to no one, a small solitary figure, and his heart went out to her. He'd help her if he could, but he'd never find the words.

Benjamin waited while someone strapped a horse to the wain and led it to the rickyard. He followed behind and lowered his head but raised his eyes to watch the stranger's every move.

At the rickyard, he helped tip up the wain. Wedging the far end under his shoulder and pushing up with his hands, he watched the shocks hurl to the floor in an untidy heap. Half the labourers began pitching the shocks onto the rick whilst the rest took the wain back to the field to start again.

Elizabeth turned and followed the wain. The sailor stalked after her, but Benjamin barred his path. 'Where are you going?'

'Back to the field,' the sailor answered in his gravelly voice.

Benjamin scowled. He wasn't about to let this man out of his sight. He planted his feet apart and crossed his arms. 'You're staying here.'

The stranger scanned him up and down, smiled, then slowly turned back.

That man irritated Benjamin like a small stone stuck in a boot, a constant irritation that had to be removed.

With the first rick now complete, Mary came out and passed brandy around to celebrate, and Benjamin watched the stranger take his glass from her. *Did he just slide his grubby fingers across her hand to grasp his drink?* She didn't seem to notice, but the stranger turned to

Benjamin and gave a lecherous grin. *Oh, he would pay for that. In time, he would pay.*

Evening crept upon them all before the ricks were secure, but Benjamin kept going, they all did, not daring to stop until finished. Finally, Mary's father called everyone to join them in the harvest supper. Now was the time to relax and celebrate. The beer had flowed all afternoon, but Benjamin remained on edge, on alert. He found Mary at his elbow.

'Leave that poor man be. I've seen you watching him. What's wrong with you? That man's worked hard all day, and he's done nothing to you. It's you that's acting odd.'

He didn't bother to reply. He knew what some men were capable of. When he walked into the kitchen, an elbow jabbed him in the side. Spinning around, he saw the stranger sidle away. The man was taunting him.

Mary called out to Benjamin, 'Help me put the boiled beef on the table; it's heavy. Let everyone find a seat around the table, and you and I can sit by the fire, out of everyone's way.'

Benjamin placed the steaming hunk of tender meat in the centre of the table and looked up and down. It groaned under the weight of food and drink. Mary had worked hard today. He grabbed a plate and speared a piece of honey-baked ham, grateful that he could sit with just Mary.

He paused. Something was wrong. Someone was missing. He scanned the room. The stranger was absent. So too was Elizabeth. A cold, numb spasm swept through his body. No need to panic. She probably went upstairs alone, but he didn't really believe it. She remained vulnerable, still needed protecting. Had he failed her? He found Mary, grabbed her arm, and asked, 'Where's Elizabeth?'

'I sent her to get more wood.'

He thrust his plate in her hands and bolted for the door. Mary called his name, but he took no notice, his own blood pounding in his ears. In his head, he rehearsed the worst. That man was dangerous, he knew it, and Elizabeth was out alone in the dark. He would save her whatever it took because his days of being passive were long gone. Now he had a choice in life—do nothing or stand up for what mattered to him.

He sprinted across the yard, but the night had closed in around him and he didn't have a light, so he used the looming outlines of the massive ricks to guide him forwards.

The woodshed door banged and rattled in the night breeze. It hadn't been closed properly, and the very sound suggested danger, abandonment, betrayal.

He reached the last rick, and a soft whimper made the hairs on his arms stand to attention and black fury rise in him that he couldn't, wouldn't control. He turned the corner and spied them. Elizabeth's lantern sat on the floor, casting an eerie distorted light into the gloom. Pushed up against the rick like an injured animal, she cowered and sobbed. Her hands pressed up against the intruder's chest, but his bulky, hulking body made her powerless. His groin thrust hard against her pelvis. He ran one vile dirty hand over her dress, over her breasts, and the other hand he clamped against her mouth.

Benjamin's vision clouded. He gave a roar like bottled thunder. He grabbed the brute by the scruff of his neck, spun him around, and butted him hard on his

221

forehead. The crack exploded like a pistol shot in the night, and the monster went down.

Benjamin raised his eyes to Elizabeth, but she stared, trembling and then turned and ran, stumbling towards the lights of the kitchen.

The rage inside him did not relent; it needed more bloody revenge before he could control it. Black spots danced before his eyes. He picked the lantern up in one hand, the man's oily grey hair with his other, and dragged him off towards the stubble field. Once in the field, he put the lantern down and wiped his hand on his trousers, desperate to get the greasy grime off. 'Get on your feet, bastard.'

The sailor stumbled to his feet, still groggy, shaking his hair. Benjamin didn't care about a fair fight, he just wanted a fight, so he rushed him, expecting to shove him to the ground, not expecting the sailor to sidestep, to produce a knife. Benjamin sucked in his abdomen as the sailor lunged for him. The knife sliced through his clothes and scored his stomach.

Panting as adrenalin coursed through his body, Benjamin smiled. *Bring it on, bastard.* He didn't care. The sailor turned and charged his lumbering body at him like a mad bull. Benjamin twisted away and aimed a kick at the hand holding the knife, sending it flying. The sailor stared at his hands as if wondering what had happened, then he bellowed and ran at him again. Benjamin waited for him. He waited until the sailor was an arm's length away, then he stepped forwards and punched him hard in the face, breaking his nose and knocking him out flat. Benjamin placed a boot on his chest and gazed down at him. Dark crimson blood spurted down his chin, starting to congeal, a purple bruise forming over one eye. Benjamin rubbed across his stomach and wiped away his own wet, sticky gore.

He snatched the lantern and went in search of the knife. A glint of metal caught his attention, and he picked up the short, wide blade, his own bright red blood smeared across it. He flicked the blade into the air and caught it by the handle. Returning to the sailor, he knelt down beside him and stuck the tip of the knife into the folds of flesh in his neck. He could kill him if he wanted, do it now. *But wait. Remember.* He was nothing like his father. He had control. He was not a murderer.

He spat in the sailor's face and wiped the knife clean on the sailor's jacket, then he stuck the knife in his own boot and left.

Inside the farmhouse kitchen, the harvest party continued in full swing, and the drink flowed like water. He spied Mary and pulled her to one side. 'Where's Elizabeth now?'

She glanced around. 'I dunno.'

'Go find her. She may be upset. Hurt. I found the sailor. Mauling her.'

'Oh God, no!' She turned to go, then paused. 'And the sailor?'

'Out cold in the field.'

She nodded at him and ran upstairs.

Chapter 30

Mary quietly opened the door and tiptoed into her old bedroom. A single candle flickered and smoked beside Elizabeth's bed. She glanced at her own bed, now cold and alien.

The dancing light revealed the curled outline of Elizabeth blanketed by bedcovers. Mary perched on the edge of the bed and rested her hand on her sister's shoulder. 'Are you awake, Lizzie?'

There was no reply.

'Benjamin told me what happened. I'm so sorry I sent you out alone, but he won't bother you again. Benjamin has taken care of him.'

Elizabeth stirred and pulled the covers off her face. 'He didn't get a chance to hurt me. Just scared me, is all. Would have been worse if Benjamin hadn't found me, but he did. So . . .'

'Yes, he did.'

'Thank him for me, will you?'

'Come down and thank him yourself.'

Elizabeth sighed and reached out to grab the covers back again. Mary seized her arm and gripped it hard. She picked up the yellow tallow candle and held it close to her sister's arm. Thin red lines covered Elizabeth's arm from wrist to elbow. Mary's voice rose in pitch. 'What are these marks? Who's done this to you? Looks like someone tried to cut you and has drawn blood, but these marks are not recent. When? Who? Tell me.'

Elizabeth's eyes blurred with tears, stared back at her.

'Tell me or I'll cause a fuss.'

'It was me. I did it to myself.'

'But why?'

'Just to know if I could still feel.'

'Oh, Lizzie.'

Mary reached around her sister's limp body and hugged her close, but Elizabeth slumped, unresponsive in her arms. 'You know I'm here if you need me for anything. Will you do it again? Don't do it again.'

'I'll try not to.'

'Promise?'

'I'll try.'

Mary heard Elizabeth's words, but they were just that, words. Meaningless if said without intention. If only she could unravel, fathom her sister's mind, but Elizabeth's actions were beyond her understanding.

Mary returned to the kitchen, but the raucous party jarred her head. She couldn't complain. She understood their desire for fun, but hers had disappeared at the sight of Elizabeth's arm. In the glow of the rushlights, she searched for Benjamin. She picked up a candle and walked to the darkest unlit corner of the kitchen and found him pushed up against the wall, perched on a stool, a bottle of brandy in one hand and full glass in the other. *Oh well, best leave him to it.*

Eliza gave a small wail from her basket by the fire. Mary crossed the room and picked Eliza up to settle her, and went in search of food.

Her father gestured for her to sit by him. 'Where's Lizzie?'

'Tired from the corn carrying.'

'Can't she just sit here for a bit and join in the fun?'

'Not tonight, Da.'

He shook his head but left it at that. A song was called for, and Mary joined in, crooning to Eliza to lull her back to sleep.

'Come Roger and Nell,
Come Simpkin and Bell,
Each lad and his lass hither come;
With singin' and dancin',
And pleasure advancin',
To celebrate harvest-home!'

A drunk labourer next to Mary slipped off his chair, bumped Eliza, and belched. Mary leant over her daughter to protect her from his stale, beery breath. It was time to leave them to it before her daughter woke. Mary returned to the spot where she'd last seen Benjamin and found him brooding and morose. 'Ready to leave?'

He slid off the chair and nodded.

She put Eliza in her basket and glanced back at the room. None of the revellers would even notice they'd gone. She closed the kitchen door behind her, and Benjamin appeared at her side with Jess.

'Wait here.' He returned in a few minutes and took Eliza from her.

'Where did you go?'

'Just making sure. That the sailor has gone.'

'Has he?'

'Yes.'

They ambled home through the dark, quiet lanes, the overhanging trees a pitch-black canopy above their heads like an underground passage. Mary jumped at a noise behind her. 'What if he comes after you?'

'He won't.'

'Why not?'

Benjamin didn't break his stride when he replied, 'He knows I'll kill him if he does.'

Mary counted the glow worms shining like green-lit jewels in the hedge but gave up after twenty. 'Lizzie says thank you.'

Silence.

'Have you noticed that she won't touch Eliza, never picks her up? Never.'

Silence.

'She's been hurting herself, cutting her arms, enough to make them bleed. I don't understand.'

They walked on but didn't speak until Benjamin murmured, 'She's lonely. Scared. Lost. Trying to find how she fits into this world. She's sad. Very sad.'

'Oh. I don't know how to help. Can you give someone something for that?'

He frowned, and his mouth twitched. 'Just love, I guess.'

Mary said nothing. Elizabeth was loved, loved by everyone around her. But he wasn't talking about Elizabeth anymore.

Later that night, after she made sure Eliza slept, she joined him for one drink before bed. He leant over to pour it for her, and she spotted an ugly stain of rusty red on his shirt. She reached out to grab it, to complain about him spilling wine, then caught her breath. His shirt felt stiff.

'It's blood!' Her voice rose in pitch with alarm. 'Is it yours?'

'It's just a scratch.'

'Let me see.'

She knelt between his legs and pulled his lacerated shirt open. The knife had scored his flesh, and crusty red blood stuck to his pale skin. 'You could've been killed.'

'Would you care?'

She went to soak a cloth in water to wipe away the rivulets of blood oozing from the gash.

Mary kept her head bent and concentrated on his taut skin but didn't reply. She rested her arms on his knees and realised he was changing. The fire in his veins that he kept hidden, suppressed, was seeping out, escaping.

That evening she wanted the beast in him to take her, to possess her. She encouraged him, and he didn't hold back. He grabbed her hands and held them above her head with one hand whilst he languidly roamed over her body with his other. He took control and made her wait. He drove her mad with desire, using his mouth, his tongue, and dear God, his teeth. Her nerve endings tingled and throbbed. He was dominant, smouldering, passionate.

When he was on the verge of coming, she whispered in his ear.

'Would I care? Of course, I would.'

Chapter 31

Another wave of bile rose from Mary's stomach and hit the back of her throat. She held her long hair off her face, doubled over, and retched. Her abdomen clenched and contracted, and she whimpered. Clutching her belly tight, she fought nausea, fought to keep it down. Oh God, she hated being sick, but it would pass. It usually didn't last long. Wiping beads of sweat from her forehead, she pushed herself off her aching knees, hung her head under the water pump, and rinsed her mouth with clean cold water, splashing it on her apron to remove the splotches of sick clinging to it. What was wrong with her? Something she'd eaten?

As she stumbled back to the cottage, the hungry wail of her baby called out from the doorway into the early morning air. She stopped and hung her head. Feeding time again. Oh, why was she always so tired? Once inside the cottage, she ripped off the apron and threw it on the floor. The smell of stale vomit that still clung to it made her stomach churn.

Benjamin paced the floor and rocked a now giggling Eliza. The sight made Mary smile.

'She's so fair, and her eyes are so blue. She looks more like Elizabeth than you. Looks nothing like me, does she?' He raised his dark eyes to stare at her.

Did he know? He couldn't, surely. Mary gulped and tied back her hair as a distraction. 'Lizzie looked just like that as a baby.'

'Sick again?'

'Hmmm.'

'You need to see the bonesetter. Go to Grace, do it now. I'll take care of Eliza.'

'No, I'm fine now. Anyway, she needs feeding.'

'I said go.'

She stopped walking towards the bedroom and stared back at him. He never ordered her to do anything. 'Was that an order?'

'Yes.'

Really? He was giving orders now? But maybe he was right. She'd been sick too much lately. 'Right, then. I'll go now.' She grabbed her cloak and left, secretly glad to break free for some time to herself. But once at the cliff path, she turned to look back, and her chest constricted. It wasn't that she wanted to escape; she loved being with Eliza, being a mother. It was just that this constant exhaustion and sickness overwhelmed her.

She pulled her cloak over her head and hurried on. Wet autumnal mists hung in the air, draping soft shadows over the rough bracken. She stared up at the bruised sky, at a mild sun momentarily trapped, waiting to shake off the swollen clouds. This murky weather wouldn't last; it would change by the end of the morning, and the sun would be free to spread its warmth.

Following the coastal path, it was an easy ten minutes' walk to Waters Cottage, but she lingered to watch the heaving surf race up the beach at Treyarnon Bay. The foaming water hid the dark jutting rocks lying beneath its surface, dangerous rocks. She rounded the headland and gazed at Constantine Bay, and there the waves rolled towards the shore in an orderly fashion, eating away at the curve of sand. The deep dark waters pulsed with a soothing surge and swell, but this bay was deceptive. Below the surface, fierce and treacherous currents swirled and eddied.

Waters Cottage was empty, she didn't have to knock to find that out. When the bonesetter was home, some part of the cottage was always open—the door, a window—inviting the outside in. Mary knocked anyway but didn't wait; she set off for St Merryn and reached the village in time to catch sight of a flapping brown coat enter Ladybird Cottage, the home where the oldest woman in the village lived. Everyone only ever called her Granny, and Mary had no idea of her real name. She lived with her husband Thomas Fox, and it had only ever been the two of them, no children. But how would the bonesetter manage to fit inside? Their cottage looked bigger on the outside than it actually was. Entering made her think of going down a rabbit hole where everything shrank in size. Granny and Thomas Fox took up such little space compared to the bonesetter.

A booming voice reached her ears before she got to the door, but it fell silent when she knocked. Strangely silent, since noise always rolled around the bonesetter and Mary knew she was inside. She tried again, rat-tat-tat, and noticed the brown paint peeling off the door. Rubbing at it with her fingertips, the drab brown paint flaked off to reveal a sky-blue door underneath. *Why hide such a beautiful colour?*

The door opened a crack, and Grace called out, 'It's only Mary.' Grabbing her hand, she dragged her inside.

231

Mary stood beside the bonesetter, crushed between her massive frame and the wall of the tiny front room, facing the diminutive figure of Granny, who didn't even reach her shoulder. There wasn't an inch to spare between the three of them and the frayed doll's house furniture. Grace looked awkward, her shoulders hunched, her head bent low. Even Mary's head scraped against the low ceiling, making her stoop, making her feel oversized, like a giant down a rabbit burrow. In front of her, little Granny Fox wrung her hands as if to rid them of something nasty.

'Tell me again. I can't understand you. Say it slowly,' Grace spoke as if to a child.

'You must promise not to tell.' Granny pointed a knotted finger up at Mary. 'You must promise to never tell a soul.'

Mary exchanged glances with the bonesetter, who raised her shoulders to shrug and bumped her bent head against the ceiling. 'Ouch. I promise.'

'And you, say it.'

'I promise.'

The old lady's wrinkled face crumpled, and her eyes disappeared behind folds of skin. 'He's dead, Mr Fox, dead, died in his sleep, in his bed.' She tilted her chin upwards, indicating upstairs, then sighed and brushed a strand of lank, wispy grey hair off her face. 'He needs to be dressed, he needs to look decent, but I don't have the strength for it, so you'll have to do it for me.'

'I'm sorry, Granny,' Grace said. 'He was a good man and a good age.'

'Oh, he was, and it was quick. I'm not complaining.'

'Well, then.' Grace pushed her arms against the furniture and heaved her body around to face Mary. 'I can't get past you, maid. I can't get past you to get to the stairs. You'll have to leave or go up first.'

Mary went up first, elbows scraping against the sides of the staircase as she climbed towards the only room upstairs. Space in the garret was even more cramped than the room below because the ceiling sloped. It was entirely filled by a small bed which, if the dark pillows were anything to go by, was meant to sleep two. Plain dreary curtains sagged across the window to make everything in the dim, airless room indistinct, like seeing with blurred vision. The outline of a body not much bigger than a child was visible underneath a stained, tatty sheet. Mary moved into the room and grabbed her stomach when the smell of fresh and stale urine hit her.

The bonesetter appeared in the doorway, huffing and panting and pushing Mary farther into the room with her bulky body. There was no escaping now.

Mary sidled along one side of the bed, stooping low as her back hit the sloped ceiling. A patch of dank, dark mould clambered up the walls behind her. Thank God Benjamin's cottage wasn't like this. As the bonesetter squeezed and squashed her bulk on the opposite side of the bed, Granny's thin voice rose up from below.

'Wait, don't touch anything; wait for me.'

Mary waited as Granny dragged her ancient body up the stairs, listening to the see-saw bump, bump, bump of her feet on the wooden treads.

Granny's wizened face appeared at the end of the bed, gasping for breath. 'The clothes is here, on the end of the bed. Oh, don't you both forget what you promised.'

'But we have to tell to report his death,' Grace said.

'No, no not that.' Granny shook her head. 'Not that. You'll see. It isn't that at all.'

Grace leant on the small bed with both her great hands. 'Right, can we get on with it? I can't stay bent double for long.' She swiped at the sheet and whisked it away without waiting for an answer.

Mary shrieked at the sight of the naked dead body. It didn't make sense, it couldn't. No, it just didn't make sense.

Grace spluttered, 'Oh my gidge.' Laughing, she clamped her hand over her mouth, then released it to laugh again before clamping it back, but her laughter forced its way out and exploded into the room.

Mary only managed a weak smile, shaking her head in confusion. Lying on the bed was indeed the dead body of old man Fox. It was him, it was certainly his face, but the body was not that of an old man. It was definitely not that of an old man.

A thin voice broke into the bonesetter's laughter. 'It isn't funny. We was very young when we met, but even so, I knew I was in love, and I'd never love another. We ran away together; we wanted to be a couple, live together, and share a bed. It was her idea—pretend to be a man, then no one will care. So, she did, fooled everyone. She wanted it kept a secret, so she has to be dressed, and you mustn't tell. Her name was Blanche. Are you shocked? Well, I don't care. They can hang me for it; I'd do it all again.'

Grace sank onto the bed, which creaked and sagged with her weight. 'You're right, it isn't funny, it's just the shock. I won't tell. We won't tell, will we, Mary?'

'No, no one,' Mary said, glancing again at the body of the dead woman.

A bony finger poked her in the side. 'The worst thing you can do with love is to deny it. You'll do anything it takes when it's true love; nothing will keep you apart. Not even the hangman.'

Was that true? If Samuel came back now, would she do anything to be with her true love?

Mary helped to dress the small body. It wasn't difficult. The gutsy, vital force that once occupied it, that had given it strength, had given it courage, had departed and left a flimsy, lightweight shell. An empty husk.

Once clothed, the body looked like Thomas Fox, a man again. But if Mary peered closely this time and scrutinised him from top to bottom, she noticed the smooth, pale, hairless chin, the complete lack of Adam's apple, the stubby hands, stubby feet, and the childish proportions. Her gaze shifted to the bonesetter. 'Grace, were you fooled? You never guessed?'

'No, I never guessed.' Grace coughed, her cheeks the colour of claret. 'I have to get out. I can't breathe in here.' She squished and squashed her great body between the bed and the wall and forced it out of the cramped room, and Mary gladly followed.

At the top of the stairs, Grace paused and took a deep breath before stuffing her broad frame down the narrow staircase. She turned to Mary. 'You can't tell. It would be a disgrace; it's against the law.'

Mary glanced back into the room and watched Granny with Blanche, murmuring to her, fussing over her wiry hair. How could such enduring love be wrong? *You*

235

can't help who you fall in love with. Can you? 'I won't tell a soul.'

When Mary emerged from the warren of rooms and stepped outside, the light drizzle had fizzled out and a sliver of pale golden sun hovered behind the billowing clouds. The bonesetter was waiting for her. 'Did you want me?'

'Yes, I've been feeling ill lately. Sick most mornings.'

'Sick, hmm.'

'And I'm tired all the time.'

'Tired, hmm.'

'Can you give me anything? To make me feel better.'

'Some advice maybe. Are you pregnant again, Mary?'

'What? No, I can't be. Eliza's only five months old.'

'So?'

'I didn't think it was possible so soon after birth, and I'm breastfeeding.'

Grace gave a low chuckle. 'Breastfeeding don't always protect a maid. It isn't only possible, I'd say it's most likely. I'll make something for you to help with the sickness.' She stroked Mary's face. 'It's a blessing, maid.' With that, the bonesetter strode away. Her vast coat swirling around her massive undulating body, she disappeared around a corner, out of sight.

Mary didn't move, not immediately, absorbing the information where she stood and waiting for all the corners of her mind to soak it up, for it to trickle through her body. Only then could she put one foot in front of the other and propel herself home. She noticed nothing on her return

236

journey, all her thoughts and senses on her body, on what grew inside her body.

Could it be true? Of course, it could. It made perfect sense. The morning sickness, the exhaustion. It was just how she had felt with Eliza. She even knew when it had happened. She'd brought it on herself, leading him into the enchanted butterfly field. What witchery it had caused. Benjamin's baby would arrive in May, just like Eliza. Did God have a sense of humour?

She neared the cottage, and something pure white flapped and waved at her and drew her attention. Her now clean apron fluttered in the breeze, drying on the line with some nappies and clothes of Eliza's. She opened the cottage door and paused in the entrance. The pattern of dusty footprints that crisscrossed the floor—all gone. A warm fire crackled and spat bright sparks that spiralled lazily up the chimney. The polished wooden chairs glowed in the reflected light, and a pan of water bubbled leisurely by the fire. Eliza lay fast asleep in her basket next to Jess.

Benjamin rose from a chair, yawning. 'You've been gone ages. What did Grace say?'

'You've done all this work, everything. I'll have to leave you alone more often.'

'I keep telling you I can do it. Let me do it.'

'But it's women's work; what would people think? Not that anyone would believe me.'

'Don't tell. Let me help. Trust me.'

She nodded and slumped into a chair. 'I think I just might.'

'Did the bonesetter give you something for the sickness?'

'Not yet, but she will.'

***

MARY WAS RIGHT about the weather. A pale sun now shone through the clouds, its balmy heat warming her skin. She walked to work with Benjamin, who carried Eliza, and longed to talk. She longed for the carefree chatter of a friend, a friend like Jenny. Benjamin would have to do. 'Benjamin, do you know Granny and Mr Fox?'

''Course.'

'Well, the reason I took so long is 'cause I met the bonesetter at their cottage.' She paused, waiting for questions, but he had nothing to say. Jenny would have. 'Their cottage is normal if you're a piskey. Everything is so small—the furniture, the rooms, tiny. Can you imagine the bonesetter squashed into such a place?'

He gave a short laugh.

'Mr Fox was dead upstairs in his bed. We had to dress him. But—I'm going to tell you a secret now, and you mustn't tell another soul ever.' She turned to look at his impassive face. Who on earth could he possibly tell? She was safe passing her secret onto him. Jenny would have stopped walking to hang on her every word, but Benjamin didn't even glance at her. So, she said it. 'Mr. Fox is—was—really a woman.'

That made him stop midstride and frown. 'What?'

'A woman. It was two women living together like man and wife. It isn't legal, you can hang for it, so Mr Fox, Blanche, pretended to be a man.'

'Well, I never.'

'It's true, saw it with my very own eyes. Are you shocked?'

He furrowed his brow, lost in thought, then answered, 'No.'

'Why not?'

''Cause no one ever really looks. No one cares enough to see the truth.'

'But two women?'

'That's love for you. I don't have a problem with it. Sometimes you have to do whatever it takes to get what you want.'

'No, but . . .' She gave up. She should have known he wouldn't be interested, wouldn't be like Jenny.

'So, we're the only ones that know. The three of us?' he asked

'I guess.'

'Best keep it that way.'

She pouted at him. 'I know I told you, but I'd never tell another, not ever.' But he wasn't listening. He'd already walked off. She scampered after him, wanting him to talk to her. Didn't he realise she was building to something even more important? 'I know something else.'

He never even turned his head, never even broke his stride. Well, this would make him stop and listen, make him take notice. 'I'm pregnant again.'

His step did falter, and he did turn to face her. 'You're what?'

'Remember the butterfly field?'

'I'll never forget.'

'From then, I reckon. Due in May. Again.'

'Oh, Mary.' He laid a hand on her flat stomach. 'My child.'

'Yes. Another one.'

He fell to his knees and pressed his face against her body, and she noticed the way his hair curled defiantly in every direction. What would his child look like? Be like?

He was silent again, not letting her know the thoughts in his head, but her own desire for conversation had dried up under the benign sun. As they walked together, he held her hand, and she clung to him, had to, to hold him back. It was as if he strained against her like he was buoyant and if she let him go, he would take off in the breeze and soar away. This was happiness. He didn't say it. He showed it instead.

Had he been like this when she had told him about Eliza? Her tired brain couldn't remember.

Chapter 32

'Garne with you; I knows what I'm doing.'
'If you're sure, Gramfer, we'll be off.' Mary paused
and turned at the kitchen door to watch her grandfather with
Eliza, who could now crawl and fast. He'd have a job
keeping up with her. *Perhaps Elizabeth would help*? No,
she still wouldn't touch Eliza. Mary sighed and joined
Benjamin, who waited outside.

He wore his almost new jacket, the one he'd got
married in. A day out was obviously a big deal to him, so
she'd made an effort too, wearing her best Sunday dress
with green ribbons in her hat. She twirled the ribbons
around her fingers. They were the last thing Samuel had
given her. Pinpricks of tears threatened, and she dabbed at
her eyes with the ribbons. She often dreamt of him. Hard
not to with his daughter around. But did she really miss
him, or was it guilt? She ran a hand over her swollen
stomach. Benjamin's child was due in two months' time,
but the thought made her tremble because another birth
terrified her. What if it was another breach? What if it was
like last time?

A fresh breeze kept them company. It lifted the
ribbons on her hat and made them flutter like flags. Fresh
but not cold and no hint of rain, which was a relief because
she intended to have fun today. How long would Benjamin
last at the fair, though? He'd never been to one, so he had

241

no idea of the hordes that would be there. He'd find it unpleasant, no, probably impossible. He would be like a ship in distress amongst a sea of people. Well, it was his idea to come, but she would keep an eye on him, would come to his rescue if it looked like he was sinking.

She played with the ribbons on her hat, and they strolled together in silence down a rough track. Once they turned the corner, they would see the fair in the next field, but the noise reached them first. The confusing clamour and roar of a thousand different voices fused with music— drumbeats, violins, accordions. It jarred with the peace of the surroundings, in total conflict with the quiet of the farm and their tranquil walk up to this point. It suggested chaos and people and disorder.

Mary glanced at Benjamin, who'd taken a deep breath, his face as pale as whey. She reached out and grabbed his hand. What horrors did he imagine lay around the next bend? He had no idea, absolutely none.

They turned the corner, and the fair spread out before them, a riot of garish colours, vivid against the dark green fields. Striped awnings in red and white were posed along the outside of the field, housing the penny peeps, marionettes, and freak shows of giants, dwarves, and bearded ladies. Beyond them were the blue and white awnings of refreshment booths, and at the heart of it all, the open cheapjack stalls, where anything and everything could be bought. Swarming like ants over everything were men, women, and children, their shouts and laughter competing with the constant beat of a drum and the shriek of penny whistles.

Mary pulled on Benjamin's hand to move forwards, but he didn't budge, rooted to the spot, shaking his head.

Oh no, he was going to panic, turn, and run. She stood right in front of him to block his view. 'It's only people, don't worry. I want to go and see, to have some fun. And I want clothes for Eliza and our new baby.'

He wasn't looking at her, wasn't listening; he couldn't tear his attention away from the sight over her shoulder.

'Benjamin, look at me.'

He flicked his eyes to her face. She could plainly see the anxiety reflected in his dark eyes, and he was shaking. 'You can do this. Do it for me. Please?'

His brows furrowed, but he nodded, pulled his hat down low, and kept his head bent to cover his face. If only he realised that no one would notice him, and even if they did, he would be soon forgotten. It wasn't just that, though; he hated to be touched or even be near other people. Not touching was going to be downright difficult here; you couldn't go to a fair and not get bumped or knocked.

She drew him onwards, towards the flapping strawberry-pink and white-striped canopies and the thump of music. The volume of noise was deafening. His hand gripped hers, his other held out in front of him to ward off people. A man in a tall black hat stepped out from a booth and shouted, 'Roll up, roll up for the penny peeps.' A throng pushed her from behind, and Benjamin held her firm and shouldered his way out.

She found a route less crowded on towards the wrestling ring. He lifted his head in interest, so she stopped at the back of the watching crowd to view it from a distance.

A snow-white ring stained the grass, and someone stood in the middle, shouting, 'Step up, step up, we need

243

one more man to enter the tournament. Come and win some money. Five shillings for the winner.'

Why weren't they queuing up for that money? Benjamin got paid seventeen pence a day; to men like him, the prize money was life changing. She whirled around to check on Benjamin. *What a ridiculous thought.* He'd never stand up in public, and anyway, he probably preferred to use his fists. Cornish wrestling was nothing like that. She'd never taken much interest in it before, but when a man stepped into the ring, she raised her eyebrows, impressed. Might as well stay and watch.

A giant of a man stood inside the ring, and she craned her neck to look up at him. A man with a neck like, well, like the neck of their bull on the farm. His inky black hair curled down the sides of his face. He wore an open sleeveless canvas jacket and shorts. Nothing else. The skin on his broad chest gleamed like bronze beneath his dark hair. God, Benjamin had muscles, but this man's were twice the size. Veins stood out on his arms like rope. He stood with his legs apart, punching one fist into the palm of his hand, his eyes sweeping the crowd. She shuddered under his piercing stare. His opponent stepped into the ring, eclipsed by the giant's shadow, and she brought a hand to her mouth. He looked small compared to the first man, but he was probably the same size as Benjamin. They were not allowed to kick or punch, no—Cornish wrestling involved grabbing the jacket and using bare feet to throw the opponent, so how brutal could this be? She would stay and watch.

The men danced around each other until the giant lunged, grabbed the other's jacket, and twisted him over his hip, throwing him on the floor with the crowd yelling for

244

more. The fight continued, and Mary frowned and turned to Benjamin, who shrugged. 'Both shoulders must touch the floor for a win.'

Mary looked back to see the larger man hoist his opponent high above his head, holding him there whilst the crowd screamed, 'Flying mare,' then slamming him to the ground. She winced. This wasn't much fun after all. More onlookers gathered behind them, and a hard elbow jabbed her roughly in the back as the mob pushed her forwards. Benjamin tugged at her hand and shoved men aside to let them through, to escape.

She guided him away from the freak shows—he would be disgusted and horrified by them—and wound her way past the theatre of puppets towards the blue and white refreshment booths. The smell of roasting meats, baked potatoes, and bread made her stomach gurgle, but they were not going to stop for food. Benjamin would never last that long. His hand damp with sweat, she dragged him on to the open cheapjack stalls to search for second-hand baby clothes or material, since that would be cheaper. But she couldn't see anything due to the mass of people in front of her, blocking her view. Then the crush parted, and she froze.

In the stall in front of her stood a trickster, a brute selling lotions and potions. The words *Dr Lamb's Medicine* loomed before her in big bold black letters. Her blood ran cold, and she turned to run, but the throng before her made it impossible. She trembled, tears blurring her eyes.

Benjamin grabbed her, turned her around to face him, and in the midst of the heaving crowd, he held her close and bent to whisper in her ear, 'I can read those words now, thanks to you. It isn't him. He's long gone. Driven out of the village.'

She took a deep breath to control her ragged breathing. She thought he would be lost today, but it turned out she was the one drowning, needing him.

'I can see a stall up ahead. Baby clothes.' He rested his chin on the top of her head, then slid his mouth next to her ear. 'You're safe with me.'

Her pulse slowed to a steady beat, her heart against his. Of course, she was safe; it wasn't even the same doctor. She raised her head to look at him. 'I'm fine now. Let's have a look.'

He nodded, but this time he led her and fought to dodge arms, elbows, and bodies. Impossible. They reached the stall of second-hand clothes, and he plucked at them, pulling a face. She laughed and caught his sleeve, pointing to stacks of material. 'I'll make them, don't worry.' After buying what she wanted, she shouted at him so he could hear her above the din, 'Can you find a stall selling fairings? I promised Gramfer some boiled sweets.'

He furrowed his brow, and she yelled, 'Follow your nose. This way.' She pulled him towards the cloying scent of burnt sugar, her grandfather's favourite treat. 'Ooh, gingerbread. Let's buy gingerbread.' The spicy, sweet smell made her mouth water.

A commotion behind her made her stop. The crowd parted to let someone through and pushed her up hard against the stall. She turned sideways to protect her bulging stomach. Benjamin moved to stand in front of her, to act as a shield, stiff and rigid as unfamiliar bodies pressed up against his back. She couldn't see what caused the excitement. Benjamin protected her from further pressure, but the jeering rabble was loud, oppressive. *If she found this overwhelming, how was he coping?* She shouldn't have come; this wasn't the fun it used to be.

Looking over his shoulder, Benjamin raised his eyebrows in surprise and shouted down at her, 'It's your uncle John. And his wife.'

'Why are they causing such a fuss?'

'I dunno.'

The mass of people swept past them at last, her uncle and aunt in the middle of the noisy throng, heading for the centre of the fair.

Mary watched Benjamin try to brush away the lingering imprint of people from his jacket and heaved a sigh. He wouldn't like it, but she needed to know what was going on. This was family.

They tagged behind the crowd, following, but she couldn't see anything or make sense of the screams and shouts. When they reached the centre of the fair where the ground rose to a grassy hillock, the horde parted for John and Sarah. Mary stood with Benjamin at the back of the crowd, watching John lead Sarah to the crest. Mary gasped. 'No, he couldn't! He wouldn't!'

John held a halter in one hand, the other end of it fastened around Sarah's waist. It looked like a leather strap used to lead a horse. John raised his arm, and the crowd fell silent. Mary grabbed Benjamin's hand. John waited, then said, 'I'm selling my wife. Her name's Sarah. She's willing in this, so there'll be no trouble. Highest bidder. That's all.'

Mary was speechless. This couldn't be real. It must be characters playacting, just a joke. She knew it was a Cornish custom to sell a wife if the marriage had gone wrong, but she'd never seen it done. She clung onto Benjamin.

'I'll offer one penny for her.'

The crowd cheered, and someone shouted, 'She's worth more n' that.'

'I'll offer tuppence.'

'Still not enough.'

'Take it or leave it.'

The crowd laughed and chanted, 'Leave it, leave it.' John raised his hand for silence. No one spoke.

Mary looked at Benjamin. 'Tuppence. Could you sell your wife for tuppence? Is this a joke?' He shook his head, put an arm around her shoulder, and drew her close.

A small, scruffy man walked towards Sarah. 'Tuppence it is, then.' But someone else in a worn-out soldier's uniform jostled his way to the front of the spectators, took off his hat, and addressed himself to Sarah.

'The name's Sobey, mam, discharged from the 28th Regiment and in need of a wife. I'll offer thruppence.'

'Four, and that's my last.'

The soldier bowed. 'Sixpence, mam.'

Sarah turned to John, not smiling. She nodded once.

'Done and sold,' her uncle shouted. As the crowd cheered, he handed Sarah's halter to Sobey, and the three of them melted away into the laughing, hooting crowd.

Mary stood still, vaguely aware of Benjamin's hands on her shoulders and the swirl and eddy of people around her. Was it real? Had it happened? Was their marriage so sour it couldn't be rescued? She wanted to cry. Something precious was lost, but what exactly? Granny Fox had told her nothing keeps true love apart. Was the opposite true? Not being in love will tear you apart? She would probably never see Sarah again, but that wasn't the reason her heart ached. If Benjamin ever wanted to do that to her, it would break her.

Mary cupped her hands and shouted at him, 'Let's get out of here.' He smiled in relief, and together they threaded their way out of the tangled knot of people. At the edge of the field, she stopped to look back and took in the noisy seething swell. She used to love it, but perhaps, perhaps now she understood that family was enough, Benjamin was enough. She broke off some gingerbread, passed half to Benjamin, and stuffed the rest hungrily into her mouth. The spicy heat was somehow a comfort.

He nodded at her. 'Let's go to Padstow. My boots need the cobbler.'

She agreed. It was too early to go home. They reached Padstow and wound their way through a narrow, crooked, foxhole of an alleyway. The wind funnelled up the backstreet and carried with it the smells of the harbour—an acrid stench of rotten fish, seaweed, and excrement—and the sound of waves exploding against the sea wall.

They reached the quay, stepping over deep gutters jammed with foul garbage. Mary picked up her skirts to avoid a steaming heap of horse manure but slipped on the slick, wet cobbles. Benjamin caught her arm and held her steady.

The reek of hot tar, mud, and decomposing seaweed fought with the stink of rancid oil, fish, and sewage, but she didn't care. These smells and sounds she was used to; they were the hallmark of labour, toil, and exertion. The chime of hammers striking iron rang out as fisherman worked on their boats; pilchard nets were draped over the harbour wall to dry, stretched out in a neat line while the cry of the saltwife, snatched by the wind, blew away with the raucous mewing call of the gulls.

Mary passed old men sat in their doorways puffing on their pipes, the breeze catching the smoke and carrying it away, up, up, up towards the belching chimney stacks. The cobbler sat on a stool at the entrance to his shop, his mouth full of tacks, tap, tap, tapping at the sole of a boot with his small hammer. She left Benjamin with the cobbler and found a sheltered spot against the harbour wall where a slant of sunshine warmed her face. She waited and watched.

A few yards from where she sat, the pilchard cellar hunkered with the big double doors rolled open so she could see inside. The floor, awash with a mosaic blend of saltwater, crimson blood, and oil drew her attention. The sunlight caught the granite walls, making them flash with salt and fish scales. Women with manly red raw hands packed the hogsheads with pilchards, chatting and gossiping, their loud banter drawing her attention.

'I have a tale to tell you all.'

'Oh good, nothing like gossip to make work easier.'

'My sister Betsy at Porthcothan told it me.'

'Go on, then.'

'They's all overgone 'cause of the new revenue man.'

'What's he doing?'

'Stopping the moonshine is what. He even knows where it's all hidden.'

'No! They never know or care.'

'He knows 'cause he used to be a smuggler himself.'

'Never!'

'Betsy says she should hate him—her old man does, wants to kill him. Says he's hard on the men he catches, cruel.'

'But?'

'But he's very eyeable, handsome. Big, muscular, said she wouldn't say no to him.'

Laughter erupted from out of the building. Mary smiled and watched them wipe away tears from their eyes to leave oily slicks instead.

'Where's he from?'

'Was in the navy, but backalong from St Merryn, I believe.'

Mary's smile froze. *No, they couldn't be talking about Samuel.* If he was back, he would be in St Merryn. He'd never be a gauger. Anyway, she'd know if he was back, wouldn't she? She'd just know.

She gazed across at the cobbler's, at Benjamin, who leant casually against the wall, jumping from bootless foot to foot to keep them out of the dirt and wet. He glanced up at her, his dark eyes searching her face, a frown passing like a shadow over his features. Her baby gave her a kick in the ribs and made her gasp.

A reminder, if she needed one, that this was her life now.

There was no going back.

Chapter 33

S at at the kitchen table with Jess at his feet, Benjamin ate his Sunday lunch, the beef so tender it melted against his tongue. He swallowed, and rich, thick juices swamped his throat. This was good. It was probably always good, and he had just never noticed before. It was eating with others that was his problem, the noise mostly. He hated it, so he ate without thinking, without tasting. Normally. He smiled. It made a change to enjoy a meal. Even a knock at the kitchen door didn't distract him from lingering over each mouthful.

The door opened, and a young man shuffled in. Benjamin looked him up and down. Sickly pale with black decayed teeth and marked with smallpox. Nothing unusual there, but his eyes darted about the room. He was nervous, dipping his head as he spoke. 'Good afternoon to you all. Do you have any food and drink to spare a poor traveller? I don't need much.'

He wore grubby sailcloth trousers tied with string to keep them up, and he kept his hands in his pockets. He looked scruffy, like he had slept in his rumpled clothes. Benjamin decided he was most likely an apprentice run away from his heavy-handed master. Sleeping rough. They were common.

'You're in luck; we got dinner to spare. Come in, lad,' Mary's grandfather called out.

The man slouched inside, sitting down and placing his dirt-encrusted hands on the table, hands that might have scrabbled through mud. He had a whiff of manure about him. Benjamin pushed his own unfinished dinner plate away.

'Tell us what you know, lad,' the old man said.

The beggar shovelled food into his mouth like he hadn't eaten for a week. His gaze shot around the room, and his knee jerked and twitched. There would often be rewards for the return of runaways, but he was safe here, provided he behaved himself.

'There's beer in it for you, but only if you know something,' the old man said.

The beggar paused, swallowing his last forkful and staring at the table he said, 'There's a wreck at Padstow. Bad weather has wrecked another ship on the Doom Bar. I heard lots of cargo to be had. It's where I'm going now.'

'A wreck? S'pose most of it will have gone by now, but still, what if you went to take a look?' Mary's grandfather stared directly at Benjamin as he spoke. 'Might be something left, something useful.'

Benjamin shook his head frantically. 'No. No, I can't. I can't leave Mary. Baby's due any day.'

'We'll keep an eye on her this time,' Mary's grandfather said.

Mary put a hand on his shoulder. 'It isn't coming today, Benjamin. You go. I'll wait here for you to return.'

'You promise?'

'I promise. Be careful, mind. Them gaugers might be about.'

The beggar spoke up. 'Not today, I believe. There was trouble at Porthcothan. Customs men decided to take on the locals, who were all armed with pistols, bludgeons, and knives. There was a terrible fight. One gauger dead.'

Mary gasped, and Benjamin turned to face her. *Did the baby kick? Did she have a pain?* Colour drained from her cheeks.

'Mary?'

She turned her face away from him.

Didn't she want him to read what was on it? Not that he ever could.

'I'm fine. Just got a kick from the baby, that's all.'

No, she hadn't. That much he did know. She always smiled when she got kicked.

The beggar glugged and slurped down his beer, then stood to leave. 'Thank you all for your kindness, but I'll be off now.' He slouched out, his dirty hands in his pockets.

'Think I will go and take a quick look.'

'If you see trouble, just leave, come back,' Mary shouted after him.

Nodding, Benjamin followed the beggar out. A fine mist hung in the air, settling like cobwebs on his face. He hadn't done this for a while—just go out walking alone.

At Padstow, he threaded his way through the narrow alleyways and stopped short of the harbour. Leaning one hand against a wall, he shoved the other nonchalantly into his trouser pocket and watched the scene in front of him.

A detachment of local militia stood to one side doing nothing. They were outnumbered, so that was a wise decision. Not much remained of the cargo, but some kegs of wine—or was that brandy? He couldn't tell the difference from where he stood—were lined up along the harbour wall. Men and women were sprawled under the wall, either out cold or too drunk to stand. There wasn't much left to scavenge, and he didn't fancy joining the crowd. If anyone saw him, insults were bound to fly about his father or his face, and he didn't want to get mixed up in a drunken brawl and get arrested. He wouldn't ignore them and walk away, not anymore.

As the sun broke through the drizzle and made rainbows on the cobbles, a woman clasping a box swayed and zigzagged across the street towards him. He didn't move, just watched, his eyes on her crate, on the bright splash of colour from the fruit inside. Oranges. Mary loved them.

The woman stopped by the roadside gutter, hitched up her skirts, and bent to pee but fell sideways, sprawled in the dirt. Benjamin's eyes never left the box of fruit.

A shrill whistle pierced the air, and the militia jumped to attention as a group of revenue men ran towards the harbour. They meant business.

If you see trouble, just leave, come back.

Amidst a confusion of shouts and scuffles, Benjamin darted forwards, hoisted the crate onto his shoulder, turned, and sprinted for the alleyway. Taking the first turn he came to, he didn't stop, ducking into another backstreet. The clatter of footsteps behind him told him he'd been seen, was being followed. Running into another alley, he dived for a dark recess, placed the crate on the floor, and stood on top of it, hidden from view with his back pressed up against a door. To listen. To wait. No gauger would bother chasing one man with one crate when there were easy pickings at the harbour.

Footsteps ran towards his alley. They slowed. They stopped.

From his hiding place, Benjamin watched the late morning shadows, dark, inert shapes thrown down on the cobbles. One moved, stretched long and wide. A shadow cast by a big man, it crept towards him. Benjamin listened and waited, a doorknob jammed hard into his back, his legs splayed wide and his feet against the edges of the crate, its strongest points. He sucked in his stomach and watched the dark shape slide ever closer.

If you see trouble, just leave, come back.

He should have done just that; now he had nowhere to go. And that shadow troubled him. Not because it was there—no, it tugged at a memory, something unpleasant.

A click of a door to his left made him flinch. *Damn, someone else to give him away*. A light tread, though. A woman, young with long dark hair and dark eyes. She stared straight ahead at the shadow. Her gaze never flickered to Benjamin, but she must have seen him. Instead, she sauntered up the alley with an easy sway of her hips, and the dark shadow gave a deep, throaty laugh before it swallowed her. Their silhouettes remained melded together until they slowly shrank from view.

Benjamin stayed still, unable to move, unable to breathe. *No, impossible*. He shook himself free of a memory. It couldn't be him; he couldn't be back, and he'd never be a gauger. *But that laugh*! Benjamin took a deep breath and counted to ten. He jumped off the crate, picked it up, and strode away.

He followed a rough, uneven wheel track across a stretch of the moor towards St Merryn and descended into the valley. High-pitched singing reached his ears. A number of young women headed towards him. His gripped his crate, his knuckles white. He tensed his leg muscles to run, but where? He'd just passed an outcrop of granite. It would have to do. Benjamin sprinted back to it and dived behind it, hunkering down, breathing hard.

Shrill voices drew closer, stopping beside his rock. He pushed up against the solid granite as if it could swallow him up just because he wished it. The murmur of female voices became louder, became shouts. His heart raced, his blood pounded, and he screwed up his eyes. *What was wrong with him?* That shadow had unnerved him. He didn't need to run now. He wasn't about to let women intimidate him; no one was going to do that anymore. *To hell with them.* He took a deep breath, swarmed up the rock, and looked over the top, then ducked back down, panting hard. *Phew.* Just a party of bal maidens who'd collided with a group of young women. They hadn't even seen him; he had nothing to do with this. He puffed out his cheeks and laughed.

A screech drew his attention. He took another look. They squabbled over a box of figs, probably from the wreck. He glanced at his oranges. They'd have them if they saw them, and he had to admit he was no match for bal maidens, with their strong arms and bodies from working on the surface of the mines. A loud shriek made him jump. He craned his neck to look, spellbound.

The women fought, rolling about, pulling out handfuls of hair, screaming and wailing with their fists flying and nails gauging. Clothes were torn, garments strewn on the floor. The previous day's persistent drizzle had made the ground slippery and muddy. He watched, riveted, as near-naked bodies writhed and squirmed, streaked in brown slush and blood, bare breasts exploding out of stays. He laughed. If they wanted his oranges, they could bloody well have them.

It took a while before the women were finished with each other. It felt like hours before one side was triumphant, but they couldn't have fought for that long. He spied the bal maidens helping each other up. Victorious, they gathered up their tattered clothes and walked off with the spoils, singing a raunchy song. He waited until the coast was clear and set off down the valley in the opposite direction. He should go out alone more often; he'd forgotten what sights could be seen.

He could see Goodtoknow Farm in front of him. He'd taken longer than intended because of the bal maidens, but Mary would be pleased with the oranges. He was near the farmhouse when a woman's piercing scream made him catch his breath. *Mary!*

Benjamin sprinted for the kitchen door, flung it open, and skidded to a stop beside the table, panting. He peered wildly about but saw only the old man slumped at the table, calmly supping a beer and smoking his pipe. A soft moan grew in intensity until it became a loud groan, a groan through clenched teeth. He recognised that sound. He stared up at the ceiling, frozen, his world slowing down.

'She's with the bonesetter, so you can't go up there,' the old man said.

In slow motion, Benjamin turned his head and waited for the words to penetrate. 'My baby?'

''Course. Soon as you left, it decided to come. But I know it isn't a breech this time. Grace told me, says it will be quick.'

Benjamin dropped the crate of oranges on the table with a thud, unable to think clearly. Surely there was something he should be doing? Another moan made him wince. He grasped the back of a chair, his knuckles white.

'Oh, don't worry. She's doing fine. Elizabeth is helping. Sit down with me; I'll get you a beer. No, perhaps I'll get you a brandy.'

Breathing hard, Benjamin wasn't listening. *His own child, his own child.* A brandy glass was pushed into his hand. The old man grasped his fingers around it, then raised it to his lips.

'Drink it. You needs to come back to the land of the living.'

Benjamin threw it back and downed it in one but never noticed.

There it was. That was it.

The very sound galvanised him, stirring his blood, bringing him back to life. The wail of a newborn. He laughed. 'My God.' He slammed his glass down on the table, running a hand through his hair. He wanted to run upstairs and see, but he waited, waited to be called.

He leant his hands on the table and hung his head, his arms rigid, his foot tapping. *Come on, let me up. Come on.* At the point he was about to explode the door opened, and the bonesetter walked in. Grace grinned at him and opened her mouth to speak, but he couldn't wait, taking off and jumping the stairs two at a time.

At the top of the stairs, he paused, not sure which room she would have gone into, but soft female voices lured him forwards. He walked up to a bedroom door, took a deep breath, and pushed down on the handle.

She was slumped against pillows, lost in her father's double bed, her hair wild and messy. Her face drawn and tired but smiling, she beckoned to him. He eased himself onto the bed beside her.

'Another girl, Benjamin. Another beautiful little girl.'

She held a white bundle out to him, and he reached for his daughter with trembling hands. *Something might yet go wrong.* He teased back the folds of the muslin and gazed at his sleeping child. He wanted to cry but gulped back the tears. She looked familiar, like her face was one he'd known all his life. He'd been waiting for her, this tiny mite who tugged at his heart. He instantly knew he loved her without limits, without reserve.

Mary touched his arm. 'I don't have a name for her yet. I was so sure it would be a boy this time.'

'I have.'

Mary laughed. 'Really? Go on, then.'

'Mary Jane. After you and your ma.'

'Mary Jane Carnarton. I'm too tired and too happy to argue.'

He undid the cloth so he could count her fingers and toes. She was perfect, and he intended to make sure she stayed that way.

A chair scraped along the floor, and Elizabeth rose to leave. He hadn't noticed her sitting alone in the dark corner of the room. As Elizabeth stood up, he also rose and made his way towards her. She backed away from him, her head down.

'Hold her.'

'No. Please, just let me leave.'

'Hold her,' he said softly.

He thrust his child at her chest and waited, not intending to let go until he was certain Elizabeth had a hold. He waited. Mary Jane squirmed in his hands and whimpered. Elizabeth's head wavered, rose to look. Her hands reached out, withdrew, then reached out again to clasp the baby and hug it to her breast.

With arms crossed, Benjamin watched. She never touched Eliza, and he would never force her to. He understood why, but this was different. He wanted to help her to heal but didn't know how. He studied her. It wasn't words she needed, it was this, this physical contact, to be needed by a helpless creature. He understood that too.

Mary raised her gaze to him and shrugged but remained silent as they watched Elizabeth bonding with their baby.

Chapter 34

Mary wandered home from Sunday church service with a sleepy Mary Jane, limp with contentment, nestled into her hip. Mary gazed down at the explosion of soft curls bubbling over her child's head like a foam of dark hair, like Benjamin's. A striking contrast to Eliza's fine, straight, honey-coloured locks, like strands of silk, like Samuel's. She leant down to inhale the smell of her, overcome by a wave of tenderness. She was a beautiful, easy child, and she loved her, loved them both with equal abandon.

Freckled sunlight filtered through the tangled trees that formed a canopy above her head, a green roof pierced by pinpricks of light. She stepped in and out of pools of sunshine and splashes of colour on the shady trail home. The hedgerows, pregnant with blackberries and alive with plump droning bumblebees, stretched their prickly brambles across the path. Songbirds burbled above her head, a sweet soothing melody. She loved these late Sunday mornings when she rambled home. The quiet solitude, the aimless drifting of her mind.

Mary Jane wriggled and snuggled closer. Mary stroked the top of her head and whispered, 'Shall I sing you a song? I think I will. Let's see now . . . Oh, I know.'

'As I was a walkin' for my rec-re-ation,
A down by the garden I silently stray'd,
I hear a fair maid makin' great lam-en-tation,
Cryin' Sammy will be slain in the wars, I'm afraid.
The blackbirds and thrushes sang in the green bushes,
The wood doves and larks seem'd to mourn for the maid,
And this song she sang was concernin' her lover,
O Sam will be slain in the wars, I'm afraid.'

From behind her, a deep male voice continued the song.

'When Sammy returned with his heart full of burning,
He found his dear Mary all dead in her grave,
He cried 'I'm forsaken, my poor heart is breakin''
O would that I never had left this fair maid.'

Samuel? Could it really be Samuel? Hugging Mary Jane, she turned to face the singer, who continued to walk towards her. His shoulders were broader, his arms more muscular than she remembered. His blond tousled hair was bleached white, and his unblinking, penetrating, vivid blue eyes were startling against his tanned skin. *Oh God, but he was beautiful.* A six-foot-tall vision, everything about him was perfect.

He looked her up and down. 'My lovely Mary.'

'Samuel.' She gasped as her legs turned molten and seeped into the ground. The deep, throaty timbre of his voice made her quiver, and a throb of pleasure pulsed in her heart. He towered over her, studying her.

'I've missed you, maid. Thinking of you was all that kept me going, that one day I'd be back for you. Did you think I would die out there and never return?'

She nodded at him, unable to speak.

'Not me. 'Course I'd come back.'

Mary took a step backwards. 'They say you're a gauger, but how could you? Against your friends?'

'War changes a man. I've seen brutal, pointless death. I didn't want to rot in that hell ship, so I took any way out. You don't know what it was like. We were anchored out of position; any fool could see that except Admiral Milne. The ship was isolated, an easy target for the Algerian gunners who raked her fore and aft. I watched men die at my feet, and I decided that what you do in life doesn't matter; it's only living it that matters. No one will remember when you're dead and gone.'

She stared at him. Had he changed, or was he always like this?

'But I hear I'm too late.'

She heaved a sigh. *Far too late. Oh, Samuel, if only.* She tried to answer, but no words came. She could only stare and remember the many days and nights she had prayed for this.

'I get you wanting to be married, I do, and thinking I might be dead and all. I told you not to wait for me, but Benjamin? That freak, that poor excuse for a man? I've always hated him. I can't believe you married him willingly. Did you?'

She closed her eyes and shook her head. She hadn't; it wasn't exactly a lie.

'Didn't think so, but what did he do to force this life on you? And you have his bairns, so he forces himself on you too. I can't bear to think about it.'

He edged closer, swamped her with his familiar scent. Instantly, the sensual memories she'd kept stacked and stored away escaped, exploding in her head.

Her eyes locked onto his full mouth curving into a hypnotic smile. How she had missed that passionate mouth, being kissed and kissing, his tongue rubbing against hers. She missed it. She craved it now. Benjamin never kissed her.

'Does he hurt you? Does he? If he does, I'll do something about him. If you want, I'll make him disappear. Then we can be together again. Just say. I'm willing to do it, to do anything. Remember, it's living your life that matters.'

He held her against his chest now. How had that happened? His hands stroked her back, and she was lost, compulsively drawn to him like a moth to a flame. It felt so familiar. Unable to break free, unable to think, breathing him in, intoxicated.

'Just say the word,' he murmured into her ear.

A corner of her mind screeched for attention—*this was important, concentrate*—but she couldn't bring herself back to sanity. Then Mary Jane squirmed against her, caught between them. She wailed and broke the spell, and Mary gasped, his words at last sinking in. 'No. No, please—don't do anything.'

'Nothing? Are you telling me you love him? And I believed you loved only me.'

'I did love you. I do love you, but I'm married now. I have bairns. It's too late.'

He drew a finger down the side of her face and left a trail of burning flesh.

Mary Jane let out another cry. 'Oh, I have to go. I have to.' With Mary Jane crying in earnest, she backed away from him.

'I'll be back, Mary. I don't give up so easily.'

She turned, clutching her baby to her chest, and ran.

'I wants you back,' he shouted after her.

Mary stopped running when she reached the headland. Still panting, she rubbed her free hand over her face and gazed out to sea. It was flat and sullen, and it reminded her of an abandoned lover.

Meeting Samuel brought back such tender, seductive memories. The times she'd had with him had been intoxicating, thrilling. But it didn't matter. What mattered were her children, and they were happy at Treyarnon Cottage. They were happy with her. With Benjamin. Life with Benjamin was different, sleeping with him was different, but it was also good. She didn't feel powerless with Benjamin—quite the opposite. Should she tell him Samuel was here? No. What would he do if he knew what Samuel had said? He'd want to fight, to see him off. There would be bloodshed, and Benjamin might come off worse. Samuel knew how to fight too, and he was bigger than Benjamin. It was best to say nothing. Keep it a secret. Another damned secret.

She turned to look at the cottage. Benjamin appeared in the doorway with Eliza holding onto him by one hand, the other holding onto Jess's ear. Mary waved to them and made her way across. Yes, this was her life now. She couldn't change it if she wanted to. And did she even want to anymore?

As she drew near, she gazed at Eliza, so like her father. It sent a yearning through her body, an ache for what might have been.

'I've planned a surprise for you.' Benjamin carried a bundle of sheets piled up in Mary Jane's basket, his eyes bright with mischief, with joy. She lowered her own. He always looked too deeply, too shrewdly, and her eyes might give away her secrets. 'I'm going to teach you to swim.'

Her head jerked up. She couldn't stop it. 'Me? Now?'

He laughed. 'Come on, it's a perfect day. We won't get another chance this year.'

Benjamin led the way down the steep, stony, shingly track, carrying Eliza and swinging the basket with Jess running on ahead. He jumped down onto the soft golden sand, and Mary jumped down after him. Removing Eliza's shoes, then his own, he threw them into the basket and reached for Mary Jane.

Mary kicked off her own shoes, then tugged off her stockings, and her feet sank into the warm sand. She curled her toes and let the sand trickle between them. Eliza stared at her uncertainly, and Mary giggled, pulling a funny face at her. She ran a foot over the sand, then burrowed into the fine pale grains. The heat retained below the surface thrilled her. She raised her face up to the mild September blue sky, closed her eyes, and let the sun's rays focus on her cheeks and nose, warming herself from the outside in. They lived near this beach. They saw it every day, but she never took the time to come down here.

Oh God, he wanted her back.

When she opened her eyes, Benjamin's trousers were rolled up, and Eliza ran around naked, throwing up handfuls of sand, squealing and laughing.

Benjamin grinned. 'The tide is going out. Let's go to the water's edge.'

Mary padded across the dry sand. Her feet sank with each step, the sand pulling her down until her legs were heavy with the effort. She looked back at their footprints, the only indentations to blemish the pristine beach.

At the water's edge, she hitched up her skirts and waded in. She watched the sea rush past her ankles and caught her breath with the shock of the cold water. The sea pulled back again, drew the sand out from under her feet in tickling eddies, and tugged her downwards. The bottom of her skirt got soaked by a wave lapping at her legs, and when she drew her feet out of the sand, it sucked her back in, and she had to slurp herself free. The surge and drag became hypnotic, soothing.

He wanted her back.

'Mary!'

Benjamin watched her from the beach as she sloshed her way towards him, kicking her feet at the ripples of water.

'Ready to swim?'

'In there?' She turned to face the waves dribbling up the beach.

'No. Not there.'

Carrying Mary Jane, he took Eliza's hand and walked towards the jutting black rocks that embraced this beach. Mary followed and rounded the rocks to find a cove where a pool of clear saltwater lay marooned by the ebbing tide. Jess flopped down at the water's edge, her fur now matted with briny water and sand. She guarded Eliza. Benjamin tucked Mary Jane into the basket and placed her in the shade, then straightened up and called to Mary. 'This pool will do for now. It's warm and not too deep. We can go to the big pool later.'

Mary liked the look of this one. She could see the sandy bottom through the clear, still water, and limpets clung to the seaweed-fringed rocks. No one could drown somewhere this tranquil.

Benjamin stripped naked, his clothes piled in a heap on the dry sand, and he waded into the pool. Her eyes flicked over his tanned skin and taut muscles, and she watched the black snake curled in the hollow of his back sink below the water. Her blood stirred, and her cheeks flushed. He was special too, different from Samuel. Like the dark to Samuel's light.

He turned to her. 'It's warm. Like a bath.'

She hesitated, scanning the rocks and beach for signs of another person.

'No one comes here. Never. No one will see you.'

She peeled off her clothes, the hem of her damp skirt now covered in sand, and waded into the pool, swishing the water around her body. Tepid, not quite bathwater but good enough. She peered down. Minute fish swam, clustered together. She reached out to scoop them up, but they darted out of reach.

Benjamin stood in the glassy water, waiting for her. 'We'll take it slow. Let's get your head under first.'

She bit her lip but nodded. She wanted to do this, had always wanted to know what it would feel like to have her whole body underwater.

269

'Take a deep breath. Close your nose off using the back of your throat. You don't need to hold your nose if you do that. Do it. See? You can't breathe through your nose. Water can't get in either.'

She swirled the water about with her hands and hesitated.

In front of her, Benjamin sank under the water, his arms spread out wide, tendrils of hair drifting about his head. He rose up again, the water streaming off his smooth skin. He grinned at her. 'Come on. Try it.'

She took a deep breath, stared at the water, and exhaled. She shook her head and tried again. The water lapped her shoulders and crept up her neck towards her chin, and her body jerked upright. She slapped the surface with her hand in frustration, spraying them both with briny droplets.

He reached out and grabbed her hands. 'We'll do it together. When I count to three.'

She nodded.

'One. Two.'

She took a deep breath.

'Three.'

And he pulled her down, her eyes shut tight as the water slinked over her mouth, her nose, and closed over her head. She stayed under until her lungs were about to explode, then pulled herself up, gasping, wiping the water from her eyes and nose. *I've done it!* She pushed back her hair, so matted with saltwater that it stuck to her face, but she'd done it. She laughed and danced around on her toes, churning up billows of sand. 'This time I'm going to open my eyes.'

'Wait! The sand must settle first.'

She did it on her own this time, and when she opened her eyes, he was under the water with her, blowing bubbles and making her want to laugh so much she had to surface. 'What next? I'm loving this so much.'

'I'll teach you to float. When you take in a breath of air and your lungs fill up, it means you can't sink. Remember that. You can't sink.'

She nodded, riveted on his serious dark eyes. She wiped the back of her hand across her mouth and tasted salt.

'I'll hold a hand under you, then you can float on your back. Stare up at the sky. Breathe.'

Using his hands, he tilted her back. She spread her arms wide, pushing back her head. She floated untethered, like the slow meandering clouds above her in the pastel blue sky. Chalky seagulls wheeled and soared, and the brackish tang of the sea drifted over her whilst the sun gently bathed her exposed skin. Her chest rose and fell in a slow, sweet rhythm. She lay suspended, happily lost.

He wanted her back.

She raised her head to tell Benjamin it was glorious, and her legs sank to the sand. He stood within reach, and she longed to wrap her arms around him, to kiss him, to thank him for this gift. He would hate the kiss, so instead she murmured, 'Thank you.'

He reached out to push a strand of tangled hair off her face. 'Ready to swim? I believe there's room.'

She nodded

'This is how you move your arms.'

She copied him and pushed the water aside whilst crouched down to propel herself through the water. In the shallows, she practised moving her legs and used her hands to keep her anchored, laughing as Eliza splashed her with water.

'Right. Let's swim,' Benjamin called out.

She waded out to where he waited.

'I'll keep my hand under you to keep you afloat. I won't take it away until you're happy. Just keep breathing. You'll float.'

She took some deep breaths as she studied his serious, salt-encrusted face, his curly dark hair now crispy and crinkly. He didn't dip his head anymore whenever she studied him; he permitted her eyes to roam, but never for long. He hated being examined, and he never allowed anyone else to stare at him. He was so different from Samuel. She pinched the bridge of her nose and shook her head free of Samuel's image.

With the feel of Benjamin's strong hands beneath her, she practised her swimming strokes, confident only because he held her steady. She could do this, she could. Gliding through the water, his hands still reassuringly under her, she stretched out her body between each stroke and managed three before she ran out of space.

Standing up, she turned and raised an eyebrow at him. 'Again?'

He nodded, and once more she glided through the water, imagining she was a fish, lightweight and graceful. She forgot about Benjamin until she stood up and looked back.

He grinned at her. 'You did it all by yourself. You swam.'

'I did? Stay there, I'm coming back.'

Three strokes, and she was beside him again. 'I can't believe it. I never thought I'd do this, ever.' She laughed and again yearned to wrap her arms around his neck and kiss him. But he'd hate her to kiss him on the face or lips. Samuel wouldn't—oh no, he wouldn't. Perhaps she could hug him, kiss his shoulder. He'd like that. She bent towards him too late. He'd already turned away, reaching for Eliza.

'We'll watch you. I don't believe we'll go to the big pool today. It's too hard to get to with the bairns.'

She swam some more and looked down through the water at the fish beneath her, one of them at last. She turned to float on her back, to watch the seagulls squabble above her, wheeling and soaring. Now, what would it feel like to do that—to fly, completely free, to let the wind take you? She closed her eyes.

He wanted her back, but he'd been at Porthcothan for at least six months, maybe more. Why wait until now to find her?

Why had it taken him so long?

Chapter 35

In the farmhouse kitchen, Mary bundled up the washing and put it into her linen basket. She wiped sweat from her brow, listening to the clink of cups and saucers behind her.

Benjamin yawned and pushed himself out of his chair, away from the kitchen table, about to leave. She called out to him, 'I'm wanting to rinse the washing in the stream this morning. Can you make sure the cows stay out of my way? I'll be at the top of the stream if you can keep them in Lower Field for me.'

He nodded at her.

'What are you doing today?'

'Spreading muck.'

She pulled a face. 'Oh, you'll need a bath after.'

He laughed, 'And a change of clothes.' He walked out with a smile on his face. He was smiling a lot lately.

Mary picked up her basket, perched it on her hip like a baby, and paused in front of the fire for a moment as its warmth spread across the back of her legs. She took the time to study Elizabeth, who softly sang to herself as she prepared dinner. Her hair was glossy and golden again, tied into a thick braid. Yes, there was plenty to smile about. The farmhouse had a contentedness about it that crept up on everyone in it. She hoisted her basket back to her hip and went outside.

A gentle breeze stirred and stroked her face, lifting and dissolving friendly October mists that had gathered in the early morning. She strolled towards the stream behind the farmhouse, breathing in the scent of ripe apples from the orchard and disturbing a gang of crows that croaked and cawed their disapproval as she set her basket down beside the broad, shallow stream. She plunged her arms, scalded red by the boiling laundry, into the cool, clear water and sighed as it quenched the heat in her skin. Reaching for the clothes in the basket, she rinsed them one by one, watching the slow pulse of the sinuous water carry fallen leaves of amber, russet, and withered brown, all swept away by the river's ceaseless energy.

She hummed as she twisted and squeezed the water out of the clothes, making her own skirt sodden, and smiled as she thought of Elizabeth and how much she'd improved lately. When a looming dark shadow fell over her, catching her by surprise, she turned around, shading her eyes, wondering who had crept up on her so stealthily. Mary caught her breath.

'Morning, maid. I said I'd be back.'

'Not here. You can't come here,' she whispered.

'Why not? I worked here once. I know everyone.'

'No. Please, not here.'

'What are you afraid of?'

Samuel's mouth formed a lazy smile as he stood over her, hands on his hips, easy in his own skin. *Was she afraid?* Yes. Afraid of giving in to him, of being conquered, possessed. It had always felt like possession with Samuel, now that she thought about it. She remained sitting out of his reach.

275

He bent closer, their heads almost touching, and held her gaze, his long eyelashes curved around his unblinking blue eyes. 'Meet me in the woods, then, the usual place. I'll wait for you. We have to talk; you know we do.' He straightened up and walked off, not looking back, not waiting for a reply. It occurred to her that he always expected to be obeyed too.

Without taking her eyes off him, she sat and watched the mist swirl around him until the woods swallowed him up. She remained still, biting her lip. Two years before, she'd have gone in an instant. But now everything was different. Now she had bairns. Now she had Benjamin, and he knew too many of her secrets. Samuel said he could make Benjamin disappear if she wanted. Did she want that? To replace Benjamin with Samuel?

God knew Benjamin was troubled, perplexing, and complicated, but he gave every part of himself to her, knowing she could break him if she wanted. He didn't try to possess her; he didn't expect to be obeyed. What he craved was her love. She wiped away the tears now spilling down her cheeks and sniffed. It was the one thing she had never given him, and why? Because she'd given her heart to Samuel and promised to only ever love him; how could it be right to break such a promise? And because she didn't deserve Benjamin. She didn't deserve to be happy after the crime she'd committed. She was still waiting for God's punishment. It would come one day. If she gave her heart to Benjamin, perhaps he would be taken from her too. She was afraid to love him.

Anyway, Samuel could have anyone he wanted, so why did he want her? Because he still loved her? She rubbed hard at her temple as an uncomfortable thought escaped—that he only wanted her to get back at Benjamin. She got to her feet and brushed twigs and leaves off her damp skirt. Glancing around, she took a deep breath and marched towards the woods. Samuel had to be told. He had to leave her alone.

As she neared the woods, her steps faltered, and she paused before entering the tangled, dense forest. What if she just turned around and went back to the farmhouse? Would he understand, accept defeat? Or would he still come looking for her? She reached out a hand and placed it on the grey fissured bark of an ancient oak tree. It stood strong and mighty, mushrooms the colour of egg yolks flowing from its base to form sweeping clumps of orange-lipped, shelf-like brackets. He didn't even know about Eliza, could never know. He had to be told they couldn't be together because she knew him, knew he would never leave otherwise. He was trouble.

She crept into the silent woods with heavy steps. The mist still clung to the twisted limbs of the trees as she picked her way over gnarled roots, across the spongy forest floor, and stopped to lean against a tree. He was just ahead of her. *Would he sense her presence like he used to*? Holding onto the rough bark, she strained her neck to watch him idly kick at the stump of a rotten tree, ignorant that she was there. She bit her lower lip, smoothed down her hair and dress, raised her chin, and left the sanctuary of the tree to face him.

His face lit up with a broad grin. 'I knew you'd come.'

She dug her fingernails into the palms of her hands and stood in front of his beautiful body, looked up at his joyful, familiar face, and tottered like a giddy child. *Why*

did he have this effect on her? She gulped. 'Samuel, I can't
. . .' But before she could finish speaking, he grabbed her,
crushing her to his body. He held her firm, bent his head,
and kissed her. And kept kissing her.

Her eyelids fluttered closed, her head swam, and
the tension wound so tight inside her snapped. Her senses
scattered at the touch of his lips, slow and hot. He prised
her mouth open with his tongue, and she surrendered,
parting her lips to welcome the languid penetration. He
claimed her as he always had, running his tongue inside her
mouth, making her body want more. Her hands reached for
his arms, for the strong muscles beneath his shirt. Her own
tongue wrapped around his, but the sour taste of tobacco
brought her to her senses. *How had he overpowered her so
easily?*

'Sam, I can't.'

He let her go and murmured, 'You can.'

She leant her head against his chest and forced
herself to breathe, to think about her children, about
Benjamin. 'No, I can't,' she stammered and pushed herself
away from him. He caught her wrists and squeezed, and she
let out a gasp at the memory of Jenny's bruised hands.

'You belong to me, not him.'

'Let me go. It's too late; you have to let me go.'

'But I love you, maid.'

'And I love you, but it's no good.'

'Tell me why you married him.'

Shaking her head, she searched for an answer, but
none came because she could never tell him the truth. He
spun her around so her back rested against the tree. He held
her arms high above her head, and her muscles screamed in
protest. He impaled her with his hips, and when she

squirmed uneasily beneath him, he groaned in pleasure. His erection, stiff with desire, rammed against her, making her legs shake. Chin trembling, she pleaded with him, 'Not like this. Just let me go, Sam, please.'

'I can feel you quiver beneath me. I don't believe you want me to stop. If you tell me you don't want me, I'll go and leave you alone.' He moved one hand down her body, over her breasts, parting her legs and pulling at her skirt. Her body became a traitor, quivering with anticipation. He kissed her again, and she couldn't speak, couldn't say no. And she was close, so close to surrender. Her body arched against him, wanting his fingers, wanting more. She closed her eyes and concentrated on her children and Benjamin because this was betrayal, and she'd sinned enough. She moved her head away and cried out, 'I have to go now, please.' He bit down on her neck hard. She moaned, not from pain, but from a jolt of pleasure. Her cries made him loosen his hold, and her clammy hands slipped free from his grasp. She ducked under his arm and backed away.

'You can't say it, and I know why. I'll keep coming back, Mary. One day you will give yourself to me like you used to.'

Gulping air to steady her breath, she turned and stumbled away, his hard laughter stalking her as she fled. At the edge of the woods, she tripped, knocking the breath from her body as she hit the ground, grazing her hands and arms that she splayed out before her, tearing her skirt, and scraping the skin off one knee. Not stopping, she rose and hobbled back to the stream, gathered up the wet garments, stuffed them haphazardly into her basket, and limped towards the farmhouse.

She shuddered. Was he watching from the woods? Did she say no to him? She couldn't even remember.

Chapter 36

Inside the barn, Benjamin stumbled against a metal bucket that lurked in a dark corner and sent it clattering along the earth floor. Further into the gloomy corner, he came across a jumbled heap of tools and flicked them with his foot. Then he found it, discarded like a piece of worthless junk. Well, it wasn't. Its qualities were not obvious until he held it, hefted the weight of it in his hands. Until he used it. For his next job, there was none better. He picked up his favourite shovel, groped his way back to his wheelbarrow, and wheeled it out into the stubble field.

At the bottom of the field, he gazed at the dung piled into heaps and covered in straw, steaming gently, the vapour rising and merging with the morning mist that swathed the hedges. A plentiful supply, about three hundred wheelbarrows, enough to spread over the field. He sniffed. It no longer stank of fresh manure; it smelt like dirt.

He removed his jacket and slung it into the hedge, where it caught. He rolled up his shirt sleeves. It was going to be a long, hard, grimy job. Dirt would be ingrained in his skin, it would lodge under his fingernails, and it would stain his clothes. He hated the dirt, but he loved the job otherwise, loved making the soil fertile, loved the physical work. He thrust his shovel into the dung and threw the contents in the direction of the wheelbarrow until it was full, then he pushed it to the other end of the field, emptied it, and spread a thin layer over the soil. He spun the barrow around to return for more and paused.

Mist rose off the field like a ghostly apparition, and black rooks scattered only to land again farther up the field, their harsh cries filling the silence. He loved this life. It was good to be alive on a day like this, to work, to have everything he wanted at last. Well, nearly. There was still Mary, but he was getting close, so close he could feel it, could taste it. He ran up the field, pushing the wheelbarrow, and laughed so loud the rooks dispersed.

At midmorning, Elizabeth came towards him carrying a basket—his lunch, presumably. He waited by his barrow for her to approach. She smiled at him and blushed. *How could someone so beautiful be so shy?* Her silences he understood. He wasn't shy, but he didn't like speaking because he simply could never think of anything to say. He could think it in his head, but there it remained.

She held out the basket. 'Lunch. I can't believe you've got so much done already all by yourself.'

He nodded. 'Where's Mary? She usually brings this.'

'Oh, she's resting her foot. She slipped by the river.'

He tugged off his hat and ran a grubby hand through his hair. *Damn, he just spread the dirt further.* 'Is she hurt bad?'

'No. Scrapes and grazes, that's all. I'll leave you to it.'

He watched her go, her golden braid swinging down her back like twisted rope. Eliza was so like her but not in nature; Eliza wasn't shy or timid. He laughed. Not words he'd use to describe her at all.

***

AT THE END of the day, Benjamin washed his grubby hands and face at the pump in the yard and ducked his head under the freezing cold water for good measure, which made his skull numb and gave him an instant headache. He shook his head and rubbed his hands over his face to bring it back to life, then made his way to the kitchen door.

When he entered, he found Mary sat by the fire, feeding Mary Jane. He joined her on the settle. He shivered, held his hands towards the leaping flames, and leant closer to the blaze. His muscles unwound as the warmth wrapped itself around his body. He turned his head towards Mary. 'Are you well? I heard you fell.'

She held Mary Jane against her shoulder and stroked her back. 'It's nothing. I'm fine, just slipped on the wet stones, that's all.'

He leant towards her to brush the top of Mary Jane's head with his hand and noticed an ugly purple bruise on Mary's neck. He rubbed his thumb against it, and she jumped at his touch. 'Does it hurt?'

'No, don't worry. I feel nothing.'

The kitchen door burst open and slammed against the wall. Benjamin turned his head to see why. Mary's grandfather stomped in, clutching one arm to his chest. A dirty rag seeped in bright red blood was wrapped around his hand. 'I was making pig skewers, whittling the wood to a nice sharp point, when the knife slipped. Just caught my hand. It's nothing much.'

Mary thrust her daughter into Benjamin's arms. 'Let me see. Oh, Gramfer, not this dirty old rag. It needs something clean. And stitches. We need the bonesetter.'

Her grandfather muttered and mumbled, 'Everything always happens in threes. You, now me, and another person will be hurt tonight, I know it.'

Benjamin rose. 'I'll get someone to send for her.' Passing Mary Jane onto Elizabeth, he hurried outside.

***

IN THE WARM candlelit kitchen, Benjamin sat at the table and waited for Elizabeth to serve up the evening meal. Somebody was talking, but the waterfall of words became blurred. He couldn't focus, and his body was loose, slumped in a sleepy suspension of peace and quiet. Hard work did that to him. A loud noise brought him up with a jerk, and he blinked, struggling to make sense of where he was. He yawned and stretched out his back as the reason for his disturbance became clear.

The bonesetter had swept into the kitchen and discarded her coat by throwing it over the settle. She made her way to the old man sat at the table across from Benjamin. He greeted her warmly. 'Put the wood in the hole and come in and have a drop of warm.'

Benjamin watched her with his eyes half closed. She squeezed and squashed herself onto the bench seat, her immense breasts thrust up against the table, then she put a hand underneath each one, hoisting them up and letting them plop on top. She turned towards the old man. 'Let's have a look at this hand, then.'

The old man held out his hand covered in a blood-soaked cloth. She unwrapped it while Mary and Elizabeth joined them at the table, silently watching. 'Hmm. Needs a few stitches.' Reaching for her old battered bag, she laid out her tools on the table and set to work.

He was cleaned up, stitched up, and rebandaged, and he never moaned, never even flinched. Benjamin shook his head. Tough as old boots, that man. Beside him, Mary rocked Mary Jane to sleep, stroking her daughter's face with her fingertips. *If she ran her hand over his face like that, he'd be asleep in an instant.* He smiled, watching his daughter fight the sleep that would soon claim her.

Mary looked up at the bonesetter. 'Stay for supper, Grace. We've plenty.'

Grace lifted her head and sniffed like a dog. 'Is that mutton pie I can smell?'

'It is.'

'I know my pies.' She ran a tongue around her fleshy lips. 'I don't mind if I do.'

The old man clapped his hands together, then pulled a face as he remembered his stitches. He rubbed his bandaged hand. 'Let's have the gossip. You can talk and eat at the same time.'

Benjamin hoped she wouldn't. He hated people who opened their mouths to reveal partly chewed food. It would put him off eating.

Grace stroked her double chin. 'Well, now, I've got news of Sarah Landeryou. Calls herself Sarah Sobey now, though.'

The old man placed a hand on the bonesetter's chubby arm, his permanent smile dropping from his face. 'Is she well, happy?'

'Don't worry, she's doing fine. She's expecting a bairn.'

His beaming grin returned. 'Jimmery-Chry! They didn't waste any time. And she's happy?'

'She said so, and she looked it to me. I saw her smile.'

'Jimmery-Chry! I've never seen her smile.'

While plates of mutton pie circulated the table, Grace said, 'And have you heard that some sheep went missing from a farm at Higher Harlyn?'

'Oh, we heard 'bout that. Thomas Clemow told us on Sunday; he was that worried, he looked like a whitewashed wall.'

'Well, constables went to the house of Francis Bassett, he lives just outside Padstow. Know of him?'

''Course I do. He's worse than a flea to catch— never home, never anywhere. I can't believe they found him.'

'They didn't find him, but upstairs in his bedroom, they found a sheep's head, some legs, and a box of mutton tallow. Now he's married to the Carbis girl, isn't he, so they went to old man Carbis next.'

'Looking for the rest of them sheep, eh? Old man Carbis, as thin as a rake, and his wife is like a bundle of straw tied in the middle. A behind like a butter tub. Mind you, sheep stealing? I'd say his name's up for that.'

'His old lady said she was ill, too ill to leave her bed, so the constables had to lift her up.'

'Ooh, I'd like to have seen them try. It would take at least four of them.'

'In her bed, they found mutton and tallow. She was lying on it.'

'Squashed flat, no doubt.'

'Then they decided to go to the son's house, Carbis junior.'

'Strong in the hand but weak in the head. Back like a barn door and feet like half-crown shovels, but slow as a coach.'

'Guess what they found?'

'More legs, most likely.'

Grace paused to scoop up some steaming hot pie, and golden gravy dribbled down her chin.

The old man turned to the bonesetter again. 'So, Grace, what happened next?'

'All found guilty of sheep stealing and sentenced. To be transported to Australia.'

Mary drew a sharp intake of breath, and the old man's jaw fell open. He said, 'I know it's against the law, but they just need to feed their families. And now I suppose it will be the workhouse for the women and bairns. Gone to Australia. Well, I never.'

Grace took a slurp of tea. 'Don't worry. The men have all gone to sea, got a boat from Padstow.'

'I said he was like a flea to catch.'

Grace sighed. 'But it will still be the workhouse for the women and bairns. The bailiff has thrown them all out onto the street.'

Slices of heavy cake circulated the table. Benjamin liked this cake; the plump currants and fruity peel stuck to his ribs. He glanced up and caught the bonesetter staring at him, so he ducked his head down. When he stole another look, Grace was watching Mary, then Elizabeth. She shifted about in her seat and clenched and unclenched her hands. She opened her mouth but closed it again. She

287

hadn't touched her cake. She raised her head in his direction but dropped it quickly. Now she wouldn't look at him?

Grace cleared her throat. 'I know something else.'

Benjamin studied her. This piece of news was going to be important, but for some reason, a coldness had settled in the pit of his stomach.

'I spoke to the bailiff recently, and he was full of news. Wrote a letter a while back to the landlord, Charles Bathurst MP. Asked him to get his son released from the navy.'

Benjamin froze. He didn't want to hear this. He wished she hadn't come.

'Samuel Treleggan is alive, then?' The old man asked.

'Alive and back, but he's not returned to St Merryn. To get released, he had to join Customs as a gauger. He's a revenue man now, works from Bude to Porthcothan.'

Benjamin clutched at his chest, unable to breathe. A surge of anger rose from his stomach, cutting off his air. He squeezed the handle of his fork until his knuckles popped and the bitter taste of hate flooded his mouth. This couldn't be happening, just when he thought he was close, close enough to reach out and touch everything he'd ever dreamed of, only to find it slip, sliding away.

Did she know? She hadn't said a word or even made a sound. Fuck. She already knew.

Despair took root inside him. He could feel it. Solid. Spreading. Sickening.

Chapter 37

L ying with his eyes wide open, Benjamin stared into the dark bedroom and strained to think, his mind in chaos. Outside the wind shrieked and roared, and the bedroom window shook and rattled, crying out at the torture inflicted by the howling gale. He wanted to scream and bellow too, his head pounding with the pain it held.

Mary twitched beside him, one hand splayed across his chest, dreaming. *Of what? Of whom?* Neither of them had mentioned Samuel's name, but the echo of his presence hovered over them, unwelcome and uninvited.

Would she go to him if he asked her? Would she leave, take the children and leave? Could she strip him of everything when she knew it would destroy him? His hand curled into a fist as his heart cried out. He didn't know; he just didn't know.

Outside, the barn door blew shut with a loud bang, and something clattered and clanged in protest. The squall blasted gusts of disorder everywhere. It would rage all night until it was spent, drained, beaten. The insistent clanging continued, calling out over the frigid wailing wind. His muscles froze. He recognised that sound; that was the toll of a church bell, the signal of a ship in trouble, wrecked on the rocks.

He slid out of bed and tried not to wake Mary, but the minute her hand parted from his flesh, she woke up. She rubbed at her eyes and yawned. 'Where are you going'?'

'Harken. Hear that ringing? It's a sign. There's a ship in trouble. I'm going to take a look.'

She cocked her head, bleary-eyed, and her eyes grew wide. 'I hear it now, but the wind is so fierce. Oh, those poor souls out at sea tonight.'

'I have to go. See if I can help.'

He sat on the edge of the bed and pulled up his breeches, then pushed his feet into his boots. When he stood up again, Mary was getting dressed. 'Stay in bed.'

'No, I'm coming with you.'

'Oh no. Stay here. Stay with the bairns.'

'Jess can stay behind, and we'll lock the door. They're all asleep. I won't be gone long, but I have to go. I might be able to help.'

He sighed. When did she ever do what he asked? She was wilful and defiant, but it was what made her so alive, so damned vital. Samuel would squash those qualities in her. Why couldn't she see that?

She waited for him by the cottage door, her cloak wrapped about her body. He reached for his hat but let his empty hand drop as the wind beat at the door with angry fists. It was not a night for hats. He wrenched open the door, and a great blast of wind tore it from his hands and smashed it against the wall. He turned to Mary. 'Ready?'

She mouthed back, 'What?'

He raised his voice so she could hear above the storm. 'Ready?' He grabbed her hand and pushed Jess back inside, then forced the door shut behind them and locked it.

The morning light had begun to tentatively scatter the darkness, which was good because a lantern was useless in this weather. Head down, he battled his way to the cliff path while the wind clawed at his clothes. He tried to speak, but his words were tossed away. He stopped at the cliff edge, planted his feet apart, and drew Mary towards him. He held her tight as she struggled to keep her balance.

Out to sea, a hulking vessel rolled in the storm, battered and bludgeoned by wave after wave, driven onto the jagged rocks at Treyarnon Beach. It had six guns on board but space for at least twenty, her booms fitted with boarding spikes. He gave a sigh. Boarding spikes could only mean one thing, one dreadful thing. Her foremast was broken, hanging in a splintered, tangled mess of rigging, her canvas shredded and useless, her mizzen completely gone. She pitched and rolled insanely against the coffin-black, discoloured sky. Wild, frenzied waves exploded against her side, discharging high spumes of white foam. Down on the beach, villagers had already gathered, but the spoils from this wreck would not be plundered. He'd seen these French vessels before, their cargo always the same because the bastard French still traded from their Breton port dark-skinned slaves from places he couldn't even name.

He scrambled down the cliff path with Mary, where they found some shelter from the storm. The wind clawed at her skirts, made them swirl and swell in a frenzy. He turned to her white face, her hair a dark, billowing halo. He held her hands and said, 'Don't come with me. It's a slave boat. I can already see the bodies on the shore. I'll go down. It will be bad.' He screwed up his eyes for a moment, brought her hands to his lips, and kissed them. 'Stay. Don't leave.'

'I will, but be careful, please.'

He searched her face. Did she mean it? Would she stay with him?

No, she wasn't answering the question he'd really asked.

***

MARY REMAINED IN the lee of the cliff, watching Benjamin skid and slither down the stony slope. He jumped onto the sand, put his head down, and ran. The wind caught his coat, lifted it up high like a sail, and pushed him sideways as he raced across the beach. He reached the opposite end, near the cove where she'd learnt to swim, where she believed no one could ever drown. The angry tide charged in this time, reclaiming it, swallowing it up. A spray of white foam soared towards the sky as a wave hit her shell-covered rocks. She remembered it as placid, but this was not placid.

A chain of men waded into the rolling surf, tethered together by rope. She strained her eyes and made out bodies, tossed around like worthless flotsam by the white-capped waves. Bodies these men reached for and passed back to the shore, where they left them face down on the sand, arms stretched out straight. A dark fringe of corpses on the shoreline. She hugged her cloak about her. *Poor souls. How many would die tonight?*

Benjamin didn't join the string of men. He discarded his coat and waded into the turbulent water up to his waist, alone. He grabbed at bodies before they were smashed against the rocks. She twirled her wedding band around her finger and wanted to shout out, 'Take care,' but no one would hear, so she closed her eyes, unable to watch. He'd be safe. He could swim. He had to be safe.

She wrenched her head away to gaze at the sea in front of her. She often witnessed the sea angry and raging, but not like this. Tonight, it was violent and menacing. She wrinkled her nose. The stench from the seaweed thrown up the beach had a bite to it. Out at sea, dark knife-edged rocks jutted out of the water like broken teeth, black forbidding teeth tearing into the sea, ripping off mouthfuls and spitting them out in a spray of froth. Mary shuddered and turned away when a sudden movement caught her eye and made her pause. She frowned. *Was that a shape in the water?* No, it wasn't possible; the wreck was on the far side of the beach where the villagers were. It caught her eye again, and her gasp was snatched away by the wind. There it was, but what was it? A piece of the wreck or another body?

She crept further down the cliff path for a better view. Shielding her eyes with both hands, she fixed her gaze out to sea and tried not to blink in case she missed it. A body the size of a child's. It clung—no, it was tied down. To what looked like a piece of wood, caught in the seething swell, driven towards the serrated jaws of the dark rocks on this side of the beach.

She turned to stare across at Benjamin, her heartbeat picking up speed. But he wasn't looking her way. No one was. Why would they? They were all too busy collecting bodies. *Stay calm.* Her pulse increased, and her head throbbed with its beat. It called to her. *Do something. Do something. Do something. Get closer.* She stumbled down the rest of the path, her legs trembling and weak.

293

Once on the beach, the wind found her, screeching and howling like a wild banshee, malicious and unrestrained. Giving up with the struggle to hold her cloak down, she untied it and let it drop. The wind caught it up and carelessly threw it back against the cliff. Sea spray and sand lacerated her face, her eyes stung and filled with tears, and her mind raced. What now? What could she possibly do?

She fought her way to the water's edge, step by slow step. Pushing against the wind, her skirt stretched out behind her, her muscles screaming with the effort. She wiped at her streaming eyes. The child was clearly there, but death called for it, waiting to tear it to pieces. She gulped. It wasn't that far out, maybe waist deep, she could wade out like Benjamin. She could save it.

Mary glanced across the beach again and held her wind-whipped hair off her face. There was no time to run for help; it would be too late, far too late. She tilted her head back to look at the brooding sky. *Oh God, what shall I do?* She closed her eyes and let the keening wind pummel her face until it was numb. The sound became the wail of a baby, and the image of Elizabeth's dead son floated into her mind and refused to leave. So, this was it, this was God's purpose for her. She'd been waiting for it all these years.

Taking a deep breath, she hitched up her skirt and tucked it into her waistband, exposing pale flesh. Taking another gulp of air, she stepped forwards, her eyes focused on a point ahead. She caught her breath as the water seeped over her boots and smacked her legs. Shivering, she held her arms around her body and clutched her stomach. Tears clouded her vision. She shook them away.

Up to her knees, the sea boiled and seethed in fury, a whirlpool of destruction. She clamped her mouth shut, but a scream swelled up inside her. *Breathe, just breathe. When I take a breath, I can't sink.* Her shoulders rose and fell as she steadied herself and kept going, dragging slim, heavy legs through the water. Past her knees and up to her waist, the breakers pounded her body, rising up before her like a wall. They crashed down on top of her, lifting her off her feet and knocking her breathless, coughing, and spluttering. She turned her head to look back at the shore. So far away. Her wet clothes clung to her, pulled her down like a great burden. Her body shook, and she started to cry. She wanted Benjamin. Wanted him to come and rescue her. She couldn't do this; she wasn't strong enough.

She took one last look out to sea, and the child surfaced, its eyes open wide, its mouth frozen in a silent scream. Still alive. A surge of tenderness swamped her, gave her strength in its fierceness. If she didn't try to save it, her past would forever haunt her, and she would never be free. She had to make amends. God was testing her.

Mary took more faltering steps further into the deep until she stretched out a hand, twisted her body, and forced one arm as far forwards as possible. Her outstretched fingers scraped against the child's makeshift raft. Grabbing onto it, she clung on, her muscles straining to hold it against the current.

The child—a boy, of course it was a boy—lay naked, tied facedown. He frantically twisted and turned his hands, fighting to free himself. She reached for the cords to prise them loose, the knots slippery in her deadened fingers as she wrenched and tugged at his hands, not caring that his skin was rubbed raw and bloody, pulling until the cords slid free. He slithered off the raft and wrapped his arms and legs around her body, clinging on like a limpet. A wave claimed the raft, tore it from her grasp, and dragged it on a voyage towards destruction. It splintered with a deafening crack against the rocks.

Turning her back to the surf, she opened her arms wide to keep her balance, to let the full force of the waves carry her back to the shore, but her legs dragged in the sand, and her body slumped from the child's fierce embrace. It would be easier, far easier, if he was on her back. She couldn't see, and she needed to keep away from the black rocks. She clutched his hands to pull them free, but his grip increased. He stared at her with swollen round eyes and shook his head hysterically.

A wave struck her back, pitching her forwards, off balance. Her feet scrabbled for traction but found nothing. She put her hands out in front of her, but the water offered no resistance and she fell. The wave crashed down on her head and pushed her under, pinned her down, spun her around. Her ears filled with a deafening roar. Her hands clawed for the surface but found nothing. Her held breath made her lungs burn, her chest about to explode. Her stomach pitched and rolled, and the darkness behind her eyelids changed from black to purple as her body jerked in its search for air.

A hand circled her wrist and hauled her to her feet. She surfaced and gulped great lungfuls of air.

'What the hell are you doing?'

Mary didn't even try to answer, could only cough and retch at the taste of salty water that hit her stomach. She ran a hand over the boy's face, and his eyelashes fluttered against her palm.

Benjamin dragged her to the shore, not stopping until they were free of the water, then he let her go, bent double, and fought to draw breath.

She spluttered and collapsed onto the sand, her arm retaining the red imprint of his clenched fingers.

Resting his hands on his knees, Benjamin raised his head and tried to speak, 'What . . .' Dropping his head, he sucked in more air and tried again. 'What the hell?'

'I had to save him. You know why. I had to.'

'Oh, Mary. Well, give him to me. I'll take him to the others.'

She shook her head and hugged the boy close. 'No, he's never going back to that life. I won't do it.' She reached up for Benjamin's hand and drew his fingers across the child's back, across the raised flesh that crisscrossed his skin.

Benjamin gritted his teeth and walked off.

Resting her cheek on the boy's head, she cried. Her sobs turned into shakes she couldn't control. The child in her arms also shivered violently. The wind's icy fingers wrapped around her like a wintry shawl, searching for her last reserves of body heat. She needed to stand, to get them both home, but her muscles were stiff, unmoving, her hands unfamiliar, not responding to her commands. They were so white, they were almost blue as if drained of blood.

Her cloak landed around her neck. Benjamin grasped her elbows and pulled her to her feet. He tied the cloak around her and the child, then added his own coat to her shoulders. 'You have to get home. Get warm. Your lips are blue.' Holding onto her, he guided her home.

Her feet were clumsy and made her stumble as she continued to shake, her teeth clicking together, unstoppable, uncontrollable. She didn't have power over her own body, tripping over her numb feet, the cold gnawing at her stomach.

Once in the cottage, Benjamin helped her to the fireplace, where she sank with the boy in her lap, her eyes closed, too heavy to open. Her heart leapt at the familiar clink, clink, clink of flint on steel and then the roar of the fire. She edged nearer, her skin hungry for warmth.

Benjamin left but soon returned with sheets and blankets. He prised the boy from her, dried him off, wrapped him like a package, and tucked him up, placing him on the floor beside Jess.

''C'mon, Mary. Get out of these wet clothes.'

She sighed as he helped her shed her clinging, cold garments. Slumped by the fire, the warmth overcame her, and the heat sank painfully into her body. A tingle ran through her hands and feet, which grew to a stabbing pain. At least she could feel them now. A groan beside her made her turn her head. Benjamin struggled to undo the laces of his boots. His fingers were uncoordinated and shaky.

'Oh God, let me help you. You're still freezing cold.' She pushed aside his icy fingers, but her swollen hands couldn't grasp the laces. Bending, she gripped them in her teeth, undid the knots and freed his feet, then yanked his shirt over his head. He joined her by the fire, and they shared a blanket. Sat without moving, without speaking, without thinking. Soaking up the heat, his arms wrapped around her. Her eyelids drooped again, safe at last.

'He may come looking for him.'

Her eyes snapped open. 'Who's he?'

'The captain. He was looking for him on the beach. Says he belongs to him. He may come looking.'

Mary stared into his eyes. 'He can't have him, not ever.'

Benjamin stared back at her for a long while. She'd do this without him if she had to, but she didn't want to. He closed his eyes and frowned. 'We may have to hide him.'

Jess raised her head and whined, unwound herself, and left the boy curled up fast asleep. She padded to the cottage door.

'I believe they're coming.'

'We have to do something.' Tears welled up in her eyes, and she thumped her fist on the floor. She couldn't take much more tonight. She wanted to sleep, to rest.

'Get dressed. I'll deal with this.' Benjamin ran for the bedroom.

Jess barked at the door and faced it, a low rumbling growl erupting from her belly. Mary left the boy sleeping and ran to the bedroom, but getting dressed took forever. *Stupid fingers. Come on, go faster.*

When she left the bedroom, she found Benjamin knelt beside the fireplace. He pushed at a protruding wall with his shoulder. 'This fireplace is larger 'cause it has a secret hiding hole. A place to stash ankers of moonshine. It's empty now. The boy will fit inside.'

'Let me see.' She ran over to have a look. It was such a small, dark hole. A crawling space, cramped and stuffy. 'Can he breathe in here?'

'Yes. Won't be for long.'

She pinched her lip with her fingers. 'He'll be scared. It's dark, and there's no room to move. It will be like a grave.'

'He's asleep.' He raised his head. 'We have no choice. Pass him to me.'

A loud hammering on the door made Mary jump and stifle a scream.

'Quick. Pass him over.'

She gathered up the sleeping boy. He had fine jet-black eyelashes, and the firelight dancing across his nut-brown skin made it glow like a copper kettle. Brushing her lips across the top of the boy's head, she passed him to Benjamin. Benjamin pushed the false wall back into place whilst the pounding continued on the door. He stood up and nodded at her, then walked to the door.

Mary perched on a chair beside the fire with her heart thumping. She turned towards the door when Benjamin called out, 'Who's there?' She couldn't hear the muffled response, only the jarring rattle of bolts being drawn back.

Benjamin stood in the open doorway, one hand on the low lintel, the other on his hip. These doorways were low to make it difficult for unwanted callers to barge their way in, but how many men were outside? Would they be armed? She plucked at the sleeve of her dress and squirmed to get a better look.

Benjamin thrust out a hand to hold back a squat, sturdy torso. 'Not him. Not the captain. He's not welcome in my home.' He shoved the body backwards, then stood aside to let someone else duck under and enter the room. He closed and latched the door.

A revenue man unfurled his body and stood erect, his long dark coat glinting with sea spray. *That had to be a fake smile pinned to his face.* His empty eyes swept the room before falling on her. He removed his hat and walked over. 'Sorry to disturb you, mam, but we're just asking around to see if anyone's seen a boy. A blackamoor from the slave ship.'

Benjamin stood feet apart, his arms crossed and head lowered. 'I was on the beach tonight, hauling in the dead bodies. How could a boy survive that?'

'To be honest with you, it isn't possible. But the captain out there is hell-bent on finding him. We've found every other slave, most dead, I'm sorry to say. It's a bad business.' He twirled his hat in his hands, and his eyes roved over the heap of wet clothes. 'Just to keep the man quiet, do you mind if I take a look around?'

'Yes. I mind.'

Mary jumped up. 'He can have a quick look, Benjamin. Won't take him long. There's not much to look at and nothing to find.' She threw out an arm and cast it around the room. 'Nothing here. Come and look in the chambers, but be quiet, my bairns are asleep.'

The revenue man nodded and sidestepped around a scowling Benjamin while Mary kept her breathing even and reached out a hand to open her bedroom door. The revenue man held onto the doorpost with one hand, the door with the other. He leant his lean body forwards and moved his head to-and-fro before he left.

Mary walked across to her children's bedroom and put a finger to her lips. 'Shh, my bairns.' She stepped in, holding the door open.

He leant in, and his thin lips curved into a slow smile. The girls lay curled up together, fast asleep. Eliza's golden hair entwined with Mary Jane's dark curls. But his eyes darted to every corner of the room. 'How old?'

'Two and three.'

He closed the door quietly behind him. Mary exhaled. *Surely, he would leave now.* Benjamin waited at the door, ready to open it for him, when Jess paced to the fireplace and scratched at the floor, whining. Mary drew in her breath, dug her fingernails into the palm of her hand, and swallowed hard.

'Jess!' Benjamin called out, but she continued to paw the floor.

The revenue man rubbed at his chin and turned to give Mary a long, intense look. Unflinching, she returned his gaze, raising her chin defiantly, but held her breath when he walked towards the fireplace, rested his hand on the lintel, and cocked his head, listening. Jess whined and leant against him, pushing at his legs.

'You're standing in her spot. Where she likes to sleep,' Benjamin called out.

The revenue man gave a small smile and made his way back to Benjamin. 'The captain of the slave ship will be gone by the morning. Back to France, I believe. Looks like without the boy. Damned Frenchies. Give me another Waterloo to put them in their place. I'm glad he can't find the boy.' He nodded at her, then Benjamin, and waited for the door to open.

Once he'd left, Benjamin leant his forehead on the door. He swivelled his head in her direction, and grinned. 'They've gone. I can hear them leaving.'

She rushed to the fireplace, tapping the wall, impatient for Benjamin to open the cache.

He pulled out the child and handed him to her. 'See? Still fast asleep.'

Tucking a hand inside the blanket, she reached for his chest. His heartbeat drummed against her palm. She swayed, and Benjamin caught her.

'Go to bed now. God knows I need to.'

She brought the boy into their bed and placed him beside her. If he woke in the night, confused and frightened, she would be there for him, would always be there for him. Benjamin gave a long yawn, which made her do the same. 'Benjamin?'

'Hmm?'

'He was tied to a piece of wood. Why?'

'A whipping post, I believe. Saved his life.'

She rubbed at her eyes and tried not to cry. 'Do you think he has a name?'

'Dunno. Probably given a French one. Maybe he only speaks French.'

'I'm going to give him a new name. Abednego.'

'After Gramfer?'

'Yes. We'll just call him Abe; it will be easy for him to say.'

'Abe, it is.'

'I believe he's about six years old.'

Benjamin stirred beside her. 'Six? A boy of six?'

'Yes, a scarred, strange-looking boy of six.'

Benjamin gripped her hand and shuddered. She couldn't stop her tears. He sniffed. 'My son. We have a son now.'

'We do. Thank you, Benjamin.'

'Me? It wasn't me that did anything; it was you.'

'You saved us. I won't forget it.'

She drifted off to sleep, fretting about the child.

Did he have any memories of his parents? Of his home? Perhaps if he pined for it, if he remembered it was where he'd last received love and tenderness, then he'd know. He was home at last.

Chapter 38

In the farmhouse kitchen, Mary turned the crank on the butter churner one more time, then had to let go and give her aching arm a quick shake. Wiping her brow, she swapped hands and continued churning when a piercing scream made her wince, followed by the clattering drumbeat of wooden spoons that ricocheted off the backs of chairs. She tilted her head to look out through the open dairy door and into the kitchen. Small feet pounded on the stone floor, and arms flailed wildly, round and round the kitchen table. She was dizzy just watching.

Abe scampered past, doing yet another circuit of the table, and she caught sight of his dusky skin, hair the colour of pitch, coal-black eyes, and a beaming, infectious smile. Her lips twitched. He was full to the brim with joy, that boy. Full of life, he never stopped moving, not even when asleep. He was alive, and he made sure everyone knew it. He'd been with them a month now, a noisy, nonstop, much-loved member of the family.

She peeked inside the barrel at the chunks of creamy yellow butter now stuck to the paddles, and poured the thin, pale liquid left at the bottom into a cold jug. She walked across the kitchen towards Elizabeth. 'I've got the buttermilk for your biscuits at last.' She stopped midstride and held the jug up high as Abe and Eliza raced past her legs, their hands brushing against her shins.

305

Abe skidded to a halt in front of the old man who slept beside the fire and poked him with a spoon before jumping away. Abe and Eliza crept back for more. Whispering and giggling together, braver this time. A deafening roar made Mary jump as her grandfather exploded from his chair and reached for the squealing, wriggling children.

The kitchen door swung open, and Benjamin stood in the entrance, holding his hands over his ears. 'I can hear you out in the field.'

Abe ran to him and clung to his legs, stuck like a burr. Mary paused to watch them. Abe would often cry out in the middle of the night, and she would go to him to be his anchor when he tossed and turned. But sometimes he fought her off and ran screaming for Benjamin. She sighed. She understood that she was occasionally part of his nightmare of nearly drowning below crashing waves; she had those dreams herself, and when she woke, dripping with sweat, her heart racing, it was Benjamin she reached for too. She'd watched them together one night through the half-closed door as Benjamin returned Abe to his bed. Abe had traced Benjamin's scar with his fingertips, tracked it from top to bottom. Benjamin didn't flinch, didn't even close his eyes. She never saw anyone else do that. He'd never even let her do that.

Now, Benjamin clutched Abe in his arms, then turned him upside down, pretending to drop him on his head. Eliza and Mary Jane queued for their turn.

She shouted to be heard above the din, 'Are me and Elizabeth the only ones working today?'

'No. I've come for Abe. Going to teach him about driving the oxen.'

Mary's grandfather swivelled in his seat. 'Oh, you ploughing in the muck today, then?'

'Yes, Gramfer. But first . . .' He eased Mary Jane onto the floor and stood with his hands on his hips. The children stared up at him, breathless with anticipation, hopping from foot to foot. 'But first . . .' He leant towards them. 'A game of mop-and-heedy.'

Mary huffed and rubbed a hand across her forehead. 'Oh, Benjamin, really? There's so much work to be done. There isn't time for that.'

'One quick game. Just one. Then back to work.'

She rolled her eyes at him.

'And we're all playing. All of us.'

'No, not me. I've too much to do, and so has Lizzie.'

'I've got time for one game.' Elizabeth untied her apron and held a flour-dusted hand out to Mary Jane. 'We'll hide together.'

'Are you playing, Gramfer?'

''Course I is. I'll help the children find a place. I know a good one.' He tapped the side of his nose and scurried for the door.

The room cleared instantly. Footsteps thumped up the stairs and pounded across the bedroom floors. Benjamin shouted up after them, 'I'll count to thirty.'

She glanced at him and shrugged. 'At least I've got some peace and quiet now. At least I can get some work done.'

'You have to hide.'

'What? I can't. I have to finish in the dairy.'

307

He walked towards her and put his hands on her shoulders. 'Have some fun. Just a few minutes.' Turning his back, he counted. 'One, two, three . . .'

Oh, this was just ridiculous. She scanned the room. What if she hid in the pantry? He'd find her first, then she could go back to work.

'. . . eight, nine, ten . . .'

She opened the pantry door, made sure it creaked and groaned so he knew where she was, and went inside. She left the door ajar to give her some light.

'. . . fifteen, sixteen, seventeen . . .'

Her eyes roved the shelves. Bottled fruit on the top, pickled vegetables in the middle, and homemade jams on the bottom. They stood to attention, arranged along the shelves according to colour from bleached white pickled eggs to dark purple plums and cherries. She rubbed a finger along a cold glass jar gleaming in the narrow slant of light, checking for dust. Lifting her finger to her face, she nodded in approval.

'. . . twenty-one, twenty-two, twenty-three . . .'

Mary tutted when she found some jars out of position. She reached across to nudge them straight and leant against the cold, hard wall, twiddling her apron strings, tapping her foot. Waiting.

'. . . twenty-eight, twenty-nine, thirty.'

Benjamin pushed open the pantry door, and she gave him a lopsided smile. 'I—'

He put a finger to her lips, squeezed inside, and closed the door behind him, obliterating all light. He leant his warm body against hers, and his hands brushed the sides of her face as he placed them on the wall behind her head.

She drew in a gulp of air and held it.

He brought his face beside hers, and his breath quivered deliciously against her skin. He moved his mouth close, grazing her cheek with his lips.

She dared not move, dared not breathe as her own mouth watered. Was he going to kiss her? It was the one thing they never did, the one thing she longed to do—to taste him. *Kiss me, please kiss me.* She closed her eyes and tilted her face up for him. His lips hovered, brushing against her own. Delicately, faintly, they whispered over hers. Her chest heaved, and she stretched out her fingertips to graze the seam of his trousers. Her lips parted, and she breathed him in, his sweet, sweet smell of grassy hay. All her nerve endings tingled and arched towards him.

'Ready, Da?' Footsteps ran above her head. 'Da!'

And he was gone.

She let out a small cry and ran her fingers over her mouth. A shudder ran through her, and she lost her balance, reaching out a hand which collided with her glass jars, making them chime together in protest. She picked up a jar of bottled cherries from the top shelf and turned it this way and that in her hand. The plump, juicy fruit looked like jewels, little treasures stored in a chest.

Smiling, she dumped it beside a jar of green pickled runner beans and let herself out, not noticing the disorder.

***

BENJAMIN HOISTED A giggling Mary Jane onto his shoulders and waited until her fingers ran through his hair, bunching up around a handful of his curls before he made his way downstairs. As he jumped down each step, her hiccupping laughter rippled through him.

He pushed his way into the kitchen and set her down on the floor, glancing up as the door to the dairy opened and Mary came out, wiping her hands on her apron. He caught her eye and gave a tentative smile. She blushed, she actually blushed, tucking a wayward strand of hair behind her ear. *Oh, Mary, I'm not giving you up without a fight. Not ever.*

The kitchen door banged open behind him, and a voice bellowed out, 'How is everyone?'

He tore his gaze away from Mary and turned to face the bonesetter. She kicked the door shut with the heel of her boot, making the door rattle in its frame, and stood with her feet apart, her hands on her wide hips, her oversized brown coat held open by her elbows. He was in awe; he was so mundane compared to her superhuman presence.

'How's this little man doing? Grown two inches already, I believe.'

Abe shrank behind Benjamin's legs, hiding his face in his trousers. Benjamin wished he could hide too. From the way the bonesetter stared, it was obvious she'd come for him.

Mary sidled up beside Benjamin and rested her hand on his shoulder. His muscles unclenched at her touch. 'He's a bundle of energy, never stops, and we don't even know what he's saying most of the time.'

'Well, send him to Aunt Dale's. You know she runs the village shop, and she now runs a school.'

'She likes her snuff, that old maid,' the old man piped up, unable to be left out of any conversation. 'She'd skin a flea for a farthing. Plain as a pikestaff too.'

'The children like her.'

Mary gave Benjamin's shoulder a squeeze. 'Why not? He doesn't have to work on the farm, not yet. Can we send him to school, Benjamin? Let him be a child for as long as possible?'

Benjamin swallowed. She had asked his permission as if he really had the power to decide. He smiled and nodded, but no words would come out. Instead, he raised his chin and pushed back his shoulders.

Abe gave up hiding and sprang forwards, prancing up and down the kitchen with a high-pitched neigh as he pawed the ground with his foot. Grace tilted her head to one side, watching Abe, her chest heaving. Benjamin watched the bonesetter. He watched her chest rise up. He watched it fall back. He dropped his gaze. He shouldn't be trying to imagine what lay beneath, restrained, waiting to burst free.

The old man called out again, 'Take a seat, Grace, rest your bones.'

'I will, but I can't stay long. I came for Benjamin.'

His heart skipped a beat. He knew it. He just knew it.

The bonesetter ambled to the old oak settle and lowered herself down. It creaked and groaned in disapproval whilst she fidgeted and wriggled to get comfortable. Rolls of fat burst out from wherever they'd been held prisoner as she undid her waistcoat and sank back. She brought her meaty arms around her chest and twiddled her thumbs.

Mary handed the bonesetter a cup of tea, which she balanced on her protruding bosom, using it as a table. Benjamin waited for Mary to take a seat beside the fire, then he perched on the arm of her chair and trailed his hand across the back, reaching for her hair to twine the strands around his fingers, waiting.

'I need a favour. King George has decided that suicides can now be buried inside the churchyard; they don't need to be left by the gibbet anymore. So, I've had a word with the vicar about moving Jenny.' Grace looked at Mary as she spoke.

Mary drew in a sharp breath. 'Did he say yes?'

'Not at first, no, but I know how to make him say yes. The gravedigger will have a grave ready tomorrow, but I can't get her parents to help, not with this. They're still broken. I need someone to go to the crossroads with me and dig her up. It has to be done at night; I promised the vicar I'd keep it quiet. I thought perhaps Benjamin might help me if he's willing.'

Oh, hell no. Benjamin arranged his face into a smile and managed to nod at her.

'Thank you. I knew you would agree.' Grace smiled back at him.

'I'll help too if you want.'

'No, Mary, no need for that. We'll be just fine.'

Mary leant against Benjamin. 'I do thank you for doing this. It means so much to me.' She wiped at her eyes with her sleeve.

He dropped his head, unable to look at her. Of course, he would help. He owed it to Jenny. Mary didn't know why he had to do this, but the bonesetter did. He was sure of that.

That was why she'd asked him.

***

LATER THAT NIGHT, Benjamin pulled his hat down low and the collar of his coat up high, but still the icy fingers of

312

the night found him, gripping him by the throat. In the gathering gloom, he swung a lantern in his left hand and held a spade against his right shoulder like a rifle, his cold breath a foggy vapour when he exhaled. Marching to the sound of his own heavy breathing, his eyes darted, watching the shadows sneaking like thieves around him. When he reached the bleak moors, a spiteful breeze stalked him. Heather and bracken, rough and course, snagged at his trousers. The few trees that dared to take root here were misshapen and stunted, bent over from the force of the winds that tore across this desolate, exposed landscape.

He glanced up at the coffin-black sky, pricked with diamond stars. What would a body buried for three years look like now? He shook his head and shivered again. He didn't know and wished he didn't have to find out.

Nearing the crossroads, his pace slowed, but the rate of his breathing increased. Up ahead, the outstretched arm of the gallows, stark and menacing against the brooding skyline, pointed at him, and the hairs on the back of his neck stood up in alert. The nebulous shape of a tall, black-hooded, forbidding figure slouched against the gibbet post. He caught the glint of an implement in its fleshless hands. He backed away, stumbling, unable to turn his back on it, but the figure swung its head in his direction and held out a bony finger, gesturing for him to come closer. His imagination was getting the better of him. It was this place, this place where they'd hanged his father. He closed his eyes and swallowed hard. He couldn't escape now, not now he'd been seen. He dropped his head, then his spade, and dragged it along the uneven ground behind him. Bump, bump, bump, he edged nearer.

The black-cloaked form pushed itself off the gibbet and advanced towards him. It came to a stop, and they faced each other. A biting wind circled and wailed around them, lifting and flapping an edge of the funereal cloak.

'Don't be afraid.'

'I'm not,' he managed to stammer.

'Good, you've nothing to fear from the dead. But still, this is a godforsaken place. Are you ready?'

Benjamin nodded and held his lantern up high to identify the place where Jenny was buried. He walked over to a small mound and frowned. Was this it? He didn't want to dig up the wrong bloody body; he had to get this right.

A voice behind his head muttered, 'This is the place.'

When he put the lantern on the floor, the pool of flickering yellow light was not much to go by, but it would do. He pulled his neckerchief over his mouth and nose—no telling what foul odours might be released—and started to dig.

He grunted with the effort, the ground hard and unyielding, but he was expecting that. He shoved the sharp-edged blade deep into the soil, gouging off the top layer of earth. The scrape of soil against metal and his soft grunts that came in time with each thrust of the spade were all devoured by the vagrant, shrieking wind.

He piled the soil up in a neat row on the edge of the grave as he worked. Once the compacted, stony top layer was removed, the digging became easier, but he didn't pause for a rest. He didn't dare. He wanted this done, to get away. He stopped only to discard his coat, to lay it down on the cold ground before jumping back into the hole. Then his spade hit something hard. Frowning, he scooped the

314

earth away with his gloved hands until he found the wooden stake. Still solid, still whole. He'd forgotten about that bloody thing. It meant he was getting close though, that he had the right grave. A finger of sweat trickled down his forehead and curled along his ear. He brushed it away with the back of his hand. He slowed his pace now, every spade of earth bringing him nearer to revealing—what?

It was her ribcage first, the stake driven right through where a beating heart would lie, the bones splintered around it. The bones were not white but creamy; no flesh remained, just flesh-coloured bones. He tugged at his neckerchief to release his mouth and sighed with relief. The worms and maggots had done their job well and picked her clean. She was just bones. She wasn't Jenny. He knelt and used his gloved hands to scrape away more soil, his breath coming easier now.

Dear God! He let out a cry and jumped up. He'd unearthed her skull. Spidery strands of copper hair still lay across dirt-filled eye sockets that crawled with worms. And the teeth, *oh hell*, the teeth remained. He closed his eyes and pictured her vital elfin face and shuddered. Bile surged from the pit of his stomach, and he gulped it down, bent double to hold it in. This was his fault; he couldn't run from the truth anymore. Acid hit the back of his throat, and he retched. He wiped his mouth on his glove. When a hand clamped on his shoulder, he jerked upright.

'Take a rest. There's no hurry. She's not going anywhere without us. Anyway, we need to talk.'

Talk? Why? No, he didn't want to talk. He could never find the words when it didn't matter, so how would he summon them now it did? Thinking curbed his tongue, and anyway, he never gave away what was going on inside his head. He dragged his legs to the lip of the pit and hauled himself up to sit on the edge. Resting his elbows on his knees, his head sank into his hands. He rubbed frantically at his scar.

Feet rustled through the short grass beside him, and from the corner of his eye, he caught a swirl of black. 'I'll tell you what I know first, shall I? Jenny came to see me before she died. She told me everything. Told me who did it and gave me his name. She was expecting his bairn. She said I was the only one that knew, but you knew too, didn't you?'

He groaned and nodded.

'Tell me.'

He was silent for a long time, fumbling for the words, forcing the voice inside his head to use his mouth and be heard. He drew some slow, deep breaths and let his gaze travel to the skull. 'I went to the woods to release the rabbits caught in the gin traps. They sound so human when they scream. I could never bear the sound. But what I found wasn't rabbits. I found Jenny. Saw it happen. Did nothing. Nothing because I was too afraid to do something.'

'But what could you do? If you'd been seen, he would've killed you. If you'd said anything, no one would've believed you. You would have lost the cottage for sure, and he still might have killed you.'

'I did nothing. Nothing! She's dead because I did nothing.' He shook his head. 'I watched without really seeing. Closed my mind to it. But I can't close my heart. I can't stop feeling even if I don't want to feel.'

Feet shuffled closer. 'He's been seen around the farm.'

His head sank into his hands again. 'Oh hell. I knew it.'

'He's been talking. He's planning to ask Mary to go away with him. He wants Mary back. But I don't believe he really wants her. This isn't about her, it's about you. He believes you were the traitor. It was you that got him arrested, planned it all so you could have Mary. He blames you, and now he wants revenge. He said no one does that to him and gets away with it. He wants to destroy you.'

'It wasn't even me!'

'I know. I know because it was me that did it.'

He twisted round to stare up at the bonesetter. 'You! You did that?'

'I did. He was never meant to come back, though.'

'Well, at least you tried.'

'Now it's your turn. You must tell Mary what you know. Warn her, let her know what he's really like.'

Benjamin jumped back into the pit, straddling the bones so he could stand up and face her. She towered above him, shrouded in the black cloak, the hood covering her face. She leant her soft bulging body against her shovel and focused her unsettling gaze on him. He shook his head at her. 'I can't tell her. She'd hate me for it. She won't believe me. I'll lose her. I was dead before my life with her. Now I'm alive. I can't risk it.'

'You'll likely lose her if you do nothing, so do something, and do it now. You have to warn her, and although terrible words will be said, the words will drift away, and love will always remain.'

'But she doesn't love me. I need more time.'

'It's too late. Mary needs to know the truth. You have to save her.'

317

Benjamin dug his nails into the scar on his face until it hurt. 'I'll warn her. I won't just stand by and do nothing. Not anymore. But I won't beg. I've done my best. If she still loves him, still goes to him . . .' He took a deep breath. 'I'll let her go, and I will leave.'

Chapter 39

B enjamin pulled and lifted a clump of potatoes out of a ridge of soft, sandy soil, brushed them clean with his gloved hand, and dropped them into his wheelbarrow. He reached for the next stalk and paused, his hand clenched as the bonesetter's remarks surfaced again, uninvited. No matter how hard he tried to bury those words, his mind always unearthed them, scooped them out and delivered them up, waiting for him to do something with them. He'd lain awake every night trying to string meaningful sentences together, words with the power to reach out and bind Mary to him. Instead, they wrapped around his throat until he choked.

He gazed across the field of undulating soil and watched the unruly wind lift a fallen heap of autumn leaves, flaming reds and burnt browns. They leapt in a spinning vortex before the wind moved on, cuffing his face as it passed by. The leaden sky sucked the colour out of the day, and without the blustery wind, this morning would be lifeless and monochrome. God, he hated not knowing what to do, not knowing what others were going to do. Had he got this far only to lose it all? He shook off a glove and wiped at his eyes. Just grit, blown up from the sandy soil. Just grit.

He glanced at his full wheelbarrow. What if he wheeled this load back to the barn and dropped into the kitchen on the way? What if he told Mary they needed to talk? Not now, but later. Then he'd have to face this shadow, this black cloud threatening to ruin his life.

Leaving the barrow in the yard, he walked to the farmhouse and pushed open the kitchen door. Stamping on the mat inside, he closed the door quietly behind him. Looking up, his breath froze.

Mary had her back to him, but she spun around to face him. As she turned, her blood-red cloak whirled around her like leaves caught in an eddy of wind. She frowned. 'What's up with you?'

He dragged out a breath, 'Are you going somewhere?'

'No.' She patted her cloak. 'I mean, yes. Back home. I forgot something.'

'What?'

'Just something I need.'

'What?'

'Does it matter?'

He nodded. *Oh yes, it mattered.* The metal jaws of a vise clamped around his chest and squeezed the air out of his lungs. He put a hand to his heart and drew a breath. So, the time had come. Whether he wanted it or not, it was now. Decision time for both of them, but he wasn't ready.

She stood staring at him, and all his carefully chosen sentences abandoned him. He rubbed at his temple, at his scar. He strove to think, but an intruder took possession of his mind. He searched for the words but found none. In desperation, he blurted out, 'Don't go. Please don't go.'

'What?'

'Don't leave me. I couldn't bear it. You're the only one that knows me. You see the person inside. The person no one else sees. You do see me, don't you?'

She bent her head and studied the floor for a few heartbeats, then raised her face. 'You don't know if I'll go or stay? Don't you know me by now?'

He hung his head. 'I don't. You never say.'

'Oh, Benjamin, really. I don't have time for this now. We'll talk about this later; it's time we did.' She took a step towards the door.

He leant his back against it, his arms outstretched, his palms pressed against the warm wood grains, and just said it. 'If you love me, or ever could love me, say it. Say it now.'

Her brow creased. She opened her mouth to speak, but the door handle rattled behind him and pushed him forwards as Elizabeth sidled into the kitchen. She stopped before a wall of stifling silence. No one moved. The seconds dragged by. Then Mary swished her hood over her head, pushed past Elizabeth, and was out the door.

He still didn't move.

'Were you arguing?'

He shrugged, rubbing a hand across his closed eyes, across his scar. *Fuck, that's not how it was supposed to go.* He'd cornered her like an animal. Made demands. But he'd said nothing, told her nothing. The bonesetter's words hammered at his skull. *Do something, and do it now. Save her.* He opened his eyes. 'I have to go after her.' He bolted for the door.

Benjamin skidded to a halt in the yard. She wasn't there, but he caught a flash of scarlet moving towards the woods, running. He lowered his head and sprinted after her.

321

She was fast, nearly at the edge of the woods when he called out to stop her. 'Mary, wait!'

Breathless, they faced each other. She stood at the edge of the woods, a blaze of colour against the dark canopy of trees. Their gnarled limbs twisted towards her, reaching for their prize.

He stood outside in the grey, washed-out light, clenching and unclenching his fists. 'I have to tell you. To let you know.'

She waited, panting. Said nothing.

'He's telling everyone I got him arrested by the gaugers. That I did it just to get him out of the way so I could have you.'

'He might be right.'

'He isn't. But what matters is that he hates me. He always has. Now he wants revenge. He wants to destroy me by taking you. This is about me and him.' He dropped his head. 'You need to know that.' His words tumbled to the floor and lay in a jumble at his feet like useless fallen leaves.

She said nothing, taking a step backwards. 'We can talk about this later. Trust me.'

'There's more.' He ran a hand through his tangled hair. *Do something, do it now. Save her.* He gulped down the fear threatening to close off his throat. 'I know why Jenny took her life.'

Mary's eyes grew wide, and she took a step towards him. 'How do you know?'

'I was there when it happened. I saw it all.' He hung his head again and whispered, 'I didn't stop it.'

'You're not making sense.'

He screwed up his eyes. 'I saw what Samuel did to her. I watched. I did nothing. But it was him. He forced her. It was his bairn she was carrying.'

Mary's howling scream made him jump. 'Liar, you liar!' She leapt at him and slapped his face with a stinging smack. His chest thump, thump, thumped under a rain of blows from her balled fists.

He grabbed both her hands and replied, 'You know I've never lied to you.'

'I know that you'll do anything, say anything to try to stop me loving Samuel. You didn't have to tell such lies. How could you say that about my Jenny? How could I ever love a man who lies? I hate, hate you.' She wrestled her arms free, an unrepentant wildness in her eyes. She took a step backwards.

'Well, talk to Elizabeth, then. Maybe you'll believe her. Come back and talk to Elizabeth.'

'Don't you dare bring Lizzie into this. Now you've gone too far, way too far.'

'Just talk to her. Please. Come back.'

'No.' She took another step backwards.

'If you leave me now, go to him, I'll . . . I'll . . .'

'What? What will you do? Nothing, as usual.'

'I'll stop loving you. I'll leave.'

She went rigid, and the bright flames of anger in her cheeks faded until her skin became deathly white. She turned her back on him and walked away.

He fought against a rush of tears but gave up, blinking them away so he could watch her. *Turn and look at me. Please turn and look at me. All I can do is stand here. I've got nothing else to give.*

She didn't turn. Her red cloak floated deeper into the gloom, and a vision swam into his head of Mary going to meet him, a predator with a wolfish grin.

She'd made her choice.

He was stupid to believe it could ever be any different.

He'd lost her.

Chapter 40

Mary came to a halt in the dark woods. *How dare he say such lies! How dare he say he'd stop loving her!* Tears of rage blinded her, and she swiped them away with the back of her hand. His words burrowed deep, bored into her heart. *Stop loving her.* That statement was like a fist, a blow to her stomach. She doubled over, gasping for air. And she had told him she hated him and just stood and watched his anguished eyes blur with tears. She didn't mean it, but what he said had to be lies, didn't it? It made her so angry, the words just spilt out. It couldn't be true; Jenny would have told her. So why did he say it and then say he'd leave? Who did she really want, Samuel or Benjamin? Or had the choice just been made? She marched up to a regal oak, clenched her fists, and pounded them against the knotted bark until her hands became red raw, pain stabbing through her, her frantic blows gradually slowing, slowing, stopping. She leant her head against her hands and wept, letting the tears slide down her fingers, her wrists, her arms. She wanted Benjamin. Could he really stop loving her? Before she could find out, before she could beg for his forgiveness, she had to make this right.

Stroking the oak with her damp fingers, she found ivy wrapped around its bark, clinging to it in a tight embrace. She followed the trail of ivy downwards until her hand grazed the top of a plant growing at the base of the

325

tree and brushed against shiny black berries. The devil's cherries of deadly nightshade. So pretty. So tempting. So dangerous. Just like Samuel.

She sniffed and gathered up an edge of her cloak to wipe her face dry. She wasn't even going to leave him, would never leave him, so why would he make up such terrible lies? She ran a hand across her throat and let her eyes drop back to the berries that looked polished like small jewels. Stop loving her. Could he? Had she lost him forever?

Mary pushed herself off the tree. She needed answers before she made any more decisions. She had to talk to Samuel and find out the truth.

Moving deeper into the woods, towards her meeting place, she left the main path and threaded her way through the trees, trailing her fingertips against rough bark as she went. The route wound and wove a route around ancient oaks, with roots splayed across the track, and distorted, twisted boughs with bony fingers caught at her crimson cloak.

Stop loving her. She prayed he couldn't do it.

A gust of wind ripped through the branches above her, forced the last of the leaves to release their tentative hold, and set them free. She stopped to lift her head, and the leaves revolved thick and silent around her. The sky was grey and dismal through the bare branches swaying and rocking above her head.

Stop loving her. A ferocious howl made her jump. The wind, just the wind. She shivered and pulled her red hood tight around her face, then paused. The old trees creaked and groaned as the wind blustered through their branches, but there was something else. Wary, she strained to hear and caught the crack of breaking twigs. Was someone out there? She held her breath and kept still. Perfectly still.

There it was again. She inched her head to the right and snatched a glimpse of a dark shape, gliding, slinking, blending into the gloom.

Her heart hammered in her chest, but she remained rooted like the trees, unable to run. *Move. Move, dammit.* In one instant, she sprang forwards and ran, ran until she reached a small clearing and came to a shuddering stop. Panting, she took cover behind a tree. Through the carpet of leaves, it padded up behind her, circled her. A sliver of fear slid down her spine and made her tremble. Panic crawled over her skin, making it pucker. She wiped her clammy hands down her red cloak and held her breath to be noiseless, invisible. It edged nearer. Her muscles tensed. She stepped away from the tree, spun around, and let out a cry. Her legs buckled.

He caught her in his arms. 'What's wrong, maid? It's only me, don't be scared.'

With a half laugh, she rested her head against his muscular chest and steadied her breathing, lifting her head to look at him and drink in his tousled blond hair and heady blue eyes. She reached up, stroked his bristly cheek, and ran her fingers across his full mouth, tracing the outline of his lips. This could never be the face of a monster. This was the face of the man she still loved but had to let go.

He bent towards her and breathed her in deeply. 'You always smell so good.' He grabbed her chin and tilted her face up to his. 'You've been crying. What's he done to you?'

She shook her head. 'Nothing, nothing. I was just afraid. I heard a noise.'

He pulled her close, his blazing blue eyes fixed on hers as he ran a hand down her back. His nails dug into her flesh through her clothes, down her spine, and over her buttocks to her thigh. He gathered up her skirt with his fingers, raising it inch by stealthy inch.

She gulped. 'I heard a rumour about Jenny.'

His fingers froze. 'What rumour?'

'That she was with child. But I don't believe it. She would have told me. She would have said if she was seeing someone. But why did she kill herself? I don't understand.'

'Maybe she loved someone who didn't love her back?'

Mary dropped her head and spoke into his chest, 'Perhaps she didn't love anyone; perhaps she was taken by force.'

'Ah, but it's too easy to put the blame on some man. Why do you think that, anyway?'

'Because she hanged herself, and so she killed her bairn too.'

'But love can be so painful, it can hurt more'n knives or pistols. I've known men to take their lives because of a woman. Why not a woman because of a man?' His eyes flicked over her, watching. 'There's always two sides to every story.'

She wanted to ask him more but was afraid, and so she shut out the voice of reason. The answers he might give made her dizzy. Samuel's fingers coiled around her skirt and hitched it higher. 'Why me, Sam? You could have anyone, someone without a husband and bairns.'

'I've told you, I love you, always have.'

'Benjamin said you believe it was him that got you arrested.'

'I know it.'

'And that you only want me to hurt him.'

A low growl erupted from deep within his chest, and his top lip curled into a snarl. 'If I wanted to hurt him, I'd break his bones. It would be easy; he never fights back.'

She opened her mouth to say he'd changed, he would fight now, but nothing came out. Samuel nuzzled into her neck, his tongue flicking over the hollow of her throat, tasting her, his teeth nipping at her flesh. His hot breath scorched her skin. Was he going to mark her as his own again? She had to tell him now that he had to leave and never come back. This was their goodbye.

Cold air caressed the back of her legs. She squirmed, but he held her firm in his powerful grip. He raised his head. 'And now I have to ask you something.'

'What?'

'Eliza. I've seen her. I need to know.'

'What?'

'Is she Elizabeth's child?'

Mary froze. 'Elizabeth's? No, why ask that?'

'Well, I know she was pregnant when I left.'

Mary gasped and pushed away from him. She stepped backwards, a cold chill seeping through her veins. Benjamin's words came back to her. *Talk to Elizabeth.* She shook her head. 'Why would you think she was having a bairn?'

'It was obvious. Sorry, wasn't I supposed to know? So, if Eliza is really yours, what happened to Elizabeth's bairn?'

Come back and talk to Elizabeth, he'd said. She'd dismissed it, pushed it away, but now those words cracked open a kernel of fear. She couldn't think straight. Eyes half-closed, she bit her bottom lip until it bled and took another step backwards. Not Samuel. He couldn't. He wouldn't.

'How old is Eliza?'

She shrugged, watching him. 'Nearly four.'

He was working it out, calculating, trying to make sense of it. How long before he realised Eliza was hers and his? Whilst he was distracted, she backed out of his reach.

'I've seen her. She looks like me.'

Silence.

'She's mine. I knew it. Mine.'

Mary snatched a deep breath and bolted.

Chapter 41

Elizabeth trudged through the potato field, her fingers wrapped around a chipped mug, the steam rising from it in smoky tendrils. 'Some hot milk for you. You haven't stopped for a break.'

Benjamin pulled off his gloves. Letting them fall to the ground, he took the mug from her. He glanced at the pale, insipid liquid. He didn't want it; he didn't want anything. He pushed the skin floating on the top aside with one soil-stained finger and took a sip. It tasted of nothing.

'Did you find her?'

He looked up and frowned. 'Yes, but she left anyway.'

'Where's she gone?' She pushed a strand of silky blonde hair out of her eyes and stared at him. Wide-eyed, innocent.

He sighed. 'She said she forgot something.' He emptied the contents of the mug onto the ground and handed it back to her, then bent to pick up two stray potatoes, holding one in each hand as if weighing them. He lifted his eyes to look at her. 'She's gone to be with Samuel.'

For one minute he thought she was going to slap his face like her sister had. To call him a liar. Instead, her hand flew to her mouth, and she staggered backwards, an arm outstretched to steady herself.

He watched unmoved as if made of stone.

She dropped to her knees in the dirt. 'No, she wouldn't do that.'

'She's gone to him before. I think she hates me.'

'No, no, she doesn't.'

'I told her the truth about Jenny.'

She staggered to her feet. 'What truth?'

He stared at her. 'That she was carrying Samuel's bairn, and she didn't want it.'

Silent tears slid down her pale skin, small clear beads that tracked down her cheeks and dropped off her chin. 'I knew it,' she whispered.

'I only told her about Jenny. Nothing else. But she hates me now. She didn't believe me.'

Now Elizabeth did rush at him and grab the collar of his coat with both of her trembling hands. 'She will, it's just that she still blames herself for Jenny's death. Go after her, get her back.' She shook him until his teeth rattled. 'Do something.'

Do something, do it now. Save her. The bonesetter's words. Much good they were. 'No.' He straightened his shoulders. 'She's made her choice.'

'No, don't give up, please. Go after her. Where did she go?'

'She said the cottage, but she headed for the woods. I dunno.'

'Go to the cottage; she might be there. Go! If you love her, you'll do anything, do anything to be with the one you love. She can't be with him. You know why.'

'No, it's too late.'

She shoved him backwards. 'So, you're going to make me do it, are you?' She balled her hands into fists.

'I'll go, then. Don't you worry, I'll go.' She turned and fled, holding her throat like an injured animal, her sobs drifting back to him on the wind.

Oh hell. 'Elizabeth, wait.' He ran after her and grabbed her arm. 'I'll go, I'll go. Get the bairns. Keep them inside the farmhouse. She won't leave without them. Keep them safe. I'll try the cottage first.'

She nodded at him, gulping back tears. 'Thank you.' She turned and stumbled back to the farmhouse.

Shaking his head, he watched her go. This was useless. He ran towards the field gate anyway, calling Jess, who bounded after him. Together they sprinted down the farm track.

***

QUESTIONS CAREENING THROUGH her mind, Mary ran through the woods, back the way she'd come, stopping once to catch her breath, convinced she could hear him thundering after her. She ran on, her chest burning with the effort, but she dared not stop. She needed answers before she faced him again.

She came out of the woods, stumbling down the farm track, and slowed and stopped by the field gate to steady her breathing. Benjamin's wheelbarrow remained, stacked high with potatoes, but he was nowhere to be seen. Never mind, she wanted to find Elizabeth first. Holding her hands to where a sharp pain stabbed at her side, she took a deep gulp of air, then another, and walked to the farmhouse, heading for the kitchen door.

Mary pushed the door open and glanced around the candlelit kitchen that smelt of freshly baked saffron cake, the gentle spices warm and inviting. Eliza and Mary Jane sat on the floor by the pantry, quietly playing with wooden dolls. Dolls she'd watched Benjamin make with the knife that had once scored his skin and nearly killed him; he now used it to whittle dolls and horses for the children.

Over by the fireplace, she found Elizabeth sitting on the old oak settle. She sat beside her and placed a hand on her arm.

Elizabeth put aside her darning and swivelled in her seat to face her. 'I knew you'd come. I've been waiting for you.'

'Lizzie.' Mary took a shuddering breath. 'I know you've never forgiven me for what I did to your bairn. For killing him. Never forgiven me for not protecting you. I'm sorry, I truly am.'

Elizabeth frowned and shook her head, shards of light flying from her plait. 'You never killed my bairn. It was born too early, too small, too weak. It could never have survived; you must know that.'

'But he was alive, we heard him cry.'

'So, it was a boy, was it? I've always wondered.' She stared at her hands before covering her face with them and sobbing. 'I killed him. I didn't want him. What bairn could survive that, its own mother wishing it dead? I'm ashamed of what I did; I didn't think of him as a life. I didn't think of him at all, I was so selfish. So, there's nothing to forgive.'

'I should've protected you, but I didn't know. It was Samuel, wasn't it? I need you to say it, or I can't believe it. Please don't hate me, Lizzie.' Mary put an arm around her sister and drew her close.

'Hate you? I've only ever loved you. Truth is, I'm jealous of what you have—Benjamin, the bairns. Anyway, it was my fault. You couldn't protect me from myself. It's you that must forgive me. I knew you loved him, but I still went to him.'

'You were a child.'

'No, I was a woman, old enough to have a bairn.'

'You were fourteen, for God's sake.'

'I went to him willingly enough.'

'Not for that.'

'No. No, but I didn't struggle. I let it happen. What was he supposed to think?'

'That you were just fourteen and my sister!'

'I've heard it said many times that if a woman's old enough to bleed, she's old enough.'

'Elizabeth, no! He was wrong. I just can't believe he could do such a terrible thing.'

Elizabeth wiped at her tears. 'And not just to me, poor Jenny Wren too. How different would your life be if you'd married him? I don't believe he would have ever stopped. But I do think he loved you. And don't forget, you still love that man.'

'No. I'll never forgive him for this.'

'But it isn't so easy to turn love off, is it? And I've forgiven him; it's the only way I can continue.'

'He should be punished.'

'Don't worry. Stay with Benjamin, and that will torment him.'

'Oh God, Benjamin. I told him I hated him.'

'But you don't.'

'No, no, I don't. I was just angry and guilty with myself. For not knowing, not seeing, and not helping those I loved the most. I took it out on him.'

'You need to admit to yourself how you really feel. Don't lose him.'

Mary twirled her wedding ring round and round her finger. 'I hated him when I married him, but then I hated myself too. He said he loved me, but I thought he made me up in his head, that he didn't see me at all. But he does, you know. He grows on you, gets under your skin. He hates people generally, and I like to protect him from them. He's so strong, yet so vulnerable. I'm the only one he lets in, except the bairns, of course, but that's different. He has this way of . . .' She trailed off and wiped away her tears. 'He has this way of . . .' Unable to finish because she couldn't stop crying, she was flooded with an urgent need to be with him, to tell this to him, not Elizabeth.

'Go and find him and tell him. Tell him how you really feel.'

'I don't know where he is.'

'He's gone back to the cottage looking for you.'

'Has he? For me?'

'Go to him, Mary. Go now.'

Chapter 42

As Benjamin approached the cottage, his heart sank. It was empty. It contained a quietness, a stillness that only existed when the cottage was deserted. But still, he flung the door open and called her name. There was nothing but silence and her scent hanging in the air like smoke.

He walked to the cupboard by the fireplace and reached for a bottle of brandy, then poured himself a full glass and gulped it down. He stood with the glass in his hand, remembering how brandy made her relaxed, uninhibited. 'Damn.' He threw the glass into the fireplace, and it shattered into a thousand pieces. He ran out of the cottage and stood by the water pump, calling out, 'Mary, Mary, Mary,' until he lost his voice.

He wandered over to the cliff edge to look out at the slate blue sea and tumultuous white-capped waves. A vast stretch of wild emptiness where seagulls wheeled and bickered in their harsh, screeching cry. Nothing looked the same anymore, knowing she was gone. Mary had changed every single fibre of his being, and he couldn't go back. Putting his hands in his pockets, he sighed and kicked at a tuft of grass with his boot.

'Benjamin!'

His eyes narrowed, then his mouth curved into a slow smile.

'Benjamin!'

The shout came from behind him. He turned to watch Samuel walk along the headland towards him.

An unstoppable explosion of white-hot anger uncurled in his gut and surged through his blood. He thrilled with the sensation and abandoned himself to it. His smile widened, but his eyes grew hard. His head throbbed with a black, brutal desire for blood. To smash, to kick, to kill. He waited for black spots to dance before his eyes, then he was ready, possessed by a savage instinct, a ruthless hunger. He welcomed it, curling his fingers into fists, waiting. Samuel strode up to him. He'd been running, he could tell from the rise and fall of his chest. *Chasing his prey?*

Samuel shouted, 'She's leaving you, leaving you for me.'

He said nothing, just flexed his muscles, the tendons in his neck taut like rope.

'And Eliza isn't yours. I know she's my bairn.'

Now Benjamin spoke, stressing every word, his eyes riveted on Samuel. 'I know. I've always known. Something else of yours that I have.'

'She's mine.'

'But it's me she calls Da.'

'I'm taking her, I'm taking everything. I'm going to destroy you. She's leaving you. She told me when she was on her knees with this in her mouth.' Samuel grabbed his crotch lewdly and laughed.

Benjamin watched his mocking sneer and locked onto his cold blue eyes. He gave a roar and rushed him. Wrapping his hands around Samuel's throat, he squeezed and squeezed again.

Samuel pulled him off balance and landed a hard fist to his gut. Benjamin's hands slackened, and Samuel pulled free, leaving him to wince and gasp from nauseating pain.

Samuel sprang for him again and aimed a savage kick at his groin. Benjamin managed to dodge so it landed on his thigh. He held his ground, reached out, and grabbed Samuel's shoulder. Jerking his head back, he brought it down with a jarring crack between Samuel's eyes, bone against bone.

Pain creased Samuel's face, and blood spurted from his nose. But he didn't go down, instead, he lashed out with his long arms. His hard knuckles mashed into Benjamin's mouth, smashing his teeth.

Benjamin reeled backwards and groaned. The warm metallic taste of blood filled his mouth. He coughed and spat blood and teeth onto the green grassy tufts at his feet. Wiping his mouth with the back of his hand, he raised another smile. The pain just fuelled his hatred.

Samuel charged him again, and he retaliated with kicks and punches. Pain exploded in his head whilst savage blows rained down on him. He kicked himself free, and Jess barked and howled, circling and nipping at Samuel's ankles.

Benjamin paused to shake his head clear, and Samuel lunged again. Another hard fist made his stomach cramp. He doubled over from the force. *Some ribs were broken that time.* Holding his sides, Benjamin tried to straighten up, but Samuel kicked at his head, his hard boot slicing through the skin above Benjamin's right eye, bruising his brow bone. Blood gushed down his face, blurring his vision. Benjamin crumpled. Hit the ground.

Thumped to earth. He raised his head, but it was like lifting a great weight, and pain flashed across his eyes.

He didn't care. He welcomed the pain. Samuel would have to kill him because he wouldn't stop now; he had nothing to lose. He hauled himself upright, panting with adrenalin, and wiped the blood from his eyes, catching sight of Samuel before his vision blurred once more.

Samuel's right eye was also swollen shut, and his broken nose still gushed blood down his chin, soaking into his shirt. *Why wasn't the bastard going down?*

Benjamin slipped his hand inside his boot and grasped the smooth hilt of the knife he'd taken from the intruder during the corn carrying. He brought it out and pointed it at Samuel's stomach. The sharp metal blade flashing with menace.

'Let's raise the stakes, shall we?'

Chapter 43

Mary sprinted for the cottage, the ache in her legs replaced with a stronger burning ache to be with him. She repeated his name breathlessly, over and over as she ran. 'Benjamin, Benjamin, Benjamin.' As if he could hear, as if he would know she was coming.

She reached the cottage and stumbled to a stop. Laughing, she scratched her head at the sight of Abe crouched down behind the cottage wall. *Now what was he up to?* She crept up behind him and placed her hands on his shoulders, making him jump. 'Following Benjamin again?'

He turned to her with round, frightened eyes. Eyes like burning coal. He pointed a trembling hand towards the cliff edge. She followed his direction and gasped, 'No!'

The fight was brutal, merciless, with savage thumps and cracks of fist against bone. Bright red blood masked their faces, ran down their necks, and soaked their shirts. They were beating each other to a bloody pulp. She reached for the wall to stop herself falling. She couldn't watch but couldn't turn away.

Making herself move, she bent towards Abe and took his face in her hands. 'Get the bonesetter, Grace. Understand? The bonesetter.' She pointed across Treyarnon Beach in the direction of Constantine Bay. He'd been there before, and she hoped he could remember.

'*Oui,* yes, yes.' He nodded.

341

'Run, Abe, run.'

He took off like a frightened animal. The look of terror on his face would be enough to bring Grace; he didn't need to speak.

Mary turned back to the two men. She had to do something to halt this madness. Perhaps if they saw her, they would stop. It was worth a try.

She stepped out from behind the cottage wall and edged nearer.

***

BENJAMIN FLASHED THE knife at Samuel's stomach. He held it in his right hand, and kept his left in a tight fist, his nails digging into his palm.

Samuel took a step backwards, his lips curling into a cruel smile, and gave a short, hard laugh. He reached inside his back coat pocket and withdrew a pistol.

Fuck. He'd forgotten flintlock pistols were standard issue to revenue men. Benjamin backed away. The range required for the shot to do damage was short, so he just needed to put distance between them.

His eyes fixed on Samuel, he watched him rotate the hammer from half-cock—*click*—to full-cock, swiping the underside of the flint with his index finger to remove any moisture. Benjamin continued to back away, running his options through his head. He could lunge sideways and hope Samuel missed or he was out of range, but then he would have to spring for him before he reloaded. Use his knife. It was the only chance he had.

His mind raced, but his world slowed down as he channelled all his concentration onto one point—Samuel's trigger finger.

Samuel lifted the pistol, his arm straight. He aimed it at Benjamin's chest, but his eyes were focused behind Benjamin's head.

Benjamin's nostrils flared. He waited. And watched. And tensed.

'Samuel, please don't do it.'

Mary's scream startled Benjamin, and his concentration faltered. Samuel's index finger twitched, but he wasn't ready. Benjamin didn't move.

The gun exploded, and sparks flew from the flash hole, black smoke spuming from the barrel. Benjamin spun around from the impact and crumpled. Falling onto his knees, he let his knife slip from his grasp. Pain seared through his body, making him dizzy. He held a hand to his chest, and blood spurted through his fingers, pooling onto the grass around him. Through his blood-soaked vision, he glimpsed Samuel priming the pistol again. He couldn't do anything to stop him. His knife lay on the grass beside him. He lamely stretched out a hand towards it but let his arm drop. It took too much effort. Kneeling took too much effort. Keeping his eyes open took too much effort. Pain ripped him apart, and he was nauseous with it. And cold. And clammy. He swayed, still on his knees.

Then Mary stood in front of him, facing Samuel, her arms wide apart. He focused on her voice. 'I won't let you do it. I won't let you kill him.'

'Mary, no!' He tried to speak, his voice a croak. 'He'll kill us both.'

343

Samuel reloaded the pistol. Benjamin closed his eyes. Helpless.

A deep rumble and growl forced his eyes open, and he squinted to see Jess launch herself with furious force at Samuel, who was too preoccupied loading the pistol to defend himself. Ninety pounds of snarling, ferocious dog landed against Samuel's chest, her front paws reaching his shoulders. Samuel stumbled, somehow remained standing, but Jess fastened her powerful jaws around his throat and held on.

Mary sank to her knees and screamed.

Benjamin took a short gasp of breath, then another. It was too hard. He slipped sideways onto the grass. Jess would rip Samuel's throat out; she wouldn't stop. Already a spume of rich red blood sprayed the back of her dark coat. Benjamin kept his eyes on Samuel, wanting to watch, wanting his last image to be Samuel's death.

Samuel's wide eyes glazed over. His arms lashed out, flailing wildly at Jess, then he stopped struggling. Samuel focused his gaze on Benjamin. Making sure he was watching, he wrapped his arms around Jess and staggered backwards.

Feebly, Benjamin called out, 'Come on, Jess,' but his hoarse voice was a whisper, drowned out by Mary's screams. He watched, unable to move, crying as Samuel stepped off the edge of the cliff, taking Jess with him.

Benjamin closed his eyes and let his body fall, giving in to darkness.

The perfect still and silent blackness of oblivion.

***

SOMEONE CALLED HIS name, but he wanted to sleep. They wouldn't stop, wouldn't let him rest. He shuddered. His eyes fluttered open, then closed. Was he dreaming? He couldn't tell. Why wouldn't they leave him alone?

'Benjamin.'

He knew that voice. He wanted to hear that voice. He forced himself to concentrate. What was she saying?

'Benjamin.'

She was insistent. Perhaps this was important. He tried again to focus on her words.

'It's me, Benjamin. It's Mary. Don't you die on me now. Not now. I couldn't bear it.'

She was crying, her hot tears splashing his face. Why was she crying? He took a shallow breath and almost passed out from the deep, stabbing pain in his chest.

'Don't you die, please don't die. I want you to know that I do see you, I do. I love you, Benjamin Carnarton, please don't leave me.'

Love? Did she say love? He must be dreaming. He lifted the corners of his mouth into a faint smile. *A damn good dream, though*.

She stroked his face and ran her fingertips down his scar. His skin purred with every strum her fingers made from his forehead down, down, down to his lips. She ran her fingers over his mouth. 'I love you. Can you hear me? Do you understand? I love you.'

He opened his eyes in confusion. She sounded so real. He could see her. What was she doing? Did she just untie a dark green ribbon from her hair and let it take off in the wind, twirling and twisting out to sea?

She bent her head towards him, her lips on his, and kissed his swollen, tender mouth.

This was no dream. He'd never had someone else's lips on his, not like this, and he had never dreamt of it, ever. Her lips were soft, smooth, and warm. His heart skipped a beat, and his blood quickened, surging through his veins.

Her warm breath entered his body, a breath of love, dissolving his pain.

Chapter 44

Grace sat in her favourite chair, her beloved view of Constantine Bay spread out before her. Her windows were wide open, a warm breath of air puffing at her dimity curtains, making them billow like a skirt.

The stretch of golden sand shimmered in the sun below her, and she smiled and hummed to herself. She closed her eyes and recalled that as a child she would kick off her shoes, tear off her socks, and run barefoot to the water's edge, testing the sea, jumping the rippling waves and wetting her clothes. She sighed. Those days were long gone. Or were they? She glanced down at her feet. *Why not*? The beach was deserted as usual. Laughing, she used her right boot to ease her left boot off by the heel, then pressed her left toes against her right boot and pushed hard. Her boot spun across the floor and hit the opposite wall. She snorted with laughter. She rolled her stockings down her legs and stretched and squashed her stomach so she could reach her feet. Puffing and panting, she pulled her stockings free, twirled them around her head, and threw them up in the air.

She planted her feet on the floor and raised herself up. The chair, fastened to her backside, rose with her. She grasped the arms and pushed down, wriggled and prised her bottom free. Stomping towards her door, she threw it open and breathed in the clean sea air, filling her mighty lungs.

347

She rubbed her hands and scurried down her path, headed for the beach. In her head, she ran like a child. She sighed as her toes sank into the soft warm grains, burrowing her feet so they were covered in sand before hefting her legs out and lumbering down to the shore.

Hands on her hips, she gazed out to sea, and childhood memories came flooding back, making her smile. Well, she'd got this far. Why stop now? She gathered her skirt, rolled it up, and tucked it into her waistband, revealing stark white, softly bulging thighs. Taking a gulp of fresh air, she waded in and slapped her thighs in joy as the freezing waves smacked her legs.

Grinning, she turned her back to the water and stared at the beach, recalling running the dunes as a child, running without stopping. Up, down, up. She shook her head and chuckled. This was her kingdom, her domain, and it stretched across the whole of St Merryn. She never left this village and had no desire to. These villagers were her life.

She'd delivered most of the bairns born there since she was eighteen, and before that, her mother, and before that, her grandmother, and before that . . . but never a bairn of her own. She would never marry again. Who would want her now she'd grown so fat? Anyway, she could never replace her lost love. So now she was the last of them, and she'd failed her ancestors by not continuing the line. She was the last bonesetter, and so she'd failed the village. She rubbed at her chin. There was no fixing this.

Then she noticed a speck on the beach, which grew bigger as it ran towards her. She waited, hands on hips, for the child to reach her. But when he did reach the shore, he stood and stared open-mouthed at her milky thighs. She glanced down to see what he saw. Blubber—flabby, fleshy, and flaccid. She sighed. It would take many years before that image stopped haunting his nightmares. She put a beefy finger under his chin and tilted his head up so he looked at her face.

He shook his head as if freeing himself of her image.

'Abe?'

He only pointed with a shaking finger in the direction of Treyarnon Bay and Benjamin's cottage.

She flexed her hands. 'Right, then. Let's go.'

***

SAT IN HIS favourite chair outside his cottage, Benjamin looked across the bay. A light spring breeze ruffled his hair, and there was warmth in the sun's rays stretching towards him from a pale blue sky. White clouds drifted lazily by, and the sea slumbered while sluggish waves crept and crawled up the shore.

You'd love this, Jess. He glanced at the grassy mound beside him, her final resting place. It was next to his chair so he could talk to her while he rested. He often caught fleeting glimpses of her inside the cottage or running for sticks by the water pump. When he dozed by the fireside and his hand dropped down the side of his chair, her wet nose would nudge him awake. She hadn't left; she roamed these cliffs and walked with him everywhere. She hadn't left.

By God he missed her. He swiped the tears from his eyes and flexed his shoulder, rubbing his chest to ease the stiff muscles. The bonesetter had done a good job on him,

349

a jagged scar his only reminder of the day he had lost Jess but won Mary. He rested his head on the back of his chair and smiled. Ah, Mary. Now he had a life worth living.

An explosion of shouts and children's singsong voices burst out. *Ha, back from church, then. No mistaking their joyful din.* He eased himself out of his chair and stood to wait for them.

'Mary Jane, don't jump up at your da, mind his shoulder.'

'It's fine. I don't mind. How was church?'

'Same as ever. You rest here, and I'll fetch the water to fill the bath; these three need a good wash.'

'No need. I've done it.'

'Benjamin! You should be resting.'

He stood before her and pulled her close. 'I'm tired of resting. I need some action.'

She wrapped her arms around his neck. 'Action, really?'

'Hmm, really.'

Mary tilted her face towards him, and he bent to kiss her.

She responded, pulling him closer, gripping him tighter.

He sank into her kiss, deeper and deeper.

Abe shouted out, 'Oh no, they're doing it again!' The children giggled.

But Benjamin didn't notice. He was lost. Lost in her caress.

And now he knew it was forever.

GET MY NOVELLA, AMAZING GRACE, <u>FOR</u> <u>FREE</u>

I love building a relationship with my readers. Many of you have said that you love the character of Grace, the bonesetter who appears in both novels. I have therefore written a novella detailing how Grace met Johnny. I will be writing further short stories until I bring her up to 1816.
If you sign up to my mailing list, I will send you this free novella and any others, once they have been written. Plus, you will be the first to know when my next novel, which is complete, will be released.

Sign up at https://dl.bookfunnel.com/hh0cssx4v9

Thank You

Thank you for reading this book.

I hope you enjoyed Secrets Of Greenoak Woods because I loved writing it and creating the characters.

I did my research for this book by reading many others and also by trawling through newspaper articles from the West Briton, Truro and British Newspaper Archive. Any of the true stories I read that captured my imagination have been woven into my novel and I hope anyone reading it will get a taste of working-class rural life in the 1820s.

As a new author, I need feedback, the more the better. Please feel free to tell me what you loved and what you hated. You can write to me at brenda@brendajdavies.com or leave a comment on my author page on Amazon and please like my Facebook page @brendajanedaviesauthor
Or join me on twitter @authorbrenda1

Finally, I would be very grateful if you would leave a review on Amazon. Reviews are so hard to come by but they have the power to make or break a book.
Thank you once again for buying and reading my book.

Acknowledgements

I would like to thank my husband for his patience, enthusiasm, and brilliant ideas.

I would also like to thank Jenny Q and Jessica Cale at www.historicalfictionbookcovers.com for the brilliant edit and beautiful book cover.

I would also like to thank the West Briton newspaper, Truro and the British Newspaper Archive (www.britishnewpaperarchive.co.uk) as sources of information used throughout the book.

Also By Brenda Jane Davies

Along Came A Soldier

When murder stalks St Merryn, no secrets are safe...

A forbidden romance...

Set in 1820 Cornwall, Charity Perrow lives a sheltered life in the village of St Merryn. She meets and falls for Jethro Ennor but soon learns their families are bitter enemies and finds herself torn between remaining loyal to her family and giving in to her growing desire for a man they hate.

A village with hidden secrets...

A battle-scarred redcoat is lurking in the woods of St Merryn. Struggling to keep a grip on his sanity, he's come home to settle an old score with those responsible for the heavy burden he's been carrying all the years he's been away. His thirst for revenge is ruthless.

An innocent man accused...

When a villager is murdered, the suspicion falls on Jethro. Now Charity must risk everything, including being disowned by her family, to prove his innocence and save him from the gallows.
But as Charity hunts for the truth, she begins to uncover secrets over a decade old—secrets that will change everything.

Chapter 1

<u>1820 St Merryn, Cornwall.</u>

From the open doorway of her father's cottage, Charity Perrow could see the whole of the village square. A few old men slumped in rickety chairs outside whitewashed cottages. A group of women gossiped in a huddle by the water pump, one eye on their barefoot babies playing in the dirt. What were those married women chatting about? Husbands? Children? She had no idea.

It wouldn't last, this sleepy peacefulness. Not on a day like today with every gate post and door draped in branches of green sycamore trimmed with cowslips, bluebells, and forget-me-nots, their leaves rippling and fluttering like dancing maidens.

A cool breeze skimmed her arms, making her shiver. She pulled the cottage door closed behind her and pressed her back up against it. She shivered again. Not from cold this time, but from the creeping sensation of being watched. From the corner of her eye, she caught a glimpse of red. It sank behind a clump of oak trees just inside the woods flanking this village. Strange, why would anyone try to hide wearing a colour even the dark woods couldn't conceal?

The steady, rhythmic beat of a drum drew her attention back to the square. A man marched past her cottage with a measured *rat-tat-tat,* leading a troop of young men and boys. They strode past with the village maypole slung along their shoulders, the smaller boys with it balanced on their heads. Charity's brothers, Tom and Joe, were amongst them. She felt a familiar tug on the cord binding her heart to her family, especially since Joe joined in on the fun today. One of the young men winked at her in passing. She laughed at him. She'd grown up with these lads, knew them too well. The rest of the villagers followed—couples holding hands, shrieking children, young women arm in arm with colourful wreaths of flowers in their hair.

She turned her head back toward the woods, at the speck of scarlet partially hidden. Who was watching?

The gangly line of lads came to a stop dead centre in the square beside the maypole clamp, and they shouted instructions at each other. At their call, the drum rolled, and the maypole swayed and rose up toward the brooding sky, clanging and chiming like the old church tower because of the school bell lashed to its top, along with crisp-white bunting that fluttered in the breeze, reminding her of clean washing flapping on a line.

She made her way to her front gate and stubbed her toe against something solid sitting on the garden path. Cursing, she bent and picked up a stone pot with a wilted, sorry-looking plant inside. Its brown leaves crumbled at her touch, but the plant still lived, the stem a dark green colour. 'What are you?' she whispered to it. But that was half the fun—not knowing until it burst back into leaf. Plants were like people; they needed love and care to thrive. If treated badly, they became twisted, stunted, even dead. Which of her neighbours had left this for her to tend?

Scanning the row of cottages one by one, her eyes fell on the cobbler's shop. William Vine slouched in the doorway, hands tucked away in his pockets. A wide-brimmed hat dotted with flowers covered most of his face. He tipped his head back, grinned, and nodded at her, then raised his shoulders in a shrug—an apology. Yes, William, good with leather, terrible with plants. Charity hugged the pot to her chest and nodded back at him, then placed it on the ground, opened the garden gate, and joined the noisy throng surrounding the maypole.

But, she edged away from the crowd, toward the fleck of red in Greenoak Woods, where dark tree trunks reached for clouds smudged black as coal dust. It was surely going to rain, and as that thought entered her head, the rain fell like cold needles.

Someone's hand clasped her arm, and Charity turned to gaze at a weathered face with eyes half hidden inside wrinkled seams of skin. The old lady gave Charity a toothless, whiskery grin and said, 'Come on, Nessa, jig with me.'

Charity gently tried to untangle their locked hands. The old lady always called her Nessa, her mother's name. She obviously thought that's who she was. Easily done, Charity looked just like her mother. Everyone said so. The old lady continued to dance to the beat of the drums, not letting Charity go. They whirled round and round together.

Charity coughed up the smell of body odour clinging to the back of her throat and the panic rising in her chest. She was a sweet old dear, but Charity couldn't look at her without a surge of dread. The old lady was a spinster, unmarried and alone, having devoted her life to caring for her parents. Charity silently begged God not to leave her with such a terrible fate and crossed herself with her free hand because it seemed the right thing to do.

The spinster's bloodshot eyes reminded her of the scarlet dot concealed in the woods. Still there. Still hiding. Still watching.

Then, Grace Partridge, the parish bonesetter, arrived and released her from the old lady's grip. Grace's beefy arm wrapped around Charity's shoulders, and she planted a fat kiss on Charity's forehead before joining the spinster in her dance. Charity giggled at the bonesetter's great bosoms as they bounced and jiggled in time with the drummer.

She left them to it, dodging children who ran squealing around the pole fast enough to make her dizzy. She crept toward the woods, her eyes fixed on the point of blazing colour. Easy to spot if you knew where to look.

That red colour niggled at her as if she should remember something. Clicking her fingers in concentration it came to her. *Of course!* Many of the young women wore red cloaks. So that's what it was—a young woman in a red cloak, probably from one of the many farms sprinkling this parish. A girl too shy to join in the fun but desperate to be discovered and invited by one of the villagers. Why else hide wearing such a striking colour? Charity wasn't shy, but she knew what it felt like to want to be included. She'd try to coax her out.

She paced forward until she hovered inside the tree line, surrounded by twisted, gnarled branches that reminded her of the old spinster's hands. The air was heavy and quiet with the forest's damp breath. She sucked in the woody scent of fresh rain, grass, and mould while watching the unmoving speck of colour.

And then the red cloak stirred.

Charity stood still, not breathing, and watched the red cloak rise and unfurl, no longer a crouching girl but someone standing tall amongst the dark trees. This was no timid girl but a man. A man in a soldier's redcoat, concealed behind a blanket of shadows, spying. But on what? On whom?

The soldier swivelled in Charity's direction, and her beating heart choked her throat until she gasped for breath. 'Stay,' she told her shaking legs. This stranger was probably harmless, but her muscles tensed, ready to run.

Her heartbeat ticked away the seconds as the soldier studied her, his own features shrouded by grey and jagged branches. Somewhere, at the edge of things, she heard children's laughter, the beat of a drum. Fear curled icy fingers around her heart, and she fell back a step, then spun around and ran for the safety of the village. Looking back, she saw him melt into the woods.

She didn't normally run from strangers, and soldiers regularly came around looking for work since they had no war to fight with France. But a cold, creeping tingle ran down her spine. The same one she got whenever she stood too close to the edge of the steep cliff paths running around Treyarnon Bay. That feeling came from her fear of heights.

What was she so afraid of now?

Chapter 2

Henry hugged his redcoat to his body, looked down at the twitching rabbit, and smiled. Caught by one foot, it lay trembling in shock and confusion, barely alive. It wasn't his trap, so it wasn't his rabbit, but he needed it; his hollow stomach, growling and gnawing at him, wanted it. He twisted the rabbit's neck until its eyes bulged and its bones cracked, then he placed one foot on the trap and ripped the body free, letting it bleed out as he carried it through the woods.

He hadn't been here in a long, long time, but he knew these woods. Being here brought back childhood memories so vivid, it was as if he'd never been away. As if nothing had ever happened. And he'd seen a ghost from his past, standing at the edge of the woods, staring straight at him. Her familiar face had sent a ripple of shock through his body. Her eyes had fixed on him as if she knew why he'd come back, as if she'd been expecting him. He took it as a sign he was supposed to be here.

Dragging himself farther into the forest, one hand in front of him, he groped around gnarled trunks and stumbled over fallen logs. It was much darker this deep into the woods, and there would be no moon tonight to guide him, but he needed to stay hidden. He could not be discovered. Not yet.

In a clearing, where the soft, boggy ground squelched under his boots, he stopped. This was where he'd

360

make a fire, with no chance of it spreading out of control. He dropped the rabbit and bent to gather twigs and sticks.

In the deep, dark gloom, he spied a shadow, slinking between the trees, and he shuddered. They had found him, even here. The beat of the drums he'd heard earlier had made his skin crawl because he knew the enemy was on the march.

At least lighting a fire would be easy. As he gathered dry moss to use as kindling, his hand hovered over the fresh, green sphagnum moss. He'd used it before, to cover wounds. The thought of using it again made him gulp. Grabbing a handful of sphagnum moss, he put it to one side.

Around him, the dark shapes grew in number. Even when he clamped his hands over his ears, he could still hear their whispered sighs and moans.

The fire crackled to life, and he rubbed his cold hands over it, then stroked the fingers on his right hand. *Eeny, meeny, miny, moe.* The smell of dust and smoke billowed around, swirling like mist, blending with another sickening smell—the smell of fear.

His fear.

He reached into his coat pocket, pulled out his jackknife, and flicked open the blade—no longer razor sharp, but it would do. He ran his tongue over his cracked lips, and, seizing the rabbit, he chopped off its head, then its feet, then its tail. The knotted ball of fear in his stomach rose to his throat. Not because of the rabbit—that meant nothing to him—but because it reminded him of what came next. He loosened its skin and ripped the rabbit apart until only the meaty flesh remained. Carefully slicing open its belly, he yanked the innards out.

They inched nearer, their blurred faces looming in and out of focus, shadows of lost souls he once knew, come to claim him. But he'd never go back, and he knew what to do next. He'd always known.

Rabbit fat dripped from a skewer and spat into the fire, as a cold sweat ran down Henry's back and soaked his armpits. A tremor ran up his spine, and his whole body jerked. He'd seen worse. Hell, he'd done worse, and he could do this now.

He gathered his tools. He didn't have much: a jackknife and a handkerchief stained with blood and phlegm, which he laid beside the fresh moss. The piece of string holding up his trousers came next, unravelling it he tied one end around the index finger of his right hand, below the knuckle. Using his teeth, he pulled the string tight—so tight the tip of his finger went numb—and fixed the knot. His hand shook when he picked up the jackknife and wrenched it open.

The faceless creatures around him melted into the shadows, watching. Their uniforms were in tatters; there was no way to tell if they belonged to his regiment or one of the enemy's. They stank of vomit and shit and melted flesh. But they couldn't have him. Not yet. He rubbed his hands up and down his arms to brush away the insects crawling under his skin.

Taking the knife, he gritted his teeth, but an uncontrollable whimper escaped, and his heart beat erratically against his chest. A scream ripped from his mouth as he sliced into his finger. He rammed a fist in it to shut off the sound, panting heavily. All around him surged a sea of crimson blood, of fallen bodies, of splintered bones. He hacked and sawed at his finger, listening to the screams of those who had fallen, and he felt their pain.

Blood spurted from his finger, and he retched and gagged and puked. He smashed the knife down onto his knuckle, and the bone cracked. With one final scream that hurled his vomit into the fire, he stabbed again and again, until his finger hung limp and bloody, held on only by a flap of skin.

Tears and sweat ran down the grooves in his face and he panted so much he couldn't catch his breath.

When Henry looked up, he saw a shadow coming closer, but he couldn't make him out. Was he friend or foe? Henry would have to kill him in case he was the enemy. As he plunged his finger into the blazing fire to seal the wound, the stranger's head exploded in a mass of flying blood and bone, and Henry fell backward into still and silent darkness.

***

When Henry woke, it was morning. A shaft of sunlight played over his face, light and dark flitting across his eyelids. He shivered and pulled his coat around him, the fire now a heap of cold ash. A throb of pain shot up his right arm, making him clench his stomach. Only a bloody, mangled stump and charred skin remained of his finger. He'd failed to seal it properly, and blood had oozed from it in the night, the grass around his hand sticky and dark with gore. But it was done, and that was all that mattered. He gathered up the moss and pressed it against the wound, then tied his handkerchief around his hand. The finger he'd cut off was missing, taken by an animal like a thief in the night, but the rabbit was still there. Cold but cooked. He grabbed it and greedily devoured the flesh, licking the fat from his lips. He picked up his canteen and drained the last of his water. No matter, he knew where to get more, but it would have to wait until darkness. For now, he had another mission.

Hesitating, he glanced around. He was alone, but they would be back. They always came back. At least now, he couldn't join them. He raised his bloody hand. Without his index finger, he couldn't hold or fire a musket. Henry laughed as if he'd just heard a good joke. Gently placing his butchered hand into his coat pocket, he set off toward the village of St Merryn.

On the outskirts of the village, he hunkered down, pulling up the collar of his coat with his left hand. He settled in to wait—something he was used to.

People he didn't recognise walked across the square. He waited until he saw her. Sarah. He'd forgotten her last name, but he hadn't forgotten her. She had been the youngest, barely twelve years old when he last saw her. So now she was—he used his fingers to count the years—twenty-seven. She looked the same only bigger, same fair hair and sharp nose. He patted his face with his good hand, felt the ridges, the grooves, the scars. He was not the same, not anymore. He had become a man broken by war, haunted by death. He also remembered her sobbing, covering her face with her hands, shaking her head in denial. At least she'd been sorry, but not sorry enough to stop it. She still had to be punished, but he'd treat her differently than the others. He would let her live.

He got comfortable, his back propped against a sky-high oak, and stared. Sarah had gone, but now he knew where she lived, and he fixed his gaze on her cottage. Planning, plotting, hatching his next move.

SECRETS OF GREENOAK WOODS

Printed in Great Britain
by Amazon